SUSTAINABILITY

TYLER HELM

 iUniverse°

SUSTAINABILITY

iUniverse books may be ordered through booksellers or by contacting:

iUniverse
1663 Liberty Drive
Bloomington, IN 47403
www.iuniverse.com
844-349-9409

ISBN: 978-1-5320-8442-3 (sc)
ISBN: 978-1-5320-8443-0 (e)

Library of Congress Control Number: 2020910110

Print information available on the last page.

iUniverse rev. date: 09/04/2020

Thanks to my editor Nicole Philp for her
time and dedication to the project

Dedicated to my son Gage

CHAPTER 1

"The industrial world takes it for granted; our most powerful manmade resource can be created completely by renewable resources and the titans don't care. The glory is in new money, selling the iPhone 18 or a reversible tablet, not old school power. Now break that down into reality... none of that technology runs, the world does not run, without power. Electricity is the ultimate fuel, even oil is a means of producing it, albeit an inefficient one."

Jim Dunsmuir, a successful American entrepreneur, swirled his Canadian whiskey over the ice in his glass while he replayed his speech in his mind. He was oblivious to the slivers of colourful light glinting across his desk from the warm evening sun as it filtered through the deep etching in the crystal of his tumbler. His calico eyes glowed as he recalled the skeptical, yet intrigued,

1

facial expressions of the world's most influential leaders, who had been sitting in a semicircle round him in the small amphitheatre at the G8 summit meeting in Riyadh, Saudi Arabia less than a week ago. Although he had been extremely successful in the real estate market, before the housing crash, and then in the oil industry after that, Jim Dunsmuir had gotten his start in the financial industry. The Wall Street Journal heralded him as an "investment savant" thanks to his unrelenting and consistent success as an investor.

Jim took a sip of the smooth amber liquid and shifted his gaze out the window. He watched the descending sun burn the horizon, in torrid mix of bright yellows, oranges and purple. The flaming ball was doing all it could to leave its mark before being enveloped by the night. Even after five years, the sight of the setting sun in the evenings and the brilliance of the aurora borealis late at night dancing over the Blue Lagoon reminded Jim that setting up shop in Iceland was the best decision of his life. The potential fallout of the speech he was reflecting on had the potential to destroy his reputation, shatter his board's trust in him, and scare his stockholders into selling their shares in his company. Jim was a risk-taker and when he believed in what he was doing, he was unstoppable. Due to political unrest during a recent trip to meet with Georgian investors in Tbilisi, Jim had narrowly escaped with his life. He owed thanks to the well-built Range Rover and his quick-thinking security team for getting him away unscathed.

Since then he had dealt with the embarrassing incident

in Las Vegas, the threatening note prior to his speech in Riyadh followed by the Molotov cocktail attack after it, and then the worst threat of all to the life of his business partner and girlfriend. These series of personal attacks had made Jim realize that he needed to start taking more precautions in life. He also felt that he must really be on to something that made someone so desperately want to put a stop to his plans.

Jim gave a low chuckle and let himself sag back into the comfort of the easy chair in his office. As he was settling in he drew the glass to his lips again. While there were days when the sheer scale and enormity of the project he was about to undertake was sometimes difficult to even comprehend, Jim would compare himself to the pioneering railroad men of the American West. When he considered what these men went through to build a rail line across an uncharted, lawless country with the primitive technology they had, he felt ashamed for his selfish thoughts. Instead of tunneling through mountains like the railroad men did above the earth's surface, Jim was going to overcome the rock within the earth. He and his team had worked exceptionally hard to maintain maximum secrecy on this project to prevent governments and industrial competitors alike from stealing the technology or sabotaging his work.

CHAPTER 2

Jim's unique style of project management was as untraditional as his first experience in investing. Instead of awarding contracts to the lowest bidder, Jim would meet with each contractor personally, interviewing and selecting a team that would be able to deliver his project, not for the lowest possible cost, but with the highest quality and success rate.

Jim's team included himself, business psychiatrist Lois Nelson, his Chief Financial Officer Ramsey King, Human Resources Chief Alexandra Griffin, environmental engineer Garcia Grey, and the brilliant Jason Evans who had degrees in electrical, civil, and mechanical engineering.

Stanford graduate Jason Evans had been project lead on some of the world's most prestigious builds in the last few decades, including skyscrapers in Dubai, autobahn roadways through mountains in Germany, bullet trains in China, and most recently, a prize skyscraper in the centre of New York City.

Jason had recently been giving lectures as a guest speaker at numerous construction and engineering trade symposiums around the world. While recruiting for his team, Jim had heard one of Jason's lectures while waiting to hear Garcia Grey speak at an Environment and Tech conference in Germany. Garcia had been advancing design and technology in geothermal electricity and her breakthroughs alone in the last five years had skyrocketed both the profile and accessibility of geothermal tech. Jim had been there to try and set up a meeting with her and entice her to join his team but was equally impressed with Jason's presentation at the same conference. While he listened to Jason speak, Jim knew Jason's experience was what he needed to complement Garcia's expertise in geothermal technology. Although Jason spoke as an expert on his topic, his delivery made obvious his passion and curiosity for learning, which was exactly the kind of open-mindedness Jim needed in his expert lead for the project.

In the subsequent weeks, Jim followed up on Jason's career to confirm his gut feeling about his fit as project lead and knew he'd found the man with the education, contacts, and drive to move big projects like this forward despite weather, physical obstacles, and bureaucratic red tape. Jim just needed to figure out a way to sell Jason on his idea and attract a man with such talent and passion to lead his team. Fortunately, Jim's reputation in the investment world and relative popularity within key financial circles enabled him to confirm a meeting with Jason in China, on Beijing's maglev train, following a lecture Jason gave at a symposium being held there. Cruising along at 430 km/hr, Jim explained his plan to Jason, and asked him if he would be interested in joining his team. Jason was a big man who stood six foot four inches tall and was nothing shy of two hundred and fifty pounds. By most anyone's standards, Jason was a very rich man, but he didn't really care for a high end lifestyle. He wore off-the-rack clothes that were well fit but never wore anything extravagant, he always said it took too much work to dress flashy and the clothes were uncomfortable anyway. He did maintain a standard cologne that had a heavy wooded scent and his thick black hair was worn long but always combed in a loose feather. His demeanour was as large as his girth, although he was not a cocky man, he made people feel that he knew what he was talking about and that he was not tolerant of having his time wasted.

Jason leaned back in the seat and said, "So basically you want to create the Super Wal Mart of European travel and electric companies."

"Precisely," Jim knew he had him hooked, now he just had to reel him in. Twenty minutes later while unloading in the glass-walled, pristine, Beijing train station, Jason said he was interested in Jim's project.

He said, "Give me a call next week, I will meet you in New York to wade in deeper."

"Make it Reykjavik, Iceland and you have a deal," Jim replied.

"Right let's get straight to it," Jason smiled and nodded. "Ok, see you there."

To be requested to speak at a German symposium on green energy and sustainable resources, by itself is an accomplishment. Being a young woman, glass ceilings aside, for a person from America or the North American continent for that matter was almost unheard of. Garcia Grey was a thirty-five-year old woman who was dressed in a conservative business suit that could not quite mask her statuesque beauty despite her obvious attempt for it to do just that. She was tall, with long dark hair that fell over her shoulders and seemed to accent her high cheek bones and long smooth neck. She wore thin, rimmed silver framed glasses that seemed to only enhance her beauty. Garcia's slender frame was not waif-like, but she carried herself with a posture that suggested athleticism, judging by her fluid movement as she moved about the stage addressing a very tough crowd of seasoned renewable energy gurus. Regardless of her physical attractiveness, this woman had made advances in the oldest form of renewable energy known to man and her research and development projects in California have put her on the world map. Germany's power requirements for its dense population and its world-renowned engineering skills, have led them to becoming the foremost leader in renewable and clean energy. Geothermal power is five hundred percent more efficient than burning fossil fuels and even more so than using solar or wind power. Garcia's latest work in Binary Geothermal energy and utilizing liquid Helium as the heart of the system had shocked the renewable energy sector.

Since she first published her successful methods of geothermal energy creation, Garcia has had European corporate suitors at her door twenty-four-seven. At this point she owns her technology and her lawyers have been working hard to patent her work. Following her speech, Garcia's assistant told her that Jim Dunsmuir had just listened to her lecture and wondered if she would have a few minutes for him. She had been turning corporate investors away like crazy, while trying to concentrate on her work, but the name Jim Dunsmuir caught her attention. The American billionaire investor was there in Germany himself, had listened to her speak and wanted to meet with her? As far as she knew he had never invested outside of rock-solid companies apart from his start up gamble with his parent's retirement fund, or so the story goes. Since then, Jim had been a public figure, less so after his wife's death, but the meeting request intrigued her.

"Set the meeting up for dinner, you know the place," Garcia replied. Her assistant smiled knowingly.

CHAPTER 3

Jim had never heard of the Good Bank restaurant. In his travels he had met people and ate at some of the best and trendiest restaurants in cities and countries all over the world. As he approached the address from the street, he questioned if he could possibly have the right address. If not for the large plain "Good Bank" sign above the door, he could have mistaken the eatery for any mom and pop book or card store. As he stepped through the door, however, two things caught his attention. The first was the walls of vegetation that seemed to be brightly lit and stacked on top of each other from floor to ceiling and the other was the long dark hair falling down the middle of the back of a very attractive woman in a fitted sweater that showed off a very perfect V back. She was speaking to the waiter and seemed to miss Jim's stumble step as he walked through the door. If anyone would have asked about the missed step, he would have blamed the strange plant walls, but it was the woman's appearance that caused him to lose focus and he knew it, despite telling himself it was not. After a second of adjusting to the strange place, Jim realized the beautiful woman was actually the gifted scientist he was there to see.

In an effort to regain his composure, Jim smoothed his navy dress shirt under his blazer and adjusted his posture. Seeing as he was about to meet Garcia formally for the first time, he decided to approach her as much from the side as possible so as not to startle her, and he professionally extended his hand as he approached.

"Ms. Grey? I'm a fan of your work and am honoured to meet you. I'm Jim Dunsmuir, thanks for agreeing to meet with me," Jim said formally. As she turned to shake his hand, her flawless profile was followed by her smile and when her eyes met his, he was once again caught off guard by her features.

"Call me Garcia. I'll admit I'm intrigued by your request. Let's have a seat and you can tell me what prompted this meeting." She responded as they followed the hostess to their table. An observer of details, Garcia noticed how the buttons on his shirt and stitching in them were a separate color from the rest of the material and admired his attention to style.

"Interesting choice of restaurant, do you eat here often?" he asked when they were seated.

"I do actually, it's my favorite, but not just for the food," she replied and left it at that. Jim had of course looked the place up online, knew the menu was organic and that it served mostly vegetarian dishes. He also discovered that the establishment left very little in the way of an environmental footprint. This was due in large part to the restaurant growing its own supplies which meant no packaging, little refrigeration, significantly reduced delivery truck needs, etcetera. Jim recognized that Garcia would likely be most interested in the science of the restaurant in addition to the choices offered on the menu.

Wanting her to expand on that comment, Jim asked, "Tell me about vertical farming, what is it that interests you or is it something else you're referring to that you enjoy about this restaurant?" As she explained the science behind vertical farming, Jim realized she had his complete attention on a topic he didn't even know he cared about; she was that engaging when she spoke. Through her explanation of how the restaurant supplied its own vegetables, he learned that vertical farming could be the way of the future. If the earth's population kept growing and food production suddenly could not keep up to consumption, ideas like high rise farming could prove to be humanity's saviour. No dirt required exact mixes of fertilizers and water sprays on plants and roots and hydroponic LED lights for year-round night and day growth. Jim had never been an environmentalist tree-hugger nor had he ever wanted to take on the cause, but he got intrigued when ideas like his project or this vertical farming idea made common and economic sense. He would never financially back a project that he didn't consider sustainable, regardless of how many "tree-hugger" activists tried to convince him their ideas would help the world out in the long run.

"So, tell me Jim, why did you ask for this meeting," she asked in conclusion to her explanation of vertical farming, breaking his train of thought.

"Why this restaurant, Garcia? Are you truly that into safe food?" Jim was curious about her motives for inviting him to this particular place.

"It's the principle," she responded, "it's a new idea, a new technology that seems so simple, it can't *not* work. It reminds me of geothermal, all that natural heat in the ground, a renewable resource that will never run out. Vertical farming simply makes sense. Growing things outdoors in dirt is the oldest and noblest of professions, but with climate change, seasons, natural disasters, and growing world population, farmable acres are being reduced at the same time when more is required. If large vertical farms could be established in uninhabitable places, the world's hunger and food shortage concerns could be put to rest. Hell, these farms could be built on the moon if need be! Obviously feasibility is the biggest concern now and much more development is required before it revolutionizes the world, but the potential is exciting."

Hearing her speak so passionately on the topic further convinced Jim that he had the right person for his team sitting beside him. He realized she was not just a crazed environmentalist, but she understood politics, capitalism and the need for sustainability. Jim was so intrigued by her. It was at this point he decided to try and bring her on board.

CHAPTER 4

"I asked to meet for a very specific reason. I wanted to pitch you a job but now hearing your thoughts on worldwide sustainable development, I have decided to offer a new proposal. I'd like to offer you a partnership." Seeing the incredulous reaction on her face to his unexpected announcement, Jim quickly went on to explain. "I have begun work on a large-scale project that very much hinges on your specialty. Although the project is a risky investment, it has almost unlimited monetary upside potential. Besides the financial reward, my proposal would be the largest single sustainable development project the world has ever seen and would change the renewable energy landscape forever. With the project already in the elemental development stages, your role would begin as soon as you're available and, if we are successful, will provide lifelong work on the cutting edge of geothermal study. With your research, intelligence, and technology, and my resources, we have a rare opportunity to alter the world's view on the reliability and use of renewable energy." Jim paused for a sip of water, giving her a moment to let the enormity of his words sink in. "Well, there's the pitch, Ms. Grey. I am certain you will have a million questions, but as I have already started down this road, I'm afraid I can't give you too many specifics without first confirming your interest and having you sign a confidentiality agreement so I can explain further. I know how that sounds, but this is an international project and business is part of the deal. A business that includes other partners that I have to look after as well as my own interests," Jim said, trying to impress upon her the reason for his caution.

Silently, Garcia inhaled deeply to calm her racing mind and deliberately turned and watched the waiter pick vegetables off the shelves for the next meal the chef was preparing, at the same time she played with the ice in the glass of her home made iced tea. She really did love this restaurant because of what it represented. Recognizing that her passion for renewable energy was a part of every fibre of her being, right down to the part that made decisions about where to eat, she realized there was no way she could turn down the opportunity to hear more about what Jim Dunsmuir was proposing, despite how mysterious he made it all sound.

"All right Mr. Dunsmuir," she said as she returned her gaze to meet his across the table, "you've got my attention.

How do we go forward?" she asked with the confidence of a woman who did not make decisions lightly.

"Well, two things off the bat. How's your schedule for the next week or so… and have you ever been to Iceland?" he asked, surprising her with the second question.

Answering the second question first, she replied, "Iceland? I can't say I saw that coming. No, I've never had the pleasure although it's on my bucket list. And I'd have to arrange a few things here first, but there is no reason I couldn't fly out on Monday. You'll have someone pick me up at the airport I presume?" She was already starting to think through the details.

"Arrangements will be made. I'll pick you up personally at the airport in Reykjavik. You'll just have to let me know your flight times."

Garcia was about to ask more about her unexpected trip to Iceland in the coming week when Jim turned the conversation to their meal. "So how do you order here? Is it like picking the best-looking lobster in the tank, or do I just ask for a salad?" He was staring at the walls of plants. She laughed out loud and promised she would order him something good, she even added grilled chicken to his entrée for good measure.

Following his lead, Garcia allowed him to distract her from the true reason for their meeting and answered his questions on vertical farming as they enjoyed their delicious, fresh meal. Neither of them realized the potential of where that conversation would eventually end up.

When she got back to her hotel later that night

and called her assistant, Amy, to begin the process of re-scheduling her life for the next couple of weeks, the conversation took an unexpected turn. Garcia was ready to talk work and Amy went all girlie on her.

CHAPTER 5

"Y ou just had dinner with one of the richest, most eligible bachelors in the world. Is he as good looking as he seems on TV?" Amy asked enthusiastically.

The question startled Garcia, who had called Amy with only flights and re-scheduling commitments on her mind. "Amy," she admonished sternly, "it was a business meeting and I need you to book me a follow up. I need to fly to Iceland to meet with him to discuss details on Monday. Can you arrange it immediately? Oh, and I'll message you his e-mail so you can give him my itinerary as he said he will be picking me up at the airport in Reykjavik."

Unperturbed by Garcia's formal tone, Amy persisted in focusing on what she considered the most important matter, Jim Dunsmuir. "You have Jim Dunsmuir's personal email? He's picking you up personally in Iceland for a three-day meeting which will take place most likely in his offices overlooking the Blue Lagoon, one of the most beautiful spots in the whole world? Does that sound about right?" Amy summarized breathlessly.

"Yes, exactly. I hear the hidden meaning in your voice, Amy Grey. This is a business opportunity and seems to be a very involved one which is why he needs the time and privacy to meet," Garcia sighed with affectionate annoyance. Sisters could be such a pain in the ass. Despite being her assistant, Amy had turned out to be more of a partner to Garcia, in her business. Like in any small business, jobs are very general and roles lack definition so Amy did everything from ordering pens to working on legal documents with lawyers. Amy was a self-declared geek and played it up. She would dress in bright, frumpy clothes, always sported an out-dated hairstyle and wore glasses that hid her adorable features and instead made her look awkward. The funny thing was she did not even need glasses, and Garcia would never understand her insistence on wearing them. Her sister was quite a quirky individual, but she was a perfect match for Garcia in their company.

"Whatever, Garcirella!" Amy exclaimed in exasperation at her sister's persistence in focusing only on business. "It sounds like Disney is writing your life story now. Anyway, okay, I just worked my magic, while we were talking and set you up to fly in at two. I will send him a semi-professional email asking him to meet you there. Any idea what this is all about?"

"No, not really, just that he talked about needing my experience in geothermal technology to help him build what I can only assume is a massive power plant. Then he spoke of a partnership and a lifelong career that would allow me to keep working on the cutting edge of geothermal scientific study for the rest of my working life. Big promises but no details yet. I'm assuming that will come when I get to Iceland! I will let you know as soon as I can. Thanks sis," Garcia said as she hung up the phone, already mentally moving on to the next thing on her list; packing.

CHAPTER 6

"We need this contract, Robin, winning it will distinguish solar power as the greatest and only renewable power supply worth using." George Anderson left no doubt in his Managing Director, Robin Harms' mind regarding the importance of the project they were working on. Robin was just putting the final touches on a solar system in Morocco, a four-billion-dollar project which would create enough solar energy to power one million homes. Robin was a no-nonsense workaholic who really had no time to listen to George's big schemes and sales pitches. Yet he did know that without George finding them new projects, he would have to do it himself and he really hated that part of the job. Robin was a hands-on man, he liked to design and build and couldn't be bothered messing around with banks, lawyers and customers' demands. Robin knew George was completely committed to the new project in Saudi Arabia; this Morocco Project had been a dress rehearsal for Neom. Neom was to be a new state-of-the-art city in Saudi Arabia that was about to go under construction. Estimates indicated the cost of the city construction would be upwards of $500 billion and its investors wanted to make the city as environmentally friendly and green as possible. Robin could feel his boss's ambition seething through the phone line from over one hundred seventy kilometers away in their Tinghir offices.

"How close are you to closing the deal?" Robin asked. George had competed in bidding meetings that were scheduled by the Saudi capitalists over the last few months. The intention of these meetings had been for the Arabians to review all major forms of renewable energy and help them find the best power resource for their new city.

In his professional career, George had grown up in the cutthroat industry of oil and fossil fuels where he learned the fine art of corporate chess. He once told Robin that in the world of oil, the Dallas TV show would have needed an R rating if the producers had JR act the way real oil men did. When George decided to move to Europe and start a renewable energy business, he put his experience working in the hypothetical gutters and back alleys of the oil industry to use and was able to easily squash the competition. The other businessmen in renewable energy were not businessmen so much as small corporate tree huggers who were actually more interested in saving the world than making a profit.

Between tricky legal deals and using and abusing many people, George had created one of, if not the largest, solar energy companies in the world. For instance, George had secured his company the Morocco project by falsifying data, paying off five Moroccan government contractors, threatening the lives of two other government officials and agreeing to give a Florida Beach house to salesmen from two competitive companies. All the two salesmen had to do was purposely make their companies' sales pitch sound less desirable than his. By getting control of the other companies' sales departments, George was able to offer services that endeared him to the Moroccan government. Without the threat of competition, George had easily been able to boost his sale price almost exponentially, which made him a fortune on the project. The scheme also got his team a practice run for what would eventually become the Saudi job.

Robin could picture George's shark-like grin that always came over his face when he was sure he had a situation under control. George had a short stature and plump was the best way to describe his physique. He dressed in high-end suits that were on the verge of gaudy, ostentatiously displaying not only his wealth but also his arrogance. He had bright white bleached teeth which were enhanced by his dark complexation that he subsidized further by his continued use of tanning beds. George was bald on top but had a jet-black ring of hair around the sides of his head that extended down into a very well-groomed beard and mustache. Ever self-assured, George replied to Robin's inquiry regarding closing the deal that he had made strong inroads in the Arabian government. In George's mind, solar energy was the only renewable resource that made any kind of sense. The city was being built in a desert for God sakes! Solar had to be the only and obvious choice.

Robin was an electrical engineer and had been a contract project lead for years. He had consulted on new designs and had provided services to major cities and power grids for years. Once his children moved out, he realized he had worked in the same profession for over 20 years and had lost the passion he used to have for his career. His interest was renewed when he attended a conference in Toronto, during a lecture he attended on solar power he got excited about energy creation and making it work. Inspired by this new challenge, Robin began studying the details and designs of the best solar systems and joined renewable energy boards and projects. It was at one of these board meetings that he met George. At the time, George's company, Blade Solar, was rapidly becoming one of the première companies in the solar world and was sponsoring many of the events. Following one of the meetings, George approached Robin with a proposal. Essentially, George wanted to tackle large scale solar projects and he wanted Robin to manage and lead that arm of his corporation for him. George said he would set up the deals and get the work but it would be Robin's responsibility to manage and lead the projects. They did a couple of solar farms in the States and Canada but realized renewable energy in North America was still only just catching on. Oil, coal, and uranium where still the big three and there was simply not enough interest in changing to renewable energy for George to make a significant profit. George saw the writing on the wall in this respect and he quickly shifted his focus to the global market. George recognized that renewable energy was already the way of the future and was fully accepted and sought by corporations in Europe. Before long, he had numerous projects in place, and they were building in Dubai, Australia, Switzerland and Germany.

This latest project in Morocco changed the scope of the company again as the enormity and the publicity it produced for Blade Solar moved George and his team into the upper cadre of renewable energy companies, solidifying Blade Solar as a world-leading company. The chances of Blade Solar winning the contract to become the electrical provider for a city such as Neom, Robin had seen as a pipe dream at best, but when George secured the four billion dollar Morocco project, and they were able to manage it with relative ease, he thought the dream could become a possibility. Not only that, but George had further endeared himself to the Eastern world by moving his company headquarters to the Tinghir Oasis, in Morocco, which is truly a beautiful spot. It is a virtual garden of Eden located in between sand and rock in a country with an extremely rough reputation.

Despite the massive cost, the country and city had the foresight to invest the four billion dollars in themselves. This would give them enough power to cover one million families' home energy needs for the next forty years, virtually maintenance free. This would be a recognized cost savings of almost one hundred forty billion over the next forty years. The savings are staggering and that doesn't count the environmental footprint savings. No burnt fuels, no pollution, no environmental spill or cleanup etc. Robin loved to build these systems, partly because solar power followed the KISS system so well, "keep it simple stupid". There were no moving parts, all that is needed is direct sunlight into a pane and it would stand for decades, not to mention easy to service. Clean and efficient. This power led into electric motors use. Electric motors are up to seventy percent more efficient than any gas-powered motor with fewer wearable parts. There was no downside to this energy source. He and George were on the cutting edge and he loved it. Thanks to George's faith in him, Robin had a renewed zest for his work and enjoyed working through the challenges George threw at him with each new, bigger project. But that didn't always mean he was ready to jump in with both feet before first considering the obstacles they would face, and he had some concerns about this Neom project George was so fired up about.

"Neom is big, George. We struggled to get supplies for the Morocco project, and it wasn't because I didn't know suppliers, but because we bought everyone's stock out around the world. We were forced to wait on manufacturing to build more panels and that was only for one million homes. Now we are talking about building a system to power a city thirty-three times the size of New York City. That's almost three hundred million homes!" Robin pointed out.

"It will be our masterpiece, Robin. I have secured banks and production facilities, all of whom are excited and ready to come on board as soon as we sign the contract. Don't forget, this is not like plugging into an existing city. This is brand new. They will bring their grids to us and we will wire the city to meet the phase needs of the solar energy. A project like this in Saudi Arabia will give us a seat on the world power stage right next to Exxon." George brushed off Robin's concerns, too excited about the big picture to dwell on the details.

"Well, I think you better play this one cleaner than you did last time. A project like this could put us in some pretty dangerous territory and not all governments and laws play by the same democratic rules we have been used to. Like you said, solar is the natural answer to a desert city's power needs if they truly want renewable energy. But bribes and threats are seen as dishonorable to many in this part of the world and violence is not an uncommon response against those who are seen as immoral. If you're as ruthless as last time in ensuring we get the job, losing a contract or being black balled will be the least of our concerns." Robin knew George wasn't going to like his warning, but "winning" a job in the Middle East using George's typical unethical tactics was starting to make Robin nervous.

"I brought you in to play with electricity, Robin. Let me play with the power," George replied in a voice that did not even attempt to hide his threat.

Robin was not phased by the verbal assault. He was getting used to George's bullying and had seen many other men bow under the pressure, but he never would. "George, you do this right, or I'm out. I know certain deals fall in grey areas, but I will not put my reputation, this company's standing, or our lives at risk just to make money."

George was quiet for a moment and appeared to be contemplating Robin's concern. When he spoke, however, Robin realized his warning had only made George more determined. "I'll get this deal and you'll build the system. Don't forget you have a wife and two kids, Robin, and I know you want to keep them safe and well-looked after, so don't ever talk to me about quitting again. Now finish up in Morocco and find out for me who the main designer is for Evergreen wind farms. I may need to get inside that company. And don't ever threaten to quit again," George said quietly, menace radiating in his tone.

Robin found himself holding a dead phone to his ear and slowly lowered it, shaking his head in disbelief. George had always been harsh but had never been threatening or out of control before. Robin was unsure if he should take George's threats to heart or if he was just hearing the ramblings of a high-strung man who had worked himself up to a boil trying to make sure he got what he wanted. Robin already knew the main designer at Evergreen as they had worked together on electric phase converters years ago. He was a good guy and they had worked well together through the complicated process of getting the phasing of renewable electricity to line up with the phases created by fossil electricity. This was necessary to get maximum safety and efficiency out of the renewable electricity as it flowed into a conventional electric grid. Robin decided to keep this information to himself for now as he had no desire to get caught in the middle of George's ruthless schemes to eliminate the competition, especially when the competition was an old friend. At this point he felt he would give George the benefit of the doubt and chalk his veiled threats up to nervousness over the bidding war.

George hung up the phone, barely pausing to think about the threats he had just made against Robin's family, but he had been serious that he'd do whatever was needed to win this bid. He never allowed loose ends and as a precaution, he'd hired people to follow all his key employees' families. If ever questioned on his motives, George would say he used the security team to protect his employees, but the reality was that the "security team" was for George's piece of mind. The team, probably more accurately described as spies, followed the employees and their families and would protect them should there be a threat to their personal safety. There was no doubt, however, in their directive that their first and foremost objective was to protect Blade Solar from corporate espionage. In order to do that they would track each employee's family's routines and contacts, that way if any of the family members or his staff suddenly changed routine or started meeting with new people it would be reported to George right away. Of course, George could also use the surveillance teams to send pictures of loved ones to his employees, send their family members threatening notes or even kidnap them if the need arose. Despite Robin's almost irreplaceable value in the company's operations, he was not an exception to George's methods, nor was his family.

In any technology sector or business that is in the rapid growth stage, corporate espionage is rampant and the solar electricity business is no different. By keeping watch on his people's routines, George was able to use the information to help him fend off potentially critical forms of attack against his company. These attacks came in the form of head-hunters, corporate theft, and false information sales. Then George would use that information to track down the people trying to steal from him and he made sure they paid the price. George himself was no stranger to stealing ideas or talented people. George was a great businessman and made many legitimate investments that had significantly built his empire, but half his paranoia, and much of his success, came from suspecting everyone else was just like himself.

Blade Solar leads the pack in new solar cell designs, phase converter technology and electrical load drop conductors. George was able to stay on top of this technology by continually spying on other companies' research and by bribing carefully selected engineers. Of course, George had figured out a way to use the information without drawing attention to himself or tarnishing his company's reputation. Through a series of media leaks, complex patenting rules and other not-so-savory methods that were not recognized by the business community, George had successfully set his company up on a pedestal that portrayed him and his business as the bench mark for the industry. He now had organizations clamouring to work with Blade Energy because it almost became a prestigious event to have Blade power in their lines.

CHAPTER 7

George knew of the men in the running that were competing against him for the Neom contract. He and three other men had been invited, summoned to be more exact, for the honor of meeting the Saudi Arabian princes in charge of infrastructure and urban planning for the new city. The monarchy of Saudi Arabia was very formal. They were about to undertake a massive project and were demanding the best. These princes were the customer and therefore deserved the best. They also had the largest and potentially most lucrative electric business project in the history of the world, so they deserved that right. George was careful to present the princes with oud and incense of the very best quality, making sure the stamps of authenticity on these culturally traditional gifts were clearly marked for all to see. Determined not to commit a cultural faux pas, George had had his staff carefully research the customs of meeting Saudi monarchs and as far as they could determine, his offering was appropriate. Whether true or not, the Saudi officials graciously accepted his gift.

George had determined the two most obvious choices of power for a desert city such as Neom had to be wind or solar. As George considered how he would destroy his competition, his mind wandered back to the meeting that had taken place in the decadent Crown Prince Palace in Saudi Arabia. The mere thought of it effectively made his blood pressure rise. The princes had that goddamn Dunsmuir at the meeting. Swear to hell, even the monarchy had been star struck by that SOB. What was it about that guy that made everyone fawn over him? Jim had that British aristocrat sounding name, James Dunsmuir, he looked like a movie star and made his fortune playing the stock market. His life had been basically a cookie cutter version of the original American dream. Now the world sees him as the corporate incarnate of David Beckham. In his mind, Jim took full advantage of this notoriety, and it made George fiercely jealous, and even more determined to best him. Like any recording artist super star, everyone brought their business and investment ideas to the great Jim Dunsmuir first. This always gave him first pick of the greatest ideas and people, just like writers pitching their best songs to the most famous singers first and then the rest of the singers having to make do with the great singers' song cast-offs. By taking advantage of these investment opportunities, Jim's portfolio seemed to expand exponentially and George had

had enough of listening to the corporate world sing the golden boy's praises.

Up until this project in Neom was announced, Dunsmuir had shown no investment interest in renewable energy and now suddenly he was short-listed to bid on the largest power contract in history with an idea that wouldn't even hardly compete with solar or wind power in a desert environment. Despite feeling personally threatened by Jim and disgusted by the public's adoration of him, George did not see Jim as real competition in this venture. Regardless, George wouldn't take any chances in his business. He had a team of professional investigators following his three competitors: Jim Dunsmuir; the CEO of Evergreen Wind Farms, Chris Buchannan; and Peter Fairchild, CEO of Naes Construction.

Despite the work he still had sitting in front of him on his desk, George needed to refocus. He grabbed his Baccarat decanter and held it up in the sunlight, enjoying the weight of the beautiful goblet in his hand and the way the amber liquid caught the light through the cut crystal, even though he knew decanting did nothing for the whiskey. George decided on a two-ounce drink and poured the liquid slowly into a Rauk Tumbler, leaving the decanter three quarters full. His nerves anticipated the bite and heat the first sip would make on his tongue.

George was twelve hours into his workday and he anticipated at least another three hours of work followed by another long day tomorrow. If he was honest with himself, and that was about the only person he was ever honest with, it would be a grueling couple of weeks as he worked toward the most extraordinary deal he had ever made. The trouble with the hours he worked was that he could not always have discussions with those he needed at the moment. As he had become more powerful in the industry, he found that the level of influence he wielded guaranteed that most of his suppliers and investors would take his calls at any time. The trouble was that he could only arrange so many meetings himself. George heavily relied on his assistant to have the contacts he needed and be able to access those people at all hours and he needed her to do that now. He pressed the speed dial on his desk phone and Sara answered almost instantly. He was not big on formalities when he spoke with anyone, but Sara was so good she had earned the extra time he spent to explain his deals to her. George also found that taking the time to explain his thoughts to Sara paid off for him in spades, she was so efficient that she could take his information and help him build a better result. This time he just needed her to set up an immediate call for him with Richard Emerson.

George did not need to express the extreme urgency that he needed a meeting set with Richard to Sara, after all the time working together, she knew it was an emergency just by reading the tone of his voice. After hanging up on Sara, while still standing beside his desk, George placed both hands firmly on the desk top, leaned heavily on both arms allowing the rest of his body to sag against the strength of his upper body while exhaling deeply. He allowed himself these infrequent breaks because he found the rest reset his senses, which invigorated his brain and increased his work intensity. Following his stretch, George flopped himself down into his deeply padded, leather, ergonomic desk chair. He reached out and snatched his drink up off his magnificent reclaimed Russian Oak desk, leaned back and poured the liquid into his mouth. Since moving into renewable energy, George had tried to immerse himself in earth-saving initiatives as much as possible. He did this to promote the illusion that his company was an extension of him and his green-earth beliefs, and that he and his company were not just out to make a quick buck as a fly-by-night business taking advantage of the world's focus on green living. George chuckled at the irony of that thought because, in truth, that was exactly what he was doing. But in keeping with the appearance of a man who cared about the environment, George's offices reflected sustainability, everything from the décor in recycled wood and bamboo flooring to donating money to global warming causes. All exposure was good for the bottom line. As he smiled at his own ingenuity and took another sip, the phone rang and Sara said, "Richard is tied up at the moment but is available tomorrow at ten, should I book you in for a call?"

George just said, "Yes please, have a good night Sara," not allowing his frustration to taint his voice.

Hanging up, George seethed inside, furious at Richard for not taking his call. These men would not scare easily and two of them didn't have any nasty skeletons in their closets that Trade Link Security had been able to find. Peter Fairchild, the third competitor, had so many skeletons in his that no one would notice one more, plus his metaphorical closet door was wide open and the social media had put him in the headlines so many times that the world just expected him to misbehave. What was worse is that they seemed to like him for it.

It was going to be complex work for George and Richard to try and discredit these men, especially the one who discredited himself almost daily. Further to that they had to keep their actions from being traced back to George in anyway. George needed to keep himself and his company's reputation beyond reproach. He needed the reputation so he could remain the gold standard in renewable energy with no tarnish dragging him down.

George tossed back the rest of his drink and then started sketching out ideas on an ivory colored writing pad, ideas that he would discuss with Richard when they spoke. They had so many scenarios to consider trying to weigh out how they could do the most damage to their competition compared to what they could get away with and not get caught. A simple science press release comparing wind, solar and geothermal power should be enough to sink Dunsmuir's chances, despite his exemplary reputation. Fairchild's plan for a water damn on the Nile could be tricky, though, as it was a good idea. Evergreen Energy was going to be hard to beat as well, there was a lot of damn wind in the desert. And none of the usual examples that discredit windmills would work in this part of the world where there are miles of uninhabited waste land where no one will be annoyed by the whooshing noise of the spinning blades. And no one would care about any birds flying into them either. Really, who cared about buzzards and who the hell knew if they flew that high anyway?

Ideally, George would like to discredit the other corporations just enough to put a seed of doubt in the Prince's heads. Doubt that would make them worry the windmills and the dam would not provide guaranteed uninterrupted power but not go so far as to raise suspicion of sabotage through a deliberate attack which could lead to sympathy and discrediting the whole bidding process.

As he poured himself a second round, a crude idea started to form in his head. If an attack could be made on renewable energy itself the small world of tree huggers and renewable energy supporters would naturally assume "Big Oil" was to blame. Investigation, conspiracy and worry would all be shifted on American oil tycoons and Saudi's rich oil sheiks. George knew in reality that even with the creation of a city like Neom, the renewable energy sector was not even an itch worth scratching for the trillion-dollar oil industry. In fact, oil may not even notice or bother refuting the fact that they had been accused of anything. At this point the petroleum world is blamed for so many bad things in the world that they barely bother to fight back, they just keep putting money in their pockets, secure in the knowledge that the world needs oil.

CHAPTER 8

Garcia's arrival time in Reykjavik was scheduled for two pm. She had never been to Iceland before but knew from the stories and recent research she had done on Google that it was quite a beautiful place and of course the Aurora Borealis was supposed to be spectacular. She had discovered, to her surprise, that depending on the time of year a person visited Iceland you could enjoy hot lake and suntan weather from mid June till mid September. Not surprisingly, it also sounded like tourist season exploded in July and August, making some of the main Icelandic attractions crowded and hard to visit.

Without really knowing what to expect from Jim, Garcia had looked into some of the top things to see in Iceland, thinking she wanted to take advantage of the situation as this might be the only time she ever visited the country. Her search found that the midnight sun phenomenon took place in June, which timed well with her trip. It also sounded like some of the whale migratory patterns would line up with the time she was there so she should get a chance to see them as well. Then there where the year round attractions; countless hot springs and fjords, the world famous blue lagoon mineral spa, coastline tours, all of which provided breathtaking views based on the pictures she had seen, and she would have to figure out exactly what the Golden Circle was. Lucky for her, a mid-June trip should make it one of the best times to take in Iceland and all that it had to offer. In addition to her schedule and the meetings with Jim, Garcia had made Amy book her an extra five days in Iceland that would give her a chance to tour and see the major sites before the tourist season started. It had been a long time since she'd had a break from work and she was looking forward to this unexpected getaway in a magical place she'd heard of, but never really planned on visiting.

True to his word, Jim was waiting for her just outside the terminal gate in a black Toyota Land Cruiser. Garcia had been betting herself he would have someone else pick her up or leave a message for her to call an Uber. She could not imagine how busy his schedule must be, so when she saw Jim hop out of the driver seat, she flushed a little with surprise. As he grabbed her suitcases and tossed them in the back, she caught herself admiring his smooth, athletic movements and charming grin, and then immediately berated herself for allowing Amy to put such ridiculous ideas in her head.

Garcia might have been initially impressed by Jim's

physical appearance, but in a matter of hours she was completely struck by him; his intelligence, leadership, and ingenuity.

Jim's experience in the industry had shown him that most anyone who worked successfully in the area of renewable energy had a general sense of optimism, love for nature and an interest in world preservation besides the more expected characteristics of loving scientific innovation and making money. His gamble on inviting Garcia to Iceland was not only to have her complete attention while he explained his proposal and tried to bring her on board, but also to get her out in the beauty of nature and let her own ideals push her towards him and his vision. Once he received word that she had booked an extra five days in the country following their meetings, he knew he had her hooked.

As they drove to the outskirts of town, Jim said to her, "Don't blame your assistant for the accommodations. It was me who suggested she put you up in a Harbour View Hotel cabin. It was the first place I stayed when I came out here and, well, it's gorgeous in my opinion. The accommodations are not typical of a luxury hotel, but neither is the Good Bank restaurant, so I hope it appeals to you."

"I'm sure your suggestion will be more than appealing. Thank you for assisting with the arrangements," she replied, surprised to find out that Jim had had a personal hand in influencing Amy's choice for her accommodation. Garcia had come across the Black Pearl in her search regarding hotels in Iceland and had assumed Amy would make her a reservation there. She was intrigued by the cabin, especially since he brought up the reference to the Good Bank restaurant. It made her realize he understood, or was trying to understand, her personal tastes and preferences. Still, she was about to embark on her first holiday in forever, and she wasn't sure she liked the sound of a "cabin" that is not "luxurious" so when they pulled up to the driveway to her own quaint little cottage, she was pleasantly surprised. She had certainly not been expecting the ultra modern residence with ocean and geyser views situated on the rocky shore of the serene cold blue sea. She stood beside the car, mesmerized by the view before her, when all of a sudden she was startled by the first geyser eruption that literally took her breath away, and she laughed in appreciation.

When she refocused on Jim, he had taken her luggage out of the car and was smiling in understanding at her reaction as he handed her the handle of the suitcase. He could well remember his first introduction to the overwhelming beauty of Iceland, but simply said, "I will leave you to settle in and tour around a bit then pick you up at six for dinner, unless you have other plans?"

Most of the executives who wanted something from her, whether it was her mind, or body for that matter, never left her alone for a minute, especially during times like this. She had prepared herself for an onslaught of high-pressure sales tactics the minute she stepped off the plane, which was partly why she had booked herself extra time in Iceland. She had certainly never expected any social time with Jim himself during the days she was scheduled to meet with him. Trying to conceal her surprise, all she could think to ask was, "How should I dress?"

"Just a shade under semiformal and wear boots if you brought them," he replied.

"I know it's Iceland, but since I was coming in June, I never thought I'd need Sorrels?" she questioned, curious about a supper that would require boots.

"Good assumption," he said, "but I meant more of a hiking or cowboy boot."

"I can manage that," she said, intrigued that he wasn't offering more information.

Garcia's responsive smile and the sudden image of her in riding gear and black leather boots that leapt into his brain paralyzed Jim so much so that he lost his professional, friendly demeanour and replied with the nerves of a high school boy who had just got up his nerve to ask a girl out on a first date. "See you at six," he said as he spun and left.

Garcia was a bit taken back by Jim's sudden attitude change as it seemed he had just basically run out on her. Then she thought maybe she was just a bit tired from the trip and was reading him wrong. Besides, a man with his portfolio likely had more business on the go besides just taking care of her. He had already done more for her personally than she had ever expected. She had fully anticipated that Jim would've sent one of his lackeys to drive her around.

As she settled in, or "nested", as she called it, Garcia decided she loved the Harbour View cabin. It felt like her own private place outside the city and it invited her to make herself at home and relax. She was also excited with what appeared to be numerous hiking trails around the cabin that she was sure would lead her to destinations where she could take in the scenery of this beautiful country on her own time. After unpacking and settling in, her attraction to nature eventually overcame her, so she squeezed a quick walk in before she had to start getting ready for dinner. As the clock wound down to the time Jim was to pick her up, she started to wonder just where they were going. She had never been to a dinner meeting where anyone had specified her footwear before. At five forty-five, her phone rang. Jim asked if she would be ok for a bit of a tour of the area before they went for dinner. He said there were a couple of things he wanted to show her before they got into their meal and down to business. She agreed immediately, since part of her plan in staying the extra week was to see as much of the country as possible, she knew a guided tour might help her decide what she wanted to see more of later on.

Five minutes later, a large helicopter was touching down about one hundred meters from her cabin. Although she was surprised, she should have guessed a quick tour of a place like Iceland really could not happen in a vehicle, it would take too long to drive between the attractions. Moments later she noticed Jim exiting the helicopter and walking across the grounds towards her door. He was outfitted in dark blue jeans and a flannel long sleeved shirt, clearly comfortable and prepared to spend some time outdoors. She smiled and felt strangely relaxed when she saw him. As he knocked on her door, she was sliding into her second boot.

"Just a second," she yelled through the door. "She made him wait two more minutes while she tied her hair up in a scarf so the helicopter blades would not turn it into a rat's nest. She loved her long hair, but wind was its natural enemy.

Jim smiled appreciatively when she finally opened the door and greeted her warmly, "Hello," he said as he held the door for her, "the scarf is a great idea," and then closed it behind her. She could not help but notice and like the way he seemed to pause when he saw her, but she knew she needed to get those thoughts out her head. He had asked her here for business and those discussions were about to start.

With the Bell 4329's propellers too loud to allow further conversation, Jim waited until they were settled inside before commenting, "I hope you don't mind flying again today. I thought an overhead view would paint you a better picture of what I want to discuss. On top of that, our dinner destination would be a two-hour car ride and as the crow flies, it's only a 20-minute flight."

Garcia nodded that the flight was fine and smiled her thanks as Jim handed her a coffee when they settled back in the luxurious leather recliners in the back of the impressive machine. While the captain gained altitude, and Garcia gazed out the window at the landscape below, Jim thought of the conversations he'd had with his team regarding his desire to recruit Garcia for this project. His initial discussion with Ramsey King hadn't been met with enthusiasm for his choice of a geothermal engineer.

CHAPTER 9

Ramsey King represented the largest part of Jim's life, both personally and in business. He serves as the Chief Financial Officer and was basically Jim's partner in Dunsmuir Energy, but he was also Jim's closest confidant. Ramsey and Jim had been best friends since high school and business partners since university. When deciding who to approach to head up the geothermal side of this project, Ramsey had initially been opposed to hiring Garcia; he thought she was not experienced enough in international business to take on a project of this magnitude despite her resume and the success she had in California.

As usual, whenever Jim and Ramsey were not on the same page with each other, they presented their position to the rest of the management team at Dunsmuir Energy for further discussion. With his name on the door, Jim could have overruled him but he greatly valued his staff's opinion and knew that being challenged once in awhile on his opinions was the best way to keep him grounded. He had hired them for a reason so he might as well use their knowledge to help him make the best decisions for the company. Once both positions were presented to the team, the final decision was that they would try to recruit Garcia. The team did not always side with Jim, however, they did in this case. The team decided Garcia was the right person for the job because the technology she used and the reliability of her systems were the bench mark in geothermal technology and they had to produce a highly efficient, solid product that would be trouble-free. Despite her lack of experience in business, her experience in system design was second to none, and that is what they needed. Dunsmuir Energy had more than enough resources and personnel to help her with the business aspect, and the team decided it would be up to Ramsey and the project leader they found to protect and guide Garcia through everything so she could focus entirely on producing a bullet-proof geothermal system.

Once the team made the decision to move forward to try and onboard Garcia, Jim had then posed the question of how they thought she could best be convinced to join them. Dunsmuir Energy's business psychiatrist, Dr. Lois Nelson, said that Jim should personally meet her. She indicated the project was his dream and that he was the driving force behind it. She further stated that it was his intensity that fueled all of them to move forward with the project in the first place, so if he wanted the best chance to convince her to join them he should fly her to Iceland and use the country's natural beauty to sell her on the project, just like he had sold it to the rest of his company.

Chief of Human Resources, Alexandra Griffen, agreed with Lois Nelson's assessment and offered her perspective at the meeting, recognizing both Garcia's talent and Jim's leadership. "Jim," she had said, "we did the research, we decided on the talent we need for this, Garcia fits the bill. Part of it is her education, knowledge and experience in designing major geothermal projects but the rest is her genius, the leaps forward she has made in her industry, her willingness to work outside the box, and a project like this is not anywhere near the box. We need her on this and if you court her we will have a 95 percent chance of signing her up, far less if anyone else does."

"So basically, tell her the truth?" Jim said, "That doesn't seem like normal salesmanship tactics to me."

Jim had considered his chosen team members, as he preferred to think of them, rather than mere staff. He had hired an astute HR Chief, an extremely intuitive psychiatrist and an extremely smart and well-paid CFO to help him lead this company and he thought together they would come up with some kind of magic hook that would help him secure the basic key to this whole project, but no they basically told him "go be yourself". Lois had noticed the doubt in his eyes and said, "Jim this project is you. It has become your world. Garcia will know you and who you are. She will know you as an investor, not as engineer or a project engineering lead. We have researched her enough to know she is not a straight up tree hugger but she is also not a green power parasite who is out to get rich off others who want to save the planet's ecosystem."

"Jim you need to tell her what you want to accomplish and how," Alexandra contributed.

"You also need to tell her why," said Lois. "I think it will be your explanation of this dream you have that will convince her. She has already opened up to you by taking you to the vertical farm restaurant. That gesture alone shows she is comfortable with you. More importantly, it solidifies our belief that she is interested in new ideas, going outside the norm and with this project we need that openness and energy."

Resolving himself to the fact that his team had just delegated recruitment duties to him, Jim followed up by asking them how he should start the proposal. Alexandra answered, "Jim you already have a captive audience. She has agreed to spend three days with you in Iceland. Basically you need to show her why you need her, convince her that living in Iceland for a decade is the greatest thing in the world, let her see the fundamental good her work on this project will do for the world, and of course offer her enough money so that she thinks it would be crazy to turn the offer down just in case her morals alone are not enough. Basically you need to make it so that it would not make sense in any logical or moral way to turn you down."

When Alexandra put it like that, Jim realized he was up for the task and started brainstorming how he would introduce Garcia to Iceland, to Dunsmuir Energy, and to the project… in that order.

CHAPTER 10

J im had planned a very quick aerial tour of some of the most amazing Icelandic sites in hope to interest Garcia and leave her wanting more; the most basic business supply and demand principals. On the way to the Fridheimar restaurant Jim had requested the pilot add the Blue Lagoon into their evening flight plan. Seeing the crystal clear water of the Lagoon from above is breathtaking. Jim knew the land mark would peak the interest of the scientist in Garcia. He thought she would be especially amazed at the wonder of a naturally heated pool that stays at thirty-eight degrees Celsius year round even when the temperature of the air drops to minus thirty-eight degrees Celsius in winter months. With her specialty being geothermal technology, this natural occurrence of her chosen profession, paired with the majestic beauty of the resort, should be an almost religious experience for her. He had then asked the pilot to pass over the absolutely breathtaking Hallgrimskirkja Church. The church's unique design seemed to never allow your eyes to focus on one element, it teases the observer's line of site so that the eyes stay busy jumping from one intriguing architectural feature to the next. The seventy-five-meter-high building is the focal point of the town square and is one of the tallest structures in the country.

From the expression of delight on Garcia's face as they hovered above the church's steeple, Jim could see his plan falling into place. Jim had been doing his best tour guide impression throughout the flight, sharing some of the facts and history that he knew of Iceland as they progressed towards their final destination, but he could tell by the look on Garcia's face the country was selling itself. By looking into her hazel eyes as she stared out the window of the helicopter, he knew she was not faking a polite interest and that she was way more interested in the view than his simple facts. As they flew on to the golden circle, Jim reminded himself that the beauty of mother nature's raw power was enough to astonish anyone, let alone an earth scientist, who saw Iceland's natural wonders, whether it was their first time seeing it or their hundredth. The endless number of geysers, waterfalls, and volcanic activity they saw offered a raw beauty that continued to reflect on Garcia's face even after the pilot banked away from the last glimpse of volcanic lava and headed further inland towards the Fridheimar farm.

After having sat on the edge of her seat for most of the flight to get a better view out of the window, Garcia slowly settled back and turned to Jim with a knowing smile. "So just what are buttering me up for, Mr. Dunsmuir? Showing a geochemist those sites are like showing a six-year-old a puppy and then pretending you might not be letting her take it home."

"It's true, the science and power that comes from the earth is amazing. Even having lived here as long as I have, I still can't help but enjoy the view, and I hope you did too. We will be landing in twenty minutes. Enjoy the rest of the flight and then let me explain over dinner. I'm not trying to be secretive, but I thought seeing the vastness of Iceland and the sparse population would better help you understand my proposal."

The restaurant Jim chose mimicked Garcia's vertical farm restaurant in that it is an organic, fresh, farm-to-table restaurant featuring tomatoes grown in a temperature-controlled Mediterranean environment located basically in the Arctic. The secret of this restaurant and the Fridheimar farm is the ground's geothermal power. The geothermal energy was used for free, by the farm, to produce an environment which replicated temperatures of some of the lushest growing regions in the world. The farm did this in a geographic location where gardening of any kind is basically impossible. As the pilot circled in for a landing about a hundred and fifty meters away from the greenhouses, the horses in the nearby coral spooked and took off for the far end of the paddock.

"So, when you said to wear boots, what exactly was your intention, Jim?" Garcia asked as she eyed the horses.

"Well, dinner first. Then if you're interested, we can

go for or a ride," Jim grinned at her obvious hesitation regarding the potential horseback ride later. "There are some spectacular sites close by and I didn't want you to miss out on the opportunity of seeing them... if don't mind riding, that is?"

She grinned and replied gamely, "Sure. That sounds like fun, and it's not like we'll run out of daylight any time soon. I'm not much of a rider, so if walking those beasts is ok with you, I should be good. Now, tell me about this restaurant because it doesn't look like a typical steak house."

Jim liked her smile and her sense of adventure that allowed her to go out of her comfort zone and try something new. He quickly explained to her how he thought she might enjoy this place as it was as close to the Good Bank restaurant in Germany as he could find and its reason for survival was geothermal energy.

CHAPTER 11

During a recent meeting in the Al-Yamamah Palace in the Capital of Saudi Arabia, Princes Sallmala and Shallans were tasked by the new Crown Prince to build and design a brand-new, state-of-the-art city in Saudi Arabia. The Crown Prince wanted a "super city", for lack of a better word. It needed to be cutting edge, self sufficient and he wanted only select country men to reside in it once it was completed. He had dreams of the city becoming a world leader in everything. Once complete, the city would be roughly thirty-three times the size of New York City. The challenge has been dubbed the world's most ambitious project. The city will be located on four hundred and sixty-eight kilometres of coastline along the Aqaba Gulf, bordered by twenty-five hundred kilometres of mountains, for a total area of almost twenty-seven thousand square kilometres.

SUSTAINABILITY

The Crown Prince had decided it was time to break their country's complete dependence on oil and balance out his investments. In order to keep Saudi Arabia as the center of the Arab world, he decided to build the super city from the ground up. He would use the city to become a global investment powerhouse and a center for world trade. Located on the shores of the Red Sea, Neom will be purposely built for a new Saudi way of life where the best and the brightest people will be moved in to live and work. Not only will the city infrastructure be brand new, but it will be carefully designed to promote advances in major water, mobility, biotech, food, manufacturing, media entertainment, culture and fashion, technology, tourism, sports, design and construction, health care, education and livability. Neom's literal translation means *new future* and that is exactly what he wanted them to design. With the Crown Prince ready to invest five hundred billion, his dream was to attract outside investors that will not only bring in foreign investment money to help finish the city but put Saudi Arabia into a more dominant world trade position. The City will be expected to function autonomously like its own country. It will have rules, laws and taxes that are self-imposed and enforced.

Although the task of building such a city on the whole was basically unfathomable, not moving forward with the Crown Prince's demand was even more unfathomable. The overarching goal of the city was to position Saudi Arabia as a country of the future by integrating it socially and financially with the world so that the country would never be thought of as an oil slave to the West. If anyone in Saudi Arabia had the ability and experience to take on such an undertaking, it was Sallmala and Shallans. The Princes took on the challenge as they would any major project, they broke it down into pieces and utilized many specialized engineers and consultants to help them determine the size of the pieces and the best place to start. As they compiled and reviewed all the information they acquired from their experts, most, with few exceptions, stated that getting adequate utilities in place first was the key to success. The recommendations further stated that the foremost utility required was power, closely followed by water, sewer, transportation, and technology infrastructure. In order to meet the Crown Prince's requirements, the city would be required to run off self-sustaining green energy which would show the world that a major Saudi city did not require oil to survive.

It was estimated that once completed, the city of Neom would require four hundred thousand megawatts of electricity per day and the Crown Prince's demand was that it be a system that was one hundred percent reliable. The new Crown Prince predicted oil could only last so long, as it is oil is already getting long in the tooth. He knew that eventually the world will either run out of crude or technology will move beyond needing it. He also knew that electric motors were vastly more efficient and reliable than combustion engines and have been so now for decades; it was only a matter of time until they surpassed traditional combustion engines.

Regardless of the time that passed since the horrific terror attack on the United States, Saudi Arabia had .

been working hard to resume a positive role in world. There are between twelve to fifteen thousand Princes and as many Princesses in Saudi Arabia. In a country of thirty-three million people under totalitarian absolute monarchy, this may not seem like a large government structure but in truth the rule of the country falls to very few senior princes. For Shallen and Sallmala to have been handpicked by the Crown Prince to build his great new city was an indescribable honor. The development of Neom would be the Crown Prince's great jewel in his very elaborate crown. It was not that Shallen and Sallmala did not deserve the opportunity. They had both studied at the best schools and trained under city planners all over the world. Together they have been responsible for the infrastructure and planning for the city of Riyadh for years. In truth, the Crown Prince would have liked to pick a couple of young new-aged design teams that would have the potential to really design an out of the box masterpiece, but even an absolute monarch has to consider his people. After careful review, he had made his selection.

As any great leader would, the Prince gave Shallen and Sallmala very strict design parameters. He insisted that traditions only needed to be followed if common sense dictated, that they needed to consult with new design teams and implement the latest technologies like the companies that built the new New York World Trade Center, the Jeddah Tower and design experts from Dubai, all the while not allowing the city to look new-age or gaudy. He insisted that the end result had to look regal and tasteful, not only in the eyes of the world today, but a thousand years from now.

The orders were tall and made the project virtually impossible, but it was a challenge the two Princes would not have passed up for the world. As time moved forward, they took their boss's dream into conceptual planning and, as recommended, they started with electricity. Despite Saudi's vast population, large parts of the desert country remain uninhabited and could easily be made ready and available for creating and storing the electricity required for the new city. Both men were wealthy and not relatively rich compared to their neighbours, but rich in a top two percent of the world rich, both have investments of well over a billion dollars each. They came from generations of well off families and were at a point in their lives where power and money would not influence them the way it would younger men. The Crown Prince knew that and needed people like them in charge of his project as there was too much on the line to allow simple greed to destroy his dream.

The Crown Prince knew these men would make decisions that were in the best interest of their king and country and that is why he chose them in the end. Prince Shallen and Prince Sallmala both have large successful families who were deeply religious, with honour and respect for the monarchy deeply ingrained in their lives. Despite their desire to do the work and please him, the Crown Prince authorized that each man could build himself a large palace on either side of the king's and Crown Prince Palace as a reward for their work. He further ordered that each palace was to be situated to overlook the shores of the Red Sea and the new city. The palaces were to have exterior looks of traditional design but remain fully functional with state-of-the-art technology. All the complexes were to connect underground and have full living quarters and pandemic supplies to support everyone who resided within the palaces. In the event of war or attack, the area needed to have complete protection for the royals, as well as have multiple defense mechanisms with numerous escape tunnels that lead to land, sea and air transportation. One amazing escape tunnel would be designed to lead under the Red Sea and surface deep in Egypt. Each Prince would also be awarded a large shipping port to add to their empires as a token for their hard work and dedication to their country.

CHAPTER 12

Shallen and Sallmala's posted tender request for a renewable energy contractor yielded them numerous bids of all varieties; sometimes new-age thinking brought out some of the craziest people. For example, they had people bidding with proposals stating they could create enough electricity out of sea weed and plant roots but they had not quite mastered the technology yet so if they could get some funding to finish their research they had no doubt they would be ready to start building in a couple months. It was not often the Princes got a chance to laugh at work, but some of the ridiculous proposals they received allowed them that opportunity. The odd bids also made them realize that as they moved forward with different tenders for the city they would have to tighten their parameters to weed out bids that only wasted their time.

Shallen said, "Can you imagine what we are going to get for plumbing and sewer processing?" The two men looked at each other and laughed. Amidst all the strange bids they did get some very good ones as well. In fact, they received four serious offers from companies that could potentially do a fine job at not only building and installing a system, but offering long term maintenance which was of upmost importance. Two of the bids were the standard offers, which they had expected and originally assumed would be their only two real options or a mixture of the two. These bids, of course, were a wind and a solar energy farm. Both ideas made sense and were well suited for a desert climate.

The third bid was little further off center but still a very plausible idea that they had never considered. This idea was to build a hydroelectric power dam on the Nile River in Egypt. The Three Gorges Hydroelectric dam in China is currently the world's largest electricity producing dam. This one facility alone produces eighteen thousand megawatts of electricity per day which would be more than enough electricity to power New York City but would only produce thirty-three percent of Neom's electrical needs. The dam in China is five times the size of the Hoover dam in the United States. The dam is two point three kilometres long, one hundred eighty-five metres high and was made of sixteen million cubic yards of concrete. The concrete needed to produce a dam big enough to power Neom would amount to no less than three hundred and fifty-two cubic yards. The challenge to create that much concrete seems impossible until Saudi

Arabia and Egypt's endless supply of natural resources, gravel, sand and stone is considered.

The Nile river has the distinction of being the second largest river in the world next only to the Amazon. The Nile has ninety- five percent of Egypt's population living along its banks. Egypt already has the Aswan High dam located at the mouth of the great river near the south end of Egypt. The Aswan is said to provide power for half of Egypt's population of close to a hundred million people. Naes Construction, a large engineering and project management company based out of the United States, would be hired to oversee and manage the project if the Chinese firm's proposal was accepted.

With this dam proposal, the Princes now had three solid tenders of which to choose from that they considered viable. The Egypt dam proposal had the potential to further tie Saudi in with its neighboring country. Deals like this had pros and cons, but on the surface it would enhance trade, foreign relations and was in many ways exactly what the Crown Prince was looking for in the development of Neom in the first place.

There was a fourth proposal, one they considered the most ridiculous, or perhaps so ridiculous that it was actually the most brilliant. If it could actually be accomplished, it had the potential to literally transform the world like nothing has since the invention of the airplane. Although extremely skeptical of the outlandish proposal, the only reason the Princes didn't toss it out of hand was because of the name attached to it: James Dunsmuir.

CHAPTER 13

"**S**o, the choices are basically tomato and anything," Garcia teased when she and Jim were seated and had placed their orders.

"Just wait till you try it, and yes, tomato plus is the menu," he replied with a chuckle. They had ordered an appetizer of little cherry tomatoes, followed by a main course of roasted chicken salad and finished with tomato ice cream and pie. They conversed easily about a variety of topics as they waited for their food and when it came, Garcia was amazed with the flavours of the meal. Although she was well-acquainted with the fact that there is nothing like the taste of freshly picked vegetables from a private garden, what was more interesting was that even all the drinks, alcoholic and virgin, that the restaurant offered were created using tomatoes. They had sipped tomato beer with dinner, washed dessert down with a "Healthy

Mary" consisting of lime, honey, ginger, sparkling water and of course green tomatoes, and then then they each took a Fridheimar Koffi to go as they walked towards their recently saddled horses. Fridheimar Koffi, as Garcia was surprised to learn, was a shockingly delicious drink consisting of coffee, liqueur, whipped cream, and the inevitable tomato syrup.

"Well if it's true that tomatoes keep the doctor away, we should live forever after that meal," Garcia quipped as she took another sip of her Koffi.

"I think that may be apples," laughed Jim, "but hey, you never know!"

As they approached the horses, Jim could see Garcia was nervous and told her that they didn't have to ride if she did not want to, they could just head back to the helicopter and continue the tour by air. Although a little scared of being bucked off, Garcia was stubborn and did not want to seem weak. Instead of cracking a joke about it, she honestly admitted, "No, I'd like to ride but may need help getting on." Her response even surprised her, making her realize she was a bit more worried than she thought. Normally she would have laughed off her concerns and would have certainly hid any anxiety about an uncomfortable situation.

Jim just said, "no problem," and didn't seem to think less of her. As a stable hand held the animal's halter, Jim put one hand out for her to step in and the other around her waist to guide and lift her up and on. The action shocked both of them. She felt him lift her like she was weightless and the strength she felt under her hand in his shoulder was surprising, she had just assumed he would be a flabby pencil pusher under his thousand dollar suits. For Jim, the hard-firm curve of her narrow waist and her athletic movement put to rest any thoughts he had of her as the class geek. She had a body she obviously worked hard to keep, and the initial attraction he had had back in Germany at the Good Bank restaurant only intensified at this first touch. Despite the fact that she was now settled in the saddle, it took him a good ten seconds to refocus. As he stared up into her eyes, she smiled down at him and relieved the awkward moment by teasing him. "Hey you're not chickening out now, are you? Or did I just call your bluff on this whole horse riding thing?"

"What? Ah no, no I'm ready," Jim stuttered as he climbed up into the saddle. "It's about an hour round trip straight walking, but there is a great place to stop and watch a couple live geysers along the way."

"Lead on," she responded. They were headed to the Selfoss geyser. As they rode, she noticed Jim get quiet. Even his body language became different like he was nervous and unsure what to do. Garcia spent the time looking around at the tundra and small pools but mostly she kept her eyes on Jim while trying to remember to hold on. As they approached the Geyser, he rode up to two empty benches, hopped off his horse and tied it to one that was close to a small pool of water with some grass beside it. Once tied, the horse immediately bent to drink. Without asking he basically lifted her down off her horse and then tied it to the bench as well. As he turned to face

71

her, he froze and just stood looking at her. Eventually she said, "Well earth to Jim, where are you?"

Then his demeanour changed and the distant look left his eyes and he was back to himself. Relieved, she followed him over to the second bench and they sat down just as the geyser erupted. Sitting next to him, Garcia watched the water shoot and the cool mist play out in waves.

Gazing into the geyser, Jim began the conversation in a ponderous tone and led it in a direction that surprised Garcia, who was expecting to hear more about the project he'd flown her to Iceland for. "Have you ever wanted something so bad," Jim started, "Something you felt was so right but yet it felt like such a long shot that you're scared not only to start but even to verbalize it, because you know that as soon as you do, it becomes real and you have to go for it, no turning back?" Until this point their conversation had been pretty light, mostly just basic pleasantries maybe even bordering on flirting. But now Garcia knew he was getting serious and with his cryptic speech she had two instant concerns. Concern one, had she just flown across the world to meet a guy who had told her he had some exciting business proposal and had she done this with no concern for her personal safety? She only agreed to the meeting because the guy was rich and famous. Thinking on it now, it may not have been her smartest decision, now she was basically in the middle of nowhere, Iceland with him. Concern two, and this may be worse, she didn't seem to care, she was starting to like Jim, really like him and she was supposed to be there just to hear out his business proposal and not think of other things.

Shaking off her ruminations, she turned to look at him and answered his questions. "Yes I've felt scared about starting new projects, about doing things differently that make people question me when really I'm just trying to get better results. In the end I usually find the self questioning to be for naught and the best thing to do would have been just to start because anything you feel so powerfully about is not going to stay inside anyway. Eventually it's going to come out and then I find all my waiting and hesitation did was waste time."

Her response surprised him. There were not a lot of people Jim met who spoke to him in a straight forward manner. His position and status in life seemed to make most people address him in very reserved and tactical ways. For the most part his relationships were all work-related, mostly formal, and therefore people would typically consider their responses thoughtfully before answering him. That was not the case with Garcia. Rather than try to guess at the response he was looking for in order to impress or please him, Garcia had just spoken from the hip. She had rattled off her feelings and thoughts without an effort to hide or make sure he was on side with her before she finished. Her response left Jim feeling even more at ease with her and he was enjoying every minute they spent together.

He turned from her intent gaze, looked at the disseminating steam, and said, "Well then, if I follow your advice I would tell you that I have a dream and it involves you. In fact, you are a crucial part of my dream and, as I said in Germany, I'd like to make you a partner in a business venture. What I'm about to tell you may sound crazy but I will preface my proposal by saying that every aspect I'm going to tell you about has been researched, studied, theorized and I have the resources in place to see it to completion. I don't want to bore you with all those details but want to give you the Coles notes first so you know your part and what the result will be. Once you decide if you're interested in going down this road with me, we can get deeper into the workings."

"Sounds like a plan to me. I was wondering if I was going to be privy to something more secretive than an indoor tomato farm and this beautiful geyser, especially since you had me sign that confidentiality agreement at dinner," she smiled knowingly.

Jim grinned in return at her intuition. "Well we have a big team and we have all signed the agreement to protect each other. Let me just jump right in… have you ever heard of the city of Neom in Saudi Arabia?"

Garcia said she had, but only in general terms. Her understanding of the city was that it was a dream created by the country's Crown Prince. He wanted to build a super city, basically a technologically advanced center, that was supposed to be self-sufficient, act as its own country but only the elite of Saudi Arabia were going to be handpicked to populate it. By doing this the Crown Prince had hopes of Neom's population advancing the world's technologies.

"Quite right," said Jim. "The Prince also wants to show the world that Saudi is self-sufficient and not completely dependent on the West and the West's need for oil to ensure its survival. Among other things he wants the city to become a central world shipping port, become seen as a major power player in global investing and above all demonstrate that oil is no longer king in Saudi Arabia. He wants the whole city powered by renewable energy, and that is where we come in. The city planning board put out for tenders to serious organizations who could build renewable energy facilities large enough to power the whole city. My team and I have submitted a bid based on geothermal power and we want you to be our design engineer." Oblivious to Garcia's incredulous reaction to his last statement, Jim went on to explain that the city is planning to be home to almost forty million people and would need four hundred thousand megawatts of power per day.

When Jim paused in his explanation, Garcia mentally shook herself out of her stunned silence and asked him the first thing that came to mind. "This doesn't add up, Jim. Why are we in Iceland discussing a project in Saudi Arabia? It only seems obvious that solar or wind power would be the go-to power for a desert-built city."

"True," Jim agreed, impressed that her first response was to challenge his thinking, "and this is where my proposal really starts to get outside the box and where you will eventually want more facts and to talk to others on my team to be sure I am not a complete crack pot." Jim went on to explain his idea in as much detail as he could. Garcia was obviously well more versed on most of the scientific facts of the subject than he was but he needed to include the information to fully present the story. He told her the idea came to him while on vacation in Iceland, during a tour he had taken of the Blue Lagoon, he learned about the naturally occurring geothermal power created within the earth by the extremely active volcanic activity present underground. Locally, Iceland had taken advantage of the geothermal power on one-off uses such as the restaurant they just ate at and on a larger scale like the Blue Lagoon itself. It was the tour that planted the seed in his mind, if he could harness the massive geothermal potential within the earth and couple it with well-designed, state-of-the-art, high-efficiency equipment, the potential could be phenomenal. He went on to explain that as he studied the idea further, he found that the earth's lava core could produce even more energy than he had originally thought. If he could figure out how to properly harness the energy and combine that with a genius in the field of geothermal design, the possibilities could be endless. It had been about that time that he learned about the new city of Neom and its worldwide request for bids on renewable energy and that is when the initial phases of the plan started to form in his head. Jim went on to say that it was at this point that he shared his thoughts with longtime friend and CFO Ramsey King. When Jim found out that Ramsey supported the idea, he pressed it further and engaged a consultant team. When the results of their findings deemed the idea economical, he moved forward.

"Interestingly, the results of the study showed that Greenland is actually a better fit for raw geothermal power than Iceland but of course if you come on board I would expect you would want to measure that for yourself," Jim suggested. "At any rate, Greenland's land is very cheap so in anticipation of moving forward with the project I bought thousands of acres along with the mineral rights located above some of the hottest deepest lava spots in the country."

"I still don't follow you, I understand you want me to design and build a large, to put it mildly, geothermal power plant in Greenland but the power is needed in Saudi Arabia. How could you ever make that feasible?" she asked, impressed by his obvious determination to move forward, but still confused by the logistics of what he was proposing.

"I see the Crown Prince request for tenders as wanting more than just a power supply. His goal is to put Saudi Arabia on the map as its own entity, not just a country reliant on oil money from the West. He wants to build a positive, safe, lucrative connection with the world and is willing to pay for it. My, I should say *our*, proposal is to build a power line. We have found a way to build concrete pillars directly into the bed rock of the earth. The power line will run from Greenland to Iceland to the Faroe Islands, on to the Shetland Islands down to London, across to Berlin, down again to Zurich, Rome, Athens, Crete, Cairo and final into Neom. All of these cities lack the tech and resources to properly maintain the needs of their people and their country's power supplies if world growth continues. My team and I have engaged the countries' leaders and they are fully behind this project because of the fact that they will one day be able to tap into the power supplied by the line. We will be looking at not only supplying power to Neom but to each one of these countries and their most underpowered cities. So far each country the line passes through with the cities I have just mentioned have agreed to come on as investors. We will just need Saudi to make the initial investment, that way we can get a facility started in Greenland. With Saudi Arabia's investment dollars, plus the use of additional funds from a resort destination agreement we are working on, the joint investment capital will allow us the resources to get the electricity across the ocean to London," Jim explained.

Garcia looked at him, amazed and somewhat dumbfounded. "That is without a doubt the most ambitious plan I've ever heard!"

"It's not done there," Jim grinned enthusiastically like a kid about to explain his winning science fair project. He then went on to explain that he had found state of the art power lines that were twice as strong and able to carry twice as much power as traditional lines with half the voltage drop. Furthermore, with the amount of electricity passing through the lines a very strong magnetic field will be created. In order to further enhance his proposal, Jim stated that his team recognized the Crown Prince's desire to enhance his country's connection with the Western world and so they decided they would encase the power lines in concrete between the pillars and then use the naturally occurring magnetic field to build four tracks that would each carry one hundred car high speed magnetic trains. These trains would travel at speeds upwards of seven hundred miles an hour which is faster than commercial planes and be able to carry unlimited cargo across the landmasses from the West side of Europe to the Red Sea, which would open massive trade routes across the Indian Ocean to India, China, Japan and Australia. The speed and efficiency of these trains has such potential that Amazon has agreed to invest in order to move its packages around the world at twice the speed for half the price.

"And that's barely the tip of the iceberg," Jim continued, standing up to pace as his excitement for his project wouldn't allow him to sit still any longer. "If it works as well as we hope it will, can you imagine if the U.S. decided to invest and they attach New York City to the rail line? The world will be connected like never before! Well not since the trans-ocean phone lines went in over a hundred and fifty years ago, anyway."

Jim paused, not for effect, but to try and read Garcia's reaction. Seeing her wide eyes and overwhelmed expression, he laughed self-derisively and sat back down beside her. "Sorry, I get a little bit carried away when I think about the magnitude of this project and how it could change the world," he apologized. "But for right now, basically what I am asking you is if you are willing to take on the task of building the largest power supply plant the world has ever seen and use geothermal technology to do it?"

Jim knew the idea would take a while to sink in. He and his team had completed the research and had a rough idea of the enormity of the generators that would be needed to create such a power supply. He could feel Garcia working over the idea in her head and he respectfully gave her the space and silence she needed to process what he had just asked of her. When she finally broke the silence, she looked at him and rather than ask him to explain more details about the project and the logistics of such an undertaking, she asked a question he never expected. A personal question that surprised him, but gave him some insight into this woman he was hoping to make a partner in his venture. "Why are you doing this Jim?" Garcia queried. "I mean, you are already rich, really rich, famous as well and very well respected in many high society circles. This sounds like a crack pot idea when you first explain it to someone. People will say you are crazy and anyone with you will be called crazy at the very least. But you say you have these countries on board already, like they've signed-on-the-dotted-line on board? Or you just have a 'yes' from a couple government members you met at men's country clubs?"

"Well there are lawyers, contracts, conditions and contingencies, but yes, as you say I have some popularity in influential circles and the clubs at the level of investment I needed are very small and very connected so I was able to skip red government tape and get meetings lots of people would not have been able to get based on my reputation. However, this will be my last kick at the cat if the project flops," he responded to her last question, first.

"I think I understand the how better than the why, Jim," Garcia pressed, "but I still don't understand why you are taking this on? What is motivating you? I think of men in your situation as more of playboys or philanthropists. You know, living the jet set good life with models and Vegas weekends or donating to hospitals and getting your name on buildings, maybe building a golf course or two at fancy country clubs…" she trailed off and paused to really look him in the eye before she continued. "This idea of yours is beyond playing. This represents a serious change in the world. It has the potential to revolutionize travel, transportation, trade and the amount of electricity being offered to these cities will change lives and standards of living in very large parts of Europe. You will likely get bad press from oil and gas companies and, at the least, be accused of biting the hand that fed you! You'll be criticized for being un-American, or worse yet, be accused of revolutionizing technology in foreign countries and increasing their ability to move weapons, even if it's not true. God I still get threats every time I work on new large geo-systems that are actually located in the States. But you must have thought of all of that already or even dealt with it if you have begun setting these deals up. Why put yourself through this? Are you an environmentalist at heart? What is your motivation?" She summarized her long speech with the simple question that Jim knew deserved more than a simple answer.

Jim leaned back against the worn wooden bench, collected his thoughts for a moment, and then turned to Garcia and began by appreciating the fact that her first question got right to the heart of who he was rather than focus on superficial details. "No one has really asked me why before," he said, "and I actually admire you for it. Most people's first questions are about how this will actually work and their second question is always about the money. How much it will cost them and how much they stand to profit from it," Jim shrugged. "That's just normal business practice. But your question clearly reflects your own motivations and character, so let me do the best I can to explain mine." When he paused again, Garcia could see he meant to give her a sincere response. She almost apologized for asking something more personal than he was accustomed to answering, but he began again before she could seriously consider reclaiming her question.

"My business partner and I work solely on paper transactions now, and I think the simple answer to your question is that I miss building things. It's not that we aren't successful at what we do now; quite the opposite in fact. Our portfolio continues to grow at a very impressive rate but this idea really excites me and I want to make it work. The idea of building something tangible again is like a drug to me right now. I have been working on putting together a strong team capable enough to pull this off. So far all of them have concentrated on design, implementation and efficiencies, not one of them has ever asked why I wanted to do this, but to be fair that's why they were hired... to make this vision a reality. Their job is to ask "how", not "why". So until now, I'm not sure I've really thought about the why before and I've definitely never tried to put it into words."

The night was cool but the warm steam that surrounded them from the geyser was invigorating. The moist air seemed to sooth their lungs and relax them as they sat talking on the bench. Garcia thought Iceland should actually sell tickets for this bench. The feelings she got from breathing the steamy air was heavenly and even at nine pm at night there was no danger of losing the sunlight anytime soon. Truthfully she had thought her trip to Iceland would be a one-time visit, she thought she'd see the sites and never be back. But now with Jim's proposal in mind she realized she was considering calling this country home, at least for the next few years. The idea of working closely with Jim excited her as well, these two meetings with him had been fun and exciting and the idea of basically finishing out her working life on what will likely be the biggest renewable energy project the world will ever see was tantalizing to say the least. The scariest part of all of this was the magnetic draw she was feeling towards Jim and she was working hard to separate the merits of the project from the endorphins pumping throughout her body. She still wanted to know that he was fully invested in the project for reasons other than just financial gain before she agreed to give it any serious thought. She wanted to know he wouldn't just shut it down in a year because of threats or a change of the political tide. "Well, I guess I feel like this project is asking for a lot of its partners. I would just like to understand your underlying motivation here," she pushed him to continue.

"Well I'm no tree hugger," Jim chuckled. "As guilty as I feel, I've tossed garbage out the car window as I drive, I've thrown plastic bottles in the garbage and not the recycle bin, I run air conditioning in my homes, I have a couple sports cars and big SUV's that definitely would not win any emission prizes and, don't tell anyone, but in the late eighties I used to use hair spray, so there goes the ozone layer."

This self-mockery made her glance at his fade hair style and smile at his ability to lighten the moment with a joke directed at himself. Jim caught her quick glance at his head and continued by saying, "Hey no judging now, you asked for this deeply personal explanation."

Laughing, she said, "Right. I'm sorry, please go on."

Jim stood again and walked a couple steps forward, turned to face her, and just as he was about to speak the geyser erupted again. The water blast shot up over his head, causing the droplets and steam to float out around him, framing him in a magical moment. He turned to watch as it finished and stepped sideways so she could see too. Garcia stood up to join him and as it finished they turned towards each other. The atmosphere and the beauty of the moment almost got the better of Jim and he lowered his head to kiss her but caught himself just in time and remembered he had a job to do. He needed to convince her to join his project and mixing romance in with a business proposal was not the best way to go about this. He stepped back, putting distance between them, and gestured that they return to their bench.

"Those eruptions are so…," Garcia hesitated, searching for the right word to describe the magic she had just experienced, knowing some of it was attributed to Jim's nearness. "Incredible. Amazing. Other-worldly. Is there even a word that can actually capture their beauty?" she asked.

"I'm glad you enjoy them as much as I do," Jim said before returning to the main topic at hand and answering her deeper question. "So as I was saying, I'm not a green 'save the world from the atrocities of big oil and pollution type person', but I'm trying to see the big picture. The world's population is almost eight billion and we grow by seventy-five million people a year which is the combined population of Canada and California. Eventually the seventy-five million growth becomes exponential and the population really explodes. Right now we are completely, or almost completely, dependent on a resource that will run out, not to mention it runs motors and equipment that are far inferior to other technologies, and of course the exhaust is dreadful for the environment. I know that once the oil reserve gets low the world will take it more seriously and jump on new products and design. I feel if we know it's coming, something should be done now. This project in Neom is the perfect place to get a head start on the change that is inevitable in the years to come," Jim said logically.

After a short hesitation, Jim continued, "I feel like my so called fame and fortune came from dumb luck, a kid messing around with computers." Hanging his head, Jim said ruefully, "I couldn't even save my wife when she got sick with cancer. We never had a chance to have kids or grow our family, but yet my financial portfolio continued to grow." Looking up, he admitted, "Garcia, I feel like a fraud. With so much unrest, turbulence and trouble in the world, I feel like this is my chance to do something good by using the luck I fell into. Yes, of course, I still want to make money and be successful but the opportunity to play a key role in getting countries to actually work together, trade and build toward a goal that can ultimately help humanity become more sustainable while giving more people access to better life styles can only be positive. I want to do this because I feel it's the right thing to do and for selfish reasons so I no longer feel like a fraud." He paused again, realizing he had just given her more of his inner self than he had shared with anyone else since before his wife had passed away. Knowing this was likely his last chance to persuade her to come on board with his project, he finished with genuine and simple sincerity. "In all my research on the subject, I've found that you have the most potential and knowledge to help me realize this dream and that's why I want you on board. So what do you say, are you interested? Will you work with me?"

Garcia had now heard all she needed to be convinced. The project had a design team, financial backing and a leader who was passionate about the result beyond financial gain. She looked at Jim and extended her right hand to shake on it. As he reached for her hand and held it longer and more gently than a typical shake on a business proposal would require, she said with a sincerity that matched his own, "You convinced me. I'm in. And for the record, you're not a fraud. If you look closer, I think your talents may be more in taking risks others would not and picking the right risks others cannot see."

CHAPTER 14

George picked up his phone. "Yes, Sara?" he asked.
"Richard Emerson from Trade Link Security is on the phone for you, George."

"Thanks, Sara, put him through please," George responded.

"Rich, how are you today?" George asked when he heard the click signifying Sara had put the call through.

"Same as ever. How about you? Did you call for a checkup or have you got something new on the go?"

"Well, yes, it's time for an update but there are a couple new things we should discuss. Where are you? Can you come to my office any time soon?" George asked.

"George, I'm in New York. Of course I can come but it's an eight-hour flight."

"Go private," George said, indicating the importance of the meeting. "Be here as soon as you can. Let me know your travel times and I'll have someone pick you up. Or should I just get Sara to arrange it for you? She's a hell of a travel agent. Will you be bringing anyone with you? When can you leave?"

Richard laughed at George's obvious impatience. "You are determined, my friend, but this will cost you. I can be to JFK in an hour, travelling alone. It will be more efficient if Sara looks after the travel details so I can wrap up what I'm doing, pack, and get to the airport. Is she really that good of a travel agent?"

"Even better," stated George confidently.

Two hours later, Richard Emerson was aboard a Gulf Stream headed across the Atlantic, mentally going over the upcoming meeting with George. Ever since his association with the man, Richard had been persuaded to take his company a little deeper down the dark path than he would have on his own, but George seemed to have a way of making Richard feel like their periodic forays into the grey area of the law were inevitable and acceptable. George paid him very well and when things were going his way, George made him feel like they were friends, even though Richard knew better than to completely trust a man like George. Richard also felt a little more at ease blurring the lines of legality with George because George mainly operated outside the States.

A few years ago, Richard had created a shell company in Morocco with George's help. With this company he had been able to funnel some of his earnings from the less-savory assignments George had given him through it in secret. So far he had left all of those particular funds in European investments and had been making some property investments in the country as well. The risk of trying to bring that money to the States was too great and he didn't need the extra funds at home anyway. Between his pension and the money he made state side, he was doing quite well financially.

As with most security company owners, Richard was an ex-cop; he had been a NYC detective who ended up in management before his retirement. He'd always been good at tracking people down, following them unnoticed and putting facts together. His superiors always said it was lucky he was on the law's side because he was way too good at thinking like a criminal. Honourable and ethical while working as a cop, Richard never once broke the law, nor had he even considered it. Since starting his own business and taking George on as a client, however, he had stretched numerous laws in the States and straight out smashed them in Europe.

Settling back in his comfortable private-jet seat, Richard thought wryly about how his honour and ethics as a cop would never have earned him the opportunity to travel in this comfort. Richard knew George was in deep on some new project but hadn't yet heard any details. George had been stressed out and neurotic over the Morocco project, but this new venture had pushed George to a whole new level of intensity, to the point Richard was worried he would give himself a stroke. George has had Richard's crew on the pay role for more than a couple months now. Richard had been required to report the movements, meeting schedules, and social activities of three men and their families directly to George, on a weekly basis. Now suddenly George was demanding that he report the information to him in person, which was not so bad, but when that meant an eight-hour flight across the Atlantic to another country, he knew there would be more to George's needs than just an update. As he flew across the Atlantic, Richard had done some speculating as to what George would want from him. He did this by reviewing the profiles of the men he was following in his head and tried to determine what George could be working on. One of the men, Jim Dunsmuir was fairly high profile, especially in the financial world. The other two were also very successful business men in their fields of green electricity. George had pushed so hard on Richard for information on these men that he had even ordered Richard to tap their phones. Richard had straight out refused this request, telling George tapping phones was beyond what he was willing to do and completely illegal. George gave in on the phone tapping order but did insist on one-minute updates on each man twice a week, each report was required to be by phone as he was adamant that he wanted nothing documented. So far, the men had not really done anything out of the ordinary as far as Richard could tell but George never told him exactly what it was he was looking for either.

Following Christopher Buchannan had been an exciting assignment for two of his men. Chris was a high roller and president of Evergreen, a windmill company that was trying to make a place for itself. In his role as president, Chris had been touring the windiest North

American cities, which meant spending most of his time on the coasts. He was wining and dining mayors and city delegates, trying to convince them of the benefits of investing in sustainable energy, and in particular, the benefits of using wind power. After his North American tour, he jumped the ocean to do the same thing in Britain, France, Italy and almost every other country that he thought might be interested in wind power. The European market was more receptive to clean energy but also more saturated with numerous businesses already well-established.

Chris kept a very routine schedule even when he was on the road. He rose early for a cardio work out, went back to the room for a shower and then would head down for breakfast. His routine mornings were always followed by meetings with government officials in charge of power and electricity. Chris would typically include the offer of dinner meetings as well in efforts to make those social situation contacts outside the work environment and had proven quite adept at insinuating himself into these high-ranking social circles. Chris was squeaky clean and didn't use the opportunity that traveling away from home gave him to get involved in affairs or shady activities. He would travel for the week and fly home every second Friday to spend four days with his wife, son and daughter. Richard's guys watched their marks closely for vices such as drinking, gambling, women, bribery, or any act that would discredit them or harm their company's reputation. On average, Richard would find information of this sort at least 70 percent of the time but so far he had nothing on

Chris. George had also insisted that Richard have a detail follow Chris's family. His children were in university and were well on their way to success, and his wife was just as clean. Chris's wife was a part time nurse at a local hospital. A background check on her had shown that when her kids were young, her days had consisted of going to work after dropping the kids at school, working nine till two, then picking the kids up and heading home. Now that both kids were grown up and off at college, she continued with the same work schedule. Everette, Chris's oldest, had played a lot of soccer after school while Lacie, his daughter, had taken up cheer leading with a bunch of her friends. Both children carried these hobbies on into University as well. The family seemed happy and healthy with no real kinks to exploit.

The only potential inroad they might have at Evergreen was through Production Supervisor Elliot Ben. In doing staff background checks at Evergreen, Richard's man Kelly Charles had noticed that Elliot did not have much of a life, no family and no real acquaintances. He had a routine of going to work, finishing his day by eating at a favourite pub for supper, then going home. He did this without exception except on soccer nights. On those nights he would stay in the pub late, drink and watch the game. Kelly had started attending the odd game night and had struck up a few conversations with Elliot as they sat next to each other at the bar, and they soon became familiar enough with each other that they would buy each other rounds and clap each other on the back when their team scored. Kelly had steered the conversation towards work a few times and Elliot had shared a few of his ideas about his work with Kelly but really tried to avoid the subject for the most part. So far Kelly did not have a strong enough relationship with Elliot to push him for more information without the potential risk of Elliot getting suspicious or bored. Elliot's nonverbal communication made it clear he did not sit in the bar to discuss work.

Richard also had men following another man named Peter Fairchild. Peter is the CEO of Naes Construction, his company specialized in engineering concrete construction, which included designing and building foundations for skyscrapers and building complexes. Beyond that his firm was revered as the standard in hydro-dam design and construction. The company is based out of Washington State and has a head office in Seattle.

Peter was a different story than Chris, polar opposite in fact. Peter had been through two marriages, and had four kids who live with his ex-wives. Peter worked a lot and didn't have time for children nor did he want to make time, he was quite selfish and work was his focus.

Peter had many of the stereotypical personality traits listed on the psychopathy checklist. He went after what he wanted, when he wanted it and treated people and possessions one in the same. He dressed in three piece suits and worked all hours of the day. Peter had a natural ability to draw people in and used his charisma to get what he wanted from them. He made people feel special, made them feel like they were his best friend and that they could be his hero, his savior if only they would do one special thing for him or get him one great deal. At the same time, the person dealing with him could be a hundred times poorer than him, but he had a way of making them feel like if they didn't help him out, he would go broke or shrivel up and die. He had a way of making people think they were his only lifeline and so important and needed that he could not survive without them, meanwhile he would already be plotting his next victim. Sometimes people saw through his ruse but mostly they would keep coming back for more. Without a doubt, Peter had talent, an ability to almost hypnotize people into believing whatever he had to say. For these very reasons, people feel compelled to sell him equipment and supplies cheaper and to pay more for his product than they would pay others. This left the competitors in his industry at a loss for how Peter just seemed to get more successful while they did the same thing without realizing the exponential gain.

Unfortunately, Peter's talent did not just apply to business. It also gave him power over friends, family, acquaintances and women, the latter of which were the cause of Peter's disruptive family relationships. Peter was with different women all the time and they seemed to provide a support system for him. He chose his women wisely as many of them had strong influential social networks where they protected him and his actions based on the level of influence he seemed to wield over them. Peter was very strategic as most of the women he targeted were in relationships or positions such that they could not reveal to the world their true feelings for him but they were proud to defend him in public and increase his status without being able to admit they were with him or had feelings for him. Somehow Peter was able to make these women feel proud to be his support system regardless of the fact he was obviously using them.

As an outsider looking in, Richard could not get over how blatant Peter's tactics were and how easily people were pulled in by him. It truly reminded him of kids at the carnival. Everyone was lined up to give their money for the chance at a prize from a game they knew was rigged. Yet once they lost at one game they would turn around and line up for the next game just as eager to get fleeced again. Richard would be able to share all this information on Peter and inform George that despite missing the application deadline, Peter had been able to talk his way into the Prince's castle and get himself bumped up into a front runner position for the Neom project. When he met with the Princes, Peter had been able to convince them that his proposal to build the biggest hydroelectric power dam in the world on the Nile river was worthy of consideration as a top bid in the tenders they'd received for the project.

Richard's file on Peter would be career-ending for most anyone else as it provided the perfect ammunition for George to use against a ruthless businessman. Unfortunately, with Peter's reputation such as it is, more than likely none of the information will help George discredit Peter. The wilder the situation or the worse Peter treated people, the more his stock rose. As far as Richard was concerned, whatever George decided to do to Peter would be less than he deserved. Peter Fairchild was one of the worst people Richard has ever dealt with, he was rotten and Peter had met a lot of awful people in his line of work. George himself was unsavory most of the time but at least George didn't fake it. George did not pretend to be some nice church going person when deep down he was just ugly through and through.

After dealing with Peter, following Jim Dunsmuir began restoring Richard's faith in humanity. Richard almost did not want to provide George any information on Jim, not that there was much to tell anyway. So far it appeared that Jim was just putting together a team. He'd been travelling Europe, meeting with geothermal design experts, and in particular seemed very interested in Garcia Grey. Richard was not a hundred percent sure what to think of the meetings with Garcia Grey. First he couldn't figure out why Jim would fly her out to meet in Iceland and secondly, his confusion was compounded when the meetings seemed more like dates than business. Richard just couldn't make sense of why an investment guru with corporate headquarters in Iceland would start bidding and investing in green energy projects, let alone a massive project like powering a new city in Saudi Arabia. Anyway, it would be up to George to decide what to do with the information. Richard signaled the flight attendant over and ordered himself a drink, realizing he might as well relax as much as he could for the rest of the flight. Knowing how George operated, Richard correctly assumed that he had not been summoned to fly across the globe simply to deliver the intel he had gathered on George's competition. George would have another task ready for him when he arrived.

CHAPTER 15

George had a driver pick Richard up at the airport in Quargagate, which was about one hundred and sixty kilometers from his office in Tinghir. The car was a black Renault SUV, a high-end vehicle built in Tangier with an environmentally friendly diesel engine. George had been buying local to show he supported the country's industries and had the additional perk of contributing to George's "save the planet" propaganda.

The Tinghir Oasis is one of the most popular tourist destinations in Morocco. Green cool relaxing space, consisting of a thirty by four kilometer park-like refuge in the middle of such harsh African terrain is therapy for the eyes of anyone who has traveled the desert to get there. Entering the Oasis and getting out of the dry, sandy, desert wind is so calming to the nerves it feels like that first deep breath of cool night summer air as you sit down on your porch after a long day. George's office had a beautiful view overlooking a large portion of the green space. Richard took one last look at the plants and breathed in the fresh air before heading up to George's office. He knew once he got into a meeting with George that it didn't matter what the view was, the situation would be intense.

Richard walked through the doors and headed for the elevator. Once Sara verified who he was through George's video surveillance system, the elevator engaged and shot him up to Blade Solar's head office. As he stepped off the elevator onto the marble floored outer office of Blade's CEO, he was impressed once again at the care and expense that had gone into its design. But as always when he visited George's empire, the beautiful office was lost from focus the second he saw Sara. George's personal secretary could literally be Jessica Alba's twin, her complexion was flawless, and her smile hypnotized him. Beyond her physical attractiveness, she seemed to be an absolutely amazing person. Normally he would not believe a girl like Sara would go for him, but for some reason Richard suspected she might like him. Over the course of his last few assignments for George, Richard and Sara had had some pretty long phone and in-person conversations that had evolved to stimulating flirtation. He guessed Sara to be in her early thirties and she was single as far as he knew. Richard could only imagine that George had hired her for her looks at the start but must have been pleasantly surprised when she turned out to be a perfect assistant. She'd told Richard that George pays her well and gives her lots of time off when his schedule allowed. Further, she had added that the two of them got along so well that she had moved to Morocco at George's request. The fact that George paid for her moving and kept her on staff during such a large restructuring said a lot about Sara's efficiency. George has said that sometimes Sara has things done before he even thinks of needing them. That compliment, coupled with the fact that he's not in a relationship with her, further justified how great she must be. Richard knew George was nothing if not famous for firing staff or letting them go for just about any reason at all, so for him to keep Sara all this time proves her worth.

Richard had been a cop, a detective, and finally a Captain in the New York City Police force before retiring to start his own Private Detective firm. Now he follows and investigates high profile people all over the world and engages in some grey area corporate espionage. Even with all this experience, at 42 years old he was still nervous about asking a girl out on a date.

"George is ready to see you Rich, go on in," Sara greeted him with a warm smile.

"Thanks, Sara. It's good to see you again," Richard replied.

"I hope your travel was ok?" she inquired, "it was last minute planning. Sometimes rushed flights aren't always the best."

"Ha," Richard chuckled, "well if I ever start complaining about a private plane and a personal pick up shuttle service, please whack me upside the head. Frankly

I was amazed how quickly you put the trip together. You may have missed your calling as a first-class travel agent."

Sara blushed at his praise and Richard allowed himself a moment to enjoy her smile before he shut the office door to start his meeting with George. George stood up, walked over to Richard, shook his hand and welcomed him to Morocco. He then proceeded to walk over to a more informal side of the office where he sat in a leather wing backed chair. He gestured to Richard that he should take the love seat. As Richard was settling in and pulling out his notebook, George jumped in.

CHAPTER 16

"Well, Richard, what have you got for me?"

Richard started with Jim Dunsmuir and relayed to George that Jim was presently at his offices in Iceland, compiling what seemed to Richard a team that would be able to build a geothermal system. He told George about Garcia Grey, the geothermal expert, and how it seemed like they were dating more than working. Although he didn't like the idea of Jim Dunsmuir getting involved in this project, George still didn't feel he was much of a threat as a competitor in the bid. To be thorough he asked, "Do you have any information on what he is building a team in Iceland for and how or where he would plan on setting up a geothermal electric plant in the desert?"

"No, nothing, whatever plans he has aren't far along or he is keeping them very secretive," Richard replied.

"Ok, well stay on him and see if you can find out what the hell he's doing," George advised.

"Next, Evergreen Wind Farms," Richard said as he switched to the Buchanan file.

"Ahh the angelic Christopher Buchanan," George said sarcastically.

"You're right, George. When most people call someone angelic, it's usually in a sarcastic reference but in Chris's case, as far as I can tell, it's true. He seems to be a devoted family man, donates to charities, has no bad habits and even calls his mom a couple times a week. He has been travelling the globe, well the windy places anyway, looking for contracts. We had a listen in on a couple of his sales pitches. They're not boastful or flashy, if anything he undersold his hardware. I think you could spend a lot of time on him and don't think you would come up with much to ruin his reputation. We've gotten Kelly in with Elliot Beam. Elliot is Chris's production supervisor, no wife, family or life other than work and cheering soccer games on at the local pub. Might be able to work an angle on him," Richard said.

"Hmm," was all George said, not appearing too optimistic at Richard's suggestion.

"Finally there's Peter Fairchild, who is basically the polar opposite of Chris Buchannan, and we've found lots of dirt on him but it's not worth much because he basically posts his own dirt on line. Peter has ruined his own reputation and all but brags about it, yet people still seem to love him. He calls himself an untamable cowboy and a risk taker willing to ride anything for eight seconds, whatever that means!" Richard reported.

"Sounds like a jackass to me, but you are right, things always seem to go his way no matter who he sleeps with or which business partner he screws over," George replied. "So Naes Construction is going to put a second dam on the Nile. That is a hell of an idea and gives Saudi Arabia and Egypt a bonding incentive. The Princes will like that idea, which means I need to make it less appealing," George reflected and then paused as he absorbed the information he'd just received and considered how to proceed.

"Okay so you got us the intel. The question is now what to do with it. I need to prove solar is better than wind power, which on its own, it's not, but in the desert sun, combined with service requirements on a solar array versus a wind farm, solar should win out. However, should is not good enough. We need a plan. I need a plan to get Christopher Buchanan out of the running completely. I also need to figure out a way to knock Fairchild out," George mused.

"What about Jim Dunsmuir?" Richard interjected.

"We will leave him be. I need to be strategic about this, which means I need to leave some competition, or the Princes will suspect me and they're very ethical in business. Playing the odds, I would say that Jim is the least of my competition. If I can eliminate the two that give me more of a challenge and make it look like there was a threat against all of us from an outside source, like the oil industry or some anti-technology terrorist group for instance, then we show the world and the Princes of Saudi Arabia that we at Blade are strong resourceful and unshakable. It'll also make the others look like they are just fly by night companies who were not all that serious in the first place about helping the Arabic people build their city of the future," George said.

"I see," Richard responded, "So what are you thinking? Do you have some people that will leak a couple stories to the media?"

"Richard this is beyond a media leak. Besides with so much fake news, media posts and blogs going on these days, no one would believe, and most wouldn't even pay attention, to a couple unsubstantiated threats. I need a way to get Buchanan and Fairchild to pull out of the race themselves or admit they're scared, which would weaken their chances when bidding on a job in a communist state such as Arabia. Arabians would look down on any form of weakness, especially for personal safety. Most Arabians live with the threat of violence every day and don't blink. That's one of the biggest motivations behind building Neom, to free their people from that lifestyle."

"How will you do that?" Richard asked. "Neither will be easy to get to and they'll not scare off on some childish death threat sent to them in a letter with words cut out of magazines in an attempt to hide traceability."

"I'm not sure exactly how to do it, but lucky for me that's not my job, it's yours Richard," George challenged him as leaned back in his chair, eyeing Richard's reaction.

"What?" Richard was incredulous. "I don't threaten people, George. I follow, track and record people. I don't threaten or use violence. This goes beyond anything I've ever done for you." Richard was emphatic in his opposition to George's suggestion.

"Richard you don't have to hurt anyone," George smiled slyly. "That's why I want you on this. I trust you and your team. All I'll require is some good acting. I need to hire you and your crew to throw a scare into my competition that's so believable they back out on the project and leave me holding it. Really, it's like a sting operation from your police force days, right?"

Richard sits back, reeling at what George was asking him to do but yet, almost involuntarily, his mind began processing the challenge and considering possibilities. It's true he was good at setting up sting operations and although the investigative part of the work he did for George was not only lucrative but filled a sense of purpose for Richard, at some level he still missed the excitement and action side of police work. As Richard recalled some of his past work, his eyes scanned George's office. George had a high level of taste and style. The office wall plaque read: "This office was designed and specifically furnished for our friend George Anderson by Restoration Hardware, Corte Madera, California." There was a signature engraving at the bottom he couldn't make out but was probably designer or the CEO. The office itself was the size of a small house so the furnishing must have cost a small fortune. It looked manly and stylish and was set up efficiently for working. At the same time, it had a comfortable feel, he felt as relaxed as if he was in his own living room. As his initial shock wore off,

Richard felt confident he could come up with a plan to get to each executive. The only question was regarding his own ethics. How far across the line this was going and once he got into it, how much further George would push him across it?

"Give me a base, George. What exactly are you wanting?" Richard asked.

George knew this question was coming and was not sure he would be able to talk Richard into helping him, but despite Richard's initial aversion to George's request, it seemed like he had Rich on the hook now. George knew that Richard and his team had the training and resources for this operation, it was just a bit more on the other side of the law than they were used to. Law enforcement officers always think bad guys have it easy, talking about how criminals don't have to follow rules or be exact in their work because no one rates what they do, nor do they have to report to anyone. George knew that was not true; if anything bad guys had to be more careful, more thorough because their price for a poor performance is prison time or sometimes their lives. Based on that alone, he thought crime was way riskier and harder than getting a poor performance rating from some bureaucrat manager in the police force.

George decided to lay it out for Richard honestly. "Here is how I see it. There are four companies seriously bidding on this project. We will need four terrorist-type attacks; one against each company. The attack on Dunsmuir should be the most visual with the most publicity but the least effective and least personal because

I do not really want him to drop out. Next an attack on Chris, I think we just need a believable threat against his family. Any threat against his loved ones and he will drop out of the competition so fast the Princes won't even believe it. There's no way Chris would risk any family member for business or money," George paused, knowing his suggested attack on Buchanan would be the most difficult for Rich to swallow since it involved family. Seeing Rich nod for him to continue, George smiled in relief and proceeded. "An attack against me should include a threat to my reputation and Blade's reputation which will somehow become completely untruthful and then allow me to donate one hundred thousand dollars to a cause that will help sustain the planet. We will have to come up with something good," George grinned in anticipation of how he was going to come out ahead in more ways than one when this was all over.

"What about Peter Fairchild," Richard jumped in when George paused to gloat over his own future success, "it's like he is immune to bad publicity. In fact, he seems to get more popular the worse he acts. With the Cowboy reputation he created for himself he has endeared himself to the American population so much so he seems untouchable. The Cowboy still stands tall as a symbol of what made America the greatest country and Peter has totally imprinted himself as a true cowboy even though he's nothing like one."

"Good question, Richard. It's one that I've given a lot of thought. Besides your firm, I've also hired a psychiatrist to study my competitors. The information I've obtained has shown me what makes them tick. I wanted this information to figure out how to outbid, out-debate and basically come out on top during any competitive session. You're right about Peter, he does seem untouchable and his hydroelectric dam proposal is probably the most feasible, so it's imperative that we block that plan. At this point, I haven't come up with a possible scenario to foil his proposal," George admitted.

"Well I think I can work out a plan for Jim and I'm sure we can discourage Chris fairly easily, but I'm going to need this psychological background information you have on Peter cause I'm at a loss. Just out of curiosity, did you also get the psychiatrist to study you? What are we going to do to make a plausible believable threat against you and your reputation?"

"I did, actually. And I've been working on the beginnings of a plan for an attack against me. I want to be accused of supporting the oil and gas industry and just using green energy as a way to make money. The accusations should insinuate that I would be willing to drop green energy as soon as the market goes south. It would also help if I'm accused of being in bed with the oil and gas industry so much so that some type of Green Peace initiative will investigate me and be forced to publish their findings, which of course will show that it was not true and will then win me the public's sympathy and support." George leaned back in his chair, reveling in the brilliance of his own scheme. "Now the risky part. Fairchild's reputation is up there in the stars and almost shines as bright as Dunsmuir's. He also has the second-best solution to Neom's energy needs so it is imperative that we discredit him in Egypt so the government there will not want to work with him. We do this by making the world see who he really is."

"Who he really is?" Richard questioned.

"The psychological assessment tells me he is an egotistical bully and that there is basically nobody higher on the narcissism checklist than Peter Fairchild, except maybe Narcissus himself."

"That doesn't give me any ideas how to bring him down. What are you suggesting we do?" Richard asked, uncertain where George was headed.

"We need to expose his true self and need to do it publicly. We need to point out to his adoring fans what he truly is. Basically, I'm gambling on my psychiatrist's assessment. We need to put Peter to the test. We need to pick one of America's favorite stereotypical cowboy traits, one that Peter should exemplify if he truly had the characteristics of a 'cowboy', and then find a way to challenge him on it and get him to fail miserably under public scrutiny."

Still not quite grasping George's vision for taking down Peter Fairchild, Richard did recognize that George was basically asking Richard to commit acts of extortion, bribery, uttering threats, and who knows what else. Not only did George expect Richard to do it willingly but to bring his whole team into the act as well. If he was honest with himself, Richard had to admit that the challenge excited him but he was not sure he could justify the means. What George was asking not only blurred the lines of ethics, it jumped them completely. Knowing George's ruthless business mind, he saw how George could talk about these ideas with the same calm nonchalance as if he was ordering a steak at his favorite restaurant, but Richard was torn and was not yet convinced he could do it.

George could see Richard's hesitation and feared he was losing Richard. Knowing he didn't have time to find a new crew, and certainly not one with Richard's loyalty, professionalism and experience, he tried appealing to Richard's ethics, rather than challenge them.

"Richard, I need you to do this for me. I do not want anyone to get hurt or seriously injured but I want this contract and you and your team are the only ones who can put a plan together and execute it safely. I know I get a little out of hand but that's why I need you. You have a moral compass that keeps me on the straight and narrow. Well, maybe on the curvy narrow," George smiled with comradery to make Richard feel more comfortable, "but nonetheless better than I would be without you. What do you say; will you help me?"

"You are asking a lot this time," Richard hedged, hesitant to take the leap across the line.

"I know." George replied simply, understanding he had given Richard a lot to think about.

"If I do this," Richard began putting his thoughts into words, "I review and have veto rights on all final plans and aspects to each scheme. We renegotiate my team's wages and you pay all legal costs for lawyers of my choice, if any of my guys get caught. I also want ten percent of your shares in Blade Solar regardless of whether you win the

Neom contract. If I do what you ask, I have to safeguard my team as much as possible and it has to be worth the risk. Can you agree to those terms??"

"Yes, except I will even do better than that," George breathed a sigh of relief, seeing that Richard was on board. He should've known. Every man has a price. "I will give you ten million dollars up front before the job and five million more if I am the successful bidder. What I won't do, however, is give up ten percent of my shares. Blade is publicly traded and I'd lose controlling interest of my company if I gave them up. If you can agree to those terms, my lawyer will write it up tomorrow, we can sign on the dotted line and start work immediately. What do you say?" George asked.

"It's a deal, but only if my team agrees," Richard said, making it clear to George that he wouldn't put his team at risk without their approval. "I can't sign before then. I'll see you tomorrow."

As he was leaving the office, Sara was locking up behind him. She said George tended to work late and sleep most nights in his office, despite the fancy penthouse suit he rented, so they walked out together leaving George alone in the office.

CHAPTER 17

"Thanks for getting me here on such short notice Sara," Richard said appreciatively.

"You're staying in the Riad Dar Bab Todra hotel. It's the best place around even though it only has a four-star rating. I've a car waiting for you to use while you're here, the driver can get you back and forth easily and knows the area well," Sara replied, giving him the additional details of the plans she made.

"That's impressive!" Richard exclaimed, never having had that treatment the other times he had been called in to meet with George. "You must have good contacts to make bookings with such short notice."

"Ah yes," Sara laughed. "And that's only travel, you should see me organize a high stakes meeting, you just don't know how Sara I am."

"I love Suits, and I bet you could give Donna a run

for her money," Richard complimented her, picking up on her reference to the popular American television show. "Have you had dinner yet? We could go to your favorite restaurant and you could finish telling me about how good you are." Richard waited nervously for her reaction, uncertain how she'd feel about his unexpected invitation.

"That will take a while longer than just dinner," she replied cheekily. "You'll have to spring for dessert too if you want the whole list. But I'm game. Let's take your car."

"Deal," Richard chuckled, pleasantly surprised at the saucy attitude that he'd never seen before in his interactions with Sara. He could not be happier, a good dinner would allow him time to take his mind off of George's indecent proposal and dine with one of the best looking girls he had ever seen. To top it off she seemed funny and entertaining. Even if it wasn't a formal pre-planned date, he could tell it was going to be an enjoyable evening.

Throughout the course of dinner, he found out Sara was from New York, her mom and dad were retired now and she had an older brother. She had majored in commerce at NYU and ended up with a business degree. She had thoughts of trying to get into law but had not gotten that far yet. It sounded like schooling came pretty easy for Sara and although she had her degree it seemed like school had been a secondary focus for her, according to her she had spent as much time socializing and partying as she had studying. Sara told great stories and although he was tired from a long day of travel, and a mind-blowing meeting, Richard was completely transfixed by what she was saying and the way her eyes moved when she laughed. Richard ordered them a bottle of Copensis Chardonnay, telling her he was not much of a wine expert but he had looked up African wine and found it to be rated highly.

"Richard," Sara said with sheepish laughter, "I'm afraid I was a party girl from New York and wasn't into sipping high end wines. For me and my crowd, it was the three M's: Manhattans to unwind, Margaritas to party or Martinis to get serious or drown our sorrows if needed." Sara looked up from her drink to see how Richard was responding to her admission. Seeing amused laughter in his eyes, she continued, "So, kind sir, your selection will be more than adequate to satisfy my wine tastes, I appreciate you helping me to expand my horizons though."

They ended up sharing a few plates of chicken and fish shish-kabobs, two skewers of vegetables and a large volcanic chocolate cake for dessert. Both were disappointed to see the dinner come to an end as they were both relaxed and enjoying each other's company. Subconsciously they ate the cake slowly, trying to drag out the evening while sipping fifteen-year port just as leisurely. Sara had to admit the port brought out the flavor of the cake and jokingly said she might have to add a P to her triple M drink repertoire.

As they walked out to Richard's car, Sara looked up at Richard in an expectant way and he reached out and grabbed her hand. As their hands touched a shiver shot up her arm and she was glad he had reached for her. She liked Rich, he was different from all the businessmen George usually dealt with. He was harder and had more depth than the suits who just moved numbers around. Richard actually had a physical component to his work and she liked that. She also liked that he was six foot two had a full head of hair with a neat stylish cut and an athletic build. Richard was in the middle of working himself up to ask her if she would consider another date with him as they got to his car.

He was opening the car door for her when she surprised him by taking the initiative. "Looks like I owe you a dinner now. I know you are only in town one more night but if you're interested…" Sara trailed off uncertainly.

Richard let go of the car door, pulled on her hand that he was still holding, and turned her towards him, bent his head down and kissed her. It was a bold move but he quickly put his arms around her as she leaned into his kiss. It was a soft kiss so their lips lingered on each other's and as she rolled her head he got to feel every millimeter of each luscious lip against his teeth as he gently nibbled on them. As they pulled apart, Richard was grinning ear to ear and Sara rested against his strong body for a few more seconds before stepping back. They were both speechless for a few seconds.

Finally, Richard snapped to and said, "I'd love to go to dinner with you again, Sara. Same time tomorrow night? I think I'll be with George anyway so we could leave right from work again?"

"Yes let's go for a late dinner. You can pick me up at my house. The driver knows where I live," she replied.

"I never expected this," Richard commented thoughtfully.

"Neither did I," Sara admitted. "But you can do your part by picking me up at my door, with flowers in your hands," she quipped to lighten the seriousness of the moment.

"Well I might have trouble finding flowers, but I'll do my best," Richard responded with a smile at her humour.

"Are you ok with not telling George about us?" Sara asked worriedly. "It's only one date and he seems to worry like a father."

"We're adults, and this doesn't affect our work so I don't see any reason to bring it up at this point. But if I don't tell him I have other plans tomorrow night, there's no telling how long we will work," Richard said knowingly.

"No problem, I know him well. I'll leave an hour before you do to get ready."

"I can't wait to see you again," Richard said, reluctant to let her out of his grasp.

"Richard?" Sarah whispered beguilingly.

"Yes?"

"Kiss me again."

Richard needed no second invitation, he tightened his hold on her as his lips found hers.

Richard went home literally high, his endorphins had obviously shot into overdrive and he really didn't snap back into reality until he woke up for breakfast the next morning. As he was climbing out of his car in front of George's office it dawned on him that he was about to see Sara again. He was on his way to a meeting to plan and discuss extortion, sabotage, industrial espionage and he had butterflies in his stomach over a girl just like he was a kid again. As Richard got off the elevator, unsure how he would greet her, Sara being the great girl she is, met him halfway across the office floor and grabbed his hand and said "Hi". The way she smiled up at him made him relax and feel at home with her. He grabbed her other hand looked her in the eyes and told her how sweet he thought she was and thanked her for the great dinner the previous night. She said she had fun too and hoped he still wanted to go out again that night. In that moment there was nothing else in the world he would rather do. Sara broke their eye lock and told him George was waiting for him in the office.

As he turned to go, she held one hand a little longer and warned him, "George is very convincing. Sometimes he loses himself chasing what he wants, so keep your eyes open, okay?"

"Thanks Sara, I will, see you soon." She tipped her head up and he was so tempted to kiss those pink lips, but he dragged himself off to George's office, knowing they had a long day of planning ahead of them.

CHAPTER 18

"Good morning, Rich," George said as Richard came through his door. George looked like he had been working for a couple of hours already, his dress shirt was open two buttons down and he was writing notes at his beautiful reclaimed Russian oak writing desk. George sat back, stood up, and came over to shake Richard's hand and asked him if he wanted a coffee or anything, before they got started. Richard said sure he would have coffee and a water. George offered Richard the same deep leather chair he sat in the day before and as Richard settled in he went over to his desk and called Sara.

"Can you bring us two bottles of water and two Kazzarr Nespressos, we need a kick start this morning with lots of planning to do." He listened for a second and said, "Thanks Sara." Richard never thought his request would cause additional work for Sara and he felt a momentary pang of guilt but at the same time he was excited to see her. Sara came in a few minutes later and took George his drink then walked over to Richard. She blocked George's view of Richard as she handed Richard his water and coffee. She grabbed Richard's hand for a second between handing him his drinks. The touch and the sight of her in a pencil skirt electrified him and he knew the caffeine would have nothing on what Sara did to him.

As Sara shut the door Richard forced himself to focus on the job at hand. "Who do you want to discuss first?"

"I need to change gears, let's just take a minute. I need to shift from offense to defense. I've just spent the last few days building a solid bid for this project." George took a deep breath, released it and looked out his large office window at the green space situated in the middle of the desert. Allowing George the mental break he obviously needed, Richard sipped his coffee and decided Nespresso was delicious. After five minutes of silence, George turned back to Richard and asked him for his preliminary thoughts.

"Well I think we need to discuss what you want a little further," Richard hedged. "I'm not sure I'm ready to do what you are thinking. The way I see it, including Blade Solar there are four companies bidding on a Green Electric Power contract in Saudi Arabia. You want to ensure victory for yourself by not only having the best offer but finding a way to encourage the competition to back out of the race or go off their game. Is that about, right?" Richard asked.

"I think you have summed it up nicely, yes."

"But how, George? I've followed and tracked all of them and provided you all kinds of information. Shouldn't that be enough for you to get ahead?" Richard asked, still uncertain as to how George perceived his role in this project.

"Richard, I know you are not entirely on board with this but we have discussed this already and have come up with a deal for payment that you agreed to. Now we don't have much time so you better have something for me or you can walk out the door now."

Richard knew it would never be that easy just to walk away from George. He knew he would have to get out of George's grip soon, but he had to acknowledge that George had a point. He had agreed to this yesterday and admittedly, he was intrigued by the turn this project was taking. Battling with his ethics, he knew he would make sure no one was physically hurt and he was pretty sure that if he backed down, anyone else George might hire would not likely have any qualms about using violence as the means to the end.

"You're right, George," Richard admitted honestly. "I'm struggling with this, but I'll be all in, if my team is."

Richard proceeded to explain the rough ideas he had come up with overnight to help George get at his competition. He went through a plan of attack for Chris Buchanan, Jim Dunsmuir, and even the false scare he would use on George himself.

"But I've no idea how to get at Peter Fairchild. I need your help with that one," Richard said.

"I knew you were the right man for this, your plan sounds exactly like how I want this done. Now, here are my thoughts on how we will get to Fairchild. Based on my psychiatrist's review, we need to break his ego, it may not make him quit but it will definitely throw him off his game. We need a plan to shame him deeply past the point of public forgiveness. If we can do that, all of his other indiscretions will suddenly become not so tolerable either. That action will set in motion a train wreck that will see Mr. Fairchild suddenly become a very undesirable investment opportunity. Without corporate support, Peter will never be able to raise the capital to bid on the project and the Princes will know it. Then if he even tries, he will just embarrass himself. On top of that the Prince's will not want to be attached to a leper." George went on to explain how he wanted Richard to get at Peter. George's plan was what a sports coach would call a high-risk, low-percentage play; almost unbelievable with no guarantee to work. It was by far the riskiest plan for Rich and his team but also the most intriguing. In fact, Richard could feel his adrenaline pumping at the thought of executing what George was proposing.

"I need you to begin immediately, you have a month until you need to go after Jim and I, but you need to start on Peter and Chris now. The plans for these two are much more detailed and will take much longer. By moving forward against them now, we can work out any contingencies we may need to incorporate if things go sideways."

"All right, I'll be back in the States tomorrow and meet with my team as soon as I can. If they are on board, I'll let you know and we'll start immediately." Richard stood to leave.

"Oh, and Rich?" George stopped him from reaching the door. "I am okay with you dating Sara, but you better treat her right, don't think for a minute I'm not watching."

Caught off guard, Richard was shocked at the evidence that George was having him followed, but he realized he should have known better. Rather than give George the satisfaction of seeing him unsettled by that realization, he simply said, "You know George, if you don't eventually trust someone you're going to end up very alone and very paranoid. Having someone watch someone who's watching someone else... even for you is getting crazy."

"You just tried to hide the fact that you were dating my assistant," George stated unequivocally. "That alone proves I'm right. You want my trust? Earn it."

"Jesus Christ, George!" Richard exclaimed, forgetting his earlier vow not to let George see him react. "My dating, or to be exact date, first date, with Sara will be tonight. She is a girl beyond anything I could hope for and I can't believe it's happening, so yes I was trying to keep it private. Not just from you but from the world. I want to see if I really have a chance with a girl like her without outside influences getting in our way. If I was ever lucky enough to have a girl like her actually decide to date me, trust me, I'd tell you. And not just you. I might shout it from the mountain tops! But until, then let us be."

"You heard me Rich," George said, unperturbed by Richard's outburst. "Treat her right. And you better not be using her to get to me, because I'll find out."

Richard shook his head. Telling George he would call him with updates, he turned and left the office.

"Thanks for the coffee, Sara. It was great," he said as he handed her his empty cup and water bottle. God, she was a knockout. She smiled and told him she would be ready and waiting when he picked her up for dinner. Two minutes talking to Sara and he had already forgot about George and what a crazy ass he was being.

"At your door, 7:30, with flowers, and if you look as good as you do now I'll also have a perma-grin for the night that you'll have to put up with."

She laughed and said, "Well now I have a challenge. See you soon, Rich."

As he walked away, Richard wondered if Sara knew it wasn't that George cared for her that he seemed protective of her and had his men watch her so close but that he was suspicious she might leak corporate secrets to his enemies. Anyway, at this point he saw no reason to upset her and she seemed to be happy working for George so he left it alone. When he got back to his hotel, he called Kelly.

CHAPTER 19

"Kelly, I'm flying home tomorrow. We'll need to meet first thing the next day, followed by a meeting with the guys after that. I have an interesting new proposal from George and if we accept it we are going to have a crazy couple of weeks. Most of the stuff will be very hush hush so we'll have to limit access which means we will need to be very hands on. I will fill you in first, then bring in Mike, Joe and Jeff for the next meeting. We need our top trusted guys only on this one."

"Will do, Rich," Kelly agreed automatically, trusting Richard's lead. "This sounds serious. Are we in trouble?"

"No, but we could be if we mess this next assignment up. Do your best to make all of this look like business as usual. In fact, bring along some of the smaller cases people have wanted us to work on that we haven't got around to. They may make a good cover," Richard said, contemplating how to safeguard his team right from the beginning. "Look, I gotta run. See you in a couple days, Kelly, and thanks."

Kelly hung up the phone in the New York office and considered the implications of Richard's phone call. Richard sounded serious and he knew their dealings with George Anderson were not always on the up and up. In fact, to say they were in a grey area was a stretch, but the jobs paid well and nothing bad had come of them so far. He called Richard's assistant and asked her to put together the outstanding job requests they had on file and then started calling the guys to set up the late morning meeting Richard had just requested.

CHAPTER 20

Finished with his calls, Richard hung up the phone and jumped in the shower. He was so excited about the date that he shaved twice. Satisfied that he looked as good as he was ever going to, he left his room and was just headed outside when he noticed the lobby of the hotel had a large vase of flowers. He did not recognize most of the varieties but the bouquet had three birds of paradise and he liked those, so he spoke to the hotel manager and he was given the flowers. As he climbed into the back seat of his car, he realized there was a good chance the flowers would probably be charged to his room. Knowing that George was paying for the room, Richard smiled. George had told Richard to make sure Sara was treated right so flowers qualified.

When he got to Sara's door and knocked, she answered almost immediately. She stood before him wearing a thin loose-fitting dress that hung down from thin silk straps over her tanned, well-toned shoulders that accented her long, gorgeous neck. The dress was not daring in the least but was definitely sexier than the office clothes he'd only ever seen her in. The dress stopped high up on her thighs which showed off her long slender legs perfectly. She had on high heels with straps that wrapped up her ankles and formed a bow about a quarter of the way up her well-defined calves. She was a complete knockout.

As he handed her the flowers, he made a sad, stammering attempt at a joke about her wish for flowers was his command. Despite the sad joke, she laughed genuinely and grabbed his hand and said thank you and then took them back into the house. He could see her dipping her head down to smell the flowers as she walked. When she turned back toward him after putting the flowers on the counter, he noticed how her long auburn hair framed her face while her bronze skin tone seemed to glow. She grabbed his arm, said thanks for the flowers again, and told him they were going for a great surf and turf dinner. He doubted very much if she ate steak, but salad and fish he could believe. He asked her which of the "M" drinks qualified for tonight and she just laughed.

The restaurant turned out to be only a twenty-minute car ride from her apartment and it was great. Richard figured that it was about as close to a Keg steak house as he would get in Morocco without it actually being a Keg restaurant. Richard had a very large bone-in fillet that was cooked slightly under medium rare with an 8-ounce lobster tail to go with it. He had asked for his steak to be charred on the edges and they did their best, but it seemed to be a relatively new concept to the cook. Sara had Ahi tuna and a very large garden salad. He was happy to see she ended up having two Manhattan's, which, as he remembered from their previous evening's conversation, she had told him she drank to relax and enjoy herself. In fact, he tried one himself, and despite living in New York they both found it ironic that his first Manhattan ever was in Africa. Richard was surprised the Manhattan had quite a kick but was fairly sweet for a whiskey-based drink. For dessert they sipped a strong, frothy espresso while eating a very rich Cream Brule. It was the perfect end to the meal. Richard could not believe how comfortable and happy he felt with her. Sara was already wondering how and if he would want to see her again when they lived so far apart. As they were riding back to her house, both were again disappointed the evening was coming to an end and even more so because Richard was flying out the next day. When the driver pulled up to the curb in front of her house, Sara asked him to come inside with her, telling him she really enjoyed the last two nights with him and wanted to know what he was thinking about the future of their relationship, considering he was leaving the next day.

"I know I sound like a needy girl, but with you leaving I just had to risk it and see what you thought?" She asked nervously, not meeting his eyes as she spoke. She looked so sweet and uncertain of herself that he reached out and lightly touched her cheek then guided her head towards his.

Leaning down, Richard kissed her gently, but with

enough force to quell any doubts she had about his attraction to her, and then barely lifted his lips from hers enough to answer her question. "Let's go in, I feel exactly the same way and I'd love a chance to spend more time with you."

Richard informed his driver he would be a while and he would call for him when he was ready to leave. The driver told Richard he would only need a half hour to get back to Sara's once Richard called for him. As the car drove off Richard and Sara held hands as they walked up to her front door. After she unlocked the door and put her key away, Richard wrapped his hands around her waist finding her body to be smooth and firm. Sara was surprised at his ardour, having pegged him as too formal of a business man to give in to emotion, but she fell into the kiss, loving how he held her and raised her hands up onto his wide strong shoulders. She had been on her own for a while now and forgot how it felt to have a man look after her or feel protected by one who cared for her and she somehow felt that instantly with Richard. That feeling just reinforced her decision to try and start a relationship with him.

CHAPTER 21

"Well, then, it's time for you to meet the team, Garcia," Jim said immediately once she agreed to join him, not wanting to give her a chance to second guess herself. "You were our top draft pick and everyone will be so excited to have you on board." Glancing up at the darkening sky, he apologized. "Obviously time has gotten away on me, sorry about that. Let's ride back to the restaurant, return the horses, hop in the helicopter and fly back to your cabin. You must be exhausted by now and I don't want you telling people I tricked you into the business through torture and sleep deprivation." She grinned, shaking her head, as he continued. "In fact, why don't you sleep in tomorrow and try to shake some of that jetlag out of your system? I'll pick you up around ten and we will head up to the offices by the Blue Lagoon. Why don't you pack a bag and try the lagoon out after our meetings tomorrow?" Realizing he sounded a bit dictatorial, Jim smiled sheepishly. "Sorry. I'm not trying to give orders. I'm just excited to have you on board and want to make sure you see all the great things here so that you're convinced to stay. I have a hunch that once you meet everyone and get fully immersed into our plan, you may need some time and space to let everything start to sink in. I swear you will find no place better in the world to reflect on your thoughts than in a private meditation pool in the Blue Lagoon."

Garcia waved off his apology, not feeling pressured in the least, but she had to acknowledge that Jim was completely right about feeling overwhelmed. Half of her brain could not believe what she just agreed to while the other half was so excited, she was already running calculations and system design plans in her head. Normally if any man, or anyone else for that matter, suggested she needed a rest or a spa day when she was trying to work would feel her wrath for insinuating she couldn't handle the pressure, but she did not get that feeling with Jim. She had worked in a trade-type of career for years now and had encountered more than one man who thought she was a weak woman who needed to be looked after or told her she was way too pretty for "this type of work". Although her guard was up at Jim's suggestions, she measured his demeanor against what he was asking of her and she did not feel like he was belittling her. She knew he was being logical in trying to prevent mental burnout before even beginning a project of this magnitude, and he was right to do so. She was tired and would need time to catch up in order to process all the information, after all this was not a normal business proposal. Plus, he knew she had never been to Iceland and was just trying to offer her a place to go to ponder this enormous project while enjoying the country at the same time. Suddenly a strange part of her brain thought maybe he'd join her in the lagoon and how great he'd look in board shorts. Mentally giving herself a stern admonishment to dispel that image, she realized she really must need to rest up because normally her feelings did not get away on her like that.

They decided to sit back and watch the geyser one last time before they rode back to the helicopter. It was well after midnight when Jim was walking Garcia to her cabin door. She had fallen asleep on the flight home and was ready for bed. As she let herself into the cabin, Jim informed her he would be back at ten thirty the next day to pick her up. Jim told her they would grab an early lunch, he would show her around the lagoon, and then they would go up to his offices at one o'clock for meetings.

Jim and Garcia arrived at the Blue Lagoon around noon the following afternoon. Jim gave her a quick tour of the amenities and explained to her that not many people realize that the lagoon is not naturally occurring and is the result of a geothermal power system built to power much of Iceland's largest city. The water flows up from six thousand feet below the surface and completely refreshes the lagoon every two days. Being loaded with minerals, the water is purported to have massive healing powers. The geothermal heat keeps the water forty degrees Celsius all year long. The endless heat, therapeutic power and the shockingly bright blue water made the lagoon irresistible to tourists. The lagoon itself was not the only amazing attraction in the resort, however, and Garcia was amazed as she walked with Jim into the Lava restaurant for lunch. The restaurant overlooked the lagoon from above and was built into a mountainous hill formed of solid lava which offered a panoramic view of the steaming lagoon and its surrounding landscape. This restaurant was the first "normal" restaurant they had been to so far and they laughed about that fact when Jim pointed it out. Lava is a high-end eatery that offers romantic or relaxing views at night and a clean polite lunch, as well as provides an early dinner feel for families on vacation.

Jim was explaining to Garcia how some four hundred thousand people a year travel from around the world to surround themselves in Icelandic beauty and rejuvenate themselves in the therapeutic waters of the lagoon. He further explained how the tourist economy alone had more than paid for the geothermal plant and its maintenance, which allowed the city of one hundred and thirty thousand to live with free electricity.

By following the Blue Lagoon model, Jim explained that he had already struck a deal with the very upper echelon of luxury resort franchises. Together they would build a state-of-the-art holiday recuperation experience. The Four Seasons would develop one side of a newly created lagoon and essentially be the flag ship to the world for the standard that would be this resort. Nobu would develop the other side, basically underlining the statement made by the Four Seasons with its own brand of luxury and refinement. In the middle, the Wynn gaming group of Las Vegas would develop a facility to provide the action and community atmosphere for those who decided to make a stay in Greenland a full holiday experience. Wynn was developing a hotel and casino complete with a fully glassed dome area that would encase and connect the lagoon to the hotel. The massive dome would contain white sand beaches, stores, restaurants and all the amenities of a high-end beach resort. The lagoon would become a massive infinity pool overlooking the Atlantic, giving vacationers the illusion that they were actually right on the ocean in a tropical climate. Basically, the resort would allow anyone using the facility to get the full Atlantis Bahama experience in Greenland all year long. They had plans to further glass in a full eighteen-hole golf course for four season play and develop a downhill ski resort. It will be an expensive place to visit but the idea will be so intriguing to people that he thought tourists would flock to it.

Although the enormity of what he was explaining was hard to get her head around, she thought to herself she could not imagine what it must be like in Jim's head. His thought process, creativity and ideas where outlandish, but yet he had the business acumen to make them obtainable. She could not stop herself from thinking he must be some kind of genius. Helplessly, Garcia could feel herself falling in love with Jim. His excitement and charisma, coupled with his crazy but scarily well-defined plan to recreate the world's power supply by linking half the world with a new way to travel, topped off with a four season summer resort in one of the coldest, most barren wasteland parts of the Artic, made her want to work with him to help him realize his dream. She knew she would do all she could to make that happen. She suddenly felt the urge to rush across the table and kiss him. The thought instantly turned her face red, so she took a sip of her iced tea.

"What I've just told you is all part of the confidentiality agreements my staff and I have in place with these companies. None of this information can be leaked or released until we have officially signed on as the new energy providers for Neom. The reason for this is that companies such as these can't be seen in business with losers. They are some of the greatest companies in the world to work with, but we can't associate with them until the papers are signed. So essentially, we need to do our part first, which is getting the contract for Neom in place. Can I trust you with my secret?" Jim asked her, already knowing he could.

"I'm all in Jim," Garcia assured him, unhesitatingly. "I'll sign any confidentiality agreement you need. This is an exciting project and I'm thrilled to be part of it. Let's make sure we win."

Jim smiled at her enthusiasm and competitiveness. She made him feel like he could do anything.

"Then let's go introduce you to the others," he said.

CHAPTER 22

Jim had a large meeting room off of his main office. Like Jim's office, the area had floor to ceiling windows overlooking the Blue Lagoon. The view alone was an inspiration for creativity and proof that their project was attainable because it had already been done on a smaller scale.

The team was already seated at the table when Jim and Garcia walked in. Jim made formal introductions. As befitting his status with the company, Jim first introduced Chief Financial Officer, Ramsey King. Next, Garcia was pleasantly surprised to meet Jason Evans, the electrical, civil and mechanical engineer. Garcia had heard of him and his brilliance, she had even studied some of his work and had been impressed, so she was excited that Jim had gotten him on board and involved in the project. Jason's involvement in the project cemented Garcia's resolve that they would be able to pull the project off; she knew Jason's reputation was that good. Next, Jim introduced her to Human Resources Officer, Alexandra Griffen. Alexandra looked every inch the professional woman, dressed in a perfectly fitted, conservative, tan, business suit. Lastly, Jim introduced Lois Nelson, the team's psychiatrist. Garcia thought a psychiatrist was a strange person to have on board an electrical project, but when Jim explained her role it made sense. Basically, Lois sat in on all formal meetings, observed the team members' interactions, and took notes. She would then summarize her findings and report them to Jim. Jim had seen too many inter-office power struggles and team break downs happen due to poor communication and conflicting personality types that he had hired Lois and asked her to help his team avoid those pitfalls. Through scheduled meetings designed to help each person become aware of themselves, as well as more understanding of each other, Lois would help the team get along and ultimately be more efficient.

Then Jim presented Garcia to the team, describing some of her previous projects and was very complimentary when explaining her recent break throughs in geothermal technology. He also made mention how European countries recognized her as a leader in green power energy design and how they had been soliciting her advice on many of their projects, obviously with the intention of highlighting the fact that she is good at what she does. Garcia was slightly embarrassed over the introduction, but took that time to go around and shake hands with everyone and then sat in what appeared to be her spot at the table. She instantly felt at home with her new team and couldn't wait to get to work.

As Jim took his spot at the head of the table, he started out by saying that with the addition of Garcia they now had their leadership team in place and that Garcia would officially be signed on in a meeting set with the lawyers for four o'clock that afternoon. Jim then called the meeting to order by asking Ramsey for an outline and update on the company's holdings. Ramsey started out by welcoming Garcia to the team and then went right into his report.

"As you know with the scale of this project and no solid confirmation dates or even confirmation as to whether we will secure the bid, it's very hard to set solid achievable goals. However, in order to be considered for the project we need to have a team and a plan in place that we can implement immediately upon signing, should we get the contract. Jim has foot fifty percent of our expenses with the rest of us sharing the other fifty percent equally. Of course, Garcia will now be added into our mix as a full partner when she signs the papers this evening," Ramsey began, providing more detail than necessary for the other members in order to help Garcia get up to speed.

Ramsey continued with explaining where their proposal was at, who was on board under what contract and who they still needed to sign. He then followed up by getting a departmental report from each of the team members to find out where they were at with their deliverables. Once he had their updates, Ramsey further challenged them to look deeper and see what else they could do to keep their areas moving forward in order to strengthen their proposal for the Princes of Saudi Arabia.

So far Jim and Ramsey had met with all eleven countries that the track would need to pass through, and all had agreed in principle to the build. The employment, usage tax and potential economic benefit the train system would create was not something their leaders could risk passing up. The dealmaker for most of countries involved was Jim's agreement to hire each country's labor force to do as much work as they could handle on the section of the track that ran through their own country. This meant billions of dollars in new outside revenue for each of their governments and citizens. As expected, no one would officially sign on until they saw that Jim had the Arabian contract secured. The other caveat demanded by most of the parties included a need to have all countries involved meet face to face to sign the agreement. There was a lot of distrust and no one wanted anyone else to suddenly back out or hold out for more money. Jim proposed that should he win the Neom contract, an immediate face to face meeting would be held with all eleven countries in attendance. Each country would be required to put up an eleven-billion-dollar retainer, which meant that if any one country backed out of the agreement for any reason they would forfeit their money to the others. The agreement was completely accepted by all involved with Jim and Ramsey volunteering to set up and host the meeting once the time came.

If all eleven countries signed on, Jim's next step would be a proposal to the United Nations Convention of Law on the Sea. Countries own the sea rights twenty-two kilometres out from their shorelines, following that the oceans become international water ways that the UN sets policy for. In principle, this request should be a rubber stamp. The UN stands on precedent and history shows that if a water way was to be used for something between two agreeing countries that was not for hostile purposes, it would be approved.

Ramsey continued his report by saying, "Right now, Saudi Arabia is only working on powering Neom electrically. Once they implement our plan, they'll become world leaders in environmental electricity production, further the project will make them a major export port for all of Europe while revolutionizing the travel industry throughout the EU. We'll of course offer Saudi the opportunity to bank roll the whole project which will essentially allow them to control the train, however we feel this method preferable as opposed to working with so many other lending institutions. We'll be ready to offer both financing options so we're able to move forward either way."

Jim and Ramsey knew the purpose for building the new city was to diversify not only the country's economic wellbeing but to try and separate Saudi Arabia from the stigma of being a one-horse show. If the Crown Prince could create a state-of-the-art city that was completely powered by green energy in the heart of the oil world, he could prove Saudi Arabia deserved a seat at the table with the other world superpowers.

"The Saudi Princes have now contacted us," Ramsey

took a second to consider Garcia and said, "Garcia I realize some of this information is new for you and I'm going through it pretty fast. I'm confident that by the time I'm done, and you've had all your individual team meetings and toured the Greenland facility space with Jim, that you'll be right up to speed, so just try and bear with me. Of course, if you have any question at all, please let us know." Garcia nodded and Ramsey continued. She was taking a few key notes and desperately trying to piece together the magnitude of this project in her mind. At the same time, she was trying not to be overwhelmed by the fact that she had accepted a role in what could become, if not a world changing event, definitely an event the world would notice and discuss. Quickly shaking herself out her reverie, Garcia told herself to focus when Ramsey addressed her again.

"Garcia with this being your first day, I've been laying out a few of the terms of reference we use for our meetings. At the end we usually hold a round table for each person to report updates and to help each other set new deliverables for the next one. What we'll need from you for the next meeting is a general schematic of a geothermal system that will be able to provide power for roughly thirty million people. You'll need to take into consideration a voltage drop as the power travels over eighty seven hundred kilometers and provide a contingency plan for massive expansion should more countries and the rest of the world want on board."

Garcia stared back at him for a moment then said, half-jokingly, "I feel like this is the moment I should choke on your words and maybe run out of the room screaming."

They laughed and declared that Ramsey had made them all feel that way when they first started too.

"I'm still sitting here trying to consider the magnitude of this thing in my head," Garcia admitted. "You all may still find me in corner, curled up in a ball, crying."

Again, they reassured her that they'd all felt the same way at the beginning but now that they were into the project, the challenge was extremely exciting.

Ramsey went on to inform her that for the next while she would work closely with Jason. Jason's engineering prowess and hands-on project management experience would be essential to her work. He informed her that Jason's role would be overseeing the project's physical construction and tying all aspects of the project's infrastructure together. Jason's duties also included having a design team draft the plans for the bridge followed by hiring consultants to work with each country to build their section of track. Further to that he would oversee an engineering firm that would design the train and control systems, along with adequate safety measures to guard against all conceivable emergency situations, either natural or manmade. Continuing with Jason's portfolio, Ramsey stated that Jason would oversee the design and implementation of the electrical superconductor that would carry the electricity she produced almost nine thousand kilometres and build the phase conductors that will align the power frequency to Neom's needs.

"Back in Greenland, Jason will introduce you to the

geotechs and construction crews we've hired to prepare the land in Greenland for your design. In many ways you will be the design and project lead for the geothermal section of the project. Jason has secured all construction teams you'll need and will be able to provide you contact information plus help you trouble shoot as you move forward," Ramsey said, reassuringly.

Ramsey then introduced Alexandra and explained her role in the company. Alexandra had a toolbox of proven processes that helped managers pick the right people for the right employment needs. She also had access to many employee pools, including eligible candidates all the way from NASA technicians to ditch diggers. Alexandra's team put the company's salary and benefit packages together and made sure all the legal paperwork was done on time. Since most of the project would be tendered out to different teams of contractors, Alexandra also oversaw the legal process of getting the documents properly written with appropriate completion of work clauses.

"As for me," Ramsey stated, "I manage the funds. Once the team meets and decides on a course of action, the resulting bills are submitted to me for review. Once I review the expenditures, Jim and I sign them off for payment." Ramsey paused, correctly reading Garcia's body language that although she was absorbing everything he'd said, she was getting increasingly overwhelmed. "But there I go again, talking too much. I need to let the others get a word in or we'll be here all day. Jim, where are you at?"

Almost unwillingly, Garcia drank Jim in as he began to address the group. A powerful, good looking man leading a group of professionals on a world-changing project that he was personally funding… she told herself that would make any girl swoon, but he had her number and she knew it.

Jim started out by saying, "Well now that the team is together, I expect big things from all of you and I know you're ready to deliver, but first I also know you need big things from me. I need to figure out a way to win us this project. We have a one in four shot right now. I've been invited to speak at the G8 summit on clean energy in Reyadh, Saudi Arabia next month. The following week I present our bid to the Princes in the same country. If I can impress them enough at the G8 it will go a long way towards helping us secure the Neom contract, so I'm going to need a great speech. Since founding Dunsmuir Energy, I have done little commercial business and have put most of my time and funds into philanthropist endeavors in the areas I like to call "sane" green energy initiatives. As luck would have it, I was invited to speak at this conference prior to the Neom's request for tenders coming out. If I can put together a speech for the Summit that endears me to the world of green energy, the Saudi Princes will be hard pressed to not choose our tender package. Jason, Alexandra, I'm going to be relying on the two of you to research and prepare a speech that will sufficiently impress the world and the Princes. It also goes without saying I'll need the same preparation for the actual interview."

Jason followed Jim's lead. He was an impressive man himself. He was a world-renowned engineer, he had numerous successful project completions under his belt, and had a way of speaking that let non-engineer types understand him. "As Ramsey said, we have a number of construction and design firms ready to work with us. Many of the fly-by-night construction companies from the construction boom have disappeared now since the downturn of the housing markets and the continued downturn of the economy. With business being scarce, construction has become a cutthroat industry and that fact will allow us to get the very best contractors for very reasonable prices based on the long-term work sustainability this project will afford us. Unfortunately, until we can guarantee work, none of them will commit to waiting around for us on the off chance they can get other work. I did talk to my contacts at three large construction firms and told them that before they take anything on in the next two months to let me know because I might soon be able to offer them a deal they couldn't refuse." Then turning towards her, Jason said, "Garcia, welcome aboard. I look forward to working with you. You and I can discuss more details in our afternoon meeting."

"Thanks, Jason. It will be an honor to work with you," Garcia said truthfully. "I have heard so much about you and your projects. I very much look forward to our planning sessions."

When Alexandra spoke next, she explained her role and Garcia realized Alexandra played a significant part of business that Garcia had never paid much attention to before. Alexandra explained how she would be the reason that Garcia and all the others got paid. Further to that, she indicated that she'd been working for Jim for a number of years and that she and her husband's company managed Jim's pay role, building rent for his office space, labor issues, benefit packages, hiring and firing of staff, recruitment and other duties surrounding staffing, legal and contract management. She said that her husband was a lawyer and he focused on the contract management and legal side of the business. Eventually, Alexandra told her, she would assign a dedicated HR officer to Garcia and her husband would assign a contract lead. Garcia would then get together with this small group and work out a plan to find staff and contractors who could take the plans Garcia and Jason would eventually put together for the geothermal system and make them a reality. She then welcomed Garcia and stated they'd soon meet and get started on a plan.

Lastly Lois introduced herself. "We'll meet and talk following your other meetings, Garcia. I don't want to get into what I do too much in this meeting, short of saying that I'm the team psychiatrist and I just want to observe the dynamic you add to the group for now. I'll then provide feedback to you and Jim as I do for the other team members. Just so you know, I only provide basic or general terms to Jim in order to maintain doctor-client confidentiality, but you'll see that after we talk."

"Well," Jim took the lead back once every member had spoken, and turned to Garcia. "That's the team, think you can work with us?"

"I can't wait to get started," Garcia replied with genuine enthusiasm. "This project represents a blank page; we'll be creating a new industry, for lack of a better description. It's exciting to say the least."

"We think you will fit right in," Jim said, pleased with her quick and passionate response to his team's introductions. "Well, then, no sense wasting time. Your meeting with Ramsey is first. There's a meeting room down the hall, you guys might as well head off. Ramsey will show you where, then you can just stay in the room and we'll rotate through."

As they stood to leave, Alexandra handed Garcia a tablet. "Garcia, take this. They're a bit of a pain but once you get used to it, they're not bad. If you make any notes or plans, please put them on it instead of in a notebook we want to be able to have access to all the files all the time."

"Sure, thanks," Garcia said as she walked out, taking the tablet from Alexandra.

"It's linked to our company's secure Wi-Fi and cloud," Alexandra told her. "With corporate espionage these days, we need all the protection we can get. It'll load with face ID, a thumb print and a password of your choosing when you turn it on. After that, all settings should be ready to go, to be used as needed."

Garcia loved tech and tablet technology. She was excited to try out the new machine and check out the internet speed. Ramsey led the way from Jim's board room to a secondary board room just down the hall. They both grabbed a water and sat down at the heavy grey table. The board room had warm lighting and a view overlooking the lagoon. The sunset over the ocean would be absolutely breathtaking from this office, as the dropping sun light hit the blue water of the lagoon.

CHAPTER 23

L ois followed them into the conference room and closed the door behind her. She grabbed a freshly brewed coffee and then sat down at a small writing desk in the back of the room. Recognizing a psychiatrist's presence in staff meetings was unorthodox, she encouraged Garcia to ignore her. "Garcia, Ramsey and the others are used to my presence in their meetings and, like I said, we'll have a full discussion following your other meetings today, at which time I hope we can really get to know each other. In the meantime, I will be here to observe your meetings with the rest of the group and understand how the team dynamic will be affected by mixing your talents in with theirs. My job will be to process how your personality will interact with the others. Although it might seem a little weird at first, I think you'll get used to me quickly and even forget I'm here, for that matter."

"It's true," Ramsey stated, "we forget she's there during meetings, but it does take a bit of getting used too. I'll be honest, as the money guy, I initially thought Lois's role was an unnecessary expense in this project, but she has become an essential part of the team." Ramsey shifted his body position to effectively turn from including Lois in the conversation to speaking only with Garcia.

"This leads me into my segway. Jim and I've been friends for ever. I was always a bit of a nerd who was good in school, took the hard classes and had high marks. Jim started out as a popular kid, the typical athlete who never really put too much of an effort into school. Needless to say we really never knew each other until after the incident in grade twelve when he became a bit of an outcast. Whatever it was in 1997 that possessed him to risk his parents' money and try internet investing is beyond me, probably beyond most of us and maybe Jim himself. There were stories around back then about people making a couple hundred thousand dollars online but lots of them turned out to be fiction. People will brag and say how they almost did and would have made millions if they had, but Jim actually did it. Jim's investment turned five hundred thousand into seventy-five million. As word of his investment luck got out, Jim started getting famous. Famous in the world and ostracized by the other students. What he had done made him different, so when you add in the extreme jealousy of the wealth, Jim found himself eating alone at lunch. Instead of fighting back and trying to stay a member of the cool kids, Jim became focused on business and began studying intensely. Mostly Jim focused on investing and found he had a real knack for it, at the same time putting way more effort into his school subjects as well. That's when he and I met. His parents ended up taking a million from the investment, which was double what they had, and let Jim have the rest. Between our high marks in school and his fame, both of us got accepted into Harvard. Jim went into marketing and I went into business law. I stayed single but Jim met and eventually married Christina. Christina's family was in the real-estate business and the real estate market was just starting to take off. People were jumping on the band wagon like crazy; everyone was buying two or three houses and renting them out, it was like investing in the stock market in the late seventies and getting twenty percent returns. Jim, Christina and I got together, did some research and formed our first company with Jim financing us, of course. As the market continued to boom, we shifted gears and went from buying rental properties to developing and building houses. With Jim's backing the three of us created a very successful construction company. We were having the time of our lives. Then Christina got sick..." Ramsey trailed off, lost in his own memories.

"Anyway," he continued, visibly refocusing himself on the work at hand, "that's a story for another day. As I said, Jim and I've been together since high school. Other than the real estate construction company, we've mostly invested in other people's ventures. Jim has worked the markets and I've managed the funds. We've had a few personal failures, but no real business failures and it's my duty to keep it that way. After reviewing your work and studying the information we received back on informal reference checks we completed, Jim and I decided you were right for this job and our team. Now going forward, I will need you to work with Jason and his team and get me a plan with numbers. Banks only respond to numbers and dates, so those are essential to the plan's success. I know you have not met with Jason yet, but we need a strong plan in a week and I am confident the two of you will have it ready for us. I need to secure the financing, Jim needs to be prepared to present to the Princes in Saudi Arabia, and we're getting short on time."

Garcia was taking it all in, and like all things that pertained to Jim, her mind side-tracked on his personal story longer than it should have, causing her to miss some of the other details in Ramsey's story. But she did catch his emphasis on the necessity of coming up with a plan.

"I'll have to crunch some numbers and see what I have to work with but I should have no trouble getting you a reasonable estimate by the end of next week, especially if Jason has crews already sourced," Garcia replied, relieved she could confidently guarantee him that much.

Ramsey was ready for her to get to work and he knew she still had multiple meetings to make it through, so he wrapped up their meeting by giving her the financial particulars she needed to know. "We have an office here for you to use and Alexandra can send for your stuff or whatever you need. She'll also set you up an expense account. At this point I don't think you'll have any payments to make so we can discuss procurement later, but there is the matter of your wages. I am going to ask Alexandra to join us so we can go through your contract with you. Unless you have any other questions for me right now?"

"No, I don't at the moment but I'm sure I will," Garcia said. "This feels like a whirlwind right now but I'll do my best. I hope I can do what you guys think I can."

"You'll be fine," Ramsey said reassuringly. "And we're here to help with whatever you need. Just make sure to ask, ok?" Garcia nodded as Ramsey picked up the phone and called Alexandra, who said she would be right there.

A couple minutes later, Alexandra walked in carrying papers that Garcia correctly assumed were her contract and the confidentiality agreements. Garcia was not at all worried about what the pay might be and she knew she would get a stake in the company as Jim had alluded to earlier, but she was interested to hear the value they had placed on her work. Alexandra explained that she would receive one million dollars over the next year and a ten percent share of the company should they be awarded the contract. Travel, per diem, expenses and health care were also provided. As she listened, Garcia came to understand that Lois, Jason, Alexandra and herself were all on the same contract. Ramsey and Jim had separate agreements, both with more risk and more reward, as is usually the case with the owners or CEO's. It had been determined that they would all have the same contracts in order to fully implement the team dynamic within the company. Garcia was more excited about the project than the pay but there was no question that the promise of a million dollars for her time if they didn't get the contract was exciting. She also learned that all their yearly wages would be reviewed after the first year if they did get the Neom bid. She signed the contract with no reservations. Ramsey went and made a copy of the agreements for her, kept the originals and left the room.

"So, as you probably heard from Ramsey, I do a bit more than HR, or I should say HR is more than just hiring staff." Alexandra began her time with Garcia by getting right to the point. "My husband and I see ourselves more like high-end concierges. We get the boss what he needs, when he needs it and do our best to cover his ass or stop him if he tries to go too far outside the lines in order to get things done faster or to get a better deal." Pausing for emphasis before her next statement, Alexandra made sure Garcia was listening intently. "I can see why Jim chose you."

Hearing Jim's name in a compliment directed towards herself made Garcia blink in pleasant surprise and although she would never have dreamed of asking Alexandra to elaborate, she didn't even get a chance to thank her before Alexandra continued.

"You seem level headed, have a personality that thrives on challenges, and your resume is outstanding. I think we'll work great together, but I need to tell you this up front," Alexandra cautioned. "My allegiance is to Jim, then the company, Ramsey and then the rest of you in that order. Not that I think it will ever be an issue, and I would assume the others would feel the same way, but I need to put it out there." Garcia nodded in response, understanding that a successful cooperation needed a certain level of hierarchy. "Now," Alexandra continued, "let's get down to it, tell me what you need."

"Well I will need to access my computer files," Garcia began, mentally checking off the things she felt comfortable asking Alexandra to assist her with. "But they are in the cloud so that shouldn't be a problem, unless it's a security risk to download them onto the technology here? I need Amy, my assistant. And I'll need my personal items and clothes if Jim wants me to stay here and work instead of going home for them?" Garcia realized that was a very likely possibility, considering the time line they were working with.

Alexandra smiled in response. "You're not in jail so you can come and go as you please but if you allow it, my team will look after all that for you, and I bet we'll be able to do it much more efficiently than you could yourself, with way less headache, simply because we have the experience."

"I'll need to talk to Amy," Garcia said, acknowledging Alexandra was probably right. Besides, she was way more excited to get working on the project than she was to jump on a plane and go back home to pack clothes. "Amy is very efficient and will be your point of contact in the States for my effects, but I'm hoping she will be willing to move here too. Once I know for sure, I'll let you know. Does that work?"

"It absolutely does," Alexandra replied. "I'll give you my contacts so if you need anything at all, just let me know. I think you'll find your office fully stocked and we have a transportation company on call here. There is an app on the tablet so just press it and follow the directions. All the drivers know us so it will be no problem, it's basically a personal ride share. I'm going to head out so you can get down to business with Jason next, but remember, think of me as your friend, sister, mother or assistant and call me for anything. The most important thing is to get this project up and running, your part is geothermal design and mine is taking life's stressors off your plate so you can accomplish that."

With that, Alexandra picked up the phone and called Jason, she told him that they were just finishing up and he could come any time. Alexandra hugged Garcia and wished her good luck. Alexandra's genuinely kind demeanor almost made Garcia weepy, normally she was not a hugger but she clung to Alexandra for an extra moment taking comfort in the friendly embrace. She was feeling nervous because she knew as soon as Jason walked into the room all of this would become real.

Almost on cue, Alexandra released her and Jason walked in.

CHAPTER 24

Jason sat down next to her, almost immediately relieving her nervousness with his enthusiasm. "Finally the fun part," he began, "I must say I've been looking forward to this part since I agreed to work on the project. I've put some design ideas together for the track and electrical conductor, I've seen some of the workings of the trains and I've been dying to show them to another engineer who will have an understanding and an appreciation for what we're designing."

Jason was as happy as a kid on Christmas and Garcia found his energy infectious. He was semi-retired and had taken on more of a teaching or consulting role, like he'd been doing at the symposium in Germany. The fact that he was here and excited meant this must be a revolutionary project. With all Jason had seen and done in the engineering and construction world, for him to be so ready to dig in and build was absolutely remarkable.

"Before I show you some of my initial schematics, tell me what you are thinking so far," Jason said.

No one had asked her actual thoughts on the subject yet and the question made her pause. Seeing her hesitation, Jason smiled knowingly. "Don't worry, I know you just got here and haven't had much time to process any of this yet, let alone begin to make plans, but based on your reputation, I'm guessing you have some initial ideas. Just tell me what you're thinking. We don't have to impress each other, we need to work together and build this thing."

"Well it's all happened so fast, that you're right, I haven't had much time to really consider details," Garcia agreed. "I'm not sure how long all of you have had to let this sink in, but my mind is reeling with questions just thinking about it. The geo system itself will have to be massive, to get it all synchronized to work together. Where to put it, what type of ground it will sit on, the heat of the earth, maintaining it once it's built, the list seems endless!"

"All good questions," Jason replied, "and that is where I come in. On my recommendation, Jim bought twenty thousand acres of land in Greenland on a very flat plane that has a granite base. So although a bit difficult for drilling, the full twenty thousand acres sits on a bed of lava not all that far under the ground surface. The heat from the earth's core should be a great natural stimulant for the geothermal process. With the naturally occurring Artic temperatures, I felt that the facility should be built in doors as much as possible for ease of maintenance and longevity of the equipment. Two of the four trains will also be serviced in a hanger created in that location as part of the deal with the local community to supply employment."

"Lava, actual lava? One thousand degrees' Celsius lava?" Garcia questioned incredulously. "Well we can use that kind of heat. It'll increase the geothermal efficiency exponentially. Sounds like you guys really know what you're doing. Harnessing that heat may be hard, but definitely doable." Garcia paused, then said, "Jason I just made a life altering decision that may affect me for the next decade and I did it overnight. So despite being very excited about this project I'm not sure I'm totally in the right head space to really make strong decisions on something this important right now. I think I'm going to need at least a day to settle in, establish a bit of a routine, talk to my family and adjust some personal stuff, so I can give this my full concentration. I promise it won't take me long, but I need to do it."

"You're right, of course," Jason said. "That makes perfect sense, I like the way you think. It's way better to look after the personal details first so you can focus on this."

"Thanks for understanding. If you're willing, I'd like an overview of your plans so far?" Garcia said. "That way I can have them in my head, when I'm settling in because my mind will be working on the project the whole time anyway."

"For sure. And don't be afraid to use Alexandra, her team is absolutely genius at getting things done. If you're like me and feel like you're using her as a maid service, you're not. In fact, she will be more upset if you don't let her help you. On top of that Ramsey will be knocking on your door asking for results and when you tell him you don't have any yet because you have been busy trying to find a place to get your laundry done, he'll get all excited and start ranting about time frames, then he'll call Alexandra and give her heck for not looking after you. Alexandra takes as much pride in her service work as we take in our designs. I'm sure she offered her help already in your meeting with her. You just need to realize it's not putting her out to help you. It's her job and she loves it. Also, I can guarantee the person she puts in place to work on your case will know you and look after you better than you look after yourself, trust me."

"Really, she goes that far?" Garcia asked, although she realized she recognized those same qualities in Alexandra in the short time she spent with her.

"Yes, she totally does you can ask anyone on the team, even Miss Quiet over there in the corner," Jason said, turning towards the psychiatrist. "Lois, am I right about Alexandra's services?"

Lois responded like she was right in the conversation the whole time, "Yes, Alexandra offers amazing services and is a genius in her line of work. You need to depend on her, Garcia."

"Ok I will," Garcia readily agreed, realizing this is how Jim Dunsmuir was the successful business man he was. Using people to their strengths was how he had built his empire. "Now show me your plans," she said to Jason.

Finally, the part Jason had been waiting for. Jason

spread out his blueprint booklet quickly on the table in front of them. The first page showed what looked like a big old-fashioned power line stretching from Greenland across most of Europe and ending in Saudi Arabia. As Jason went through the pages and got into the finer details, she was as amazed as she thought she would be. Maybe even more so. She could see Jason's reputation was well earned.

Jason's design showed the track pedestals infused into the bedrock of the earth. The pillars themselves were built of a cement poly mix that would keep corrosion and decay away from them for a lifetime. Sitting on the pedestals was a four track system that actually floated above the pillars in order to provide a smoother ride for the trains and to allow for tectonic shifts in the earth's core. The track would be initially built attached to the pillars in order to line things up, but then once Garcia's power started flowing, the track would separate from the pillars magnetically.

Next Jason showed her pictures of the trains themselves. They were designed for passenger comfort and cargo. The amazing thing about the cars was there really was no cargo weight limit like planes or even trucks had to deal with. Most importantly, and hopefully never needed, was that each car had a built in parachute so if there was ever an accident the train car would end up floating safely in the water where a GPS locator would call out a position location and ask for help. Jason went through a number of other safeties that would also be installed as well.

The speed and efficiency this train would bring to Europeans was going to set markets on fire. Garcia could only imagine that in a couple decades the world would be completely connected by these trains. When she thought of jet fuel and tanker ship pollution versus the clean burning, more efficient, cheaper to run and faster transportation system they would install, there was no contest. Jim's idea was genius. What amazed her the most because it was connected to her work, was the super conductor Jason had installed within the track. The interior of the track would be cooled to minus two hundred degrees Celsius and the electric flow over the eighty-seven hundred kilometres would have nearly zero voltage drop. In fact, the voltage drop that would occur would be harnessed as extra power to assist in helping the train float magnetically along the track.

Garcia looked at Jason after he finished speaking and humourously told him he should take a bow because his plan was an incredible work of art. Jason thanked her but told her none of it would work without her power flowing into it. They were going to need a way of not only creating enough power, but getting it to flow safely into the track and all the way to Neom. Garcia knew he was right, and her mind already started detailing plans for her design.

Jason then said that he thought that was enough for the day. He knew Garcia had to meet with Lois and Jim yet and then fly off to Greenland with Jim for a tour of the land where she would build her electric plant. Jason called down to the other board room and told Jim that Garcia was ready for him. As soon as she heard Jim's voice on the phone, she got nervous, plus she realized she had been out all day and thought she needed to freshen up. Garcia excused herself and went to the rest room while they waited for Jim. As she fixed her hair, touched up her makeup and readjusted her clothes, she could hardly believe she was doing this for him. When she got back to the room, Jason had left and Jim had not yet arrived.

In order to avoid an awkward silence, Lois got up to go to the washroom. As it was her job to notice such things, she could tell Garcia's demeanor had changed since hearing that Jim was on his way to see her, as well the evidence of freshly applied make up and perfume she had applied while in the restroom. She thought to herself this could be an interesting dynamic for the entire team if Jim and Garcia fell for each other. Lois was realistic enough to recognize the possibility as Garcia was lovely and had a personality that would appeal to Jim.

While she waited for Jim, Garcia set up her new IPad, then used it to start designing a geothermal system on the machine's 3D cad app. Her biggest concern was going to be maximizing the lava's heat to create as much electricity possible. Combined with that, she would have to figure out the proper size and number of generators required to effectively and efficiently produce the amount of electricity required to power Neom. She would also need to build in room for significant expansion, because it was a guarantee that no matter how much electricity she created now, in five years the city would require more. As she was finishing her thoughts, Jim and Lois walked in. Lois went back to her desk and Jim joined her at the table.

CHAPTER 25

"Well, what do you think of the team so far?" Jim asked as he sat down across the table from her. "Can you work with us? And more importantly, do you think we can pull this off?"

"In short, yes," she said, "I really like the team dynamic you've created. Everyone seems genuinely interested in achieving the final goal and seems willing to help each other, which is refreshing. So many large corporations are filled with employees who are only looking to get ahead, even if that means stepping on someone on their climb to the top," Garcia said, having sincerely received a different impression from Jim's team. "Of course, everything is still new, but after getting to know everyone a bit today and spending the last couple days hearing your vision, I can say I'm excited to be part of the team and this project. I believe the engineering and building may be the easiest part though. I can't imagine the logistics that must've gone into getting countries to agree to allow this track to be built across their nations."

"Initially, Ramsey and I thought the same thing," Jim agreed, impressed at her intuitiveness. "We were worried that there was no way it would happen, but we just kept throwing around the idea and finally we decided that we either needed to do something about it or quit talking about it because it was wasting our time. So after much deliberation we went for it. By capitalizing on my reputation, I was able to secure meetings with all the country's leaders. Richard and I were more than surprised by the acceptance and excitement our idea generated. The economic down turn has been worldwide, each country's leader was eager to sign up for a new industry that would create outside investment and employment opportunities for their citizens, especially one with the potential for long term economic return. The tax money or usage fee each country would charge would be a great new revenue stream. Competition between countries proved to be one of the strongest marketing tools for us. The fear of missing out on such potential and letting a neighboring country get ahead of them was something the leaders could not risk so in some respects it was an offer they couldn't refuse. The countries and banks had to endorse the contract for our proposal. If they didn't sign the guarantee to build, based on Saudi Arabia accepting our contract, then Saudi would never even let us compete." Jim paused to take a sip of water, then finished by saying, "the good news is everyone has now signed and we'll know one way or another in a month's time."

"What are the next steps, then?" Garcia asked, knowing she needed to be clear on his vision for her role. "Do I start designing immediately, are we helping you put together a bid, or what do you need me to do?"

"Well tomorrow I'd like to take you to Greenland just to show you exactly what you will be working with for space and terrain. It's about a thirteen hundred kilometer flight so we'll take the helicopter because the chopper's maneuverability offers a better view than you can get from a plane window but the only drawback is that the ride takes longer," Jim said.

"That's great," Garcia replied, enthusiastically. "I'll bring a camera along and get a few pictures of the area which will help me with design planning." The idea of sitting and visiting with Jim alone was anything but a bad idea in her mind plus the trip sounded exciting.

"Good. I'll pick you up outside your cabin door tomorrow. We'll land in the same place we landed in when I picked you up for dinner that first night. Avoiding airports will put our schedule on about the same time frame as if we took a plane anyway."

With that decision in hand Jim stood up to leave, but then turned back to her when he realized he hadn't responded to her question. "To answer your question, Garcia, I'll need a bit of both. I need estimated costs for building, start up and o and m planned out for the next 20 years. In addition, I need a blue print. I need to be able to show the Princes tangible plans during my proposal.

You and Jason will have two weeks to put that together for me. I'll leave you with Lois now. Have a good talk and a good night." Jim turned to Lois, "You too, Lois." Glancing once more at Garcia on his way out the door, he said, "Garcia, I'll see you at seven."

As he walked out the door, Lois was already moving up to the table to sit with Garcia.

"Tell me what you're thinking so far," Lois said, kindly.

"To be honest," Garcia admitted, "I'm all over the place emotionally. I'm excited, scared and anxious. This project is beyond out of this world, yet here we are doing it. I'm not sure exactly what answers you are looking for from me, but I feel ok about this so far and I know I'm up for the challenge. I'll be honest, having Jason as a leader helps me relax but I'm not sure how much pressure that puts on him. Jason's work and experience in the field just makes the project feel more solid. After the preliminary designs he showed me, I believe it will work. What do you think of me so far?"

"My observations of your interactions with the senior leadership team today left me with no worries you seem like a perfect fit," Lois said, dispelling any lingering doubts Garcia had "except that I do have one concern."

"Really, what is it?" Garcia asked, worriedly.

"I'm blunt sometimes, Ms. Gray, especially when it comes to business concerns. I feel it's best to just get them out in the open so here it is. What are your feelings towards Jim? Your body language in his presence today leads me to believe they may run deeper than just professional?"

Normally Garcia would deny the insinuation, especially when she barely had time to asses exactly what her feelings were herself. But Lois was a doctor, obviously quite good at it to recognize Garcia's feelings so easily, and Garcia knew she needed the help navigating these feelings she had towards Jim so they didn't affect their working relationship. So she decided to confirm Lois' suspicions and see what she thought. "Yes, Lois, it's crazy. I was almost instantly attracted to him at first sight. I know he's a rich, famous, billionaire and as cliché as it is, I'm attracted to him and the more time I spend with him the more I feel it."

"Well, you're both single adults but before you profess your feelings for him or even contemplate starting a relationship, it's my duty to point out that if you pursue him or a relationship with him you need to consider what your work life will be like if you break up, if he doesn't reciprocate your feelings or if he starts dating someone else while you are still under contract to work for him for the next decade." Garcia just about choked on Lois's words. Between admitting feelings for a man to a stranger, and then have that stranger force her to consider a relationship with him followed up with how it might feel to get dumped and to see him with another woman all before they even started dating or she knew if he even liked her in the first place was an emotional roller coaster she had not been ready to discuss.

"I can just imagine the lineup of women he must be able to choose from on a daily basis," Garcia said in an attempt at humour. "It's crazy to even consider this. I don't know what I think of him and I doubt he's actually even noticed me, so I'm really not that concerned. Your warning is noted though. Yes, I assume it would be awkward, but I'd never quit unless he fired me. I think this is an amazing project and I'm happy to be part of it."

"Garcia that's a perfectly fine way to look at the situation. My role is not to parent or police, just to help point out personality and communication conflicts and then help the team solve them so the project can stay on track and finish more efficiently. In all honesty, Jim is a great man and I hope someday he does find someone to love again. My role is also to help you guys talk through issues and get emotionally set so you can focus harder on work each day. Remember if any issues come up from a relationship with Jim to Ramsey looking at you cross eyed, don't let them fester. Call me immediately and we'll talk it through. I have once a week meetings set up with each team member to discuss life and work but you can and should call anytime. Are you ok with that?" Garcia said she was fine with the meetings and realized she liked Lois and could see how beneficial it would be talking with her on a regular basis. That was it for her meeting with Lois so they shook hands and exchanged numbers.

Relieved that was her last intense meeting for the day, Garcia was ready to get home. She needed to call her sister and see if she was willing to move to Iceland and really needed her sister's ear. Garcia had just made the biggest decision in her life in a forty-eight-hour time frame without taking time to mull things over or consider the consequences. As she was leaving the office, Alexandra caught up with her. "Your driver is downstairs waiting on you. I've given him instructions to take you to a great restaurant near your house cause I'm sure you'll want to get home and get settled. If you email me a list of any items you need, food, clothes, etcetera when you get a minute tonight I'll get them delivered to your house. I also have a courier service ready to pick up your stuff whenever you're ready and to ship it over for you. I presume you will want to discuss the move with your sister and family, I spoke with Jim if you do want to bring Amy on board, we're fine with that. Many staff will be needed as we go forward."

Garcia smiled and thanked her. It seemed like this might turn out to be her dream job after all. It was very obvious that Alexandra may be as good as advertised. Garcia had a quick supper at the restaurant Alexandra had suggested and she'd been right, Garcia had been able to grab a healthy meal and it only took a half hour for her to get her food, eat and be back on the road home. Her driver got her back to her cabin in good time and once she settled in she called Amy.

CHAPTER 26

The sisters had sent a couple check in texts to each other since Garcia arrived in Iceland but had yet made time to talk. Garcia knew Amy would have a ton of questions and she had a couple of her own so a call was needed. Garcia filled a glass of water from the sink and took a sip. Definitely some of the smoothest water she had ever tasted. Garcia moved into the living area and sat down in the easy chair as she got her phone out. It was nine pm in Iceland so it would be one pm in California, a great time to call Amy as she would be just done lunch. The phone rang twice before Amy picked it up and said it was about time that Garcia finally called her. After their usual gossip, with Garcia fending off a few direct questions regarding how hot Jim was in person, Garcia was able to explain the situation to Amy in about ten minutes with relatively few interruptions. Amy was in shock that Garcia had agreed to such a life changing move and career choice in the span of a couple days. When Garcia broached the idea of Amy moving out to Iceland with her, Amy said of course she would, the sisters were best friends and worked well together so if the business was moving, so was she. In a way Garcia couldn't believe Amy's quick decision to move but deep down she had thought she would. Amy was adventurous and this was about as big of an adventure as they were going to get. They did a bit more planning, including Garcia giving Amy Alexandra's phone number. Together Amy and Alexandra would work out the details of the move as well as getting all of Garcia's personal, financial and business affairs in order so they could relocate to Iceland without any major concerns.

Garcia told her that she would talk to Alexandra and get her to call Amy to set up their move to Iceland. Garcia said that Alexandra could be trusted, and her team would easily handle the task with Amy's help. Amy thought the job and the new opportunity sounded amazing. She said she would organize things with Alexandra and then get to Iceland as fast as she could. The sisters made plans to talk again soon and hung up.

Garcia got ready for bed but found herself too wound up to sleep so she began designing the new electricity plant in her head. A four hundred thousand megawatt plant was almost unfathomable yet she decided she would look at building a plant that could produce five hundred thousand megawatts per day with infrastructure that could be vastly expanded to meet eventual demands of nearly double that. She thought that if she could design a plan for Jim to show the Princes that the geothermal electricity he would deliver to Neom had almost limitless potential, it would be a great help in his proposal. Garcia also needed to consider the amount of power three ultra-luxurious resorts such as Wynn, Nobu and The Four Seasons would draw, not to mention the plan to maintain a full sized indoor golf course, beach and convention area. The electricity required for these hotels would be a drop in the bucket next to Neom's requirements, but significant just the same.

The steam she would create using direct lava heat will make the Greenland facility easily the most efficient clean electricity producing facility in the world. The fresh glacier water that melts into the oceans that gets wasted every year will now be put to good use, albeit a very small percentage.

The plan she was forming in her mind included using the naturally calving artic ice sheets. She would take a small percentage of the ice bergs, corral them into a hanger where instead of letting them melt out at sea naturally, she would melt them using geothermal power. Garcia would then use the newly created glacier fresh water to supply the water needs of the resorts, golf course and greenhouses created in Greenland for the tourists to enjoy. On paper the ideas were so simple and straight forward, but she knew the geography, climate, remote location and terrain was going to cause massive delays and challenges in the project. The equipment and supplies she would require to build the system in an all but desolate country in the Arctic Circle would be no easy task to procure or get delivered. She knew they would need pin point accurate seismic and x ray technology to find the most productive heat areas along the tectonic plates and the research would need to be completed quickly so they could get buildings constructed for the drillers to be able to work indoors out of the arctic elements.

It would be good for her to physically see the terrain so she could understand the harsh conditions and climate her crews would be working in and the challenges they would face. By understanding these concerns, it would make her more empathetic to the building needs and be less likely to make design mistakes for simply not understanding the naturally occurring topography and challenges it creates. Too often engineers had to go back to the drawing board during projects for the simple reason that they didn't take the time to understand the environment before design. Garcia was going to need to speak with Jason, she'd need his help to determine the best equipment to use and figure out how to get it to Greenland. As she was finally forcing herself into bed her phone lit up, Jim had sent her a message to confirm that he would be landing around eight am to pick her up. As soon as she saw his text, she started worrying about what she would wear the next day. She wanted to look good when she met him but professional as well. Garcia shook her head, thinking she must be exhausted she was supposed to be thinking about work, not men. Finally, after ten minutes of unsuccessfully trying to take her mind off Jim, she gave up, telling herself that if nothing else her interest in Jim was jump starting her interest in building the geothermal reactor. At this point any push was good because the two-week time frame Jim had just given her was short and success in the next couple weeks was critical to living out the next decade of her life, and her sister's life, for that matter. Garcia fell asleep thinking of sunsets out on the California coast and how far away she was from them. The funny thing about all of this was that she didn't feel homesick, not yet anyway. So far she really liked her new partners and the fact that Amy had agreed to move with her was icing on the cake. Garcia knew her parents, friends and family would come and visit and knew that she and Amy would return home to visit as well. She fell asleep happy about her decision.

CHAPTER 27

Garcia got up at six the next morning and went for a run. Iceland's air was clear and fresh, and with clear skies and no wind, it looked like the day was shaping up beautifully to tour Greenland in a helicopter. She did a forty-five minute run across the photogenic landscape and got back to her cabin in time to shower and eat with fifteen minutes to spare before Jim was scheduled to arrive. Garcia grabbed her plans and ideas she had scribbled down last night in hopes she would have time to run them past Jim. She wanted his opinion to make sure she was on the same page as him. Just before eight she heard the rhythmic whirling noise that only helicopters make and Garcia glanced out her living room window as she was putting her boots on and watched it land. A few moments later she saw Jim jump out and start walking to her door. Garcia could see confidence in his movements and liked watching him walk. Dressed for a day of traveling, Jim was wearing dark jeans and a fitted hoodie. Garcia herself had on fur lined leggings, knee high boots, a collared dress shirt that she left unbuttoned maybe a little too far, and a black puffy jacket over top. Jim had only made it halfway to the cabin when she ran out the door. The unexpected movement caught Jim's attention and the sight of her athletic body, long hair, fashionable sunglasses and welcoming smile hooked him instantly. Without thinking, he opened his arms to greet her with a hug and a smile. For some reason the act just felt natural and she fell right into the embrace. After a moment, they both jumped back awkwardly.

Jim asked Garcia if she was ready to go and she just nodded in reply and turned toward the helicopter. The walk to the helicopter was quick with Jim thinking how amazing she looked as the blades of the helicopter tossed her hair. Once she climbed inside, he shut her door, sealed it, then ran around and climbed in on his side.

The helicopter rose up and took off into the wind with the massive rotor dragging the rest of the machine up with it. Luckily for Garcia, the angle gave her a panoramic view of the coastline as they ascended. Last time they'd taken off to the East and flew inland so she had missed the ocean view. As they headed out over the Atlantic toward Greenland, the rising sun from the East was providing a brilliant back light that illuminated the ocean in a spectacular sparkling blue. Garcia was already excited to see her first iceberg up close. She'd read that some icebergs can be up to two hundred meters square and seventy-five meters high. The largest known iceberg to have calved off an ice sheet happened in 2000, when a four-thousand-mile square iceberg was discovered in Antarctica. Each year fifteen to forty thousand bergs calve off the Greenland Ice sheet and a piece of ice had to measure five meters square to be considered an official iceberg.

Garcia turned from the window for a moment to look at Jim and found him intently watching her rather than the scene below. Blushing slightly, Garcia covered up her momentary shyness by asking about the icebergs. "Is there any way we could take time to view a couple large icebergs, I've never seen one up close before? I can only imagine how terrifying they must be to come up on if you're in a ship of any size."

"For sure," he replied unhesitatingly, "and I think you'll find them quite a site. I'll have the pilot circle around one up close so you can get a feel for the enormity of them. They really are quite majestic to look at." As Jim called the pilot on the headset, Garcia took a moment to appreciate the helicopter she was in. Jim had told her it was a Belle 429. She'd been in helicopters before for work and tours but nothing like this. Most of the machines she'd been in had fully open cockpits, everyone had to wear ear defenders to protect their hearing from damage and to be able to talk with each other through the headphone speaker system. This helicopter, however, made her feel like she was riding first class. The cabin had deep leather reclining chairs, a fully stocked fridge, a coffee maker, thick rich carpet and was whisper quiet. There was pleasant symphony music playing in the background coming from speakers that were part of the surround sound system hooked to the TVs and infotainment system. She needed to remind herself to enjoy these luxuries when she got the chance because they're not a normal life occurrence, well, not her life anyway. Jim finished talking to the pilot and informed her that the pilot said he would come in close enough to take a good look at a couple of the bergs and even land on one if it looked steady and safe enough.

"That's great, Jim, thanks," Garcia said appreciatively. Recognizing that he probably had better things to do with his time than spend the day playing tour guide, she apologized. "Sorry, I probably shouldn't have asked. I'm sure you're bored with sight seeing and icebergs and just want to get down to business."

Smiling, Jim shook his head. "No, I hired you for your expertise. I need to trust you on the work part. In addition, getting you acclimatized to this country and this part of the world is going to need to happen eventually and in my mind the sooner you understand all aspects that affect the job, the more detailed you'll be able to make designs for our project. Anyway I still think the bergs are pretty cool too and honestly I have never landed on one so this will be a first for me as well." Garcia smiled at his attempt to make her feel better about her request and realized, again, how much there was to appreciate about this man. Her rose-colored glasses were set on high right now and focused completely on Jim Dunsmuir.

"The pilot also told me that he's had reports from other aircraft in the area that they've seen a number of whales moving around today. I don't know if you have watched them swim before but I find it quite relaxing. I know whale watching really has nothing to do with work, but if you don't mind the distraction, I wouldn't mind taking a few minutes to watch?" Jim asked.

Garcia had never watched whales swim before but had always heard of people doing it on tourist excursions and thought she might as well take the opportunity. "I've never had a chance to watch them swim before, sounds great."

"Well you're in for a treat, in my opinion anyway. There are some things that nature can provide that just can't be duplicated or out done by manmade technology." He looked over at her and smiled. "But I guess I don't have to tell you that, your life's work is all about harnessing the raw power nature provides and converting it into something good. The more I investigate, the more I believe electric motors and electric power is the way to go. Electricity is just so much more efficient than combustion power, the first electric truck beat a Porsche 911 off the line for, god sakes! When battery technology and infrastructure catch up, electric vehicles will dominate the roadways and once that happens the switch over will be inevitable," Jim paused, clearly lost in thought about the future. "I guess it's not the technology so much as the cultural and capital shift required for us to switch from gas stations to charging stations. With the proven efficiency of electric motors, can you imagine where we'd be at if the same amount of research that has gone into combustion engines had gone into electric motors? That doesn't even account for home and building heat or the indoor vertical farms that you seem quite fond of. I just feel like we're right on the cusp of something great and just can't get there fast enough. I think that's why I find your work so amazing. You really cut out a niche market for yourself and have made it your own," Jim vehemently slapped his knee with his hand, emphasizing his point. "God I'm excited for this project. We need to get the job, Garcia. We simply have to."

Garcia was struck by Jim's intensity on the subject, she obviously had developed an attraction for him as a person but had no idea he was so passionate on the subject of electric power. He was showing more than just a simple desire to get his name on something or to show off his money and power. She'd met rich people before and while many of them seemed normal for the most part, once she got to know them she often saw a fierce underlying need to kill, to be the best, to get the best and win. Maybe it was because they were still working to achieve more but most likely it was ingrained in their personalities. The difference she saw in Jim could be the social statures between millionaires and billionaires, but his personality was a mystery to her and she wanted to know more about him, hell at this point she wanted to know everything about him.

Questions flooded her brain and she tried without avail to ignore them. Finally, she thought, screw it, she was just going to ask. They were having a personal conversation to the point of him explaining his philosophical beliefs and she would build a way out of the conversation for him into her question in case he didn't want to answer.

CHAPTER 28

"Jim, I know talking about money and finances is kind of a taboo subject to bring up with people but you're famous for yours and for how you earned it. You don't have to answer if you don't want to, but are all the rumors true? I've heard the stories about you risking your parents' retirement fund and then just knowing the financial markets and how they were going to react before they did. Ramsey started to tell me some of the story yesterday during my meeting with him. It seems like such an amazing story! But you're probably sick of telling it and in that case, don't feel like you have to just to appease my curiosity." Garcia knew by the time she was done talking that she was basically babbling and felt so embarrassed for asking.

Jim stared at her for a few moments, the question took him back, he hadn't been prepared for it. The story was his and he'd never really put it fully into words before, despite the number of reporters who had asked for his personal account. Christina and Ramsey knew the story and had lived it with him, well Ramsey had, anyway. Christina had been part of it until she passed away in 2003. In all honesty, most of his fortune was built during a period of mind-numbing grief. At the time his carelessness for life following the devastation he felt from losing Christina had left him unfocused, just floating through life. He'd moved his money around to places he thought were good investments without much real care. He was hesitant to answer her question at first but then thought maybe it would do him good to put that part of his life into words. There was something about Garcia he felt like he would be missing out on something if he didn't get to know her better, plus it was not like his life was any national secret, so he decided to tell her.

"Well to be honest I can't truly say that I've ever put this story into words before. With the exception of the financial results I'm not sure the story will make me sound like much more than a drifter jumping from one job to another. Mostly reporters and bankers just like to hear the parts when I shifted from one investment to another and how much my portfolio increased with each move. For me, though, it really was just my life and how it unfolded. I'll do my best to tell you about it, but just be sure to stop me if you get bored," Jim joked modestly.

Garcia smiled, relieved that he was not mad at her for asking and teasingly replied, "I very much doubt your life will bore me, but I promise to stop you if it does."

She followed by softening her demeanour and saying, "I would really like to hear your story Jim."

Her words gave him the resolve to tell her his story. The last thing he wanted to do was cry in front of this beautiful woman. All the interviews and analysis that he'd gone through had cemented many of the dates in his head so keeping the facts straight wouldn't be an issue. He felt adding in the life part might be where he'd struggle.

"Okay here it goes. I was born in 1979 to Lynn and Don Dunsmuir and we lived in New York City with my younger sister. My grandparents were born in the United States but my great grand parents came over from England. My father is a doctor, a general practitioner, and my mom was a nurse. Mom worked out until I was born and then she became a stay at home mom. We were not rich by any sense of the word, especially in a city like New York, we didn't live on the Upper East Side or summer in the Hamptons, but we were more than comfortable and my sister and I were very well loved and looked after. Being a GP, dad had regular office hours except for his on-call shifts which he always took for extra money and to keep his skill set up. I remember happy times as a kid. I did well in school and played sports. At the time, my goal was to follow in my father's footsteps and become a doctor. Dad had attended Cornell but I was not quite as dedicated in school so I probably would have been lucky to get into a medical program at a lesser known school. I'll never forget my parents bought me a BMW Z3 for my sixteenth birthday, just like Pierce Brosnan drove in

Goldeneye." Jim paused and stared out the window for a second, then turned back to Garcia and continued.

"In my opinion we lived a normal mid to upper class lifestyle. Stealing, rebelling or acting out really was not something I did. As a teenager I never felt a need for anything or restricted by parental rules, but maybe that was the problem. I felt invincible without knowing it. Somewhere around 1995 dad upgraded our family computer and hooked us up to the internet. Dad was an electronic and gadget lover so his new after dinner hobby was transferring as much of our lives to the Information Super Hi-way as possible. Then once he felt safe enough with online security systems he transferred his banking and investment portfolios. Dad was a conservative investor and never used a money-managing firm, he had always invested his money himself. Now with the internet, he was able to get into day trading which was really just gambling. Dad knew day trading for what it was but liked it and did a little bit just for his own entertainment while secretly hoping to make it rich, of course," Jim grinned ruefully at the memory of his dad, hunched over the computer in the evenings.

Jim looked over at Garcia, determined that she still appeared interested, and continued. "Then I started using the internet myself, I quickly found a fast way to research school papers without digging through library books. The school system at the time had not made the shift to recognize the information available on the internet and plagiarism was made simple, my marks went up. I started emailing friends, looking up things on line like sports stats and hot girls. Eventually that got old so when I overheard kids at school talking about internet stocks and how these tech companies were jumping one thousand percent overnight and then going broke the following day it interested me. I guess the information I learned from dad and his investment hobby rubbed off on me so I stated looking into stocks and investing. Whether I had a talent or not, I found that watching stocks and predicting their movement was quite easy to do. My father either didn't have a pass code back then or in those days, it would have been something easy like his name so I was easily able to get into his accounts. It took me about two minutes to figure out how to buy and sell stocks. I ended up watching the markets, focusing mostly on technology and internet stocks. These were the stocks everyone was talking about and were the ones that moved around fast enough to actually entertain the short attention span of a teenager. At first I never really thought much of it, life went on, I was in school, had friends to hang out with and girls to chase, games to play and after school practice. I never even thought about actually investing. Then something happened. Maybe I was between sports and had more time or who knows, but I started watching the market more closely. I seemed to be pretty good at predicting which ones would go up and make money. As good as I thought I was, basically every single internet company went up with a drastic rise and then would go broke just as quickly." Jim laughed at himself and continued.

"But with my limited or non-existent knowledge of investing I thought it was simple to make money and suddenly the idea started to form in my head. I was a little conservative myself so I practiced a couple times, I moved five hundred dollars of dad's money in and out of tech stocks, made a couple thousand dollars and sold out. I never told him, I just did it and he never noticed. I do remember trying to talk him into investing in the Nasdaq a couple times but he'd just say no. He thought the investments were too risky. To this day, I don't know what came over me it just seemed to happen. Suddenly there was new stock out selling for ten cents a share and I was absolutely sure it would go high. Dad was away at a medical conference, in my mind the stars aligned, it was fate or so I thought. I took all of mom and dad's retirement fund and bought five hundred thousand worth of shares in a fly-by-night internet company, getting dad five million shares. God for all I know it might have been my investments that triggered the stock to rise!" Jim chuckled at the thought of his naïve investing prompting a chain reaction. "As I recall it sat even for a couple days and I was sick because the other funds I had been watching usually jumped immediately, so I was starting to get scared. Then suddenly the fund spiked and within a week the stock shot up to fifteen dollars a share and I was so scared I sold out right then. I put seventy-five million into my dad's account that day and that made me even more afraid because now I knew I was going to have to tell him what I'd done. I took the seventy-five million and invested it into Amazon, a strong steady tech company at the time. I did this mostly because I wanted to be safe and I had no idea where else to invest all the money, dad was away and I could not remember the other stocks he had before, so I just did it. Amazon shares were just over eighteen dollars apiece at the time."

"Oh my God," Garcia exclaimed. "That's like beyond winning the lottery," Amazed at what she was hearing, Garcia realized that it was starting to seem like the Jim Dunsmuir urban legend might be true. "How did you break the news to your parents? They must have been shocked."

"Shocked, mad, happy, dumbfounded... I'm not exactly sure the best way to describe their emotions, but they were something all right," Jim laughed. "I tried to ease the shock as much as I could but really there was only so much I could say. I started by telling them I figured out how to make stock trades and had made a few thousand dollars doing it while they were away. They were mad and gave me a speech on gambling hard-earned money that was not mine to touch in the first place. Then, as dad was logging in to see what I did, I had to tell them that those investments were not the only ones I made. Basically, I said, mom and dad, there is something I need to tell you. As I was saying that, dad's portfolio popped open on his screen and when his total came up, his mouth dropped open and he just stared. Mom had never been on the system so she just looked perplexed. After a minute or so dad said, 'what the hell?' and he started clicking back and forth in and out of his account trying to get it to reset. Mom started asking him, 'Don what's wrong? Don what is it?' Dad wouldn't answer her, he just kept staring. Finally, mom broke down and started crying. I was too scared to speak and answer her. Dad whirled around in his chair and looked at me and said pretty threateningly, 'no jokes or lying, boy. is this true?' I just nodded.

He looked at me a minute longer then he reached out for mom's hand and a smile started to creep onto his face, then he started to laugh and cry all at the same time. Poor mom probably was thinking she was going to need to jump to my rescue to prevent dad from strangling me. Finally, dad pulled himself together and questioned me again. 'Really?' He asked. I knew I was not out of the woods but felt I was about to get some reprieve, having seventy-five million in the bank was going to make them quite happy once they knew for sure it was true and legal. Dad spent the next ten minutes explaining the process to mom and she fell into total shock. The next few weeks were chaos as mom made dad check with every accountant, lawyer and banker she could think of to make sure the money was totally ours and totally legal." Jim said, grinning at the memory of his mom and dad's reaction.

"Did you ever get in any actual trouble?" Garcia asked, hung up on the part of the story where he'd taken his own parents' money without them knowing.

"No, not really. I don't think they could really figure out exactly what to do with me," Jim admitted ruefully. "They did send me to a psychiatrist to get me treated for gambling addictions and to talk through how everything in life would not always be so easy. Whether I had a true problem or not, I'm not sure but the doctor did help me map out and make a life plan for myself. It was during these sessions that I realized I liked business and had some aptitude for it. Now that we had money, I was free to pick a University of my choice. I applied for, and was accepted, into Harvard business school. I ended up going into commerce and got a double degree in accounting and marketing. I'll get to that later. Back to the investing part of the story... Amazon kept climbing steadily and reports predicted strong growth so dad left the money in the company. By 1999, Amazon was sitting at sixty-nine dollars a share, so we had basically made another fortune. Then the stock started to slip, dad thought it would bounce back but by 2000 the price had dropped to forty-six dollars a share. It was at this point that he decided he needed to diversify and for the first time put his money into a managed fund. He ended up putting most of the funds in Berkshire Hathaway. Dad studied all the investing information he could get his hands on and all the reading he did pointed him towards Warren's company and he's been happy with the result ever since. Of course, he had almost two hundred million to invest following the Amazon sale," Jim stated matter-of-factly.

"Jim that is such an incredible story," Garcia said admiringly, shaking her head at the ludicrousness of it all. "When did you start to get recognized for all of this?" She asked.

"Good timing for that question," he replied. "It was about then that the story got out that we had made all this money. Without even thinking about it, Dad let it slip that it was me that had done the investing and that's when I made the news and ended up with my picture in the papers. Then I got to meet Warren Buffet and get my picture taken with him for the cover of Forbes. What a great and humble man, by the way. From the Forbes picture, I became a national interest. During that time, I lost most of my old friends and made a new one in Ramsey so down sides have their ups as well. Life became harder for me in some ways. I felt everyone had their eyes on me and I was so paranoid about screwing up. I felt like the world was just waiting to pay me back; I was so scared all the time. I ended up going back to my psychiatrist and we talked and he got me to realize my life had changed and I couldn't unchange it. He helped me understand that if friends or acquaintances left me because of my good fortune, then they were probably people I didn't want to associate with anyway."

Pausing, Jim gazed into Garcia's eyes. "I can't believe I'm telling you all of this," he said, somewhat embarrassed. "Short of telling my doctor, I've never verbalized this much detail of my life to anyone. Do you still want to hear more or should I wrap it up?"

Garcia was surprised he couldn't tell she was completely spell bound by what he was saying and wanted to hear more. She wanted to hear everything he was willing to share, she wanted to know him and was honoured he felt comfortable enough with her to tell his story, so she said, "Jim you don't have to tell me anything but I'd love to hear your whole story, every detail. I'm curious what made you tell me more than you usually tell others but really would like to hear it all."

"I want you to know *me*," he said. "For some reason I care about what you think of me, and that's saying something because I quit caring about what people thought or said about me years ago." Seeing her sincerity, Jim continued. "After I got semi-famous, the party offers were nonstop, but Ramsey and I focused on school and then work and I was able to ignore them. Then when I was with Christina, it was like.... It was like my life became balanced. She was the bright white light I was meant to follow and I was so happy." Jim spaced out and stared out his window. Garcia reached over and grabbed his hand. It was strong, but clammy with his emotions, and she felt bad for him and reassured him, saying, ""It's ok you don't need to say anymore."

Jim turned and looked into her eyes then down at their hands. Garcia thought she might have gone too far by holding his hand. She expected him to draw it back but suddenly he squeezed her hand tight and started to speak again.

"After Christina died, I fell apart, I sold everything and got out of control. But that's not the part of the story we're on to yet. If you really want to hear it, I should at least tell it in order." He sat for a moment, gathering his thoughts.

"Please, Jim, go on," she prodded.

"Well Ramsey and I got into Harvard, like I mentioned. He was on an academic scholarship and dad was paying my way. We were working hard, getting good marks but neither of us were completely sure what we were working towards. Somewhere in my second year I met Christina and well..." Jim looked up at Garcia and felt guilty but said it anyway, "my world changed. She fit right into my life, or vise versa, but suddenly it went from Ramsey and me to Ramsey, Christina and I. Ramsey and Christina became good friends and we spent all our time together. Christina gave us a goal, her family was fairly well–off and worked in real estate. We used her family business plan as a model for an assignment in one of our classes and the idea took off from there. We were set to convocate in the spring of 2002, we had a business plan drawn up and had already gotten a loan approval from the bank to start our own real estate business, it was at that point I felt comfortable enough with my life plan that I proposed to Christina and she said yes. When I told my parents we where engaged they were so happy for us, they loved her almost as much as I did," he said with a grin.

"Besides wedding planning, dad was also interested in the new business we were getting into. As I explained our business model to him and showed him a copy of the bank loan contract we would sign to get the business up and running, he decided to back us. He said if the banks determined we were a good investment how could he not support us, so he gave us half the investment money. He said no sense paying interest to the banks when he could help us out. I was shocked that he was willing to trust me with his money after what I did the first time, and I wanted to do him proud. Christina, Ramsey and I poured over the business plan, working out all the benefits and efficiencies we could, finally deciding to convert our company's business plan from buying rental properties to new home construction on land we purchased from cities. We had such a tight plan, and although it seemed expensive, the new home construction phase was just taking off so we got a few blocks of land very reasonably priced compared to a few short months later when everyone else was getting into the business. Our spec houses sold quickly for astronomical prices and we just kept building higher end homes and selling them for more and more. The demand was literally out weighing what we could produce. Before long, our company developed a great reputation and cities were actually requesting us to build in their municipalities. Without having to make interest payments or pay back principle, we just kept expanding and building. All we did was work, but we loved every second of it. We built thousands of houses all over the major U.S. cities. Things were going so well that Christina and I were talking about starting a family. Ramsey and I seemed to be able to read the markets, we had strong dedicated contractors who stuck with us through the boom, a time when anybody with a hammer and a measuring tape could start building houses and make money. Our people were our team. We paid them well, set up training, medical coverage, pension plans and organized crews so they could have time off. We looked after each other and I think that is why everything felt so good and worked so well. But all good things come to an end and so did this."

Visibly shaken as he started into the next part of his story, Jim took a breath, and then dove back in. "Christina booked us a doctor's appointment, just the basic checkups to match blood types and make sure we were healthy. Normal stuff to do before starting a family. A couple days later, the hospital called and asked Christina to come back for a follow up appointment. We just thought it was a normal follow up, an extra check for the hopeful mother to be, so she went in herself and I went to work. I was in a meeting, sitting in a black leather chair at a dark stained walnut boardroom table when my phone rang. I can remember those details because I was staring at that table when my life changed forever. I almost didn't take the call; it was from a number I didn't recognize. When I answered the phone, it was our doctor on the line asking if I could talk. Maybe deep down I knew that something was wrong, but self-preservation would not let my mind go there. I excused myself from the meeting and went out in the hall. The doctor told me that he had shared some concerning news with Christina and that she was in no shape to drive home. He was wondering if I could come and pick her up and he wanted to discuss a few things with me as well. Christina was a tough woman." Jim shook his head. "No, scratch that. She was the strongest person I knew so for her to be upset to the point she couldn't drive left me shaking and wondering what was going on. I quickly ran back in the meeting, whispered to Ramsey that I had to leave, apologized to everyone else and flew to the hospital. The doctor had given me his floor and office number so after parking I ran up to his office. When I entered reception, the doctor's assistant quickly ushered me into the examining room. Christina was sitting in a corner, talking to a woman I'd never met. Christina's facial expression showed so little emotion I barely recognized her, and she was in so much shock that she was white as a ghost. The doctor was at his desk and he waived me over to sit across from him. I had a feeling I should go to Christina, but she was mid-conversation so I went and sat down, feeling worried and confused. Once I was seated in front of him, the doctor said, 'Jim I've something to tell you but I need your attention, ok? Focus. I need you to listen carefully'."

"I will never forget how he demanded my attention at that moment. His words punched right into me. I wanted to ask what the hell was going on and that was when he blurted out, 'Jim, Christina has cancer.' I can't imagine the look I must have had on my face when he told me. Despite him telling me he needed my whole attention, I really don't remember much of the conversation that followed. To this day I remember certain words about white blood cells, platelets, stage four, inoperable and months to live."

Jim's hands were shaking and he withdrew his from her grasp and clasped his own hands together. It almost seemed as though he was telling himself the story and had forgotten Garcia was there. She could tell he was off in his own memories and she felt sick for him and Christina. How awful a shock it must have been to go from planning a future and children to a complete end-of-the-world moment.

"I'm sorry, Jim," Garcia whispered quietly, trying not to disturb him. "I really didn't mean for my question to make you relive that time."

"It's ok," he said, "it was almost twenty years ago, I... it shouldn't bother me much anymore."

"Well, I'm sure it's not really a consolation, but in my opinion I find it very romantic that you still feel so strongly. And if nothing else, Christina would have passed away knowing she was loved as much as any person could be."

Jim looked at her, and she could see him refocus and come back to the present. When he was ready, he began his story again. "I'd like to be able to say that I jumped up from the doctor's desk, ran over to Christina's side and started comforting her but instead I froze. My mind started running. First I thought, how could I have left her to come and get this news on her own? Then I thought, maybe the tests were wrong or mixed up, because we were supposed to be starting a family. Then I felt a hand on my shoulder and I looked up and Christina was standing beside me, looking down at me. That's when I snapped out of it, jumped up, grabbed her and squeezed her so hard. My emotions instantly turned to anger, and I spun on the doctor and demanded treatment and retests. Then in the midst of my angry tirade, I remembered Christina and I made her sit down. I wanted her to relax and take it easy but I couldn't contain my anger. I spun on the doctor again and was almost out of control. He was ready for my reaction and told me that the lady who had been talking to Christina when I first came in was one of the resident oncologists at the hospital and he introduced me to Doctor Astar. She had been going over Christina's test results and would definitely run another set of tests on Christina to make absolutely sure all of the original tests were accurate, plus a number of other tests in order to fully diagnose Christina's condition. I asked the doctors how long for the new test results to get back, they said they would have them back in a couple of days. I called and told Ramsey to cover us because we needed a couple of days off."

Then, smiling at his own memories, Jim said, "Christina called him back and said never mind. Both of us would be in first thing in the morning. She was like that, pushy, stubborn, and perfect. Over the years I realized that Christina and I never really got out of the honey moon phase. We went from dating in university to marriage and successful business people, then to complete disaster. That's why I've still got such a perfect opinion of her, or so my therapist says. When we got the new test results back, the diagnosis and prognosis remained that same. We took turns breaking down mentally and emotionally. There were so many nights we screamed, cried, and comforted each other. I felt so guilty for being such an emotional wreck when I was the one who got to live, but I still hurt more than anything. Ramsey took over the business for me while I spent my days calling doctors. We put Christina in every trial she could handle at every hospital from Johns Hopkins to the Mayo Clinic. I basically went to them on my knees with my checkbook open, begging for every treatment possible. In the end it was the ethical standards of those two facilities that ultimately sent us home where Christina could live out her last few weeks as normal as possible. I was ready to offer millions, but the doctors politely told me they would not take any more of my money. They were sorry but there was nothing else they could do. Christina took a few rounds of chemotherapy with little to no progress and the drugs made her so sick that it just wasn't worth it. It just goes to show how bad a disease is that the potential cure can make you just as sick as the sickness itself."

"Once she got the cancer drugs out of her system, she came back around to her normal self. We took a week and rented a place on the lake. We walked and talked and even almost forgot about the cancer for a couple of days. Well, not exactly forgot, but pushed it away from our minds. Then towards the end of the week she started pulling away from the holiday and started drifting back to reality. She was being strong while I was slowly being brought to my knees. She spent her last couple of days at the lake planning her own funeral, making lists of all the people she wanted to visit, figuring out the days she wanted to spend with her family... basically organizing her last days on earth. She even made lists for me so I could take care of myself and her parts of the business once she was gone. I literally couldn't take it. I begged her to quit planning her own death, but she just kept going. Never have I lived through such hell, seeing her prepare for the end, trying to deal with it myself, feeling guilty for feeling selfish."

Jim turned to look at Garcia and was surprised to find her watching him with tears welling in her eyes. "God, sorry, Garcia I really went off, didn't I?" He said, self-derisively with an attempt at a smile.

"Jim," she said gently, "it's ok. Really." She felt compelled to touch him and reached for his hand again, hating the defeated look on his face. "It was obviously a traumatic event for you, to say the least. I can still see the pain on your face and in your eyes. I really didn't mean to make you relive all of it again. I didn't know Christina was so intertwined in the story when I asked to hear it. I should have realized she would've been a large part of your history and I'm sorry to have put you through that. I'd love for you to finish telling me, but only if you want to. I've heard that talking about tragedies such as this really helps the healing process."

"Healing aside, you deserve to know my story Garcia." Jim squeezed her hand, appreciating the anchor it gave him to keep him in the present. "You've hitched your professional and your sister's professional life to my wagon now and you deserve to know I'm not just a gambling risk-taker who got lucky. I'm an investor and very good at it, I did work hard to get my Harvard degree and to build my real estate business. Yes, we had strong financial backing from my investments, but Ramsey, Christina and I worked ourselves to the bone, took calculated risks and we were successful, very successful. After Christina passed, I tried but could not go back to real estate with any passion. Building housing and commercial real estate had been her dream, her family's legacy, and that's why we started there in the first place. Ramsey was my partner so I told him I needed out of the business. He tried to talk me into staying on, saying it's only been a couple of months, and that I shouldn't make any rash decisions, but my mind was made up. I offered to finance him and sell him my share, but he didn't want it. He told me that he had been struggling without Christina too and said if he had to lose both of us, there was nothing in it for him either. Ramsey said it seemed to him like he and I needed to stay together, and I felt the same way. So we put the company up for sale. With our reputation and the real estate market as it was, we had people lined up to buy us out. It made me so proud because I felt like it proved just how great Christina's business model had been."

"It was 2004 when we liquidated everything. My share of the sale was around seven hundred million. Once we had our money, we needed a place to invest it. There was not much going on in the markets at the time with the only upside being real estate and we weren't about to invest in something we just got out of. Ramsey was talking about starting another business but I wasn't in the mind set to create something new. I continued to study the markets, looking for a place to invest our funds and eventually I came across gold. Gold had really tanked a couple of years' prior and was at the lowest price it had been in decades. I'd never invested in precious metals before but my research seemed to say the price was way undervalued for the market's demand. Further research showed me that not only was the metal undervalued but that gold had been on a slow steady climb for the previous two years with no drop off. It would be a risky investment, however Ramsey said he had faith in me when it came to investing, so we invested every dollar we had in gold at four hundred and thirty-five dollars an ounce, basically with the understanding that if it dropped below four hundred we would sell. As luck would have it, gold continued its rise and so we left our money invested in the precious metal market and watched it grow."

"Although financially it appeared that I was about to make another huge chunk of change, I wasn't doing well emotionally." Jim hesitated for a moment, seeming to consider his next words, then went on with his story, sticking to the facts while avoiding the emotional side of his life. Although an entertaining story, Garcia found herself wishing he would feel comfortable enough to tell her everything.

Jim continued by simply sticking to the facts of the story and leaving out the emotions. "I needed out of New York, so I moved to California where I took a job in the oil industry. I needed a change and the job would give me a chance to see if I had any talent in my chosen profession of marketing. Between my reputation and Harvard degree, I didn't have any trouble getting hired. My job was a consultant of sorts, working with the company's marketing team to try and rebrand oil's reputation in California. At the time, anti-oil slogans and protest groups were all the rage and California was the leader of this movement. In order to do my job properly I started studying all the effects oil had on the world, basically researching oil versus renewable energy. Oil is so simple and easy to sell. The tech is old, fire is the basic form of heat, power, even gunfire. All of our machines are set to run on oil and they are relatively easy to fix and maintain, plus we all trust it inherently. Renewable resources still have space-age uncertainty. People don't understand or know how they work, their grandfathers don't have old used solar panels in the garage they pull out and tinker with like they do combustion engines. Lack of understanding, trust and change has kept renewable resources back every bit as much as big oil and gas-powered engine companies have been blamed for its slow adoption.

"This information really made my job easy. Speak to people about tradition, tried tested and true machines, remind them about exhaust filters, fuel efficiency, make them proud to be doing their part for the environment, while still being able to burn oil and people feel content. Just like after a big Thanksgiving turkey dinner, you know you should get up and walk or stretch but it feels so good just to go on visiting," Jim grinned.

Garcia laughed out loud at his uncanny, witty analogy. People are not looking to change when they are happy with status quo, especially if they can feel good about how and what they're doing.

Enjoying her laughter, and relieved he was able to turn the story in a more upbeat direction, Jim continued. "Despite having the superior product, renewable energy is going to need to not only convince people to change their way of thinking but to spend lots of money converting to something they are unsure about that has a considerably weaker support and infrastructure system."

At that moment Garcia knew there would always be gas power at least until oil ran out or the governments mandated a no oil world order. Jim went on to say that the more he studied renewable energy the more he started to consider its benefits and possibilities beyond just solar powered cars. It was during his time working for the oil industry that plans started to form in his head for ideas like indoor heated golf courses in the Arctic Circle.

"I had these thoughts and dreams but no ambition or drive to start building anything. I was tired, I already felt like I cashed in on Christina's death because I sold out of the housing market a couple of years before my business would have been wiped out during the housing crisis. Ramsey and I were saved and Christina was dead." Jim stumbled over the word dead and his voice cracked, but he kept going. "So I just kept on working selling oil. Ramsey had started a consulting firm and he was doing well helping people start up and build businesses. He and I stayed close, we got together a couple of times a year and spoke on the phone often. I continued to watch the markets and in 2009 we sold out our gold shares for just over fourteen hundred an ounce which left me with a net of somewhere in the neighborhood of 2.3 billion. I recommended the sale to Ramsey because I saw an opportunity in the crude market. Oil was sitting at forty-six dollars a barrel and it had been climbing steadily. Ramsey said I'd made him a fortune and he would follow my investment lead anywhere so we reinvested our funds into oil. Oil had a couple quick initial price jumps which put me in a position that I was ahead money and could afford to watch the market. I'd been working in the oil industry since 2005 and although the steady work was nice, renewable energy was now in my system and I could feel some ambition coming back. I wanted to build again. But I needed help and my best friend just happened to be in the business of building businesses, so I gave him a call and we started planning.

By 2012 we were ready to get going, Ramsey sold out of his business, I quit my job and we sold out of oil. I needed the startup capital and if we were going to start a renewable energy business, I didn't want to be heavily invested in oil. As it turned out, oil was sitting at one hundred dollars a barrel at the time and my net worth jumped to almost four and a half billion dollars. So there I was, thirty-three years old, a self-made billionaire as the papers called it, starting a new career under the title of Dunsmuir Energy and, well, the rest you know. Ramsey and I spent time researching and finding a project we wanted. When we came across Neom, we knew that was the one, and we immediately started building towards it. Despite a lot of variables, we were able to get the financial backing we needed, by getting business owners and country leaders to sign on with us. From there we started recruiting and signing the right team to help us build the project. Now we just need to figure out a way to convince the Crown Prince that our idea is the best."

With perfect timing, as Jim finished talking, the Captain cut in.

CHAPTER 29

"Sir," the pilot's voice came through, "another craft just reported a pod of Narwhales in the ice flow not far off the coast. You still want us to fly over?"

"Absolutely, Captain!" Jim replied. Turning to Garcia, he openly shared his enthusiasm for what they were about to watch. "Garcia, you are going love this. These are such amazing creatures. They can dive over one and a half kilometers and spend upwards of twenty minutes under water without coming up for air. Narwhales don't stray far from the continent so not many people have heard of them, in fact they're nick-named unicorn of the sea because of a long tooth that sticks far out of their mouths that looks like a horn. Some of the whales have a tooth that grows almost ten feet in length and they're basically an endangered species so they're not always easy to find or see."

Garcia was astonished over Jim's boyish excitement about the whales. He'd just explained his life story to her about how he'd become a billionaire with less enthusiasm than he was showing over the whales.

"We'll be approaching the whale pod in about ten minutes and if you look out your windows, you'll notice the ice flow is just starting," the Captain reported.

CHAPTER 30

ollowing the flight back to New York, Richard's ride share car dropped him off at his house around nine pm. Once he settled in and ate, Richard called Kelly to double check and make sure the meeting was set for the next morning. Kelly said all was ready for eight am then asked if Richard could update him on what was going on so he could be better prepared for the meeting. Richard started to talk and then hesitated.

"You know what, Kel?" Richard said, "let me mull it over for the night. You deserve to hear it personally from me first so why don't we meet at seven? I'll outline my plan for you then and give you a chance to critique it before the others come in."

"That sounds good," Kelly agreed. "I'll get there a bit early and put the coffee on, see you in the morning."

"Night Kelly," Richard said, hanging up the phone.

He tried to make plans, but his mind kept wondering to Sara and how she looked and felt in his arms. Each time he realized he was in fantasyland, he'd shake his head back to reality and start the planning he needed to do all over again. After about four attempts he gave up, picked up his phone to call her and completely second guessed himself so he went into the kitchen for a drink of water. While in the kitchen he built up his resolve to call her and thought honestly, what does it hurt she's in Morocco? If she doesn't want to talk, she doesn't have to answer. It's not like they would run into each other by accident or even on purpose any time soon. Plus, he really needed to make the call to get it out of his system or he'd never be able to concentrate on his task at hand. Finally, he made up his mind, went back to his chair and dialed her number, completely forgetting about the five-hour time change.

"This must be an incredibly important business request for you to call me at 3:00 am," Sara said drowsily when she answered the phone without even saying hello. Embarrassed at being so obviously excited to talk to her that he'd failed to consider the time difference, Richard considered hanging up, but then realized she already knew who was on the line due to call display. Feeling sheepish, Richard was still struggling with what to say when she saved him by saying, "Rich, is that you? I've been hoping you would call."

"I'm so sorry," Rich stammered, "I don't know what I was thinking. I wanted to talk to you and totally forgot about time changes, I'll let you go back to sleep."

"No, it's ok really," Sara said, "I'm half-awake now and, like I said, I did want to talk to you." Truth be told once she realized it was Richard waking her up, she got a smile on her face. It was weird but she missed him already.

"Well seeing as I've so brazenly woken you up already, I might as well keep pushing my luck," Richard smiled, hoping she could tell through the phone line how happy he felt just to hear her voice. "I just finished setting up meetings and I was trying to plan out directions for my staff tomorrow but my mind kept wandering over to you and a kiss or two that we shared. Basically, no matter what I tried to do to shift my concentration, my thoughts kept going back to you. I'll try not to make the late calls anymore, but do you think it's ok if I continue to call you at a more reasonable time?" Richard asked her.

"Rich," Sara reassured him, "my mind has been on you too. In fact, I've been trying to figure out if there is a way I could see you again sometime if you're interested? We live so far apart but I can't tell you how happy I am that you called. I've also been worried about you, I know what George asked you to do, I know some of the things that George has done, and his actions border on criminal. I want you to be careful, ok? George is charismatic and he has a way of talking people into doing things they may not normally do or think is right. Please don't take this as I'm trying to tell you what to do, I'm just ... I just like you and I don't want to see anything bad happen to you."

Touched by her concern, Rich also respected her moral compass which prompted her to caution him. "Thanks, Sara. You're right about George. I do have some reservations and quite honestly, I think I would have turned him down except I truly believe he'd just get someone else to threaten his competition if I didn't do it. I've already made sure my plans will not harm anyone physically. I also won't make up or publish anything that is not true, so reputations will only be ruined if the men react in ways that would ruin them in the situations I put them in. I'm not sure I can guarantee someone else George hired would do the same for his intended victims. I also feel challenged by this assignment and now I really want to try it just to see if I can, it's like a crazy adrenaline rush. Like playing spy when I was a kid, except in real life. I'd never admit that or tell it to anyone else, but I want to tell you so you know me and because I want to get to know you."

"Don't feel bad, Rich," Sara said. "I know George's business methods and I still work for him. You don't need to explain yourself to me, but I'm glad that you want to. I can't tell you how glad I am that you called and hope you don't regret it either. Can we plan to talk again soon because I would like to catch a few more hours of sleep before I have to get up for work?"

"Regret it, god no. I was worried you would see my number and not even answer. This was the sweetest call of my life. Would you let me kiss you again if I was there?"

"I'd demand it actually," she answered, laughingly.

"Hmm... nice," Richard said, imagining the feel of her lips under his. "Text me when you have time to talk and I'll call then, ok?"

"I'll send you something tomorrow. Good night Rich, I'm glad you called."

He loved that she had started calling him Rich. "Sleep well Sara, talk soon," Richard replied as he hung up the phone and scolded himself again for calling her so late.

Now that his mind was settled, he felt alive and ready to plow into his assignments. When he was in the police force Richard had set up stakeouts, surveillance and even a few sting operations. The first part of all these ops would be familiar territory for him. First, get the guys to gather information on their marks, he'd need their schedules, routines and social plans for the next couple weeks in order to make solid plans. Richard would make two plans for each subject, a primary scheme and then a secondary or back up plan. He'd then have his team act out both scenarios for preparation. Tomorrow he'd have Kelly review and critique his ideas and then they'd start developing plans of attack. He'd need to inform Kelly about the psych reports and explain George's basic ideas so Kelly would be able to properly help him build the best plans of attack. Richard knew they'd only have a couple days to finalize their plans once the guys brought the info on their marks back to him. Richard knew if anything went wrong, it would be in shoddy planning due to the limited time frame they had, so he was going to need to be extra careful. He spent the next hour jotting ideas down in a rough outline. Richard went to sleep around midnight with Sara on his mind once again.

Richard was up at five am the next morning, following a quick half-hour workout he was showered and eating breakfast by six. Five minutes later he was heading out the door to start his commute to the office. It was only a ten-minute drive from his home, five minutes at this time of the day, but Richard wanted to get in early.

George had picked Richard not only for his company's reputation but for the fact that his headquarters were on Long Island, Bay Shore to be exact. The Long Island Governor of the day was very progressive and already had an off-shore wind farm south east of Montauk under construction. The contract had, of course, gone to Chris Buchanan who was a long-time house owner in the Hamptons as well as a well-known philanthropist in the area. George knew the location would allow his investigators to access the area without any undue attention, if Chris was even looking for anyone that might be following him. Most summers Richard had men out in the area following allegedly cheating spouses anyway.

True to his word, Kelly had coffee ready and was waiting to meet with Richard when he walked through the office door.

CHAPTER 31

"That was a whirlwind of a trip," Kelly said, looking at him questioningly when he walked in. "Africa and back in three days with immediate meetings scheduled for us and our top guys? What's going on?"

"Grab your coffee, Kel, and let's sit down." Richard's offices were not the same calibre that George boasted in Africa, but they were nice just the same. The Trade Link Security offices were contemporary in style, with glass walls and mass-produced high end ergonomic office chairs. They sat in the board room and Richard brought Kelly up to speed on George's plan.

"This is beyond surveillance, Richard," Kelly observed. "It's a planned operation which is beyond what any of us had in mind when we signed up for this job. Ironically, it's also outside the law, which is something all of us signed up to defend at one point in our lives."

Completely understanding Kelly's hesitation, Richard was determined not to make his partner feel obligated in any way to agree to the job. "I know and I've decided to go forward with it, that's why I am presenting the case to you. But I can't do it alone and I will not do it if you, Mike, Joe and Jeff are not on board with me. This needs to be a team initiative with members we can trust and count on. I'm not prepared to bring anyone else in at this time. If we decide to do it, our biggest hurdle will be time. In saying that, there's not much time for you and the guys to discuss or mull it over. It has to be a snap decision because we need to put things in motion in three weeks', time which means a lot of preliminary recognisance and work to prepare. I'd say you have about fifteen minutes to decide yes or no before the others start rolling in and if you're out, I'm not even going to bring the opportunity up with the others. I'll leave you alone to think it over. And I need you to know, Kelly, that I respect your decision whichever way you go."

As Richard stood to leave Kelly said, "I already have my answer, but give me ten to think it over on my own. I owe it to the guys to give it some consideration before making a gut decision."

"You're a good man, Kelly, and a good leader. The men respect and trust you. I'll be back soon."

Trade Link's location on the second floor of a two-story building allowed Richard an office with a balcony that looked south east over the ocean. They were not ocean-front, but the building was situated in a way he could look out over the town and see the sun shining off the ocean as the day started to build. If they took this job and were successful, he thought he might take some of his earnings and move their office closer to the ocean. The guys would deserve the upgrade if they all didn't decide to retire with the bonus pay they'd get from completing this assignment. Richard finished the last of his coffee and returned to Kelly in the board room. Richard had a feeling Kelly was going to want to do this job. The money made it more than worthwhile, and beyond that, the action, and the chance to do more than follow people around and watch them cheat on their spouses was going to be so appealing it would be like a drug. The idea was going to get his adrenaline pumping just like it had got to Richard's. Kelly was writing out work orders when Richard sat down at the table.

Kelly finished up and said, "My immediate feeling was that I wanted to do this and after I thought about it and weighed the pros and cons, I still feel the same way. I'll want to see George's name at the bottom of a contract with all the agreed to terms that we discussed from the money to lawyer fees to us having full autonomy etcetera."

Relieved, but not really surprised, that Kelly was on board, Richard reassured him. "George told me he would send a contract over as soon as we agreed to take the work on."

"Well I'm not sure I totally trust George, but if the guys agree to the job, I say we get them out on surveillance immediately to start gathering information. Then once George sends us the contract and our lawyer goes over it, we can put our plans into action."

"Do you think the guys will want to do this with us?" Richard asked.

"They'll be intrigued for sure but we'll need to give them till after dinner so they can at least take some time to process what it is they are signing up for. After all it will be them doing the dirty work and they'll have to be able to live with their actions," Kelly said reasonably.

In complete agreement with Kelly's assessment of their team, Richard started thinking out loud about strategy. "The hard part about pushing and threatening people is they need to believe the threat so they actually do what we want them to. If they realize we can't back up our threats or take them further, we not only lose, we might get caught."

"Exactly. That's why planning and execution will be so important in this operation, Rich. I see Mike and Joe are here and Jeff is just walking in. How do you want to tell them?"

"Well, we're partners, so let's tell 'em together," Richard said. "This is about to be the biggest, riskiest job offer they've ever gotten, so for them to feel safe I think they should see you and I are on the same page and in agreement. What do you think?"

"That's exactly what I was thinking, I'll call them in," Kelly said. Kelly went to the door of the board room and waved them in, then came back and sat down beside Richard. The men took seats at the table, all the while giving Richard the gears about all expense-paid vacations to Africa and asking him if he met any cute girls on his African Safari. Once all the informalities were out of the way, Richard hesitated. They were all such loyal people and all close friends; he was not sure if he wanted to really ask them to join him in this endeavor. He looked over at Kelly, who gave him a nod of encouragement which was enough to get him going.

Richard started out by saying, "Men I have a proposition for you. I'm going to do my best to give you the facts and not try to sell it one way or another. Once I explain things to you, time becomes of the essence and you'll see why. I've already explained the job to Kelly and he and I have agreed that it's worth exploring, but not without you guys on board because we need men we can trust and who're really good at what they do. That's why I need you."

The men took a bit of a double take and glanced at each other; they enjoyed their work and it was serious at times, but never had Rich or Kelly been so formal about a job.

"Gee, Rich, you better fill us in. You guys are being way too serious. You'll end up with ulcers if you don't get it out," Jeff spoke up, trying to ease the tension at the table.

Richard knew there was nothing else to do but lay it out for them. "Ok boys, here it is. George called me down to Morocco for an in-person meeting, that's why I was in Africa the last couple of days. You all know the businessmen we have followed for him the last few months?" Seeing their nods, he continued, "Well it turns out they're in competition with him. They're all finalists in a multi-billion-dollar bidding war where the winner will be awarded a contract to supply renewable electricity to a brand new city that will be built in Saudi Arabia. The city is called Neom and it's projected to be thirty-three times the size of New York City. George's company represents solar power, which he feels should be a shoo in to win with the endless supply of sun in the deserts of Saudi Arabia. In saying that, he doesn't want to leave anything to chance, so that's where we come in. He wants us to run interference. For example, Chris Buchanan is also in the group of finalists; he'll of course pitch wind power. Peter Fairchild has a bid that includes putting a dam on the Nile River and Jim Dunsmuir will be representing geothermal power. They'll be meeting in the Crown Prince's Palace in mid August to present their cases and try and win the contract." Richard paused, took a drink of lukewarm coffee, then continued his explanation.

"What George wants from us is a series of precisely executed scare tactics against all four of the bidders. George is deadly serious on this. He's already had psychological assessments completed on each bidder. Using that information, coupled with the information we've provided him, allowed him to build base plans of attack which he shared with me. Now he is asking us to take his base plans and produce precision blueprints that, once executed, will force two of George's competitors out of the race and scare the third significantly enough to throw him off his game during his presentation to the Princes. Of course, George will know the attack on him is just a rouse but completely necessary to keep suspicion off him, once the other three are attacked." Richard paused again and looked at his men, trying to gauge their level of interest. He didn't have to look long to see the sharpness in their eyes and it was then that he knew they were going to vote to do this with him.

"Now here's the tricky part," Richard continued, "what we must do involves kidnapping, extortion and threats, all of which are serious criminal offences, and I don't have to tell this group what that means, that's why the operation calls for meticulous planning and execution because we can't get caught. As part of the negotiations, George has agreed to pay all legal fees if we get pinched, to allow us the right to abort the mission any time we see fit. Although this assignment means breaking the law, we'll not be expected to hurt anyone, we'll take the plan only so far and if the mark doesn't break, we end the mission. For the time we spend working on this project, all our living and business expenses will be covered and your wages will be doubled. Further to that, you three get one million dollars each and Kelly you get two million. If we're successful and George is awarded the contract, each of us will get an additional million for services rendered." Richard concluded his brief summary of the job. "That, gentlemen, is the proposal. With the contract meeting coming up in August you can see why time is not our friend on this one. Kelly and I are going to leave you now to discuss this amongst yourselves. After your discussions, I want each of you to go for dinner separately and come back here for one thirty. At that time, we'll hold a secret ballot where everyone can vote yes or no. I want us all in or we're not taking this job. You're all good men and I don't want to lead you into something you won't be able to live with yourselves afterwards. Do you have any question before we leave?" Richard asked.

"The turnaround time is very quick, but no questions for me," Joe replied.

"It absolutely is and that's why we need your answer so soon," Kelly agreed. "We'll see you all back here at one thirty." With that, Richard and Kelly left the room and headed up to Richard's office. The morning was shaping up into a perfect spring day, so they went out on the patio to enjoy the sunshine.

"Well, what do you think they'll decide, Kel?" Richard asked.

"They're a lot like us," Kelly grinned. "I bet their gut feeling will be to jump in. It's new, it's exciting, and the reward is big and instantaneous. I have to say your secret ballot vote idea was an interesting addition."

CHAPTER 32

Richard leaned on the steel railing, looked at Kelly and said, "I meant it when I said I only want to do this if we're all on board. I don't want peer pressure or anything else to force anyone into something like this. If everyone's not in, then it's too risky to try. I want you to vote too. Once everyone has voted, I'll take all four votes back to my office and count them. No one will ever know if one person voted it down or if all four did. Now, let's go grab a long lunch while we wait for their decision. At this point I'm ninety percent sure we will be accepting the job so let's start planning the first phase while we eat." They had some time so they drove to Nicky's on the Bay. The trendy restaurant opened at eleven and they'd be just on time. On a day like this, Nicky's would have a line up out the door by eleven forty-five. After ordering their meals, they began discussing what actions to take first.

Kelly began with Chris Buchanan. "Well we know Buchanan will likely spend most of the summer in his house in the Hamptons. Not only is he a family man, but with that big wind project of his out by Montauk, he'll want to be on hand to oversee the project and at the same time see if he can gain further corporate or government support to build more wind farms around the country. The biggest money in the world spends its summers in the Hamptons, so if Chris can add a couple more clients from there, they'll be massive accounts. What are you planning for him?"

"Well if he's on holidays his schedule might be a little harder to nail down. Let's send Mike out to tail Chris. Chris may seem easy-going, but we better not underestimate him. There is a reason he's in the position he is," Richard said thoughtfully.

"You're absolutely right. We can't take any of these men for granted and we need to remember that," Kelly agreed. "And if any of them are like George, they'll have bodyguards following them at the very least."

"George's psych assessment on Chris says we need to threaten his family and make it clear to him that the only way to save them is to withdraw from the Neom bid," Richard explained George's base plan for Buchanan. "Our threat will have to leave no doubt in his mind that harm will come to his family if he doesn't comply. This means the plan and acting will have to be perfect because the truth is that we're bluffing and can go no further than the threat."

They ordered a dozen pacific oysters on the half shell

as a starter. While waiting for his drink, Richard wondered why people liked to order things from far away. Here they were, sitting on the stunning deck of a luxurious harbour, admiring yachts, on the Atlantic coast, but felt the need to order oysters from the other side of the continent. When Richard pointed out that fact, they both laughed at the simplicity of the human psyche. Despite their thoughts on ordering the foreign oysters, they still tasted perfect when mixed with the right amount of brine and Tobasco sauce. The oysters where served drizzled with lemon while sitting on a bed of fresh ice. After tapping their first set for luck, the men tossed back a couple more oysters each, then settled back to enjoy a freshly poured draft beer served to them in chilled frosty mugs.

The summer season was just starting and soon the roadways, beaches, summer houses and estates would be packed with commuters, tourists, summer dwellers and, of course, the locals. For the locals, the late spring to early fall season was their bread and butter. Like any resort or tourist town, great service and efficiency was required during this time of the year or they wouldn't make enough to subsidize themselves through the winter months. Eighty percent of the tourists and cottage owners could look forward to grid lock traffic to the tune of a five-hour commute from New York to their Hampton destination, if they were forced to drive during the busy season. Of course, the affluent would charter jets into the East Hampton airport where they would be shuttled to their mansions by a private car service. The trick for Mike's assignment of tailing Chris was going to be fitting in to the social circles and being accepted by them in order to even get close to Chris and his family. Despite the size of the area, the Hamptons have always been a close-knit community with many of its residents looking to find some privacy from their normal world or to mix and match only with close friends and relatives.

Most houses boasted thick high hedges to keep prying eyes out and privacy to the maximum. Richard was thinking he might need to get Mike a place so he could have a base for operations and wouldn't be thought of as a suspicious wanderer amongst the Hampton elite. It would be expensive, but George had given him an open expense account, thinking he needed to double check the contract to be sure, if they signed. He was just about to ask Kelly about the idea when the waitress brought their soup and salad. Kelly had the seafood bisque while Richard preferred clam chowder and both had the Caesar salad. The view at Nicky's was amazing, peaceful and relaxing and the men enjoyed it, almost like the calm before the storm. Despite having a deadline and anticipating the possible excitement of a real mission, neither man had a worry in the world at that moment. They just sat back, picked at their delicious food, and watched the boats float by.

Kelly smiled, "You know we're both retired we could just find a beach somewhere and do this day in and day out."

"True," Richard replied, "but we couldn't afford these types of places. I have to say I'm excited to try this project if the guys agree. In fact, I was thinking if Mike is going to get close to Buchanan, we are going to have to rent him a place in the Hamptons or he'll never find his way into the right social circles."

"I was actually thinking along the same lines. He's going to need an appearance of someone who fits the lifestyle so as not to draw any suspicions. It will be expensive," Kelly cautioned.

"Let's send him in with the guise of looking to rent or buy a property. He'll need a good back story," Richard contemplated, "real estate agents likely do extensive background checks and tell the neighbours everything about a person before selling or renting anyone a property in that area."

"So that's a start," Kelly affirmed. "Mike'll work on Chris Buchanan. What are we going to do to George?"

"George wants a public display. Basically he wants us to tar and feather him using false information that shows he's in bed with big oil and could care less about the environment. We need to show the world he only wants to line his pockets by using the green energy industry but leave him an easy out so he can prove himself as a world leading environmentalist."

"Let's get Joe to work on George," Kelly said. Then he thoughtfully added, "We'll need to base our attack on George here in the States if we want to maximize media attention. George'll need to fly over and let us know his schedule in order for us to plan something. Despite his knowing something is coming, we'll be framing him, so we should make our attack on George as much of a surprise as possible that way his reactions never look staged. If you tell George to fly to the States and set up some high profile for meetings for himself, then give us his schedule for that time, we can choose one of the events he is attending to plan our attack."

"You're right on it, Kel, thanks," Richard said, feeling somewhat relieved to have another brain helping him figure out the details. "I've been apprehensive about accepting this job and the potential impact on the guys and haven't spent a lot of time thinking about the actual steps we will need to take, so I'm glad you're running with it."

"You got us this job, Rich, and you're going to have to deal with George and all the administration that comes with a job this big. You need a deputy who can run the operation so I need to step up on this one," Kelly said confidently. "Now what's our plan for Jim Dunsmuir? Jeff has already been to Iceland and doesn't report very much going on out of the ordinary. What's George recommending we do with him?"

"Jim is an interesting case. George doesn't want to completely knock everyone out of the running, just his two biggest competitors. He believes suspicion will be thrown his way if three quit and he is the only one still bidding. George wants Jim to be shaken up but not scared off. He believes Jim's proposal has the least chance of being accepted, even though we're not yet clear what it'll be, so he wants us to make sure Jim is off his game but still shows up to bid," Ramsey explained.

Kelly was dumbfounded at the thought. "George is

shrewd isn't he? I'd no idea business worked like that. It's way beyond just cut throat, it's downright ruthless."

"Extremely. And you haven't heard the worst yet. You and I, well mostly you, get to deal with Peter Fairchild and this one is unbelievable. We have to sewer a person who lives for his bad reputation and George's idea for him is beyond ruthless." Richard was about to go into further detail when their burgers arrived so he paused in his explanation.

"For a place famous for sea food, they make a damn good burger," Kelly remarked, leaning in to take a bite. By the time they had each finished their last fry, both men were full and feeling pretty good. The day was beautiful, both were sitting back in their chairs simultaneously thinking they should forget the whole deal and sit here and relax on the deck all day. Then they could each have a couple more beer, more food and enjoy the sites of the evening. Neither man shared with the other what they were thinking. Pushing those thoughts aside, both knew they had a team that would soon be waiting for them back at the office and more than likely some strategic and sensitive assignments to hand out. As they drove back to the office, they decided they'd assign each person's case separately and instruct the men not to talk with each other verbally or electronically until the operations were complete and Richard and Kelly cleared them for communication. This would give each of them some deniability and keep them from becoming conspirators in more than one crime should the worst case scenario happen and they get caught. Only Kelly and Richard would take the risk of knowing each man's assignment and even they would split the info up between them as much as they could.

As Richard and Kelly walked into the board room, Richard's excitement grew on a couple of levels. One, the money would be something that would set him and his staff up comfortably for life. He knew money was relative and the more you had the more you wanted, but at least now their wants would only be for material things. If they were successful in this mission, they wouldn't have to worry about retirement savings or food bills ever again. Secondly, Richard was most excited for the chess game, or maybe a better description would be poker game. He needed to bluff three very smart businessmen with threats so severe that they'd back out of the business deal of their lives. Backing down was not something men like this did easily. He was ready and wanted to test his wits against theirs even though he'd have the upper hand because they didn't know he was coming. When Kelly and Richard entered the board room, Mike, Joe and Jeff were already seated and waiting.

CHAPTER 33

Kelly asked, "Well guys, what have you decided? Are you saying no or are we going to vote?"

As always, Mike spoke up on behalf of the group. "We're in. I'm not sure we need to go to a secret ballot but if you think that makes it fair, we're ready."

Before handing out the ballots, Richard wanted to clarify there was no pressure to commit to something that had the potential for risk. "Guys I know you're all friends and I know you well enough to believe any one of you would be willing to speak up in front of the others, but this is serious. It's a lot of money, has the potential for violence and maybe criminal convictions, so I want you to be absolutely sure. I've made four ballots, one for each of you, I want each of you to take the ballot back to your office, in ten minutes I'll start calling you one at a time. When I call, you'll leave your office, bring me your ballot with either yes or no checked off, put the ballot in the hat and then return to your office and close your door. Once I know you're back in your office I'll call the next person and so on until each of you has voted. Once everyone votes I'll count up the ballots and call you back to my office to reveal the results."

With those instructions, Richard gave them each a ballot and they all left the board room. He was going to have to get the contract from George today and get it signed if the guys said yes. Richard was worried George would dump them completely if they said no, without a doubt he was their biggest customer and without his business Trade Links' bottom line would suffer.

Back in his office, Richard grabbed a bowl and put a bunch of blank ballots in it, now when the guys dropped their votes in they wouldn't know if they were first or last to vote. Once the bowl was set up, Richard sat down and called Mike. Mike was also retired from the police force; he had left the department as a detective. Richard and Kelly had retired as Captains from the NYPD, both had moved up to management from the rank of detective. They'd worked together as detectives, becoming good friends as they bounced thoughts and ideas off each other while trying to solve cases. When they both became Captains and each took their own department, they continued with what worked and maintained their relationship, talking with each other every day, sharing ideas and helping each other through difficult cases. As they found out, being a police Captain had less to do with hands-on crime fighting and more to do with staffing, managing overtime, public perception and budgets. After twenty years in the service they became eligible for pension and decided to start a private detective business together. Richard was single so he became the president and in the two-person operation did most of the work. The men were ambitious and still relatively young, and before long they were turning work away, which is every businessman's dream, so they began putting more hours in to accommodate the extra work. They already had guaranteed pensions so they were able to pick and choose their cases. Kelly took cases that kept him around home that involved little to no travel which allowed him to stay close to his wife and kids. Richard continued to take on more cases including corporate employment, which eventually led them away from finding estranged family members and following cheating spouses, to dealing with corporate espionage. That's where he met George.

With the work George and other businesses were sending their way, Richard and Kelly realized they either had to expand their business or give up the corporate stuff. The opportunity was the perfect fit for the business, with Kelly wanting to stay closer to home he took on the administrative office duties and Richard kept investigating. Fortunately for them it was around this time that Mike, Joe, and Jeff had decided to retire from the NYPD. Mike and Joe had worked under Richard as detectives, Jeff was a fellow detective from a different department that Mike and Joe were friends with. When Kelly started looking around for employees it wasn't long until he was deep in negotiations with the three detectives and shortly thereafter with new staff hired, the business was booming for the private detective agency.

Prompt as usual Mike, was at Richard's office and knocking on his door within a couple minutes of being called. Mike had a personality a lot like Kelly's, both men were strong and steady, black and white in their thinking and unquestionably loyal. Mike was still married to his first wife and had a couple of kids in college; he was happy and truly believed he had a great life. Chris Buchanan would be the best assignment for Mike, it would allow him to stay close to home and if they rented a Hampton house, the cover of his wife and kids would be a great way to blend into the culture of the place.

"Richard, I'll cast a vote, but I'd be more than happy to straight out tell everyone my opinion," Mike said, looking Richard directly in the eye, signifying he had no problem being honest and forthcoming.

"I know you would, Mike," Richard replied appreciatively, "but I want to be absolutely fair on this and let everyone have the chance to back out if they want. I don't want anyone to feel coerced."

"I understand that. You're a good boss, Rich. I appreciate you thinking of us." Mike walked over and dropped his vote in the bowl and then turned and left the office. Richard hoped he was doing the right thing leading his team into this assignment, because he was reasonably certain the vote would be unanimously in favour. Once he was sure Mike was back in his office, he decided to call Joe down next.

Joe was a great PR guy. He had a very outgoing and

likeable personality and people always felt at ease with him. Over the last few years, Richard and Joe had talked a lot and developed a solid friendship. Joe was currently single; he'd been married early in his career but his wife left him after ten years. As a homicide detective, Joe had worked on too many cases where children were abused, used and murdered. Whether it was PTSD or not, he couldn't bring himself to agree to have children for fear of what could happen to them. His wife tried to understand and accept this but eventually her want for a family versus his desire to not have one broke them apart. Being a detective, Joe had tracked her down a couple of years later and she was already remarried to an engineer, had one child and one on the way. Richard knew Joe kept an eye on her even to this day. As far as he knew, Joe had never attempted to contact her but probably still loved her as now, 15 years later, he still hasn't been able to move on.

Joe was at Richard's office and knocking on his door a couple minutes later. Richard smiled to himself at how seriously the men were taking this vote; no one usually ever knocked on his door, they usually felt comfortable enough to walk right in. In fact, his office door was rarely ever closed because everyone always knew everything everyone else was working on or it didn't matter if they did. Richard only shut his door when clients were with him so they could feel more important and that their information was more secure. But today with this new phase he was leading his team into, suddenly he was closing his door, his staff were knocking, he was planning things out to give his people maximum deniability, and asking them to vote on whether or not their company should participate in an illegal job. There's no question that this was not their normal working conditions. Joe would typically sit and talk any time he was in Richard's office, but this was not one of those times. Everyone was excited and nervous, so he just glanced at Richard as he cast his vote, told Richard he supported him, and then headed back to his office. Two votes down; two to go.

Richard called Jeff next. He had never worked with or supervised Jeff while on the police force like he had the others, but Jeff came highly recommended by people he respected and trusted. As it turned out, the recommendation was a good one. Jeff was also single and Richard wondered if it maybe had something to do with the job that three of the five of them were single. Jeff seemed to be extremely close with his family and spoke often of his two brothers and a sister. One brother was married, as was his sister, and both had kids that Jeff was a favorite uncle to and he spent a fair amount of his off days babysitting. He and his other single brother would take holidays together. They would go to Vegas or down to Mexico to unwind and have fun. Richard had found Jeff extremely easy to talk to and he was great investigator. Jeff was the first of the three who actually didn't knock, he just stuck his head in and asked if it was ok to enter. Richard smiled and waved him in.

"Whichever way this vote goes, Rich, I just want to say I am glad you hired me and that I took the job offer. I know this assignment is concerning for you but if we take it, the guys and I will pull it off. No one will be hurt and I have confidence that our bluffs will work."

"Thanks Jeff," Richard replied, again impressed by his team members' support and loyalty. "You know if it goes forward, you'll more than likely be headed back to Iceland or where ever James Dunsmuir ends up."

"No problem," Jeff grinned, "Iceland was pretty incredible. And look at the time frames, we'll be busy as hell for a couple months but then either way it'll be over. In the meantime, I get to travel to places people talk about but rarely go. I've got no complaints." Jeff put out his hand and Richard shook it. Last on the voting list was Kelly. Richard called him up and Kelly cast his vote. Once Kelly was done voting, Richard walked over, picked up the bowl and sat back down at his desk. He invited Kelly to sit down and started to mix the ballets up with his hand while Kelly took a seat.

"What do you think, Kel, will we be doing this or not? Are there four yeses in this bowl?"

"I bet a million bucks there is," he replied assuredly.

"Well let's see." With that Richard dumped the bowl over and immediately he saw three yes check marks. After a couple of seconds search, he found the fourth yes. He showed Kelly the four ballots and said, "looks like you won the bet. The vote's unanimous."

"I better call the guys up. We just gave ourselves a lot of work to do," Richard said, grabbing his phone off his desk. He and Kelly moved into the board room about the same time the guys arrived from their offices. Once everyone was seated Richard formally announced that the vote was in and they would be going ahead with the mission.

"Because we will be operating on the edge of the law, this will be the last full team brief we have until this whole event is complete. I'll be assigning each of you a case that only you, Kelly and I will be privy to everything on because, as you know, lack of knowledge can sometimes protect. I'll be formally accepting George's contract later today and after my lawyers review it, I'll sign. In the meantime, I need you to start your assignments. So head back to your offices for now and Kelly and I'll be by to hand your assignments out in detail in a couple minutes. Any questions?" The men shook their heads and headed out. "Good luck guys, and thank you," Richard added as they left.

When the men were gone he picked up the phone and called George. Sara answered on the third ring. Damn. He kept doing this to himself, forgetting Sara would likely answer the phone, and then being momentarily flustered when he heard her voice on the other end of the line. The tone in her voice and the noticeable effect it had on Richard made Kelly take notice and he continued to watch Richard's facial expressions as he spoke with George's secretary. Richard was smiling as he exchanged pleasantries with her but then seeing Kelly's perusal, promptly informed her she was on speaker phone with him and Kelly and then he asked to speak to George. Sara explained George was away for a few days but wondered if there was anything she could help him with. Richard told her that his company had decided to take the job

George had offered them and wondered if she had a copy of the contract and if she could send it to him. She said that George had told her to expect his call and had given her the go ahead to send the contract out upon Richard's request. Sara indicated she would email the contract immediately for Richard to sign and return. Richard told her he'd need to have his lawyer look it over before he signed but would likely have it back to George by the end of the week. Richard then asked Sara to tell George that he was working under the assumption the contract would be fine so he was going to get his men started immediately. Sara thanked him for the information and told him George would be happy to hear that because he was already starting to worry about how short time was getting. They'd barely hung up the phone and the email from Sara with the contract arrived in Richard's inbox. The men took a quick look at it, curious how a contract could be written with terms that requested illegal activities. The contract read more in the form of services rendered for further investigative work, mixed with subject contact and specific time frames for meeting and finishing said work. They could see how the contract steered clear of all illegal activities but Richard still sent it to his lawyer for review.

"Once we send the guys out, I'll call the firm and explain to them over the phone under client privilege exactly what the outcome of the contract needs to be, that way they'll know what they are looking for in their review," Richard said.

"Good idea," said Kelly, "so how are we going to do this?"

"Let's go talk to Jeff first. He needs to get himself back to Iceland," Richard decided.

Once they were seated in Jeff's office, they explained to him that he would need to figure out Jim's schedule for the next couple weeks, then plan and execute a failed attempt on his life. Richard told Jeff he would need to work out the best plan he could and it needed to happen before Jim went to the bidder meeting in August. The attempt would have to be public and credible or it would not sufficiently shake Jim up enough to make him question himself about why he was getting into the Neom deal. The tricky part would be making sure Jim was shaken up enough to throw him off his game but not so much that he withdrew from the bid so it would be a tough assignment. Jeff said he was up for the challenge and would make it happen. Richard told him he needed to call in with his plan in two week's time so they could go over it in order to make sure the outcome would be what they needed. Kelly reminded him to stay out of contact with the others for the duration of the assignment and to report to him over the phone only. Kelly asked Jeff to update him every two days unless he needed help, then he was to call immediately. Jeff indicated he was ready to go, he just needed a plane ticket and he'd be on the next flight headed north. Richard and Kelly wished him luck and moved over to Joe's office. Joe was ready for them.

"Joe, you're going to need to set up the most believable, yet least effective rouse of all," Kelly began. "George will be in Texas in two weeks. He has deliberately set up meetings with numerous energy companies, both renewable and non-renewable. He'll be campaigning, selling the idea of his solar power systems. Renewable energy is probably the least-used power supply in the southern states and definitely the least-popular in Texas. George will be meeting with oil companies offering to supply solar panels to some of the more isolated drill rig sites."

Richard interjected, adding to Kelly's explanation. "Giving the Spreads access to electricity will allow them better efficiency, which in turn helps them produce more crude. The oil industry doesn't care about competition. Oil is king and if solar power can make them more money, it's just business. George has spun a web that will make it look like his business dealings in Texas are completely supporting the oil industry and you know how the renewable resource community loathes businesses it believes are only in the industry for money and not in it to save the world. In actuality, most of his meetings will be assisting start-up solar companies in Texas. On the surface, the meetings will be philanthropic in nature but underneath he'll be scouting out the best new company to come back and invest in or buy. You'll need to tar and feather George on behalf of the renewable energy community. Once you do that, he'll be able to flip it around, let the truth out, and show up as a big hero who has made the first step in moving Texas towards renewable energy as opposed to the fake news condemning him for getting in bed with big oil. The world will notice if Texas makes even the smallest shift towards renewable energy, especially if the oil companies back it. George will gain huge positive publicity for this and the Princes in Saudi Arabia will hear about it and like it." Richard paused to strengthen his point and then continued. "The absolute biggest and most crucial need in this assignment is to get the word out to the world that big-time environmentalist George Anderson is just a money-grubbing fraud. Then once those rumors soak in, we need to get the truth out in such a way that George looks like he might not only save the earth, but every endangered animal and plant on it. He needs to become a beacon for renewable energy so the Princes of Saudi will not only want his product but desire the benefit of having his fame and positive name stamped on their project as well."

Kelly added to Richard's instructions. "Although you have the easiest attack to make, you have the hardest assignment in that we need worldly attention. In order for this to be successful, George needs to be in national and international news, not just local radio and pod casts. We'll help you, but you need a few ideas of your own as you know how tight our time frames are."

"But no pressure, right?" Joe said, jokingly, knowing that the opposite was true. "I know this is serious and that timing will be everything. I'll head down to Texas and get something set up."

"Thanks, Joe," Richard said, grateful for his employee's confidence. "Report back to us every two days till we get through this, ok?"

"I can drive down in two days. I'm going to book

myself a few appointments here during that time in places where receipts are given and have someone go in my place. That way it'll seem like I was in New York the whole time," Joe said, impressing Richard and Kelly with his foresight and the obvious planning he'd already done. The men agreed that the more off the grid they could get, the better off they would be if something ever came back at them legally.

"I'll grab a couple burner cell phones and drop one off for you on my way out tomorrow. I'll take cash as well to help stay off the grid. We'll get reimbursed, I'm assuming?" Joe asked.

"One hundred percent reimbursed, yes," Richard confirmed.

"Ok. If that's all, then I'll see you in the morning," Joe said as he prepared to leave the office to go home and pack.

Joe was out the door so fast, Kelly and Richard were still sitting in his office when he left. So far they were happy with the staff's response; the men seemed to understand just how tight the time frames were and grasp the repercussions that could come back on them if something went wrong. They left Joe's office and moved down the hall to Mike's. Mike was ready and waiting for them. The last two assignments were the big ones. One was threatening a powerful man's family and the other was kidnapping. Richard and Kelly decided they'd look after the kidnapping themselves but the threats on Buchanan's family had to be delegated and they had picked Mike for the job.

"Mike, we're going to give you a dream summer with the exception of the job you have to do." Richard began. "As you know from the information you've provided us, Chris Buchanan will be summering at his home in the East Hamptons while overseeing his most recent project's construction. This will also give him the chance to spend the summer with his family. We need you to figure out how to scare him off the Neom project, and according to George's intel, family is the best way to get to him. You need to follow him and figure out just how to do that. George thinks if we push Chris hard enough, he will drop right out of the contracting bid."

"Guys, you know summer traffic to the Hamptons will never allow that. I'd be driving back and forth all day and never get anything done. Then between actual security and those high hedges the Hamptons are famous for, I wouldn't even be able to spy on him, let alone get close to him. The place is basically built for privacy," Mike said, already thinking through the obstacles.

"That's why I said we're about to give you the best summer ever. We need you and Marcy to go to the Hamptons on the pretense of buying a house. Once you speak to a few realtors you will decide to rent for a summer first to see if you like the environment and atmosphere. Then you find a residence as close by Chris's house as possible and rent it for the season. You and Marcy can stay there, tell Marcy you're following a high profile client's wife or husband and all she has to do is enjoy the area. Get the kids to come out for a couple of days to complete the family vacation look. We could cover their expenses and even pay them for a couple of days. Your job will then be to use the house and live the life style of a Hampton elite, endearing yourself into Chris's social circles far enough so that you can plan an effective attack. The hardest part is going to be acting out a scenario against a man you will probably really like." Kelly told Mike about the strategy he and Richard had come up with over lunch that day to get Mike into the Hamptons.

"Well, I guess that goes with the job and I signed up for it. Any way I look at it, though, there's no way it will be a one-man operation. How do I handle that?" Mike asked.

"We need you to be in contact with us every second day to update your progress. Once you develop a plan, we'll figure out how to get some staff together, but it will need to be as few as possible because we can't risk this getting out," Richard answered.

"I know I don't have to say this, but a house in the Hamptons and the lifestyle won't be cheap. Are you sure I just go ahead? George will cover expenses like that?" Mike questioned.

"Mike, you're covered. We have an account set up, ready for you to draw from. None of the expenses will even come to us. The only concern is the timeline, can you make it work for you, Marcy and the kids?" Kelly asked.

"Yes it will work. I'll get started tomorrow," Mike affirmed.

"Perfect," Kelly said. With that, the men stood up and shook hands and Mike was on his way out the door to go home and talk to Marcy about the interesting summer they were about to have. Richard and Kelly returned to the board room by Richard's office to begin planning their attack against Peter Fairchild. The offensive against Peter was different in the sense that they knew what they wanted to do to him while the others had to follow their targets and make plans. Kelly and Richard's biggest challenge was that they needed to execute their operation within the next two weeks. In order to make that happen they were going to need an iron-clad plan, all kinds of equipment, a building, rental cars, weapons and so forth. From an overview perspective, it all seemed so simple but the actual details were seemingly insurmountable. Richard and Kelly were worried they wouldn't be able to get the job done. Finally, Kelly said, "Ok we need to break this down into steps and move forward one step at a time till we get a workable plan together with time frames. Now let's think, what do we need to do first?"

Richard knew Kelly was right. He took a deep breath, reassured himself that his team was capable of this, and mentally stepped back from the big picture of his and Kelly's plan in order to focus on the small steps that would lead them to success.

CHAPTER 34

As the helicopter approached the ice flow, the view was mesmerizing and Garcia found she couldn't take her eyes off the glistening ice. Some of the bergs were big enough to be islands and the patterns they moved in looked made them look like a gigantic jigsaw puzzle. The ocean current created a natural roadway that the floating ice chunks followed out to sea. Jim called up to the pilot and asked him to find an iceberg that would be suitable to land on so he and Garcia could get out, eat their lunch, and watch the whales. Today was supposed to be about work, but this area would be Garcia's new home for the foreseeable future and in Jim's mind the more she fell in love with the place, the happier she'd be, which would increase her productivity. Jim also wanted to spend more time with her alone, or as alone as they could be on a barren iceberg with a flight crew waiting on them. As they moved along the ice flow, the Narwhale pods came into view. There was a dozen or so whales per pod and the animals were enjoying themselves in the sun and calm water. The sight made Garcia smile as they reminded her of puppies jumping all over each other, nipping and chasing, then falling asleep, exhausted and wrapped up in each other for warmth and safety. There was one large pack forming as about eight feeder groups of whales were converging in a large open expanse of water between a couple of massive icebergs. From above, Garcia could see the herds on the outside slowly moving towards the large group like they were all joining a large family reunion. As the helicopter passed over them, it flew up the ice flow right to the massive Greenland ice shelf. Hearing the ice cracking inside the cockpit of a machine that had a cabin that was virtually built to be noise free let them know the power Mother Nature possessed. Jim had witnessed the ice shelf calving before but was still amazed as he watched chunks of ice bigger than some towns he'd been in break off from what looked like the Greenland land mass and float out to sea. He looked over and smiled when he saw Garcia's mouth literally drop open as she saw the ice break off and fall into the ocean. Jim reflected for a moment in appreciation of the advantages his wealth provided him. Not many people would be able to have the opportunity to see such natural wonders or share them with someone. Jim picked an iceberg below them next to the gathering group of narwhales and, speaking of advantages he enjoyed, he put his landing request into the Captain.

The helicopter hovered over the ice field for five

more minutes while they watched the mammoth sized ice chunks break off and plunge or slide into the water. Garcia looked like a tourist snapping photos out her window with her IPhone; Jim couldn't blame her for her enthusiasm as he'd done the exact same thing when he first saw the occurrence. It was amazing how much he enjoyed watching everything she did. The helicopter took a long slow bank up over the Greenland ice shelf and then headed back towards the whales. Most people think of icebergs as jagged, rocky mountain-type objects but most are large and flat. A commonly known fact is that ninety percent of an iceberg's mass is located under the water, which only proves how large they are. A good sized iceberg contains twenty billion gallons of fresh water and weighs upwards of two hundred thousand tonnes. As they flew back they could see the pods of whales had all but joined up with each other and they were fully at play now. The helicopter landed on the iceberg that Jim had suggested, about two hundred yards from the edge, and quickly killed the motor. As Jim and Garcia exited the machine, the co-pilot handed Jim a large Hudson Bay blanket and an old fashioned picnic basket.

"Thanks," Jim said as he grabbed the food. "Pass me the other one, too." As the co-pilot handed Jim the other basket, he smiled and said, "Good luck, boss she seems nice."

Jim just grinned. He was so fortunate to have such a good group of people that worked for him, in many ways they were just as much friends as employees. Seeing Garcia's honest excitement over the whales and ice put

Jim in a position where he could no longer not make his feelings known. As sappy as that sounded, it would also put all the cards on the table, which would allow Garcia to quit and move on if he offended her with his advances. If she did quit, it would be difficult for him and his team, but he'd still have time to find a new geothermal scientist to finish the project.

It was a perfect day to explore and tour around an iceberg. There was no wind and the temperature was ten degrees Celsius, or fifty Fahrenheit. The arctic fresh air was incomparable to anywhere in the world. It was cool, fresh, completely unpolluted, and totally invigorating. The smell of a Tahitian rain shower or of freshly turned dirt on a Canadian farm in the spring might compete, but Jim thought the ice would win.

"Garcia, wait. You better wear these," Jim called out to her as she moved away from the helicopter, intent on exploring this once-in-a-lifetime opportunity. She turned, thinking she was already properly dressed, wearing warm hiking boots, fur lined yoga pants and a Thinsulate hoody. Jim was holding out a pair of odd looking sunglasses and explained how they'd be snow blind in a minute if they didn't wear them. Seeing that Jim was already wearing his, with a blue tint to them and leather sides to shade the sun, Garcia recognized that she wasn't entirely prepared. Relieved that the lenses were large enough that the view was not disturbed, Garcia noticed the brand name on the side of the glasses identified them as Vuarnet. She'd never heard of the brand before but once she put them on, she knew they were good. It was like she suddenly had 3D vision. The terrain ahead of her popped up into view with such clarity she could not believe all she had missed on first glance without the glasses, not to mention the aesthetic appeal the lenses gave to her surroundings. The color enhancements the bright blue lenses gave the ice reminded her of the effect Maui Jim glasses had on Hawaiian scenery.

As she thanked Jim and put the sunglasses on, she asked, "How does it work, can we go anywhere we want on this iceberg? I'd really like to go and see the whales up close and take some pictures."

"The pilots have been landing on icebergs for years. Tour companies and research expeditions they charter for require them to know the best bergs to land on. We got lucky with this one because it's big and flat so we can get right to the edge of the water and the whales will be swimming right beside us," Jim explained.

"Thanks for this stop over, Jim," Garcia said, smiling appreciatively. "I know you're busy and this really has nothing to do with the job."

"Garcia you are a key component, if not *the* key component, to this endeavor. Without a highly efficient renewable energy source, built by someone with a great reputation in the field, we've nothing to sell and nothing feasible to offer the Princes in Saudi Arabia. You're giving up your life as you know it to take on an amazing challenge. A couple hour detour for you to get to know your new home is hardly a poor investment. I'm glad you enjoy it, and don't forget, come wintertime living on the edge of the Arctic Circle may not be so appealing. I do what I can to offer my team as many amenities from home as possible, but it's still not the same," Jim said as they walked towards the whales.

They were now only a few hundred feet from the edge of the iceberg. Garcia had expected walking on an iceberg to feel like she was on an ice cube, bobbing up and down in a glass of water, but she was pleasantly surprised to feel like it was solid ground. Garcia guessed the reason was a couple hundred thousand tonnes of compacted ice and snow.

"Are you hungry yet or do you want to watch the whales first?" Jim asked her.

"I'm starved," Garcia laughed, "but I need to see these whales and get some pictures before I do anything else. I want to enjoy this before I get too used to it. You know what I mean, it's like vacationing in the Bahamas, the first day is paradise but by the end of the week you get used to it and sometimes even have complaints about the heat and the sun. I don't want that to happen to me here. I want to enjoy and not be spoiled."

"I know exactly what you mean," Jim said, recognizing that this was yet another aspect to Garcia's personality that he found attractive. "Let me put this stuff down and come with you."

It took him a few minutes to spread out the massive rubber backed insulated picnic blanket then place a wool one down on top. People picnicked on ice and snow in this region but it took planning to stay warm and dry. Once he had the blankets placed, he strategically placed the food baskets on top of the blankets to protect them from blowing away while they were whale watching. Once they got to the edge of the iceberg, Garcia started snapping pictures like crazy and the whales seemed to be posing for her. Garcia even made Jim pose for a couple selfies with her that had ice, ocean and Narwhales in the background. Watching the pure joy radiate from Garcia as she tried to take it all in was infectious. Jim couldn't remember a time he felt so refreshed and alive; he felt like he could conquer the world. As reality came back to him, he realized he would need that feeling to help him win the Neom contract.

"Ok, Jim, now I'm really starving," Garcia exclaimed breathlessly after about 45 minutes of whale, water, and ice watching. "Let's go eat." Reacting to her rosy cheeks and bright smile, Jim led her back to the blankets and food. He opened the big basket containing tossed salad, turkey sandwiches, vegetables and fruit. He had water and burning hot tea along as well. There was even two rather large pieces of New York cheesecake for desert, and Garcia was impressed that he was so well-prepared. By the time they were both full, they'd only eaten about half the feast that was packed for them. The day was so perfect that they sat back talking and looking out over the water as they let their food settle. While they were talking, Garcia turned and smiled at him, her smile gave Jim a spark that made him think she had feelings for him too, so he decided to take a chance. He reached out, put his arm around her waist, and gently tugged her towards him. He'd taken his sun glasses off and as she slid towards him, he dropped his lips to hers. After a cool, fresh kiss, the kind that can only be experienced in the serenity of the outdoors, Garcia smiled shakily up at him, surprised and uncertain about his unexpected embrace. Knowing honesty was probably in their best interests, she whispered, "that was nice, Jim."

He continued to hold her tightly, and spoke softly in return. "I have to be honest, Garcia. I have felt like doing that for awhile now but was worried about mixing business with a romantic relationship. But after that kiss, though, I am so glad I did," he grinned down into her upturned face.

"I've been feeling like this for awhile, too, Jim. I'm glad you did, too," she said, her lips gently turned up in a graceful smile.

"I brought my mystery basket over there just in case I got the nerve up to tell you how I feel," he said, somewhat sheepishly. "Of course if you slapped me and quit the job on the spot because your boss tried to assault you, I wasn't going to open it."

She laughed with delight, both at the obvious planning he'd put into this day for her as well as at his humility and uncertainty. Who would've thought billionaire and successful tycoon Jim Dunsmuir would have any self-doubt? "Well," Garcia teased, "It looks like I'm stuck here on an iceberg with you so let's see what the famous Jim Dunsmuir does for a date other than helicopters, icebergs and whales."

"Well, madam," Jim said, mimicking her mocking tone, "I'm not sure if you like it, but I brought us caviar and small Bellini pancakes. The experts say caviar is to be served off mother of pearl spoons and washed down with ice cold vodka. I wasn't sure straight vodka was ideal for a first date so I brought us a dry rug champagne instead," Jim said, and then turned serious. "Besides, a first kiss from you deserves a champagne celebration."

Touched once again, Garcia turned and picked up the spoon, loaded it with rue, and ate it, visibly enjoying each bite. They both laughed as Jim popped the cork and poured them each a flute. Raising hers, Garcia toasted, "Well, here's to champagne wishes and caviar dreams, Mr. Dunsmuir."

The couple then spent the next two hours laughing, kissing, and touching, lost in each other's company. Eventually, Jim stood up and told Garcia they'd better get moving, he wanted to show her the raw land and the base of operations she'd be working out of before they needed to head home. The land Jim was about to show her in Greenland was barren; nothing but rock and ice and during the winter it was completely snow-covered. Jim would be asking Garcia to use her knowledge and expertise to harness the heat from the lava flowing beneath that landscape to create enough power to not only create a tropical paradise in the Arctic but create enough electricity to power a city thirty-three times the size of New York located thousands of kilometers from where she'd be creating it. Jim texted the pilot and told him they'd be ready to leave in thirty minutes. Garcia helped Jim gather up the blankets and food baskets then they took off for the helicopter.

CHAPTER 35

By the time they walked back to the craft, their pilot was just finishing his pre-flight check and the rotors were just starting to turn. The view of the helicopter profiled in the sun sitting on the ice waiting for them made Garcia smile. Had her life now become private helicopters and caviar? Then she realized she was only there because she was expected to create the most massive clean energy source the world has ever known and make it efficient enough to work halfway around the world. She was terrified, but god it was so exciting. And now she had just kissed a man that she had stronger feelings for than she'd had for anyone else in years, possibly ever. Maybe this will be the best decision she'd ever made in her life… she mentally shook her head and ruefully thought that damn champagne had gone right to her head.

Forcing herself to think more objectively, Garcia

wondered if Jim would like her without her abilities to make him money, and she realized she was going to need to find out. He seemed quite genuine, but she'd met good talkers before. After all, any business man was in sales; if he wasn't then he wasn't going to make any money. As they climbed into the helicopter, Garcia noticed the pilots had strange smiles on their faces. Garcia was suddenly aware that Jim may have planned a potential romantic situation with a little more detail than she thought. The idea of him taking time to plan something for her made her heart trip with anticipation, but her realistic nature made her wonder just how many bimbos he'd treated to this same mind- blowing date in order to just get them in bed or get whatever he needed from them. Sighing, Garcia knew that the champagne was really hitting hard now because her mind couldn't stay focused on the potential negative reasons for Jim's actions. Rather, she suddenly found herself wondering what Jim would look like in a tuxedo standing at the altar while she walked up to him. Damn, being a human female was not easy. All these emotions and feelings.

Once they got settled in the helicopter, Jim was back in business mode, although he did give her a knowing smile that was warm enough to melt her heart. The smile put her mind at ease and allowed her brain to shift back to work. As they lifted off and headed back up the ice flow towards Greenland, Jim explained that the land he purchased was on the East shore just below a national park. The plan was to have Garcia's energy plant be the foundation for as many of the resort buildings as possible.

Since the canvas for their masterpiece was a large ice-covered island, they'd need to work around the ice and drill into rock to support the structures. With Garcia's geothermal plant serving as the base, the resort hotels would have a solid platform for construction. With full three hundred and sixty degree views being available from the top penthouse suites to normal suite options of tropical resort or ice flow, aurora borealis and ocean views, there wouldn't be a room that didn't appeal to the eye. Jim further explained that each room would also have digital black out glass that could be turned on and off by the occupant. This option was available for guests sleep comfortably during the times of the midnight sun, allowing them to completely darken their rooms.

"We're coming up on the mainland, Mr. Dunsmuir, and will be flying over your property in about five minutes' time," the pilot's voice interrupted Jim's description of the resort rooms. "What I'll do is circle the outside of the perimeter so you'll be able to look down from the port side window and see the border of your land as we go. Does that sound good to you?"

Jim looked at Garcia and surprised her by laughing. "In here he calls me Mr. Dunsmuir, on solid ground it's Jim, James or sometimes Jimbo. But anyway does the tour route sound ok to you?"

"Yes, of course. Is there anything I should be looking for?" she asked.

"Well, yes and no," he replied. "You're going to see a whole lot of barren ground made up of rock and ice. This project is not going to offer anything near normal working conditions, especially not for you and Jason. You and your crews will be going in to work this land and climate in its rawest form and I need to prepare you as best I can for the obstacles you'll face. So here we are." Jim turned gestured for Garcia to look out the window with him. The ice flow continued north and she could see the snow building up as she looked forward. The helicopter flew into Greenland airspace, reduced its speed, and dropped down a couple thousand feet to hover over the mainland. The pilot then tilted the machine, offering them a better view and began the perimeter tour. Jim was right, Garcia was astonished at the uninhabitable location Jim had chosen for this project. It looked like they would be building right on top of the Rocky Mountains, well maybe not quite that bad, but close, she thought. As far as she could see, the only thing in sight was rock, snow, ice, a few scrubby brushes, hills, holes. The difficulty of the work she had signed on for just became very real.

In her initial discussions with Jason, he'd spoken about planing off an area at a level that required less earth movement. His plan was to ignore the natural terrain, put pilings down through the ice and snow directly into the bedrock of the island and then build a massive sub floor on top of the pilings which would reach a number of meters above the worst of the natural terrain. The subfloor would have the same effect as the over water huts in Bora Bora, only instead of blue ocean water under the floor, it would be arctic rock and ice. From her observations now, she thought Jason had the right idea, the natural elements in this place would be too much to contend with. It was not her area of expertise, but she could only imagine the work surveyors and munitions experts were going to have to put in just to drill the pilings and she was only thinking about her building, not even counting the scope of work required to build the resorts. As they rounded out the tour, Garcia thought twenty thousand acres didn't look that big from the air when seeing it framed against the rest of the massive island. If she put it in perspective, though, landscaping twenty thousand acres of untamed arctic land was almost unimaginable except that is exactly what they had to do. After circling the perimeter of Jim's Greenland property and then flying up through the middle for a further look, they returned to the ice flow and then the pilot set a course back to Iceland.

Garcia leaned her head back against her comfortable seat, feeling overwhelmed with emotion and completely exhausted. The surge of adrenaline that had kept her going from the moment she stepped off the plane in Iceland two days ago – was it only two days?! – was finally waning and reality was setting in. The new job, aerial view of Greenland, calving icebergs, landing on an iceberg, a couple glasses of champagne, kissing Jim, realizing her near impossible task and now preparing to head "home" left her feeling numb. Sensing her emotions and sensitive to her obvious need for some time to herself, Jim simply held her hand and offered her his shoulder to put her head on. She felt bad not engaging in conversation with him on the way back, but she appreciated his understanding, laid her head on his willing shoulder, and drifted off to sleep.

With the weight of her body completely relaxed against

his, Jim felt complete satisfaction in the opportunity to hold and comfort Garcia. This was exactly what he needed and it felt right. For a man who had made many successful decisions based solely on his instincts, he trusted his gut feeling when it told him something was right. Jim realized he, too, had a moment to relax and he rested his head back against the seat, allowing the memories of the day to soak in before he forced his mind to shift to work. Tomorrow he was going to have to start making plans with Ramsey for the speech he needed to give in Riyadh in a couple weeks' time. The event would be a great place to further raise the profile of Dunsmuir Energy, and he knew he had to be in the zone during his presentation as it often took more than just facts to make sales.

"Sir, we're about halfway home. Any further plans for the night, or what is our destination?" the pilot asked.

Without raising his head from the back rest of his seat, Jim replied. "Just take us home. We'll drop Garcia off first near her cabin where we picked her up, then back to the airport for us."

"Sounds good sir, I'll let you know when we're ten minutes out."

"Thank you," Jim responded. He was just starting to think of his speech again when Garcia nestled further into his shoulder, getting even deeper into her sleep. Her quick and easy lapse into sleep surprised him, so far she had seemed like a bundle of energy and if anything he thought he'd be sleeping before her. As he looked down at her face, he saw how relaxed she looked and incredibly pretty she was. After watching her sleep for a minute, he put his head back and closed his eyes too. The next thing he knew, the pilot was calling back to him saying they'd be landing at Garcia's in the next ten minutes.

Jim gently woke Garcia and together they watched the ocean change into land through the helicopter window and Garcia's cabin soon came into view. Once they landed, the pilots opened the doors and Jim walked Garcia quickly to her front door. Jim asked if he could call her tomorrow and she answered him by taking the initiative, putting her arms around his neck and giving him a long kiss. They pulled apart and smiled at each other as Garcia went inside and closed her door. Jim stared out toward the ocean for a minute, then jogged back to the whirly bird and moments later they took off for the airport. Garcia barely had her boots off before she was phoning her sister to tell her what had just happened with Jim.

Once back on the aircraft, Jim called Ramsey and set a meeting for the following morning to start planning his speech. Following that, he called Alexandra and asked her to make sure they had decent accommodations in Riyadh. He told her it would likely be Ramsey, himself and Lois attending the event. Knowing it couldn't be avoided, but recognizing the need for complete disclosure, he reluctantly called Lois to tell her about the relationship he'd just started, or had potentially started, with Garcia. Jim was not overly comfortable telling her, but he'd hired her for just such situations so if he didn't utilize her services himself, how could he expect his staff or partners to. In the end he was glad he called, Lois was great to talk to and did not make a big deal of the situation. They had a great discussion, Louis ended up telling Jim that she wasn't at all surprised that they formed a relationship. In fact, she indicated that she fully expected a few romances to arise within the group. She explained her reasoning by saying that the team members were likeminded, highly successful individuals that have bonded together to create a world-changing project. She figured that stress and emotions would most likely become a factor at some point. Lois's bigger concern was the potential for break ups to rock the team and the efficiencies of the project. Jim knew it was true; most relationships ended and few of them on good terms. Jim knew that professionally, he should end it before it started with Garcia, but he also knew at this point no matter how many times he told himself that, there was no way he was going to keep himself away from her. It was late before he went to bed that night. After making those phone calls, Jim was back in work mode and spent most of his time putting together talking points for his speech on renewable energy. Jim woke up early the next morning so he went for a jog to clear his head. As he ran, he thought about Garcia, and then refocused himself on work. He got into his office around eight am, and found Ramsey already there, putting facts together on renewable energy to include in Jim's speech.

CHAPTER 36

As Jim walked into the board room Ramsey was using, he said, "This really is our chance, Ramsey. I'm not naïve enough to think the speech is going to change the world, but giving it without backing a political platform or shamelessly advertising my company and our industry, I really believe gives us a chance to do something that will have an impact in the world. How many people can say that they have accomplished that in their lives? I don't want to run oil down, no one is completely sure of the effect it's having on the environment, but I do know that oil is not renewable and it'll run out eventually, especially with human population growth as it is and the standard of living increasing around the world. Renewable energy and electricity is so much more efficient. It gives off millions of times less pollutants and the city of Neom being built in the heart of the oil industry is a shining example of forward thinking, not only for Saudi Arabia but for the world."

"You're right Jim," Ramsey agreed. "It's not about shameless self promotion at the summit, it's about the promotion of renewable energy. But to be honest, the salesman in me needs you to get as much positive publicity as possible from it. The more popular and respected you can be on the world stage, the more the princes will want to hitch themselves to you. They have an amazing opportunity with their new city. They want to break out of having the stigma of a war torn country that is in constant turmoil and is only rich because of the Western world's need for oil. The Princes want to build a community for their people to feel safe, to work, to socialize, and to live in. By building industry and personal success for themselves and their families, they hope to attract business, trade and investors and then once the world sees a steady economy, I see them wanting to align with wholesome, stable well-respected institutions. And that, my friend, is what you represent. But you will need to shine at the summit in order to fully achieve that status. If you can make Dunsmuir Energy the beacon for universal clean energy, it'll not just be the Saudi Arabians who will want in bed with you, but the rest of the world as well. Everyone wants a high end product."

"We have all the facts, Ramsey, and they should be convincing on their own. All we we need now is for Alexandra to polish this up for us because you're right. The speech needs to hit home and resonate with everyone in attendance. That will be the only way we can truly trademark ourselves."

Knowing there was little left that he and Ramsey could contribute to the speech, Jim called Alexandra and told her they'd need her help finalizing the speech. Jim explained that he wanted the speech to sound unrehearsed and to be presented in "normal speak," yet still convey a powerful message on the need for the human race to embrace renewable energy if it was going to be able to continue its exponential population growth and continue to improve its high standard of living. With her usual efficiency, Alexandra came through for them by finding a couple of extremely talented motivational speakers and speech writers. She informed Jim she would have them on site in Iceland in a couple days and then they would help to make his speech brilliant. Satisfied they'd done all they could for now, Ramsey updated Jim on the business financials, after all a billion-dollar portfolio had a lot more going on in it than just working at building a new energy project.

Ramsey reported on the status of the Neom project as well saying that he'd reconnected with his contacts in the banks, the private sector and their government partners and could confirm that all were still on board to help finance the track system if Dunsmuir Energy was awarded the contract. Then they discussed the possible liabilities of the Neom project, the main point of concern was if word of their project got out, the possibility of others trying to sabotage the deal for some kind of personal gain was very real. With a project this large and widespread, keeping strong loyal ties with investors was tough because in business everyone was ultimately out for themselves. They agreed the best way to combat this was for Jim to make personal contact with as many of the investors and partners as he could in an attempt to solidify and maintain those relationships.

CHAPTER 37

"Sara, I need to go to Texas, Dallas then Houston," George demanded as soon as Sara walked in the door Tuesday morning. "I'll be setting meetings up for Monday so I'd like to fly in on Friday and enjoy the weekend. I'll need a week in Dallas and then will need to fly into Houston the following Saturday."

Accustomed to George's demands, Sara didn't even bat an eye but replied over her shoulder as she strode to her desk. "The travel will be no problem, but from what I understand about your plans, wouldn't it be better if you were invited to Texas to meet with the oil companies as opposed to you inviting yourself?"

"Yes, optically it'd be better for the success of the operation I need Richard to complete, but with such short time frames I can't get that set up in time," George explained.

"That's why you have me," Sara grinned slyly. "I'm part of an online chat group that connects the Assistants of Presidents and CEOs of energy companies all over the world. We message each other advice and best practices. More importantly, we keep each other up on industry events. If I was to message them that you were setting up tours and had important information their bosses might need or want, they'd likely be able to get their bosses to invite you out. The thing is, you'd actually need to have very relevant information to pass on or the others would black ball me from the list and I wouldn't have the benefit of belonging to this group for any future projects."

George stared, shocked, but knowing he shouldn't be. He'd become so used to her efficiency that he sometimes forgot just how good she really was. "Hell of an idea, Sara. Get on it. I won't disappoint. The new solar panels are so efficient and can be set up and moved so easily now that I could easily set up a system to power a whole drill site. In fact, I'll even offer set up crews for large customers. I was going to use the system as a reason for cold calling them anyway. If you can get me invited, though, I'll give you a raise. You can rest assured you won't get black balled from your group. Some of the larger companies will take me up on the offer because they are national or international and are always interested in showing they are reducing their carbon foot print."

"Really?" Sara asked, surprised. "The oil companies care about the environment?"

"They care more about the environment than the rest of us do. They have to because they have such bad reputations and the governments regulate them harder than anyone else just for publicity's sake. Some fossil energy companies are actually more environmentally friendly than we are. It's not about not using oil," George explained. "It's about maximizing efficiency."

"I'll put the information out to my contacts in Texas," Sara said as she turned on her computer. "I should have no trouble getting you at least four meetings per city."

"See if you can get me four meetings in Dallas that first week and then set up another four in Houston the following week. I want the second meeting in Houston to be with the largest oil company you can find and I want that meeting to be on Tuesday. Tuesdays are the slowest news days of the week so it'll give us more of a chance to make all the headlines." Now that George had gotten excited about Sara's idea, he was also getting very particular.

"I'll set the meetings," she said, trying not to roll her eyes at his demands. "Plan to fly out Thursday around noon. I'll set up your schedule and let you know, just make sure you have a great product to sell or we'll get cut off from a major information supply."

"Sara, if you get me in meetings with eight companies that think they invited me to come and speak to them and pay my travel to boot, I'll send you on the holiday of a lifetime. Three weeks, anywhere you want to go." George paused then said, "Regardless of what you think of me Sara, I do have a moral code. I'd never do anything to hurt you and if you don't believe that, I know you believe I'd never do anything to hurt myself. Losing you and your connections hurts my information flow and your loyalty, both things I depend on greatly."

"I like this job, George, and I wouldn't stay here if I didn't. I'll get you your meetings. You get working on the sales pitch because I want that holiday," Sara teased. "Be ready to fly out Thursday and, like you asked, your biggest meeting will be Tuesday morning. Be ready."

George knew Sara would be true to her word; she was the best assistant he'd ever had.

"Robin, I need sales sheets on the new panels for Wednesday night at the latest," George announced into his office phone a minute later. Robin was his right hand man and he knew Robin would have all the information he needed to give a good lecture to the oil companies on their latest technology and services.

"What the hell are you up to now? We can't take on another project at this time and we don't even have the new system fully tested yet!" Robin's exasperation was loud and clear.

"All part of the plan Rob," George chuckled as he reassured Robin. "We're going to begin offering beta testing partnerships to oil companies in Texas. Can you think of a better industry to break into with solar power than oil? I want them to use our tech on their oil rigs. Right now they use generators. If we could offer them silent, maintenance-free solar carts that transport just as easy and set up faster than a generator, we'd have the potential to sell them on an industrial scale. Not to mention offering full service transportation and service contracts. What do you think?"

Robin was pleasantly surprised by George's idea. "Brilliant," he said, "sounds like a great idea, boss. By the time those guys decide to commit, we'll have completed our other projects and be looking for work. I'll get you the information sent up right away. Do you want a speech prepared as well or will you wing it?"

"Send me the info and some talking points too. I only want to give a twenty-minute talk but need to be prepared for questions. Give me the highlights for the speech, cost, recovery, usability, perception and service, but I'll need a detailed facts sheet for the tech guys."

"Will do," Robin replied. "I'll email it your way before noon tomorrow. How serious is this? Do you want me to shut down here for a couple extra days to come and help you out?"

"No, if you get me the info, I'm good to handle it myself. Thanks, Robin. Good luck down there in the meantime and I'll let you know how it goes," George said and hung up the phone.

CHAPTER 38

True to her word, when Thursday came Sara had George on a plane to Dallas and as promised she'd set him up with four meetings. Each meeting was scheduled almost exactly 24 hours apart and was with a Field Division Head from each company. George didn't know what holiday destination she'd pick but she had definitely earned it, he thought. The only down fall would be the three weeks she was gone. It was a fifteen-hour flight from Morocco to Dallas. After Sara was done working her magic with the companies, three of them had gotten together and chartered him a flight on a private air line. Not only was the private plane significantly more comfortable for a half-day flight, but more importantly it was ready to leave early in the day, which meant he would be able to get settled into his hotel at a decent hour upon his arrival in Dallas. His potential clients were putting him up in the Fairmont Downtown Dallas which was a central location for all four meetings.

Ever ambitious, George thought, these meetings in their own rights could actually prove quite lucrative for Blade Solar. He knew his product would instantly become a recognized efficiency for the oil companies if they chose to use it. As with any new technology, the start up cost was high and the companies already had the standard generator equipment in place so he'd have to talk them out of the "if it ain't broke don't fix it" mentality. He'd need to get them excited about the long term profitability of the tech and the positive publicity of moving towards sustainable development and reducing their carbon foot print.

George's meetings in Dallas were scheduled for Monday, Tuesday, Thursday and Friday with a flight scheduled into Houston for Friday afternoon. The second meeting in Houston was with a top three oil giant and it was going to be the perfect stage for Richard's team to launch their attack. George called Richard while he was in the air to get an update on Richard's complete game plan. He wasn't worried about Richard's plan or execution of the op, they'd worked together enough for him to know Richard wouldn't miss a thing. Richard was a tactical genius and probably missed his calling in the military somewhere, but the military's miss was George's gain, and probably Richard's too, financially speaking.

George gave Richard his itinerary for the next two weeks and told him the second meeting in Houston needed to be the attack day. Sara was releasing information in certain business and social media circles about his upcoming meetings with the oil companies in a vague enough way that they could be interpreted to mean almost anything, including collusion with "big oil". Richard confirmed with him that he'd seen the posts online and agreed they were the key to launching an attack. Richard said he was quite concerned over the cost associated with the move they were planning against Chris Buchanan but George quickly put that to rest, saying all business deals had expenses. George was most concerned about Richard's play against Peter Fairchild. There was no way around it, the plan was illegal and if they were caught they'd end up in prison with substantial sentences. George was even more worried about himself if he was linked to the operation. Not only would he lose the Neom deal, but he could potentially end up in jail himself. George had Richard spell the plan out for him and he knew it was as solid as it could be and that Richard had ensured all the bases were covered. Knowing Richard and his team were ex-cops and that Richard himself was handling the kidnapping personally put George's mind somewhat at ease. It gave George some anxiety that he was forcing Richard to step way over his ethical boundaries, not because George had moral guilt about it, but because he was worried that Richard might not go far enough, which could lead to mistakes and ultimately capture. Like any shrewd business man would, he began working on a contingency plan for just such an event. Once he hung up with Richard, he settled in and went to sleep, knowing jet lag would be coming for him and that he was about to have a couple of long weeks so he needed to stay rested and sharp.

Following his call with George, Richard immediately called Sara. Not only did it give him an excuse to call her, but from his experience working with George and other bosses, he knew that the executive assistant would have George's exact agenda and for operations like this, second by second planning could make all the difference. Although the attack on George would by far be the easiest assignment they had, he thought he might as well plan it now so he'd be free to concentrate on the three legitimate operations his team would be performing. Sara picked up on the second ring and sounded happy to hear from him. They flirted a little and then fell into a very enjoyable conversation. Richard felt he could really connect with her, but she was the type of person that anyone could probably talk at ease with. Reluctantly, he eventually switched the conversation over to business. Just as he thought, Sara had George's exact itinerary for his time in Texas. She provided him with all the details he needed to create his plan; hotel room number, dinner reservations, car service, meeting times and locations. With this information, Richard would have no trouble helping Joe plan an attack that would publicly embarrass George, which was just what they needed. Once they finished discussing work, they returned to talking about themselves. Sara was tempted to ask him to join her on the three week holiday she'd just earned but thought better of it since they'd barely been on a date and didn't even live in the same hemisphere at this point.

Instead of outright inviting him to commit to a three-week excursion, she nonchalantly brought up the topic of a holiday. "You know, Richard, once all this settles out I'll have some holiday time coming. Is there a chance you'd want to take some time and meet up with me for a couple of days? I really haven't planned anything yet, but if you had time I'd like to see you again," Sara hesitated, unsure of herself. "I really hope that didn't sound too desperate, not exactly playing hard to get here, but I like you."

Disbelieving the uncertain tone he heard in her voice, and eager to reassure her of his interest, Richard said, "I couldn't think of a better way to spend a few days off than with the most attractive woman I've ever met. You may not want to sound desperate but I'm desperate to see you again. Just tell me when and where and I'll be there. Wow if talking to you makes me this happy, seeing you might make me crazy. Ha, how sappy did that sound?"

"Not at all, Richard!" Sara replied, smiling. "That was the perfect answer. Exactly what I needed to hear."

"Sara, I know you know this," Richard turned serious, "but some of these jobs I'm doing for George aren't exactly legal. I'm not even sure how I ever got myself into them, but if I get caught I won't just get a slap on the wrist. I'm not sure how to say this, since I'm going ahead with it and won't back out, but what I'm doing now for George is not the real me, not me ninety percent of the time. I took the job for two reasons, first it's a challenge, and the financial reward is undeniable. Second, George is ruthless and becoming more so, I'm worried how far he's willing to go to win this contract. I fear that if I don't do this for him, he'll retaliate against me, my staff or their families. I also believe I can keep all the victims safe while still accomplishing George's goals and I've instructed my staff to make sure no one is mortally injured, no matter what. I wanted to tell you that so you knew the truth about me and how I operate. I like you, but I don't want to lose you later if you find something out about me that you don't like."

CHAPTER 39

With a soft and understanding voice, Sara responded to the truth in Richard's concerns. "I get it, Rich. George is charismatic and scary at the same time. I know most everything he does and by working for him, I endorse what he does. So how could I ever judge you when I do it myself? I'm like you, I enjoy the thrill working with George provides. He's always on the move and is so animated it's addicting. Please don't tell him this, but as much as I enjoy the adrenaline rush of trying to keep up with him, I know I'm going to have to break away from him sooner than later or I'll lose myself."

Relieved beyond belief that Sara understood, Richard replied, "we need to be able to talk and trust each other if this relationship is going where I think it is… or am hoping it is, Sara. What I've told you could put my team in as much danger as what you've told me. I didn't do it to compare, I did it so that you know I'm not keeping things from you nor will I ever use information you tell me for my own gain."

From the unpleasant discussion on George, the couple moved on to a more pleasant topic which included solidifying a plan to meet up for a few days during Sara's holiday. Among other ideas they both seemed to agree on a relaxing trip to the southern United States, somewhere beautiful but off the beaten path from their current life. After hanging up the phone, Sara smiled to herself and thought about how much she liked Richard and was happy that they seemed so at ease with each other. She was starting to worry for him, though, knowing that what he was about to do was more than just risky.

Richard felt a sense of relief following his conversation with Sara. He knew what he was doing was not something many women would respect or want anything to do with. Sara seemed willing to not only accept his career decision but support him in it. His excuse for accepting the assignment was keeping the victims safe, but he knew that the right thing to do would be to turn George in and distance himself from all of it, not act out the crimes and get paid for them. Sara seemed to think she was in the same boat, both drawn in by George, enticed by the money, power and adrenaline rush.

Richard was excited for the vacation time they'd just planned but knew he had to focus on work. If he and the guys didn't get these plans right, they could end up in jail or dead and then he'd never see Sara again. Now that he had George's exact itinerary he could finalize some details. He searched up a number on his phone and dialed, Joe answered on the second ring.

"Hi Rich, good to hear from you," Joe said in greeting. "I'm just crossing into Texas and should be in Houston in a couple hours. Do you have a plan for me?"

"Yes I do," Richard answered. "George has numerous meetings set up over the next two weeks but our focus is his second meeting in Houston. It's with the largest oil company and will generate the most media coverage if done correctly." Richard went on to fill Joe in on George's plan.

"I was thinking about it," Joe began, "what if I also tipped off some of the more respectable environmental groups to the fact that Blade Solar CEO George Anderson is meeting with and investing heavily in Texas oil? I won't give them the whole itinerary because I don't want them to have time to figure out the truth, but if they got to the last meeting in Dallas and then saw that the second meeting in Houston was with a major oil company, chances are they'd focus an attack on George for that day and not even take time to truly research what the actual meeting is about. I'd think the environmentalists would eat that up. George is a hot ticket right now, being one of the successful candidates to bid on Neom. What do you think?"

"Excellent idea," Richard stated. "What exactly do you have in mind?"

Joe had been thinking about the operation on the long drive to Texas. He'd found several leftwing political activist and environmental lobby groups in and around

Texas. He did some research and found four groups that were quite action orientated and well-funded. Each group operated as a real business with offices, were open five days a week, and had twenty-four-hour tip lines. Further research showed that the groups organized and planned monthly protests. Being located in Texas, oil companies were their favorite target.

Now that Richard had endorsed his idea, Joe planned to leak George's meeting itinerary to the environmentalist groups' tip lines along with a damning fake news story. The story would reveal that famed Blade Energy CEO George Anderson, who was recently shortlisted to bid on the largest green energy project the world has ever seen, was about to partner with eight oil companies over the next two weeks. The invites George had to the eight oil company meetings over the next two weeks could easily be interpreted as a request to partner Blade Energy with the oil business.

Joe's hope, and what he and Richard decided on, was that he'd call in and pass George's itinerary on to the four activist groups in hopes of spurring at least one of them into action against Blade Energy.

CHAPTER 40

When Joe called in to the tip lines, he established himself as a reporter working on the Neom super city story. He stated that he'd been trying to get interviews with the CEOs of the successful bidders for the new city's amazing new green power supply, but George would not for some reason grant him a sit down. He further told them that he'd recently learned that George was flying to Texas for business and had reason to believe that George was trying to partner with oil companies to amass the capital he needed to successfully complete Neom, should he be the winning contractor. Joe was quick to add that he felt the oil companies being involved in a project like Neom was putting more power back into the fossil fuel burning company's pockets. Joe further indicated that he didn't want to see Blade Energy get away with such a tactic and thought that strong environmental groups might want to know the inside story and look at exposing George if possible. The lobbyists were very interested in his information and even more so when Joe was able to produce documents on company letter heads indicating the meeting details.

Joe leaked the information that indicated the Tuesday meeting in Dallas was one hundred percent for sure and that he was only about ninety percent on the other dates. Once he had the information shared, he was very confident that one, if not all, the activist groups would raise some type of protest with the information he had provided them. His next call was to the news agencies informing them that he'd reason to believe George Anderson of Blade Energy was about to start on-boarding oil companies to raise capital for his Neom bid and it sounded like environmental groups had already got wind of the meetings and were preparing to meet him as he left his meetings on Tuesday the following week. The news agencies showed a lot of interest in the information and even more so when Joe again showed the proof by having George's itinerary. Joe was not in the least bit worried about the press showing up for the event. In this day of social media, everyone was a reporter and if anything happened it would be recorded and all over the news whether the actual media showed up or not. Joe's hope was that he'd provided enough information to spur a large revolt against George that would be well-documented in official media. The idea seemed a little crazy to him, but George was the boss and that's what he was paying them for.

CHAPTER 41

George was feeling good when he arrived in Texas. The private flight to Dallas had been comfortable, he'd checked into his hotel, and had some time to look over the presentation Robin had sent over. Robin had impressed him, not only had he included financial numbers but he'd also presented some new good tech information to help get everyone excited. George borrowed a hotel board room to practice his presentation. He wanted a power point but didn't want to rely on it, just use it to accent his comments. George wanted to make his speech more personal than just letting a slide show do the selling. He was the president and face of Blade Energy and if the companies were meeting with him, he needed to know his stuff inside and out to instill confidence.

George's primary goal in Texas was media recognition and to prove he was the subject of a slanderous attack, just like the other bidders would soon be. His secondary plan was to actually get the oil companies to buy his product and install them in all the drilling and service rigs sites in Texas. He knew if he broke into the Texas market, the other oil camps around the world wouldn't be far behind. With two days to wait until his first meeting, George thought he should immerse himself in American culture. He'd been away dealing with other countries and foreign investors for so long that he realized he needed to get himself back up to speed. There was a reason America was the most powerful economic nation in the world and there was no room for second best or bull shit when dealing with these superpowers. George knew he didn't have time to get to the King Ranch but he went to the Fortworth stockyards.

The Stockyards are a symbolic place, now a tourist attraction that represents Texas history. If a person took the time to think of the grit it actually took to be a rancher back when the country was young, only then could you begin to understand the tenacity that was built into Texans. Following the stockyard visit, George took time to visit the JFK memorial.

As a visitor looking in, a person could marvel at the romanticism of the American Cowboy and the sensationalism of the assassination of one of the most beloved political figures in all American history. George realized this history could be taught and learned but couldn't be internalized into people who didn't have to live through it firsthand. Texas, and Dallas in particular, was even the base for one of the most popular TV shows in history, a show that was so popular because it portrayed the stereotypical views of a people and an industry. It became a benchmark for some to live up to and initiated trends that became popular internationally. With all that history, it's no wonder many in Texas call themselves Texans first and Americans second, even if they don't mean it, they have earned a reputation of being a strong group.

During the meetings George explained how partnering with his company would offer massive long term bottom line savings. The Texans, like any other businessmen, were interested in what he could give them and if the ROI would be worth it. The only difference being there was no need for flashy words or trendy perks, Texans were old money, especially the companies George was meeting with. They had all the money and access they would ever need and had always had it. None of them were against environmental initiatives, as media would lead the world to believe, in fact quite the opposite. They know oil is a finite resource that will eventually run out. As strong business leaders they were looking for new opportunities. These companies have large shares in the world energy market and were excited for the opportunity to invest in new energy. After all, they already had distribution and marketing initiatives in effect. The only thing changing would be the type of product but the result was still the same. Instead of gas powering vehicles it would eventually be renewable electricity. Starting slow was the order of the day, three of the four Dallas companies ordered solar plants for some of their oil rigs on a trial basis. Basically, they wanted to test George's service promise out and capture some positive media attention for implementing green initiatives.

CHAPTER 42

Tuesday afternoon was a scorcher. There are few hotter places on earth than downtown Houston on a cloudless summer day. It was three pm, Joe could literally see the heat waves wafting off the mirrored glass skyscraper that George would be exiting any minute and he couldn't have hoped for a better result. Two of the Green activist groups he'd called had assembled with signs denouncing Blade Energy and George Anderson as a fraud. A flash mob request had been sent out to the locals and people were turning up by the hundreds. The media was there, and Joe couldn't imagine the police were far behind. To be honest, with the growing frenzied mood of the crowd, Joe was beginning to get a little worried that George might get hurt. He got on the phone to Richard and explaining his concerns. Richard indicated he'd shoot George a text but he fully expected George to have prepared himself for some potential fallout even though it had to look like a surprise. Joe agreed to let the situation play out and said he'd update Richard as soon as he could.

Twenty minutes later, police arrived on scene and set a perimeter around the protesters. Joe was thankful for this at least, knowing that with police presence, the mob mentality would not be able to take over and let George be injured. Fifteen minutes after the police barricade was put in place, the front doors of the office building opened and George and a few oil company executives stepped out into the hot street. At the sight of the CEOs laughing and talking like old friends, the crowd erupted, slapping George with the stigma of being nothing but a capitalistic pig instead of the environmentalist he claimed to be, and the media caught it all. The story made prime time news and trended on all social media sites, going viral within hours. In true newsworthy style, if it bleeds it leads, and with this event it appeared George was bleeding, perhaps from the jugular. The media had found its scape goat and although George made a few initial feeble attempts to save his honor, public perception condemned him further. While the social streaming was having a field day with George's reputation, George was continuing to build his net worth. With his new oil company partners and their teams of lawyers, George was building a press release that would not only shut down the media frenzy but let them all come out smelling like organically grown roses.

Together they decided that George would agree to a media interview with the largest news network that wanted him and let himself be interrogated on national television by the investigative reporter of the network's choice. All the lawyers agreed this was one time the absolute truth would set them free. It was almost comical to everyone in the know how far off the allegations were and yet the world seemed to believe them like gospel. The only truth the slanderous stories had was George's itinerary, which included the meeting times and dates he had for each company. The rest was just made up bullshit that grew from the flash mob outside the building. George was ecstatic with the result when he called Richard from his hotel later that evening.

"Richard, as far as I can tell, this couldn't have gone any better! I'm in the middle of it, though, so how does it look from the outside?"

"The media has made you out to be a hypocritical ass, which is exactly what we're shooting for, so in that regard the operation was a success," Richard said, dryly. "Are you looking for loopholes in the plan now?"

"Yes that's exactly right I need you to help me see if we are vulnerable anywhere. As far as I can tell, the attack you and Joe orchestrated was right on point. The negative media fall out has been almost better than I could've hoped for. The oil companies and I have gotten closer together and our lawyers are on the same page, all agreeing to the same defense. They want me to go on air and defend our position. All of our meetings were well documented and the contracts were signed and dated. My speech and proposals can be handed over as most of it was based on the power point that I showed in each office and computer records would confirm. The contracts themselves show I'm supplying the oil companies with solar powered electricity which they'll use to run their drilling and service rigs instead of the large diesel burning generators they currently use. Once this information is out, my reputation will be saved and big oil will get a big green initiative boost. I know the Saudi Arabia princes like media, so from where I sit this looks like a win," George paused in his explanation, then realized Richard was in a better position than he to be objective. "What do you think? Do you see any holes or vulnerabilities from our side? We can't get caught."

"From the surface it's a solid plan," Richard said, confidently. "There's no way to trace Joe back to being the one who called in the tip, let alone trace him back to me or to you. Your itinerary went to eight businesses in Texas so who knows who else may have gotten ahold of it or how? Listening to your details did give me a thought, though. Why stop with breaking even? Instead of punishing or suing the protesters and the activist groups, why not build them up, praise them for trying to save the planet, offer a donation in their name to some environmental research project at a university somewhere? Then not only would you get positive press but the oil companies would come out looking good and guaranteed all of that would ring home world-wide, even to Saudi Arabia. You spoke about something like that before, I think this is an excellent opportunity to do it."

"You're right, Richard," George said, excited about the benefits of Richard's suggestion. "An investment in a nonprofit organization is tax deductible and would go towards building market awareness and technology in solar energy and that would help all the way around."

"Plus a donation to a university keeps the money out of the environmental lobbyists' hands, which will also make your oil company clients happy," Richard added.

"Well aren't you earning your pay in dividends today?" George commented. "If this keeps up, we're going to need to talk further about your interests and future potential with my firm."

"Don't get too carried away George," Richard said modestly. "I appreciate the offer, and enjoy celebrating wins, but the battle still remains. One step at a time and let's keep our eye on the prize."

George's comments had Richard worried. The last thing he wanted to do was endear himself to George when he knew he needed to do the opposite and distance himself from George following this assignment. So far they'd only completed part one of four and it was the most legal of all four parts, there'd only been a little bit of collusion and fraud involved.

CHAPTER 43

As he clicked off following his conversation with Richard, George knew he'd been right to bring Richard in on this venture. Although the next assignments were much more detailed and risky, this one was well planned and went off without a hitch. Truth be told, George knew, the rest of this Texas assignment was up to him. He needed to finish off the con and sell it to the world, and he knew just how to do it.

George called Robin and set him to finding out which university had the best environmental and renewable energy study program in Texas. Once he found the right institution, he instructed Robin to call the Dean and ask him "hypothetically" if he was to receive a large donation towards his renewable energy study program, would he feel compelled to put the money towards solar power studies. It would need to be their decision entirely of course but should they decide to put the money towards solar power research, they could very well see themselves in a partnership with Blade Energy and have the potential for larger grants in the near future. Robin had understood exactly what George was getting at and set out to find a strong partnership. The University of Texas in Austin would likely be the best choice. Robin already knew that the U of T had been seriously involved in renewable energy studies and would likely be very thankful for a large grant. Robin didn't waste time and it wasn't long until he found himself on the phone with the Dean.

Following that phone call, George got to work preparing his speech for the media. Since news of the protest rally against him broke, coupled with the fact that he was shortlisted to bid on the Neom project, he'd been approached by several talk shows and newspapers looking for his story. George eventually decided on meeting with the Houston Chronicle and a subsidiary of CNN for a tell-all interview. He'd been working with his lawyers and had made a few statements online to indicate the whole thing was a big misunderstanding, but had deliberately not given them anything strong enough to deter the accusations against him, and had instead strategically just said enough to ignite the fire of the environmentalists and keep the fight going. As he'd hoped, the story had picked up steam and that was when the serious news media syndicates began calling, which was exactly what he'd been waiting for. George was scheduled for his interview at two pm the following day. He'd been working with a publicist that Sara had found him. He had to be careful, he didn't want the interview to look like a polished soliloquy, but he also didn't want to come off as a moron in the news like some of the recent politicians kept doing.

CHAPTER 44

Mike had no trouble talking his wife into a summer vacation and even less talking her into a free one, in a mansion, in the East Hamptons. Despite their working class jobs, Mike and Marcy had always felt they'd had a fairly affluent lifestyle but they'd certainly never even considered vacationing in the Hamptons. Marcy was quite excited to have the opportunity to tour the area and eventually pick a house of her choice to live in for the summer, it was like winning a luxury vacation that you'd never consider spending your own money on.

Mike was happy that Marcy was excited; it helped to ease his guilt about his actual assignment and the cruelty of what he had to do to make it successful. Chris Buchanan, as it turned out, had an estate on Marine Boulevard which was a high-end location, even by Hampton standards. In order to portray the part properly, Mike and Marcy flew into the East Hampton airport on a Lear jet. They had a meeting set with a real estate agent who promised to show them the best estates available along the Atlantic coast. Mike informed the agent that his wife was looking in the East Hampton area.

Kim Edwards, a fifteen year veteran Hampton real estate agent, met them outside the terminal and took them in a tram to the helicopter hangers. On the ride over she explained that most of the estates had heli-pads or large enough grounds to land on. Utilizing a helicopter would allow them to view all the houses in a timelier manner and skipping traffic would allow them to get the full Hampton experience from the air. Kim loaded them into an R-66 turbine helicopter and once safely aboard, they took off to the South West. Kim said she wanted to show them the East Hampton Shoreline and to point out a few landmarks and celebrity homes as they flew over. The forty-two acre Jule Pond Estate, originally built for Henry Ford and currently for sale with an asking price of one hundred and fifty million, was definitely the high light of the tour. Marcy was enthralled with the landscaping; the grounds were absolutely stunning.

Kim then flew them up the coast to see Marine Boulevard and the estates within. From the air, Mike was able to pick Chris's house out quite easily. He'd been studying maps and Google Earth images for hours, looking for paths and venues on which he could orchestrate chance meetings. There were two houses in the area that had potential. One was actually two houses over from Chris's and was also beach-front like his. The other was a block over and two streets back from the ocean. Both were beautiful houses and offered dream summer escape opportunities. Obviously, the house on the ocean was substantially more expensive. As they continued the tour, Mike and Marcy wrote down about five potential houses located throughout the far East side of East Hampton. From the air they could see the island south east of Montauk where Chris was planning to build his massive wind farm.

"Well that about sums up the houses in the range and area we spoke of on the phone beforehand," Kim said. "I can show you others, of course, but they'd be further away. Before we head back, did anything interest you enough to go back and take a second look? This is the great thing about the helicopter. We can see any house again in five minutes' time, just say the word."

Mike made a show of conferring with his wife then said, "we picked five houses we'd like to take a second look at. If we flew over them again, I bet we could narrow it down to two or three and then start negotiating."

"That's exactly what I was hoping you'd say," Kim responded with a smile. "Let me see your map and I'll have the pilot fly over."

Mike passed his map forward and asked that they fly over the Marine Boulevard houses last. As the pilot banked the helicopter back south west, Mike looked over at his wife with mixed feelings. He was proud he could offer her this lifestyle even if it was only for a summer, but deathly scared at the price he may have to pay for it. As they flew over the houses a second time, Mike knew that he'd have to pick the house two doors down from Chris's in order to have any hope of connecting with him. The Hampton yards were close in proximity to one another but thick bushes and tall hedges were planted between houses to maximize privacy. Even from the air Mike could see that unless you were invited to someone's house, there was no way you could stumble onto their property by accident without raising suspicion. Besides the hedges, most of the houses had relatively long driveways with gated front entrances.

Mike already knew the house he needed but thought he'd do his best to get the best deal he could, meanwhile keeping up appearances of a millionaire looking for a relaxing summer home so no one got suspicious. At his request, the helicopter landed on the front lawn of the house next to Buchanan's, just before the sand of the Atlantic shoreline started. The dwelling was a five thousand square foot wood finished mansion. It was the poster child for the traditional Hampton residence, the best way to describe it without a picture would be to tell someone to imagine a beach front Hampton home on a post card and they would basically come up with it every time.

They disembarked from the helicopter and stepped up onto the long wooden sidewalk that led from the beach to the small acreage. Marcy grabbed Mike's hand as they walked towards the house. They had been together a long time and he could read her barely contained excitement. Mike could hear the ocean roar while the sea breeze blew through his hair. As they walked towards the house, he could already tell the views would be amazing. Despite the traditional look of the house, the ocean side consisted mostly of glass walls which were accented by brick and wood.

The house sold itself, but Kim did her duty and pointed out small features that were not so noticeable, such as the fact that it sat on a one-acre lot and the property line extended five feet into the ocean, which meant no one could ever build in front or sit on the beach without permission. The house itself was surrounded by a huge cobblestone drive and patio. There was a heated swimming pool and Jacuzzi located in the back yard, which was basically an outdoor living room and kitchen that could easily handle a party of one hundred and fifty or so guests.

Despite its age, the home's designer obviously had a timeless sense of class and had created an overall look of gentle elegance that would never go out of style. The interior, however, had been completely updated. It was a fully operational smart home where everything turned on with voice activated sensors. Boasting marble floors, dimmable windows and zone-controlled temperature for each room, the house was breathtaking. When they got to the second floor, however, Mike and Marcy were speechless. The impressive elegance and beauty of the architecture inside couldn't compare to the majestic view the house offered of the natural beauty beyond the picture windows.

Experienced at her job, Kim had given the couple some space to explore and talk, but was now walking back towards them with a knowing look. The place really did sell itself and she knew it. "Well what do you think?" She asked, with a grin. "I know the views and location are without equal. The house was designed and built to resemble the traditional Hampton look. It's quite a contrast to the boxy contemporary ones around, but if this is the style you like, you won't find anything better."

Marcy looked like she was going to cry, she was so in love with the place. Mike laughed to himself. He knew he wouldn't get far negotiating a deal if the agent saw her face.

Mike decided to go for it and lay his cards on the table. "This is the house we want, Kim. We're up in the air on buying, though. I'm sure for most of your clients these type of houses are just an addition to their collections, but for us it is a very serious purchase. It'll literally be our second home and take a large chunk of our retirement fund. Chances are we'll like it, but we really want to be sure. Regardless we need to talk some numbers. Do you have a sell sheet for it or how do we move forward?"

"I know you need to get back to the city," Kim said. "Why don't I put together a price for you on the way back to the airport and we can discuss further when we land? Or if you need some time, you can take the quote with you and call me if you are interested."

"You're right, we do need to get back. I just wish I could get more of a feel for the place. Obviously it looks amazing, but it's a lot of money to spend," Mike said, beginning to lay the foundation for his request to rent rather than buy when they began negotiating terms later.

"Well if you're ready to head out, let's go back down to the helicopter and load up. I don't want to be responsible for you missing your plane," Kim said.

As they made their way back to the helicopter, Mike was lost in his own thoughts. He hoped he had put up enough resistance that Kim would offer a buy price and a rental price. It was late spring and Mike knew most Hampton sales happened in early spring or mid-winter for those trying to get deals. This fact gave him the thought that a rental deal may be in the cards because at least that way the house would have some profit for the year if it wasn't sold. As the helicopter turned towards the Atlantic and lifted off into the wind, Mike gazed out at the original infinity pool. The ocean steadied his mind and he started planning the next stages, well aware that none of them would be near as pleasant or innocent as today had been. When they landed at the East Hampton Airport, Kim led them over to her car.

On the way, she handed Mike her IPad. "I worked out a couple sets of numbers for you guys. Take a look and let me know what you think. I'll wait in the car while you discuss, just come get me when you're ready or if you have any questions."

"Thanks, Kim," Mike said, grateful that she understood her clients' need for privacy. "Let us talk it over." Mike and Marcy looked at the prices. Kim had the house listed at fifteen point five million, which made Mike wish he could just buy it outright for Marcy, he'd seen the way she had looked at it and wished he could get it for her legally. Then he flipped to the next page and there it was. Kim had heard his hints and had given a rental option. She wanted sixty thousand a month rent but they would have to sign a three-month lease. Richard had told him to pay what he needed, but he thought he better check in prior to agreeing.

"Marcy, you keep looking this over. I need to make a quick call to Richard and make sure the client is willing to pay 180k for three months' rent just to track a guy. If Kim asks, I got a business call, ok?" Marcy nodded to him and Mike walked away to call Richard.

"Mike, how are you making out?" Richard answered on the first ring. "I've been hoping to hear from you."

"Rich, I'm in the middle of negotiations on a house but I snuck away to call. We were only able to find five houses close to Chris Buchanan's and only one of those would work for what we need. Trouble is, it's a fifteen million dollar plus home. They'll let me rent it but I need to sign up for three months at sixty grand a month. Do I take it? I thought I should check."

"That real estate is unreal, but George said to do what it takes and basically gave me carte blanche on spending. Go ahead and rent it. Use that company check I gave you. With any luck, this mission will go as planned and you can spend two of those months actually vacationing," Richard replied optimistically.

"Well I can tell you if that happened, I'd be in the good books with my wife for the rest of my life," Mike laughed. "Thanks, Rich. The price was so high that I got nervous. But if you're sure, I'll sign on the dotted line."

"Mike this isn't going to be an easy job so don't stress

over these details and expenses. Your real job is next and that's the one you need to focus on."

As they hung up, Mike was grateful to Richard for helping him refocus his priorities. Richard was right, he'd been letting himself get too involved in the small stuff. Right now he just needed to get his tools in place so he could concentrate on his main objective. One of those tools was this house. He needed to close the deal and move forward. If he let himself get bogged down in the details he would never meet his time frames. He still couldn't help but smile as he walked up to Marcy, because one look at his face and she knew they were getting the house, which made her burst out in grin of her own. Marcy hugged him hard, then Mike went over and knocked on Kim's door.

As she stepped out of the car she asked, "well what do you think?"

"You're a good agent, Kim, so I'm sure you already know our decision. I see you heard me loud and clear about the uncertainty of buying outright. We'll take the three-month option. That way we can get a feel for the place and make our final decision in a couple months. Our only stipulation is that we'd like to move in immediately. Would that be a problem?" Mike asked.

"The owners of the house have purchased a property in Spain and, much like you, wanted to try it out first. They've decided to buy and to sell this property. So what I'm saying is, there is nothing preventing you from moving in tomorrow if you like. Other than signing the papers, of course," Kim said as she handed him both the papers and a pen with a smile.

"Well, I better sign quick then before somebody beats me to it," Mike replied as he took them from her.

As Mike and Marcy flew home that night, Marcy started planning their move while Mike was in his own head, planning the next phase of his operation.

CHAPTER 45

Jeff was back in Iceland and had booked into the same apartment he was in before. It didn't take him long to pick up Jim's trail. For the most part, surveillance was needing to know the person you were following. That way you didn't have to tag along a couple steps behind the mark everywhere they went. In some instances, where the recognizance was long enough you could actually start beating the person to the place he was going, and the challenge of outthinking his marks kept his mind from becoming complacent. All people have routines and not many veer very far from them. The most organized people are like clockwork, but even disorganized, easy-going people tend to stick to the same paths, generally speaking.

Despite his success, Jim was fairly normal and seemed like a decent and down to earth guy. His schedule was pretty standard, he would get up in the morning, eat, fit an exercise routine in, and head off to work. His workdays were the most irregular part of his life. He was always working but could be jetting off to Europe one day or meeting with architects at the Blue Lagoon another. Most days, though, he spent in his office. Jim was not an overly security-conscious person. He never seemed to have issues discussing his business openly at restaurants and coffee shops with whomever he was meeting. Jeff had been able to blend into the crowds but always got close enough to hear lots about his plans and schedules.

Jim had recently added a social element to his calendar. He was now dating Garcia Grey, the well-known and stunning geothermal scientist he'd recently hired. Jeff discovered that Jim and Garcia were going on a trip to Las Vegas prior to flying to Saudi Arabia for the Summit meeting where he knew Jim was scheduled to speak. It sounded like the couple would be spending about a week in Vegas. To Jeff it seemed like a strange time to start a romance, right before making a major speech to world leaders, but Jim lived in a different world than Jeff and maybe that was how guys like him did things. Jeff knew Jim had a suite booked at the Wynn and so he booked himself a room there too.

Jeff now had two things he needed to discuss with Richard. The first was that he was considering beginning his attack early. He reasoned that some minimal threats in Vegas to set the stage, followed up by the big blast in Riyadh, would help to get the point across. The second issue was his growing concern over how the hell he was going to procure and deploy a bomb in Riyadh that would be effective enough to produce the results they needed while still avoiding capture. He couldn't even imagine what the punishment would be in a place like Riyadh for disturbing the peace or attempted murder when Saudi Arabia was hosting a world event, so he picked up his cell. When Richard answered, Jeff got straight to the point.

"Hey, Rich, just calling with an update date and a couple questions. Is now a good time to talk?"

"Absolutely, Jeff," Richard replied. "What do you have for us?"

"Jim seems to be fully engaged in a relationship with that new scientist he hired to run the geothermal side of his corporation. They must have it hit off immediately because they're sure spending a lot of time together. From everything I hear, Jim has barely had a date since his wife died so it must be serious. He's booked a trip with her to Vegas for the week prior to his scheduled trip to Riyadh for the conference he's attending where he's giving a speech on clean energy. The trip seems odd to me because usually all he does is work and I'd have thought he'd be sweating the details of his keynote address right before a big event like this. Who knows… women can get guys to do things so maybe she wanted a getaway before the event, it just really seems odd to me given his personality," Jeff mused aloud.

"I agree," Richard said thoughtfully, "it doesn't sound like Jim at all, but hardly any of this project fits his profile for that matter. A big fund investor who's now buying real estate, bidding on world changing environmental projects, and completely changing his profile. We need to find out what gives. Follow him to Vegas to see if you can find out what's going on. See if it's just some romantic high-rolling vacation or if there is a mixture of work in there as well. I'm guessing it's a bit of both."

"My plane tickets are already booked and I'm staying at the same hotel on the strip as he is. I was thinking maybe I send a few subtle, or not so subtle, hints his way in Vegas. Something about using his fame and fortune to sway the masses away from gas and oil use. Basically, I want to make him think the oil and gas industry is telling him to back off his Neom bid and this green energy wave he is so vigorously supporting or else there will be a price to pay. It'll let him know that if they can get at him in Vegas, and then more seriously in Saudi Arabia, that they can get at him, and those he cares about, anywhere. By following him around the world and steadily increasing the warnings should prove that they are serious about wanting him to back off. I need help, though, because I don't know how I'm going to be able to get a bomb in Riyadh. How will I ever get the workings to build or buy one in a place like that with no contacts, especially at a time when the country will be on high security alert for an event like a G8 with all the world leaders there? Security will be unreal."

"I've actually been thinking about that, too, Jeff," Richard replied thoughtfully. "I've been wondering if you had something figured out or if you were going to come to me with this. I do have a thought regarding Riyadh. First, though, I love your idea for Vegas. Just keep in mind cameras are everywhere there and a guy like Jim will have no trouble getting police or other hotel and casino groups to help him out if he needs to see anything caught on video. I'd say notes and small vandal type things, slashed tires, deep hood and paint dings, but whatever you think's best. Then for Saudi I think you go with a Molotov Cocktail. Not only are they easy to build but you can control them and make them relatively safe. A Molly will cause fire, a bit of an explosion and significant burns if it gets on anyone, so you'll have to be careful, but overall it should scare the hell out of anyone it almost hits. Use it to wreck a vehicle or two at the most but don't hurt anyone. Also, you build Molotovs with oil which is a perfect reminder of who we want Jim to think is after him. What do you think?"

"Crude but effective," Jeff said in agreement. "An attack like that would be scary and extremely personal. I should have no problem finding a couple of gang members willing to throw a fire bomb or two for a few hundred American dollars each, especially if my instructions are to make sure no one is hurt. I'll keep an eye on the situation, if they take my money and run I'll have one on hand to throw myself if it comes down to it. I'm glad you agree with the Vegas plan, that means we are on the same page. I think a sustained and progressive attack leads to the intensity of messing with his mind. Jim will be waiting for the next shoe to drop, wondering how far his enemy will be willing to go. I'm sure it won't be enough to make a man who wants to win a multibillion dollar business deal quit, but if it puts doubt in his mind and throws him off his game, that's just what George wanted."

"What does Jim's schedule look like for his stay in Vegas?" Richard asked.

"He's a class act as far as I can tell, he has a suite rented in the Encore at the Wynn, nothing showboat fancy, but as high-end and elegant as you can imagine. He already has chairs booked for supper at SW steak overlooking the waterfall and pool, but of course he managed to get second level seating which is basically a private balcony overlooking the diners and the water. I'm not even sure most people would know there is a balcony, I didn't," Jeff said.

"Well make sure you see who he meets there," Richard advised.

"On the third night they're staying at Caeser's, but in a hotel within the hotel called Nobu. I understand the stay at this hotel is supposed to be an almost religious experience," Jeff said.

"You've heard right, a stay at Nobu is a vacation itself," Richard agreed. "Basically, a philosophy all of its own. Even the restaurant experience is unique, the waiters discuss and plan your meal with you based on time, mood, company. It's very intimate, though, so if you follow him there make sure you get seated in a place you can hear but not get noticed. There's a good chance the restaurant will be booked; it's quite popular, so I'd call and try and book now if you can or you'll never get in. On another note, I agree with you that there is something going on with Jim... There's no way he'd be vacationing in Vegas right before a meeting like this with how much he has invested. See what, if anything, you can find out. And keep me posted with how the scare tactics go."

"You bet, thanks for letting me bounce these ideas off you, Rich," Jeff said in closing. Once he hung up the phone, Jeff immediately started planning ways to get at Jim. This mission wasn't going to be easy. He desperately needed to not get caught, put significant blame on the oil industry, and make sure Jim was not actually harmed in any way. Not an easy gig. Jeff was flying out in the morning so he jumped online and began trying to get dinner reservations at two of Las Vegas's classiest restaurants. Although Jim Dunsmuir had not had any trouble getting reservations, he felt he may need to do a little more work to secure himself decent seating, or any seating at all.

Richard was happy three of his four objectives were well in hand and he had a meeting scheduled with Kelly in an hour to further discuss how they were going to move forward with their plan against Peter Fairchild. In all honesty, the only two guys who deserved to get kicked out of this bidding race was Peter and, ironically, Richard's boss George. Jim and Chris were stand up solid businessmen who supported their family, staff, and clients. Whereas George was extremely ruthless and underhanded. George supported his clients, not so much because he worried about their success, but because he needed them to be happy so he could keep his own reputation especially in the world of environmental energy. Right now the renewable energy sector was all about world-saving initiatives and strong ethical values, basically the opposite of how business works in the traditional energy sector.

There'd been too many fly-by-night companies that were ran by little more than hippy drug addicts who'd first tried to get renewable energy started in the world for no other reason than to "screw the man". They'd been unreliable people with unreliable technology, offering no warranty or guarantees and many times were not in business long enough to finish the job. It was these people that gave renewable energy a lousy reputation, especially in North America, going right back to the 1960s. To their credit, it's been men like George and Peter who revitalized renewable energy and gave it a credible name, even if they weren't credible people. The evolution of renewable energy was now shifting to men like Chris and Jim who had long standing, strong reputations in the world with business plans and customer service that people could trust.

CHAPTER 46

"We still on for a meeting?" Kelly asked, standing in Richard's office door.

Richard looked up, surprised that he hadn't even noticed Kelly walk in. With his mind on the business model of renewable energy, he felt guilty for being off topic.

"You caught me daydreaming, I'm afraid," Richard admitted, "but absolutely get in here. We need to plan this thing out and I know you've been making progress. Let me hear what you have so far."

"Peter's back in Seattle right now. He's working with his people preparing the Naes Construction presentation and bid for the Prince's meeting. Let me outline my plan for you. See what you can do to spot its vulnerabilities. What I'm planning is illegal, so I know there'll be holes. We just need to make them hard enough to find so that if they figure out what we're doing, by the time they catch up to us, we can be gone without a trace."

"Ok, Kell, I'm ready. Lay it out for me," Richard said as he grabbed a note pad and prepared himself to write down any concerns he may have with the plan.

"I flew to Seattle. We have a man there following up on an insider trading deal so I set a few meetings with him to legitimize my reasons for travel. Then dressed in the best inconspicuous disguise I could think of, I did some online searching from an internet café that had free Wi-Fi so there's no traceability. I found five high rise apartment buildings that had the qualifications I was looking for in the vicinity of Naes offices. All five buildings are currently under construction; however, they're still renting out apartments. Through a burner phone I rented an apartment in each building using money orders I picked up from various pay day loan shops around the city. I paid for the first, last and three months' rent for each apartment, which was the going rate. In each building I took an apartment on a floor directly above the floors that are under construction. The good thing about each of these buildings is that under renovation means that the rental markets are so poor the construction has been on hold for months now, which means boarded up empty floors. I took the stairway down in each building and broke my way into each construction area. There are no cameras or signs of any kind of surveillance systems. The doors were boarded up, but with the right tools I easily gained access and then repositioned the barricades so it looked like no one had entered. I then placed supplies in each area. Fortunately, the land lords never found the need to turn the power off to the vacant floors. My thought is I'll have a main plan with 4 backup buildings to choose from because you never know which building you may need to run to when it comes down to an actual kidnapping. In each building there's at least one empty floor above and below the areas I prepared. Screams for help would be muted at worst and unheard at best. In saying that, for our safety and theirs, I think we keep both of them gagged and tied up most of the time," Kelly paused in his explanation. "Are you with me so far, Rich? Don't let me keep going if you think I'm way off."

Richard just nodded as he jotted down a few notes and told Kelly to keep going. In truth, he was quite impressed with the plan so far.

"Now here's how we do it," Kelly continued. "Peter uses ride share services for any and all small trips around the downtown area and that plays right into our hands. We can easily track any taxi or Uber that picks Peter up after lunch. We will pull it over on the way back to his office, blind the taxi driver, chloroform Peter, and slip away around a corner where we change vehicles and leave the taxi. At that point we're home free. I'll have a moving company booked to move furniture into my new apartment and Peter will be sleeping in one of the boxes they haul up. We'll basically do the same thing to his daughter except we'd grab her on the way home from school. They'll be allowed to see each other so Peter knows we're not bluffing, but then they'll be separated for a couple days in separate rooms. We'll have to torture

Peter, at least a bit, and fake-torture the girl. I refuse to
hurt her in any way and if that ruins the mission, so be
it," Kelly said this with defiance on his face. Richard saw
there would be no changing his mind on that issue, and
he was actually relieved Kelly felt so strongly about it
because he felt the same way.

"Once we start in on Peter we've got to get him to
break and give up his daughter's life in exchange for his.
We'll need to get him to do this in a short time frame and
with what appears to be minimal damage to his person,
and capture the whole thing on video. That way the
world will see Peter Fairchild for what he is, a bully who
puts himself first and not the "true" American cowboy
everyone loves to forgive. Once he gives her up to save
himself, we then release the video to the public and ruin
him through social and traditional media. After that we
blindfold and chloroform them again, haul them back
out, and leave them downtown in a car somewhere far
from where we kept them," Kelly paused again to see if
Richard had any questions. Seeing Richard motion for
him to continue, Kelly finished off his explanation. "The
only safe way I see to do this, though, is to do it in house.
We don't have time to recruit and trust others. We need
to call our guys in for the job. I think we know that Mike
is going to need the same help with his operation too.
Once the initial ops are complete, we'll be able to hold
our own and finish the job, but we need the man power
for the initial phases, unless you have another solution?"
Kelly said.

Richard was impressed with the plan and told Kelly

so. Not only the plan but the actions Kelly had taken to move it forward. If Richard used his own men for this operation he'd need to reconfirm swearing them to secrecy. It wasn't that they weren't trustworthy, but because once they dropped the victims off unharmed without any ransom demands, the police would likely lower the priority on finding the kidnappers. If anyone involved let down their guard once the heat was off and let something slip they could still get caught. The police would soon have more pressing emergencies to handle than finding out which one of Peter Fairchild's long list of enemies hated him enough to go so far as to publicly embarrass and discredit him, but if they had clues they'd get followed. The most dangerous thing they'd have to be on the lookout for was Peter himself. Richard knew if Peter was like George, he'd stop at nothing to regain his reputation and pay back his attackers with extreme vengeance.

Seeing no other option than to agree with Kelly, Richard shared his thoughts. "I don't like the idea of using the guys but I've been thinking about it and I agree there is no way to execute this with only two people, especially with such short time frames. Even if we had more time I'm not sure we could do it without help and you're right that Mike is going to need help too. There's just no two ways about it. If we pull the guys in to help us, Mike will have even less time to plan his attack, which compounds his timeframes and puts him in the position of needing more help too. What about if we give up trying to do this separately and do it as a team instead. Call in the guys, how soon can we go?"

Nodding in agreement, Kelly said, "I was hoping you'd agree with me so I booked tickets for everyone to fly into New York tomorrow. We just need to tell them to get on the planes. Once we brief the guys, each of them will then fly on to Portland and from there they'll drive to Seattle and rent cheap motel rooms for cash. We'll meet them at the motel and finalize plans for the next couple days. Once we have a plan ready, we'll do a practice run, pick up a few more supplies, make some tweaks to the plan, conduct another practice run the following day and jump into the real thing on the third day. I don't see that we have any more time than that," Kelly took a drink of water, checked his notes and then continued. "After it's over the guys can drive back to Portland, fly back to New York, and then with the exception of Jeff who needs to get to Vegas, go out to the Hamptons with Mike. Mike will fly private to keep up his appearance while the others will drive out to the Hamptons and rent as non-descript hotel rooms as they can for a week with Trade Link security credit. We'll need to find a case to put them on "officially" in the Hamptons so we have an alibi for them being out there while they're helping Mike. Once the guys help Mike, George's other jobs will already be complete so they can stay in the area and investigate whatever rich spouse is fooling around with the tennis pro or lawn boy case we have," Kelly finished outlining his strategy. "Now let's go over whatever else we may need for gear and get ready to get to Seattle."

CHAPTER 47

"Jason and I are off to Vegas in the morning," Jim updated Lois, Jason and Ramsey. "If either company has questions, I can speak to all aspects in general terms, but if they want to get technical, Jason can detail the how. I'd like you guys to be on standby when we're in meetings in case further information is needed and we can give you a call."

"Jim," Lois interjected, looking him directly in the eye. "I think you should take Garcia with you as well."

"Why would I take her along?" Jim questioned, confused at Lois's obviously adamant suggestion. "Jason can easily speak to the detail any investor will want to hear on geothermal technology. Ramsey," Jim said, dismissing Lois's comment to refocus on the task at hand, "do you have those confidentiality contracts from the lawyers? I need to remember to get each ownership group to sign them. This is a deal that needs to be released to the public in the right format and to the princes first."

"Yes they're right he…" Ramsey was cut off by Lois.

"Jim you know what I mean," Lois said abruptly. "You don't need Garcia for technical support, you need her for mental stability. You two just started a new relationship. I don't know if you've told the others yet but it's my job to point this out and there is no time for subtlety. We all know what happens in new relationships; half a person's brain or more is gone for at least the first three months, all intellect is lost somewhere between lust and love. If you don't take her along, neither of you will be at your working best and you know that. But if you're together, you'll be on an endorphin high and there'll be nothing that you can't handle. In a way, her presence will enhance your presentation, which is good for the business in my opinion. On top of that, it'll give her and Jason more time together and I think she could benefit from his experience and listening to his answers when you meet with these companies. I don't think any of you can tell me I'm wrong," Lois smiled confidently and challengingly at the group, "but feel free to disagree."

"Well I was trying to think of a best time to tell everyone," Jim said sheepishly, "but trust Lois to rip the band aid off."

The guys around the table chuckled awkwardly and averted their eyes. They knew Lois was right, she was always right, and they didn't care if Garcia went along. But men being men, they shied away from discussing relationships.

Not wanting to discuss his relationship any more than the others, Jim recognized he at least needed to be honest with his team. "This is a huge business deal, folks, and I'm trying to stay above board with you guys. Garcia and I seem to have had an instant attraction. We've not really discussed what we are yet or where this is going, but I wanted to get it out to Lois and to you guys. No way I want this deal jeopardized because I tried to hide something."

"Lois is right, Jim," Ramsey said, reluctantly being brought into the discussion. "That's why we hired her. We need you on the top of your game. What's the saying, 'this is your brain on love'. Sometimes the euphoria feeling helps a person accomplish things that you would never think possible and we've all seen it, even if we haven't experienced it. Not saying you guys are a couple or will hit the Little Church of the West in Vegas, but proximity in these cases can comfort the mind and we need you at your best right now."

"I can't believe we're talking about this when we have so much to do and all these deadlines to meet," Jim shook his head at the turn the conversation had taken. "Yes I'd be happy to have her with me on the trip, provided she wants to go, and I appreciate you offering me the opportunity. Now if Garcia's accompaniment puts your worry to rest about my emotional stability, can we move on to business?" Jim said, trying not to sound exasperated at the interference in his love life. "Jason, you've been quiet. Please don't feel your opinion isn't welcome or valued. Ramsey, Louis and I have history and tend to banter on sometimes but you're integral to this team and we need to hear from you."

Jason responded with his typical candor. "I appreciate that, Jim. As for your relationship, I'm good either way. Ramsey is right about Garcia, though. She and I need to get some plans together. I'm not sure about me mentoring so much as us working together on a design. I think she would be an asset on the trip for the business."

"It's settled, then," Jim finalized. "I'll call and ask her to come along. I don't know if she had plans but I imagine she'll make herself available. She knows the whole deal rests on us getting this bid."

Garcia excitedly agreed to go to Vegas the minute Jim called. Not only was she going to get to spend some personal time with Jim, she was also going to have a week to work with Jason, which would be any engineer or scientist's dream. She was packed and ready to fly within minutes of Jim asking her if she wanted to go along. They met at the office and then Jim's car drove them to the Reykjavik airport. They flew first class to New York and then on to Las Vegas.

CHAPTER 48

Jeff arrived in Vegas the day before Jim's team and checked into his hotel. His contacts had discovered that Jim and his entourage had two meetings set, one at Caesar's Palace and the other at the Wynn Hotel and Casino. He had a couple ideas he thought would allow him to victimize Jim while he was in Vegas but he'd need to wait and see how Jim and his crew travelled the city. As Richard had cautioned him, Jeff knew Vegas was a city of cameras and tourists which would make it hard not to be caught on film. He'd learned that Jim liked to eat at Oscars and watch the lights on the roof of the old strip. Jeff took a risk and booked himself a table on the only night of Jim's trip he knew that Jim didn't have a meeting. Jeff guessed Jim would take his colleagues there for dinner. In preparation for that evening, Jeff purchased five high end drones that he'd been able to synchronize and control from his phone. With his phone, Jim was able to make the machines take off, fly in patterns and operate in spaces anywhere from two inches to fifteen feet of each other.

One good thing about Vegas was the unlimited access to anything imaginable. Jeff went off the strip in order to purchase his goods but still had no trouble obtaining what he needed. He knew surveillance off the strip was good, but it wasn't the cutting edge security they had on Las Vegas Boulevard. Anyone who knows Oscars knows the restaurant has the look of an old town water tower. Only in this case the bubble was a glass walled high end steak house that overlooked the original Vegas Strip. From its windows the guests dining in the restaurant could look down the old strip and watch all kinds of entertainment. The street never had a dull moment, people were zip-lining the length of the street and the ride ended not far from Oscar's windows. The whole street was covered in a dome that had a continuous show of lights and pictures with an endless supply of vendors and entertainment under it and between the casino doors that lined both sides of the street.

Jeff rented a room overlooking the old strip and opened his window to not only watch and listen, but to create an airport for his drones. Then he pulled a table up next to the open window and set all 5 drones on it. Drawing on his experience from the police force, Jeff was able to concoct five small explosive devices, each with a detonator he could trigger from his phone. He'd also had two large banners and a bunch of confetti-type advertisements made up. He rigged a bomb to each drone, then attached a confetti-filled bag to each of three of the machines and a ten-foot banner to each of the last two drones. Each drone had a forty-five-minute battery life. Jeff was able to pre-set a course for the drones that would have them attack Jim and then fly out over the desert and self-destruct. Jeff was taking a big gamble that Jim would show up at Oscar's restaurant, but figured, what the hell. When in Rome… he thought.

CHAPTER 49

His hunch paid off. Jeff was just ordering his main course when Jim and his group walked into Oscars and sat down at a front row seat next to the glass overlooking the strip. His conscience bugging him, Jeff shoved aside his mixed feelings about acting against Jim, knowing he couldn't let his team down. Jeff decided to let the group settle in and relax before he made the attack. He knew the wider range of emotions people felt after such an attack, the more they would be affected.

Once Jim's party finished ordering, they settled back with their drinks to watch the sky show over the strip and that's when Jeff pulled out his phone. Jim was sitting with his two engineers and he was obviously pretty close to the geothermal scientist. He couldn't blame Jim, Garcia was a knock out. Forcing himself not to think of his targets as victims, Jeff activated his program. The first two drones rose up out of the window of Jeff's hotel room and flew down the strip towards the restaurant windows. They hovered about twenty feet out from the glass, right in front of Jim's window, and lined up side by side to deploy their payload.

Two bright red, ten foot banners unrolled from the belly of each drone to dangle with crisp black letters on full display for all the restaurant patrons to read. One banner said, "Drop Neom" the other next to it said, "or die". As the drones started flying closer towards the restaurant, everyone was staring by now and had their phones out to record video and take pictures. Jim and his team looked shocked and uncertain. They just sat there, staring at the signs. As the drones started moving towards the restaurant, the other three rose from Jeff's hotel room window and followed the path of the first two. As they moved into position behind the first two drones, all five hovered menacingly in front of the windows, obviously pointing directly at Jim and his team.

The longer the drones held their positions, the more the people in the restaurant became uneasy and started to panic as fear of the unknown was setting in. Most of the diners didn't know what Neom was and it really didn't matter to the Oscar's employees. The staff flew into action; they had contingency plans for just such events, the police were called, they pulled customers back from the windows, they tried to escort their patrons out, but with human curiosity what it is, most refused to go.

The lead drones rose, dropped their banners and flew out of sight as the remaining three moved closer.

Suddenly three clouds of party streamers shot out of the remaining drones and exploded against the restaurant's windows and then in turn flew off in pursuit of the first two. Each confetti streamer had an identical message, "You have been warned, Jim." There were at least five thousand streamers. After bouncing off the glass, the steamers drifted down into the street and landed in front of the tower entrance.

Jeff did his best to fit in with the crowd exiting the restaurant, but kept one eye on his phone. Each of the drones flew out over the desert and one by one exploded into tiny pieces. The small charge Jeff had installed worked perfectly, completely destroying each unit. Jeff had proof each drone was destroyed when he lost the digital camera feed from each craft. One second he was looking at desert through the drone cameras, the next, blackness.

The Las Vegas police arrived on scene. Some got busy setting up a perimeter while others began investigating. Still other officers escorted hysterical people away from the area. Oscars was the picture of great customer service, for those patrons who wished to stay, their meals where quickly comped as well as their hotel rooms for the evening. For those wishing to leave, gift cards were presented for the next time they came back.

Jeff allowed himself to be escorted out of the building and accepted a free meal coupon along with the other customers that were leaving. Cautiously, he'd already erased the drone app from his phone. Not completely sure the drones hadn't been spotted flying out of his hotel room window, Jeff didn't return to his room. He'd checked in under a false name and had worn a wig, hat, glasses and a full fake moustache. Not knowing exactly the technology the old strip had, he'd made sure to slouch a bit more than usual and walk slightly pigeon toed just to further hide his appearance. He had done all these things earlier when purchasing the drones and streamers.

Jeff eased himself slowly back out of the crowd that had gathered around the base of the strip and watched for a moment as Jim and his staff began talking to the police. People were filming the incident and snapping pictures and once Jim's identity became common knowledge, people began gathering around him while he spoke to the lawmen. Almost everyone had picked up and read the wording on one of the streamers. Many tourists were even taking them as souvenirs. An ambulance arrived on scene and the media vans were right behind. Jeff left the scene with the knowledge that Jim would now have this attack on his mind and hopefully it would shake his confidence in his Neom bid. With a successful first phase out of the way, Jeff was ready to move into phase two.

CHAPTER 50

The reaction Jeff sparked in Jim was fury, not fear. At first he was shocked at the drones and their reference to the new city. Then as they hovered towards the restaurant, he understood it was a personal threat directed at him. He didn't need the thousands of streamers to point it out, but they just served to enrage him further. He was on a day between meetings so at least he wouldn't be forced to cancel anything, but he didn't like the idea of bad press. Jason and Garcia waited along the edge of the crowd while Jim let the police and then the media interview him. He couldn't afford bad publicity at this point, so he did his best to shield the project and his company from any negative fallout. Following the interviews, he would need to contact Ramsey and Alexandra to decide what kind of a response they were going to need to give the world to settle this issue down. They'd need to make sure it didn't damage their chances for Neom.

Back at the hotel, Jim quickly arranged a conference call with Ramsey, Lois and Alexandra. Ramsey began the conversation by filling the group in on other news. "George Anderson was recently accosted down in Texas by an environmental group. He was accused of getting in bed with big oil. As it turned out, George's intentions were quite the opposite and he had the oil companies investing in solar technology. That left the environmentalists with egg on their faces, not only for having false information, but for disturbing the peace and setting themselves up for a law suit. George came out smelling like a rose. He even took the high road, which is a little odd for his normal behavior, but I'm guessing it's because he's hired a good PR person. George ended up forgiving the environmentalists on a TV interview, telling them that their beliefs are strong but their intel and actions need to be cleaned up and then he donated a million dollars to a Texas University in the environmentalist group's name to go towards furthering renewable energy studies. Of course the university he donated to is most famous for their work on solar power, but all in all he came out of it shining like a star. What's most interesting is that there was a fair amount of discussion surrounding Neom in his case. I can't quite figure out why, but it's sure been good for his reputation. As far as I can tell, the attack has come out nothing but positive for George and his company. It seems odd to suggest the two assaults have anything in common, but I can't help but find it suspicious considering they involve the two of you and both of you are bidding on the Neom project in little over a week. I'll keep an eye on the news to see if anything more on Neom, Chris Buchanan or Peter Fairchild comes up now, just in case. Anyway, that's just my conspiracy theory. Alex has a couple ideas to run by you, I think you'll like them."

"First thing first, Jim," Alex jumped in. "You need to make sure that Garcia, Jason and even you are ok. We can't afford any of you to be off your game and the company cannot afford for anyone to be reacting emotionally to this situation. I need all three of you to call and talk with Lois following our discussion here, ok?" Alex asked out of formality but they all knew they weren't really getting a choice.

"You're right, Alex," Jim agreed for everyone. "I'll get them to start calling her now." Jim put the phone down and told Garcia and Jason that they needed to each have a private call with Lois to discuss the events of the night. Then he got back on the phone with Alexandra and Ramsey. "Ok guys what have you got for me?" Jim asked.

"First, you need to offer a Dunsmuir Energy night at Oscars. Pick up the tab for everyone's meal and offer thousand-dollar casino vouchers for all patrons that evening. We need to stay in favor with our hotel partners. Next, and this might surprise you, but we just leave it be. You were helpful to the police and media on site, no one was hurt, it was an obvious attack against you, personally, and we're not suffering in the news right now. If anything, this just gave us a little publicity. What do you think?" Alexandra concluded.

"I'm pissed off, is what I think," Jim said, not intending for his anger to be directed at Alexandra. "I mean, what the hell? That was personal. Someone knows me or too much about me. I didn't even have that meal scheduled! I had only just decided to take everyone there for dinner last minute. Yet it was well orchestrated and planned, definitely not a spur of the moment attack. Obviously, I'm not going to back out on Neom, so I think we need to prepare for what is coming next because there was no way that was just random. Am I risking our lives staying in the process?" Jim's thoughts and emotions were obviously all over the map, so Alex responded with wisdom and a calming tone of voice.

"Jim, that's why you need to talk to Lois," Ramsey took over. "You need to decide if you want to continue. If you're not committed 100% to this project, you have no chance of being the successful bidder. The competition is too steep to beat if you're only pursuing it half-heartedly. You need to make a great speech in Saudi Arabia at the G8 and then an even better one to the princes a few days later. If you're not mentally prepared for both, we'll be cut to shreds in the interview and you know it."

Jim shook his head, sat back in his chair, and sighed with frustration. "You're right, guys. I'm not focused. I'll talk with Lois." Jim tried to relax, but then couldn't help express his cynicism out loud. "This is where capitalism fails. I know that's the pot calling the kettle black, but people get so eager to get rich they're willing to maneuver instead of making better products or cut corners instead of meeting emissions tests. Everyone's focused on immediate gratification instead of what's good for future generations and the health of the world. I got into this business and this project in hopes of working with people who were thinking the same way as me. Now I just feel like business is all the same. The best salesman and the cheapest product will always win out. It's so disheartening. Businesses like ours need to get together if we're ever going to make serious changes with long term goals. Now instead of working towards something positive, we have to worry about publicity and physical threats. I believe our system could be world changing. We just need the buy in!"

CHAPTER 51

Jim spent an hour and a half talking with Lois after Jason and Garcia finished talking with her. Without breaching any confidentiality, Lois informed him that for the most part Jason and Garcia were just fine. She indicated she would follow up with them in a couple days and get them to talk through it again but at this point she didn't foresee either of them having any problems. Both seemed understandably upset but believe it was just a passing threat from the oil companies. Lois was a bit surprised that Jim seemed to take the event the hardest, not that he was scared so much as disappointed in the world. Lois understood that the project was his baby and now it was tearing him up inside because he'd never put his staff's safety at risk for a job before, yet he didn't want to give in. He wanted this project so badly. Jim seemed to think that someone put a lot of deliberate planning and effort in to threaten him in the restaurant, which made him think further attacks were imminent, and that's what concerned him the most. Jim was obviously shaken by the event and Lois had to focus a lot more on bringing him around again than she thought she would have to. She gave him set goals that she wanted him to work on overnight and said she'd call him the next day to discuss them with him and to plan next steps. Lois's plan worked. The idea of working towards something seemed to calm Jim's nerves, which allowed him to focus on the upcoming presentations.

"Jim," Lois said, after giving some thought to his schedule. "You have two days left till you fly from Vegas to Saudi Arabia. You know your presentation inside and out. Ramsey and Alexandra will clean up any little tweaks that you might need, so I'm ordering you to take Garcia out on the town tomorrow. There's nothing you can't get or see in that town. Plan a day with her and enjoy it. Let your mind be free for a bit while you have the opportunity. You're going to be extremely busy soon enough and you know as well as I do that a shift in thought processes will often times help a person do better with their main concerns. This is the perfect chance to make something of this relationship."

Jim was astonished. "You can't be serious, Lois! Take a day off and wonder around in Vegas before the biggest couple of days in my life? Especially after last night's attack? Are you kidding?"

"Especially *because* of last night's attack," Lois contradicted. "Jim, it's my job to study and keep you and everyone in this company on track mentally and emotionally. Right now you're not in good shape emotionally. You need to shift gears and reboot. I think a "relax day" with your new girlfriend is just what the doctor ordered, and since I happen to be the doctor, I agree," Lois said with an attempt to lighten Jim's mood with a bit of humour. "Jim, this is common practice amongst high achieving people and studies show it works. Athletes have light work outs the day before games; they rest and take on hobbies to distract their minds so they can bring themselves back up to full speed on game day. You're in the same type of position, only more serious because your event is completely mental, whereas theirs are mental and physical. You need to present with energy, enthusiasm and be ready to take spur of the moment questions or deal with whatever else may come up. A recharge is what you need. Trust me," Lois implored.

"Well it's true that with my mind where it's at right now, I feel like I'm just going through the motions in planning my speech anyway," Jim admitted. "I'm not really making any head way so maybe I should take your advice. I doubt I can truly take my mind off all of this, but this is your job and I do trust you."

"Jim, you'll never be able to take your mind off what's coming," Lois acknowledged. "The goal is to reduce it to background noise while you focus on the here and now for a few hours. If you can do that, you'll go into those meetings feeling alive and refreshed. I promise you."

"You've convinced me," Jim said. "I'm off. I can feel it. I'll give it a try. I just hope it works."

Lois had put the same type of idea in Garcia and Jason's head as well. She ordered them all to try and relax for the next day and a half and then start bringing themselves up for the presentation on the flight over to Arabia. They too were iffy on the idea of not having a massive planning session over the next couple days the same way Jim was, but she gave them the same advice she gave Jim. Both Garcia and Jason are masters in their fields. They already know what they need to say and have the info they need to provide Jim. Too much stress just wears people out and she knew they needed some time to decompress.

When Jim informed Garcia that Lois told him he needed to take the day off and asked her to tour around Vegas with him the next day, she readily agreed. Jim asked if there was anything she liked doing in Vegas and if he could take her anywhere special. Garcia considered his request and a thought popped into her head. She could see the tension in his face and his movements were more stiff than normal. She knew it was a combination of nervousness about his upcoming meetings and the stress of personal threats against himself and his company. She didn't quite feel comfortable enough yet to ask him to discuss his feelings, but she recognized them for what they were and she wanted to help.

"You know what, Jim?" Garcia said on a spur-of-the-moment hunch. "It's my turn to take you out. Be ready to leave at nine am tomorrow morning, dress casual and bring sunglasses. I want to show you *my* Las Vegas."

Jim looked at her, about to deny her offer and insist

that it was his duty to take her out, but at that moment he didn't have the energy to argue. He could also tell by the look on her face she wasn't going to take no for an answer.

So he just laughed and said, "Well I feel cheap letting you take me out, but honestly the idea sounds perfect. I'm off to bed, then. See you at nine." As he turned to walk away, Garcia called out to him.

He turned back towards her and realized what she was offering. Grinning in anticipation, he walked into her open arms and let his lips fall on hers. She kissed him hard and squeezed him tightly, then stepped back. "Good night, Jim," she said and then turned and walked away, satisfied that she'd given him something else to think about when he went to bed. She had planning to do, and even though it was late, this was Vegas so she knew she'd get it done.

Jim stood open mouthed as Garcia walked away from him. Her kiss had floored him and he was stunned. It took a second, but he realized he was standing alone in the middle of the luxurious Wynn hotel hallway, staring into space with his bottom jaw unhinged. He quickly looked around to see if anyone was looking at him standing there like an idiot and then quickly walked off to his room.

CHAPTER 52

After a surprisingly good sleep, Jim was up around seven the next morning. He ordered breakfast in and had a short conversation with Ramsey. Despite focusing most of his efforts on this energy deal, he was still the final sign-off on all major transactions for his company's investments. He was also the guide that determined the company's global direction, and Ramsey needed his help to steer the ship. Following the conversation, Jim showered, shaved and headed down to meet Garcia in the lobby. She'd texted him that she'd picked him up a coffee and said she was ready to leave as soon as he was. Jim got off the elevator and found her by the concierge desk. As promised, the coffee was hot, but so was she. Her hair and eyes were more of a welcome jolt to his system than the scorching caffeine.

Excited about her plans for the day, Garcia told the

concierge that they were ready to go. The concierge was well dressed in a conservative Wynn suit. He led them out the front door and loaded them in a black Escalade.

"Are you going to tell me what we're doing today, or is it a surprise?" Jim asked, noting she hadn't been forthcoming with her plans for the day.

"Well it's sort of a surprise," she said, smiling up at him. "I know we're not supposed to work today, but there are a couple places I've wanted to tour in Nevada that have never been high on the priority list when I've been down here before, so I hope you're ok with it."

"Well I'm not sure I could totally get my mind off work anyway, so anything interesting may help me prepare for my speeches. Just don't tell Lois," he winked.

It was a short trip to the McCarran airport and the driver pulled them up to the private field where a helicopter was already waiting for them.

"It's not as fancy as your machine, but it's all I could get on short notice," Garcia commented. "Come on, let's get in. First stop, Hoover Dam," she said with the enthusiasm of a tour guide.

The helicopter took off and gave them a tour of the strip. They could see Vegas was just waking up; street venders were out and the running shoe people were out for their early morning exercise. She'd booked a night fly-by as well once they returned at the end of the day. Part of the full day helicopter tour that Garcia had scheduled included landing near the dam where they were picked up by a personal tour guide in a golf cart that ran them quickly to the top of the dam. The engineering marvel built by hand, in the midst of the great depression, was a seven hundred and twenty-six-foot dam forged in devastatingly hot desert conditions at a time when the next closest competition was less than half the size of what this wall was.

Jim was inspired by the tour. He discovered that if all the concrete in the dam was laid out in a straight line, a road could be built with it across the entire United States. The dam produced two thousand megawatts of electricity per day and cost one hundred and forty million dollars to build in 1930, which in today's dollars would be equivalent of almost two point eight billion. The dam's inspirational story was enough to reinvigorate his own dream. He loved Garcia for taking him on this tour, knowing she'd chosen it for this exact reason. The underground walk in the coolness of the deep caves, seeing the massive generators at work, and listening to the history of the construction was relaxing without him even being aware.

Jim thought if this dam could be constructed in the middle of a barren desert with 1930s technology and equipment, he knew for a fact his team could construct a geothermal plant in the barren Arctic with 2020 technology.

Garcia was watching Jim and the tour seemed to be having the effect on him she that she'd been hoping for. He seemed to have a bit of a smile on his face, his eyes looked happy, and his posture was more relaxed. Once the tour of the dam was completed, the tour guide took them back to the helicopter and they once again lifted off. This time they flew over the Grand Canyon. They circled the glass observation deck that reached way out over the side of the Canyon for tourists to walk on and then flew down into the pit of the canyon where they landed on a small island in the middle of a flowing stream. Garcia saw this picnic package advertised by the helicopter company and could not resist. From an ice picnic to a desert picnic she loved the idea.

"Your dates are ice and mine are fire," she told Jim, grinning with pleasure and he laughed at her obvious enjoyment. "Helicopter picnics seem to be our standard date," she said teasingly. "What do you think of this place?"

Jim grabbed her around the waist as she was turning to grab the picnic basket out of the helicopter and pulled her to him. "Thank you for this day," he said, gazing into her eyes. "I feel better. The Hoover Dam was absolutely inspiring and renewed my faith in the fact that we can make this project work." He held her tight and kissed her deeply as the great cannon walls shaded them from the desert sun.

After eating lunch, they boarded the helicopter once more and took off for the Stillwater Two geothermal electrical plant. When they arrived, the plant manager met them on the helipad and personally escorted them around the facility. Garcia was treated like royalty based on her fame for geothermal designs and work in the industry. This geothermal plant happened to be one of the largest plants in the country and produced forty-seven megawatts of electricity per day.

The tour was very thorough, and Garcia and the plant

manager got into very specific details, which was great for Jim to hear. He was able to follow along, get a feel for the technology, but was not on the spot in the least nor was he expected to be. For once he was not the center of attention in a business event, Garcia had taken that roll here and Jim was grateful. This day was getting better and better for him. The sun was just setting as they flew off from the geo-plant and the night sky was up as they approached the city. The lights were bright and the light from the roof of the Luxor led them home. As they circled the strip they could see the running shoe people had been replaced with the high heel and wing-tipped crowd. Vegas was in all its glory, as it was every night.

Once back at the hotel, they changed and met down at the SW steak house for a meal that was unparalleled. In true Vegas extra style, they listened to a big green frog in a cowboy hat sing Garth Brooks' Friends in Low places while sitting on top a massive waterfall while they dined. Following the meal, they walked the casino floor and finally headed up to their rooms. Jim walked Garcia to her door and kissed her again and said good night. As he turned to go, she grabbed his hand and pulled him back into her arms and then into her room.

Jim was up early the next morning. They were flying out to Saudi Arabia that day and he wanted to get mentally prepared. He was down in a coffee shop having breakfast and could not help but think of the day before and would probably remember it as one of the greatest days of his life. Lois's encouragement and Garcia's plan had refocused him and he was ready to take on the world. Jason joined him for breakfast and they talked business. Jason had met up with some engineering buddies the day before and had started putting together some ideas for companies to use in the event they were successful in the Neom bid. After breakfast they returned to their rooms to pack up and planned to meet in the lobby in time to share a ride to the airport. It was a twenty-hour flight from Las Vegas to Riyadh, Saudi Arabia. Jim hadn't booked a private flight for this trip but they each had their own pod and he knew from experience that the ride on a long international flight was sometimes a lot smoother on a large plane than on smaller private jet and the service they received in first class was good. The only downfall was the long wait in the airports. The private airport lounge made the wait more bearable, allowing them time to work together to polish up Jim's speech.

CHAPTER 53

Richard and Kelly met up with Mike and Joe in Seattle. With the limited time they had, the men drew on their case file experience from the police force and forged a plan to execute two kidnappings with as much detail as they could, using all the information Kelly could provide them from the surveillance he'd completed. The following day they staged a dry run and then returned to their hotel rooms and made a few tweaks to their plan. Mike and Joe would do the actual kidnapping. Everyone seemed prepared and they were as ready as they had time to be.

"Get ready," Richard was giving his team a pep talk just before they left their hotel room the morning of the kidnapping. "We can't hesitate or second guess ourselves at any point. This has to be exact and we have to use maximum force when dealing with each victim because we need them to feel scared and hopeless. Flight or fight will kick in for any cornered person, just like an animal. If Peter thinks he sees a weakness in our actions he'll try and exploit it with everything he has. Remember, we might know we're not going to hurt them, but they don't. Peter and his daughter will be scared for their lives and if anyone is a dangerous opponent it's someone who thinks they're gonna die, so don't underestimate either of them."

The group nodded their understanding, their silence indicating the seriousness with which they were about to approach this task.

Mike and Joe positioned themselves and their vehicle just off the street that Peter's ride share would take him back to work on. It was an out-of-the-way alley Kelly had found and as far as he could tell had no official cameras of any kind. They had two large magnetic tarps, a cloth with a chloroform bottle, masks to protect themselves from the effects of the drug, and a special tool that could shoot out a knife and instantly puncture car tires.

Richard gave himself a crucial role, knowing that if his timing was off they'd miss their chance to kidnap Peter and they wouldn't get another one. He had to get it right and he had to do it by dealing with two major unpredictable variables, the driver of the ride share and the Seattle noon hour traffic. First Richard would force Peter's Uber off the road and distract the driver, then while Mike and Joe grabbed Peter and plied him with chloroform, Richard would take off to track down Peter's daughter and help Jeff abduct her from school.

CHAPTER 54

This was it. It'd been a long time since Richard had been both this nervous and excited about a mission and he'd never been on this side of the law before. Driving his new secondhand car he had bought for cash at one of those shady corner used car places, Richard's vehicle had no registration and just an old license plate that had not been renewed in ten years. He was parked ten spots up from the restaurant where Peter was having lunch and was watching him get in a yellow taxi. As the cab pulled out into traffic, Richard pulled out ahead of it and led the way down the street. Richard knew the route the cab would take back to the office building. Things were shaping up nicely, traffic was steady but flowing, he was staying roughly two car lengths ahead of the taxi and they'd been synchronized as they passed through two sets of street lights. The turn off onto the one-way street was approaching on his right, two hundred yards out. This was a crucial cog in the plan. If the taxi didn't turn down this street, their plan was bust. Trying to keep himself positive, Richard thought there was no reason why the driver wouldn't take this route, short of fate working against him and his team, but stranger things have happened. The two-hundred-yard drive was the longest of his life. He stayed two car lengths ahead of the cab and now he was a hundred yards out. At fifty yards Richard put on his turning light and got into the right lane. In a moment of panic, he thought the cab wasn't going to follow, but then the driver signaled and moved into the turning lane as well. At the ten-yard mark Richard signaled again and turned onto the far left lane of the two lane street. The cab followed his turn but stayed in the right lane a couple lengths behind him.

So far so good. Richard needed to force the cab to turn onto the upcoming side street two blocks ahead without causing too much of a commotion. As a police officer he'd been taught driving techniques that included safe apprehension of suspects fleeing in motor vehicles. In those cases, he had other officers in cars with him, but in this case he needed to make the plan work alone. Because the cab driver was not fleeing anything, just taking a fare back to work, Richard decided to make the move as civilized as he could. He put the cab into his car's blind spot, which any seasoned driver would quickly recognize, especially a cab driver who spent his days transporting people and avoiding collisions in order to keep his insurance premiums low. With any luck when

Richard suddenly pulled into the cab's lane, the careful cab driver would see it as his lucky day and turn right up the side street to avoid a collision. If not, Richard would be forced to jump out of his car and commandeer the cab at gun point. Richard was in full disguise but really didn't want to rely on it. The more interaction there was, the greater the chance of getting caught or letting Peter escape.

With half a block to go, Richard pulled into position just ahead of the cab. Just as they broke into the intersection, he swerved right. The cab driver laid on his horn but Richard kept going. Right on cue the driver twisted the wheel and turned up the side street. Richard hit the brakes and started backing up. The driver in the vehicle that was behind the cab was shaking his head as he pulled out to the left and drove past Richard's car. Richard followed the cabbie down the back alley. It was a single lane and came out one street over. As he had hoped, the cab driver had decided it would be easier to just go around then to back up and try to get going on the one-way again. With Richard following behind at a safe distance, the cab driver didn't get suspicious. Peter was still ranting about the asshole who basically forced them off the road and swearing some people should not be allowed licenses when the cab driver swore and hammered on the breaks. Right in front of the car in the middle of the road was fifteen or twenty large cinder blocks barricading the entire road.

"What the hell," Peter yelled when the cabbie slammed on the breaks, then looked up saw the blocks and swore again. "Well we're going to have to move them or back up," he instructed the cab driver. Both men were just opening their doors when the world went black. Mike and Joe threw the large car covers over the cab and the magnets held it in place perfectly. Joe ran around and popped all four of the cab's tires while Joe cut a hole through the tarp, broke the back window, and sprayed chloroform into the cab. Both Peter and the cabbie were lights out within seconds. They grabbed Peter, tied and gaged him, put him in a mover crate, gave him another shot of chloroform for good measure and then put the crate into the back of their truck. They took the tarp off the cab, stole the cabbie's cell phone and radio, left the windows open so he could get air, and took off to the rental apartment where they would join the workers in progress as they moved Kelly into his new apartment. The whole operation took less than five minutes and the team breathed a collective sigh of relief that the first phase of their plan had gone smoothly.

Once the cinder blocks were moved, Richard left the scene and headed towards Peter's daughter's school. It was a private school that offered its students a shuttle service. The service chauffeured the privileged children home or to their after school activities during times when their parents were too busy to drive their kids themselves. Jeff was already at the school when Richard pulled up. Jeff pointed out that eight-year-old Cindy Fairchild had boarded the second van in the line of shuttle vehicles and told Richard that if things went according to plan, she would be dropped off at The Seattle School of Music in about ten minutes. Jeff further indicated that once the driver saw Cindy safely enter the school he'd move on to his next stop. Timing would be everything for Jeff to successfully execute Cindy's abduction. He needed to be walking out the door of the school just as she walked in and flash her with enough chloroform to make her look like a sick or extremely tired kid. He'd then pick her up and carry her like she was his own daughter right out the school doors and load her into Richard's car.

Richard pulled out, passed the student van, and drove on ahead to the school of music. Richard let Jeff out of the car a few blocks from the school so no one could identify the vehicle. This part of the plan was the riskiest for Jeff and Richard because the school had security cameras. Jeff had to look respectable enough not to draw attention but far enough from himself so that he'd be unrecognizable on video. Richard had to admit he wouldn't recognize Jeff if he didn't know him. Not only was he wearing a convincing disguise, he'd even adjusted his walk. The student van was just pulling up to the curb as Jeff walked through the school doors. Cindy was the only student to get off the bus and as any eight-year-old kid would, she took her time meandering her way up the walk. At one point Richard wondered if she'd even remember to go into the school. She was singing to herself, dancing in circles, looking at the sky, then the ground, then the sky again. Finally, in about double the time it should have taken, she went through the front door and the bus driver sped off. He took off in a hurry, obviously annoyed at having to wait so long for her too. About thirty seconds later, Jeff came walking out of the school with what appeared to be a sick kid in his arms. He was using his stooped-over, adjusted gait, which meant things must be going according to plan if he had time to concentrate on disguising his walk. Jeff walked right over to Richard's car, which was parked around the block from the school and safely out of any camera sight. He loaded himself and the girl in the back seat and Richard took off. By this time, Cindy was sound asleep from the effects of the chloroform. Jeff folded down the back seat, got out the small moving box and gently put the girl in it. He then changed into a pair of mover's overhauls and jumped out behind the moving truck with the box in his hands and walked into the building and went right up the stairs to Kelly's apartment.

Richard took off and parked the car on a side street blocks away then walked back to the apartment. If the car was still there in a week's time, he would use it to take Peter and his daughter to the drop off point. The movers were just finishing up as Richard walked past them and entered the building. He saw their truck pull away from the curb as the elevator doors closed to take him up to Kelly's apartment. Jeff had just got off the elevator on the ground floor as Richard was getting on. They tried their best not to acknowledge each other as they passed by. Jeff was on his way to catch up with Jim Dunsmuir and his crew as they headed to Saudi Arabia.

Richard got off the elevator two floors above Kelly's and then followed the staircase down to the renovation floor. Mike, Joe and Kelly had their prisoners bound and gagged when Jim got there, both were still sleeping off the effects of the chloroform. When Cindy started to stir, Mike gave her another breath of the drug so she would stay under longer. They needed her dad to see her before they separated the two. When Peter woke up, only a well-disguised Kelly was in the room. As predicted, Peter struggled to break out of his restraints but once he realized his efforts were futile, he concentrated on Kelly. Kelly simply pointed towards Cindy and waited for the recognition to come into Peter's eyes. Once that happened, he signaled for the others to take the girl away.

CHAPTER 55

"Peter we know who you are, we have you and your daughter. You have no idea where we are or even what city we're in, let alone what date today is," Kelly was laying it on thick. "Here's the deal, Peter. We've gagged you for two reasons; one to save our ears, the other to save your voice. Now I'll take the gag off soon and you can yell and scream all you want but no one will hear you because we're in a remote location. It's up to you if you believe me or not, but the better you behave, the sooner this will all be over. I'm going to lay this out for you short and sweet, so pay attention. We've hacked you. In ten hours, your company will go on sale in the corporate market place. We already have three bidders lined up that we've been talking to under the pretense of being you. The bidding will close in twelve hours and we'll pick our winner in fifteen. Of course, unknown to them, the winning bidder has already been established and we'll accept their check through a proxy. You'll then sign the sale documents from here and eventually the check over to us where we'll then quickly disperse the funds into our offshore bank accounts. Yes, you'll be flat broke, but you and your daughter will be returned home unharmed."

In order to make the charade believable, Kelly had devised a fictional yet very detailed robbery story. The tale consisted of Peter cheating him out of a very lucrative business deal that left Kelly for broke while Peter raked in the cash. This was the type of situation Peter had been a part of many times over in his career so he knew the idea would be believable. Peter also had to believe the kidnapper was not just out for money but wanted to actually hurt him. Peter had to be taken past the fact that this kidnapping was a negotiation or a business transaction. He had to be broken to be made to believe he had two choices. Either A, give up all his money or B, his daughter would be killed in front of him for refusing. He had to understand there was no room for negotiations; it was all or nothing, black or white with no middle ground. So, Kelly continued.

"Peter, you cheated me out of my entire life's work and left me with nothing. It's taken me years to get revenge, but now it's my turn to repay you, and I intend to do just that. Just like you left me with nothing, now, I'll leave you with the same." Peter glared at Kelly as he was forced to listen.

"Peter you need to know this, and I want you to really hear what I'm about to say. You're going to walk away from this with no permanent physical damage. Your daughter may or may not. If you pay, she goes free. If not, she will be tortured and killed. You need to know this is not a negotiation, it's an ultimatum and you have a choice to make. Your company's gone either way once it goes on the market. If you don't sell you will be tied up in legal battles for years. You're rich but these Capital Equity funds are richer. You can't beat them, and they can't afford to look weak. Your choice comes down to your money or your daughter's life, period. We're going to give you ten minutes to think because I know this is a lot to take in, and then I'll be back so you can give me your decision. And Peter, I want to make this very clear. We're dead serious. To prove that I'm going to leave you with something to consider." With that Kelly nodded at Joe. Joe walked up, grabbed Peter's baby finger on his left hand and broke it. Peter howled in pain, but the gag muted it to a small hoarse cry. Joe then pulled first aid supplies out of his pocket, set and splinted the broken digit. Then they left Peter alone.

Peter was absolutely terrified and furious all at the same time. How the hell could this have happened to him and who were these guys? He pulled at the ropes that bound him to the chair, wiggled his face to try and get out of the gag, soon realizing it was an impossible task. A large digital clock appeared and was counting down ten minutes right in front of him. He couldn't believe these assholes had Cindy. How the hell was that possible, he thought again. His hand hurt like hell, but he needed to think how he was going to get out of this. He needed to cut a deal. There was still eight minutes on the clock, but he wanted to talk now, god dammit. He itched all over, his head was spinning from the drug they gave him, and he was sweating like a pig. At this rate he'd pass out before the ten minutes was up. He needed to calm himself and prepare to negotiate.

Richard, Kelly, Joe and Mike observed Peter's actions on camera. He was restless and mad. They'd locked Cindy up and told her she would just need to wait for her father. They told her he was in a meeting and he'd take her home as soon as he was done. The guys had made her a very nice playroom, full of toys and snacks. They knew if she didn't get scared or worried she'd be fine. She was already playing with dolls and had been eyeing up the IPad that was loaded with games. At the ten-minute mark, Joe went and stood behind Peter again. Kelly stood in front of him, both men were extremely well disguised, and Kelly had adapted his voice. He nodded his head at Joe, when Joe walked up to Peter's chair, Kelly saw Peter cringe which was just the reaction he was hoping for. Joe reached out and removed Peter's gag. Peter glared at Kelly but didn't say anything.

"Well, Peter what have you decided? Before you answer, keep in mind this is not a negotiation. Your answer needs to be one or the other. I'll not entertain anything else so don't even try. Now what's your decision?"

Peter continued to stare at his captor. The room had dingy lighting at best and it was located in some kind of construction or renovation area. He'd not heard any outside noises so it was obviously a secluded location or very well insulated. The men seemed to be very well organized to the point of military precision and their actions confused him. Normally people want some type of personal gain in situations like this; why would anyone take this risk without demanding a reward? Not only did it confuse him, it worried him because these men really didn't seem to want anything except to see him suffer. In Peter's world, though, he believed everyone had a price and he needed to figure out what that was. He knew he was working from a weak position. But any amount of payment would be better than losing his company, or worse yet, losing to these bastard thieves in general. Finding out people's price, negotiating and cutting deals was Peter's forte and he was determined to use that to his advantage here.

"Why are you doing this?" He demanded, trying to gain the upper hand by making it sound like he was in control. "What do you gain by hurting me and my daughter? I don't know what you're getting paid for this, but I'll double it. You said I ruined your life and your business, so rather than hurt me, let me make it right. I'll buy it for whatever you think it's worth, or better yet, make you a partner and you can run it yourself. What do you say?"

"I say I gave you a choice, Peter," Kelly's voice was furious and he was clearly out of patience. "I told you this was binary, black or white, A or B, and warned you that you needed to understand that. I'll give you ten more minutes to let it sink in then, I'll ask you the same question again. If you still don't answer, the next time it won't be you who suffers." As he finished threatening Peter, a TV monitor turned on and Peter could see his daughter in a pink room playing with toys. Kelly's hint was obvious. The monitor went black and Kelly turned and walked away.

Peter saw Joe approach him and turned his negotiating skills on him. "Good, he's gone," Peter said quietly. "Let's make a dea…". Peter never got the rest of his word out when Joe reapplied the gag, reached over and broke Peter's ring finger. They both heard it snap like a yellow number two pencil breaking in half. Peter howled into his gag once again. Joe reached into his pocket and, in a very similar fashion, reset the finger, applied a splint and walked casually off to the meeting room. Joe was doing his best to make Peter think breaking his bones was as meaningless to him as tying his shoe, but he sure hoped that would be the last finger. He wasn't cut out for the part of ruthless villain.

The throbbing in Peter's hand had extended into his arm. His discomfort was incredible and seemed to escalate with each heartbeat, as did his panic. Peter could tell his mind was failing him due to the stress and pain; he wasn't able to hold any form of concentration that would allow himself to plan a way out.

He knew he had to keep his business and his money. He thought these guys were pros but didn't believe they'd ever hurt an eight-year-old child. His confidence rose when he realized he'd caught their bluff; they'd played their hand too early in the game. When he tried to buy them again and they didn't hurt Cindy, which he knew they wouldn't, he'd win, and the negotiations could truly start. When the timer ran out for the second time, Joe and Kelly resumed their positions and Peter's gag was once again removed.

This time he started the conversation. "Okay, guys I've thought about this and I'm sure you have too. Getting away with all this won't be easy, so let me help you. I can offer you such a good deal, tell me a price and I'll pay double it, no questions asked. I won't investigate or press charges, just let me out of here and I'll set up any type of payment plan you want," Peter said, keeping his voice calm and relaxed, like a good salesman.

Kelly just started shaking his head, motioning his disbelief at Peter's stupidity. The TV monitor came back on showing little Cindy playing in her cell. The door opened and she looked up towards the figure standing in the doorway. The camera showed Mike as he entered the room and walked towards her. Kelly glanced towards Peter and saw a nervous look cross his face and then looked back at the camera in time to see Mike pull his foot back and kick out with massive force, striking the child right in the middle of her face. Her head snapped back and she went flying against the wall. Peter heard a sickening scream from the room and was shocked into silence. The monitor turned off and the screen went blank.

Peter lost control. He surged and roared against his gag and bindings, his face was a picture of purple rage. The captors waited patiently for him to regain control of his emotions. Once he reined himself in, Kelly walked back up to him.

"Peter this seems to be a hard concept for you," Kelly said patronizingly. I thought it would take you some time to figure out this isn't a negotiation, but you didn't seem to get it. I can see by the look on your face it's starting to sink in now, though. I'm about to give you fourteen hours to contemplate your choices. At that time, I'll be standing in front of you with papers to sign and a check for a couple hundred million and you'll have a choice to make. Freedom for you and your daughter or freedom and no daughter. It'll be a nasty court battle for your company or your daughter's life. I want you to think hard on this."

"A few hundred million," Peter mocked. "Are you idiots? I'm worth closer to a billion and if I was selling my company, I'd get a billion."

"This is a fire sale, Peter, we needed to make sure the sale was fast and easy with no risk for the buyer. You sign it over and you and your daughter walk free. If you don't, she dies. See you in a few hours," Kelly said then turned and left the room.

Joe stepped up, after re-gagging Peter, Joe reached out for Peter's hand, causing Peter to jerk so hard against his restraints Joe thought he may have done Joe's job for him and broken his own bones. Joe just patted Peter's broken hand and walked out of the room. The men could see the tears and terror that had formed in Peter's eyes from the monitors in their makeshift office.

"Good work, Mike," Richard complimented. "The kick in the face and scream was Oscar style acting. It made me sick to watch and I knew it was fake. All right guys let's settle in, we have a bit of wait. Mike can you go tend to Cindy? Tell her snacks are in the fridge, her dad will just be a little longer. Let's pray this works."

CHAPTER 56

Jeff found out that Jim and his crew would be leaving Vegas the following day on a flight to Riyadh. He decided there was no sense in him flying back to Vegas just to follow Jim out to Saudi Arabia so he booked himself on a flight from Seattle to New York and then on to Saudi Arabia. Jeff was feeling the pressure; he didn't have to be as successful as Mike or Kelly had to be. He didn't have to get two men to completely back out of a massive business deal. He did, however, have to orchestrate a credible looking attack on the life of Jim Dunsmuir, in a communist country, during an event when the eyes of the world would be on this very event. The Arabian government wouldn't put up with a terrorist type attack that would make them a target of the world's shame. If he was caught, punishment would be severe and he tried not to think of the consequences. His flight time from Seattle to New York was six hours and from New York to Riyadh was another fifteen hours on top of that. His jet lag was going to be tremendous so he knew he needed to get his planning done early on the trip while he was fresh, so he could rest up for his mission.

CHAPTER 57

Jim and his team landed in Riyadh around two am, but even at that time of night a limousine was there to pick them up for the half hour ride to the Four Season hotel where they would be staying. It was a beautiful hotel and the venue for the G8 summit. Once checked in, they all headed straight for their rooms, desperate to just get settled in and go to sleep. No matter how great the accommodations are on a plane, jet lag always catches up. Knowing this, Jim was anxious to sleep it off so he could be fully prepared to give his speech in two days' time. Once in his room, he turned the bedding down and took a moment to call Garcia and Jason and made plans to meet up with them at nine the following morning for breakfast. Laying down, Jim closed his eyes and willed sleep to come.

Jeff landed not long after Jim and company, but he

didn't follow them to the Four Seasons. He knew the Four Seasons had state-of-the-art security and the chances of him getting caught would be greatly enhanced if he stayed in that hotel. Based on that knowledge, Jeff elected to stay at a run-of-the-mill hotel a few blocks away from the Seasons. He also went to bed as soon as he checked in, but like his targets, was up early with work to do. Jeff didn't have the luxury of taking time to sleep off his jet lag; he had supplies to buy and needed a way to implement his plan. Jeff had already decided to go with Richard's Molotov cocktail suggestion. There was something terrifying about those bombs; they were crude, unsophisticated and deadly and they had the same scare effect that staring down the barrel of a loaded shot gun did. There were so many more sophisticated weapons in the world, but few could strike fear into a person like hearing a shot gun rack and having a big scatter gun pointed at your chest. The same could be said about a Molotov cocktail strike as a victim thought about burning to death.

Jeff decided to make his cocktail a virgin. Instead of using a standard oil-based product as a fuel that could not easily be extinguished, would burn for many minutes at high temperatures, and rapidly spread upon explosion, he decided to use a petroleum-based fuel instead. The petroleum compound would give the bomb the same dramatic flair but the fuel would burn off fast. If it did happen to land on someone, its high flash point would burn off quickly and leave minimal damage. First thing tomorrow, he'd buy himself what he needed for clothes and props to fit in as a local.

Luckily for Jeff, a loose-fitting "thawb" was the style in Saudi Arabia and while wearing one he could easily conceal his bomb. Jeff would buy what he needed to make it look like he had his right arm in a sling, thinking that with a fake injured arm, he could conceal his real arm inside the thwab and still be fully able to throw his homemade cocktail around it. The disguise would be as good as he could muster and would hopefully take any suspicion off him if he was seen on a camera or noticed by authorities after the fact before he had a chance to get away. The second part of his plan would be to pay a kid in the street to deliver a message to the Four Seasons. The message would simply say, "You were warned in Vegas, last chance."

The following day was a busy one for each side. Jeff vs Jim, each was preparing for the main event. Like in horse racing, each champion was carrying his own lead weights to make the competition fair. Jim was unknowingly invited to the race, but not only did he not know he was in a competition, he was also not introduced to his adversary. He was, however, being treated like royalty in the country of Saudi Arabia, preparing to give a state of the Union Address to the G8 on sustainable development. Not only was he there to advocate for renewable energy, but he knew he had to take advantage of this opportunity to try and sufficiently impress the Arab Princes by subliminally convincing them that he and his company were the correct choice to power Neom. Jeff, on the other hand, had the benefit of knowing his goal and his adversary, but he was a visitor in a country that had little tolerance for strangers, let alone a foreigner trying to disgrace a world-class event that was of extreme importance to its Crown Prince. His lead weight was that he had to operate with such extreme caution and precise timing that he could easily miss his opportunity. Worse, if he was caught, life in prison was likely the best he could hope for.

CHAPTER 58

For being an ancient city dating back to the mid-1500s, Riyadh was quite beautiful and a lot more modern than Garcia had anticipated. As she and Jim walked the main streets surrounding their hotel, while waiting for Lois, Ramsey and Alexandra to touch up Jim's speech for the final time, they tried to beat the 40°F summer heat. Even though they were dressed for it, they continually stepped in and out of well air-conditioned side stores to get some reprieve as they toured. Despite the uncomfortable heat, the couple walked along holding hands and simply enjoyed each other's company.

When Ramsey eventually sent Jim the finalized version, Garcia and Jim stopped at a Starbucks, ordered iced coffee, and sat down at a table to review the recent revisions. They had a corner table so Jim read the speech out loud to Garcia to see how it flowed from his lips and to see if the wording felt comfortable. He had it memorized for the most part so he didn't need to read much, which would make his presentation that much more effective. Alexandra had also created a digital display that would run in the background during Jim's speech that would start out boldly with symphony music, then gently quiet down to gentle background noise for the entirety of his twenty-minute speech. As he stated his last line, Jim would key the remote and ramp the music back up for a memorable finale. Through the entirety of the speech, green landscapes, clear blue oceans and pristine ice flows followed by majestic pictures of renewable energy plants of all kinds would be on display in rotation on large screens behind Jim. The goal was to get people excited about the future and all the possibilities going forward for mankind, with renewable energy as a focal point for those advances. The speech was incredible and the landscape photos were exceptional; Jim's team had helped him create an amazing keynote address.

While Jim and Garcia were able to explore and enjoy the better parts of the city as well as stay cool in some of the high-end shops, Jeff was trying to navigate his way through a rough section of town. He'd spoken to his hotel concierge and found out which parts of the city he should go to as a tourist and which ones he should avoid. Once he had his bearings, Jeff had a cab take him to the edge of a prime tourist spot and then walked out of the main area and lost himself in a crowd of locals who were sketchy at best. This area was exactly what he was looking for, knowing that if there was any camera coverage, it would be spotty at best. Jeff decided to buy a couple of wardrobes from a local street vendor and he quickly changed into one to help him blend in better and he kept the other in the package to wear during the main event. It was unbelievably hot. Jeff could see the cabby had the air conditioning on in the car but he was still sweating in the back seat and when he stepped out of the cab into the heat he could feel the heat waves burning at his lungs with every breath. Jeff had waited until early evening to do his shopping, hoping the forty-degree heat would've subsided a little bit. If it had, he was glad he had waited because he doubted he would've been able to make it far had it been any hotter. Jeff would've waited until even later at night but knew the streets would be too dangerous for him to be out on at that time. By going out just before supper there was still a bit of a safer crowd around even if he did have to endure the heat.

With his new clothes on, Jeff was set to shop. He needed two glass jars, one that would fit inside the other, a cotton rag about two feet long, hi-test gasoline, some flammable petroleum jelly, a bottle cork and a good lighter. Most cocktails are just a gas soaked rag that gets lit on fire and when the glass bottle breaks it splashes its flammable liquid all over its target and catches everything in its path on fire. Jeff wanted to make his bomb more of a show and less of a danger so he needed a different design than the typical Molotov recipe.

Once he had his supplies safely packed in the nap sack he'd also purchased, he headed back to the right side of town and caught a taxi back to his hotel. Once back in his room, he stored his purchases in his closet, had a shower to cool off, then went down to the hotel restaurant for a late dinner. While he was waiting for his main course to be served, he sent Richard an update on his progress. Richard's response was almost immediate, indicating that Richard understood and approved Jeff's actions. He also stated briefly that things were progressing on their end as well. Jeff understood Richard's response to mean that things were advancing with Peter Fairchild and his daughter but were obviously not finished yet.

Jeff had ordered a mix of wheat, rice and lamb; not a meal he'd normally order but thought he'd try it and was pleasantly surprised. Following the meal, he returned to his room, made sure to double lock the door, and then retrieved the nap sack out of his closet and removed his newly purchased items and placed them on the hotel room desk. As Jeff assembled the virgin Molotov cocktail, he mentally played out how he would deploy the device. Once the bomb was complete, he started to work on his fake arm and sling. The Arabian robe was the perfect attire for hiding his device. He'd purchased a shoulder and arm sling from a pharmacy, used a couple of small rods and towels carefully woven together to create a very believable looking injured arm that he could attach to his shoulder with the shoulder sling. He then wrapped the arm with a sling that made it look like his hand was inside the dressing. The fake injured arm also provided him with extra room under the robe to easily carry his bomb. His disguise worked better than he thought it would, which boosted his confidence. For a final touch, he sliced the robe under the injured arm and affixed Velcro to hold it together. He'd now be able to open the gown, throw the cocktail and then re-hide his real arm with very little disturbance to his clothing. The disguise was perfect, right down to a fake beard and turban, and Jeff knew that it had to be. In a very real way, his life depended on not getting caught. Jeff was ready. He had a map of the Four Seasons grounds, knew where Jim would be parked and roughly the time he'd be leaving. Jim would have his entourage with him, but that's what was great about a Molotov, no timers were necessary, just a high toss up over the guard's heads and it would land with a bang at the victim's feet. His plan was set.

CHAPTER 59

Peter's time was up. Kelly knew he had to play the bluff now or lose the edge. They had the fake sale papers and check in hand, drafted by a known investment capital firm, all they needed was for Peter to believe it. Kelly and Joe re-entered the room and could immediately tell Peter had lost his edge. It had been around fifteen hours since he'd been kidnapped and during that time he had been drugged and had bones broken. That's not even considering the mental anguish of having his daughter kidnapped and assaulted. Peter looked broken and exhausted. Interestingly enough, however, he had yet to ask about the condition of his daughter, which played into the kidnappers' hands. Joe took up position behind Peter's chair once again and Kelly stood in front of him.

Peter had been trying to think of a way out of this mess for the last few hours but hadn't come up with any definite plan. He'd done so much negotiating in his life, figuring out angles and leverage usually came naturally to him, but in this case he was lost. He didn't know how much of what they were saying was a bluff or the truth because he didn't know what they really wanted. Yet the way he was taken and the precision to which he'd been handled led him to conclude, as he'd assumed earlier, that these men were no amateurs. The choice between all his money and his daughter's life seemed ridiculous, yet there it was on the table. He didn't believe they'd really kill a young girl, but they'd thought nothing of breaking his bones and striking her in the face.

His money had to be their goal, Peter thought. If he was going to win, he had to take a page out of the government's book and not negotiate with terrorists. After all, what would stop them from killing Cindy and himself if he did sign the papers? In the end, Peter decided they must want his money. Going through with all of this was simply too risky for them not to have a massive pay day in mind. In his final hour of solitude, Peter had solidified his decision not to cooperate and held that decision in his mind as his captors reappeared in the room, positioning themselves in the same places as before, one in front and one to the rear.

As he stepped towards Peter, Kelly pushed a small table in front of him and placed the legal papers and check down on it.

"The choice is now, Peter. Sign over your company and walk out of here with your life and your daughter's or walk out of here on your own, with your company intact, but then start preparing a funeral for your child. Let me remind you for the last time. Don't try and negotiate with us. There's no negotiation. It's black or white. You saw what happened when you tried before. If you choose to sign, you will no doubt want confirmation that we'll keep our word, so here is what will happen. We'll gas you again and you'll wake up in a car with your daughter in a busy parking lot. A gun will be on both of you and we'll be set to gas you again. Our team will exit the car and the papers will be given to you to sign. If you sign, our team will disappear immediately and you'll be left to work your way out of the restraints. If you try anything else, your daughter will be shot and you will be left. Secondly, if you choose not to sign, your daughter will be killed and you will be released now. Two choices. As I said before, your gag is coming off. I need a decision."

"Fuck you guys," Peter growled the second his gag was out. "No way I'm signing my company over. I'll hunt you down and kill you for this."

"No, Peter," Kelly said, sighing with impatience. "You'll be released in the next 10 minutes if you don't sign."

"And Cindy?" Peter asked.

"Cindy won't survive. I told you the choices," Kelly reminded him.

"That's no choice. Money or family. How can I make that?" Peter asked.

"Most people would make that choice easily, Peter," Kelly scoffed. "But I'm not here to bargain. Choose now."

"I won't choose," Peter stated. Joe stepped up and put his hand on Peter's shoulder.

"You need to choose, and you need to do it now, Peter. There is not a third option," Kelly reiterated.

"I have other family that need me and my resources besides Cindy," Peter began to whine, recognizing he was beat. "What about them?"

Kelly could feel Peter cracking. "Peter, many people get along in life just fine without a couple hundred million, I'm sure you will too," Kelly had finally lost his patience and his temper. Slamming his hand down on the table, he yelled. "Enough of this. Choose now."

With that the camera to the playroom came on. The screen showed a masked man holding Cindy from behind. His hand was on her little shoulder and he'd forced her down on her knees looking away from him. He had a gun pointed at the back of her head. Peter stared in shocked horror. He couldn't believe these men had gone this far. Never for a moment did he think they'd go so far as to put a gun against his daughter's head execution-style.

"Your choice needs to be now, or we take it from you. Your daughter will be executed, your money will be gone, you'll become a severe cripple, and you will bear the responsibility of knowing you had the choice and decided to lose it all instead of saving some. I'm not negotiating. You have ten seconds to make a choice." As Kelly finished speaking, the big screen on the wall lit up and started counting down from ten. "When the clock hits zero," Kelly said, "your time is up."

Peter stared at his daughter on the screen and said in a whisper, "take her."

"What'd you say?" Kelly asked in disbelief, despite the fact that this was the reponse they'd not only expected, but had banked on.

Peter still didn't think they'd kill his daughter and felt he could call their bluff on that, but he also couldn't risk his company. He already had plans forming in his head on how he would hunt these men down and slaughter them. "You heard me," he said. "I said take her and let me out."

"Is that really your choice Peter?" Kelly asked, loud and clear, wanting to make certain the cameras were capturing Peter's final decision. "You're willing to sacrifice your daughter's life for your money?"

"Shut up and do it, I want out of here," Peter burst out.

Kelly acted, astonished but Peter had played right into their hand. "I'll give you one last chance, Peter. Sign the money over and you can spare her life."

"I made my choice," Peter said with conviction. "It's up to you now, big man," Peter mocked, still feeling mostly confident that he'd just called these men's bluff.

Kelly keyed the mike and said, "do it."

With no hesitation, the trigger was pulled, the gun shot echoed, and the child lurched forward and fell out of the camera view. Peter screamed. The cameras were shut off, Peter was chloroformed once again and put in a moving trunk.

The computer-generated image of his daughter's murder had worked just as well as it had when Peter had watched his daughter getting kicked in the face. The kidnappers gassed her as well and put her into a large suitcase. The men went up the stairs to a floor in the apartment that was not under construction and took the elevator down to the main floor. Richard and Joe quickly changed back into their moving man overhauls and face disguises, took the two items out the front door and loaded them into the large moving van they'd rented. They drove out of the district and after a forty-five-minute drive, pulled into a large big box store parking lot where they parked beside an old car they'd stashed in plain sight. It was dark so the men were easily able to open the suitcase and moving box, get the two people out of the containers and move them quickly into the back seat of the car. As far as they could tell no one had noticed or cared about their actions and there were no cameras close by that they'd been able to identify when they had surveyed the parking lot weeks ago. The two men then drove off in the truck with very specific plans to dispose of it.

CHAPTER 60

Richard had been carefully monitoring the news while he and his team held the father and daughter captive. The kidnapping became statewide news within hours of the event taking place. Cindy's school had quickly alerted the police when she was found not to be in attendance, after completing customary checks and she was still not found, the emergency alert system was activated. As the police investigated further, they found Peter's drugged out driver and following a quick interview with him, confirmed the theory that Peter had also been kidnapped. That's when the story broke nationally. A child victim meant a full red alert, a manhunt was instantly initiated, roadblocks and check points were quickly established, call centers and search teams were all set in motion. Cindy's mother and Peter's company offered significant rewards for their safe return. The prize was substantial enough that almost every bounty hunter and private investigation firm in America was on their way to Seattle to try and track down the prize.

News reports indicated that Peter's driver stated he'd been bumped off the road by a vehicle that cut into his lane. During the course of the interview the driver further stated that he couldn't remember the make of the vehicle nor did he have a description of the driver. He thought the situation seemed innocent at the time because he was in the blind spot of the other car and it pulled into his lane. He'd been worried about getting side-swiped so he swerved down a back alley intending to use it as a detour. Instead of backing up and turning around, he followed it along until he ran into a bunch of construction blocks in the middle of the street. He was just getting ready to back up when his car suddenly blacked out. Then all he really remembered was waking up in the front seat alone with no phone or money.

Cindy's school offered little more in the way of helpful information. The school's surveillance system showed what looked like a tired little girl being carried off in the arms of an unidentified man who walked with her until they were out of the school's camera range and from there it was anyone's guess what happened to her, presumably she was loaded into a vehicle and taken away. The news continued to report updates on the search but with no ransom demand and the kidnappers unusually silent, the authorities had little to work with. It was hard for them to track down clues with no motive to follow up on. After all, what was the point of kidnapping a billionaire and his child if money wasn't the goal?

Richard had been relieved that Kelly had found an apartment building located far enough away from the abduction site which situated the safe house outside the main search area. He'd also been happy to see that the story had basically gone viral so when they eventually released the recordings of Peter giving up his daughter's life for his money they'd have a national platform to put it on.

Richard and Kelly had been able to edit the tapes to perfection. The video showed Peter being abused to the point of realizing the kidnappers were serious, then being offered repeatedly the opportunity to save his daughter's life and walk away from the situation with both of their lives intact, all he had to do was give up his money. The video displayed how Peter watched with little to no reaction to his young daughter being brutally tortured. It then showed him watching the kidnappers put a gun execution-style to his daughter's head and how he told the kidnappers to kill his daughter so he could keep his money. The video actually showed Peter tell the kidnappers to kill his daughter a second time when they offered him another chance to walk away with his daughter. In the end it showed Peter watch as his daughter was executed for his greed.

Richard recorded the finished video on numerous flash drives, placed them in envelopes and worded them with Peter Fairchild's name. Email and media could easily be traced so he delivered them via a courier service he'd found in downtown Seattle to a couple major news agencies and numerous subsidiary news agencies.

CHAPTER 61

The story and video were just breaking publicly as Peter and his daughter were waking up in the back seat of the unmarked car. The video also contained same time footage of Cindy in a separate room while a look alike doll was being used as part of the torture scenario that Peter watched when he made his choice of money over his daughter. Peter would soon find out what the rest of the country knew, that his company was not sold; he still had his company, money and power, and that he'd been completely duped. No one would know why, but the world would see him as a weak man who willingly gave up his young daughter's life for his money in a complete act of cowardice. Peter's reputation as an American hero or cowboy was forever destroyed and he was nothing now but a disgraced has-been. Peter would spend the rest of his working career trying to rebuild his credibility. The story was picked up worldwide and the princes in Saudi Arabia soon heard about Peter's humiliation. Needless to say, Saudi's government was severely disappointed. They'd been excited about Fairchild's dam proposal and thought it was a great idea, but it was too late to find another bidder and they couldn't tie their country in with a man like Fairchild now. They quickly put out an official statement saying that they'd no longer be accepting a bid from Naes Construction for the Neom power build.

George was ecstatic over the news; his biggest competitor was out of the race. Richard and Kelly were beyond relieved to have the job over with, they and their team were headed home no worse for wear. The men were completely mentally and physically drained from the stress of executing the kidnapping, yet they still had one more job to do, not to mention Jeff's main attack on Jim in Saudi Arabia. Despite his exhaustion, Richard knew that there was no time to rest now. He could not afford to let his team lose their edge; they needed to move full steam into the next operation. They had a day to repack and reorganize their gear and then it was up and on to the business in the Hamptons.

CHAPTER 62

Jim was only an hour away from going on stage. Garcia was still shaken from the note that he'd received from a local who had just delivered it to their hotel that stated, "Remember Vegas, last chance". The note had upset Jim too, truth be told he was glad Garcia had also seen it because it gave him a chance to busy his mind by reassuring her that everything was alright, insisting it was just a typical threat some activist group was using to try and get a name built for their cause.

Jason had already called and did his best to give Jim a pep talk. Jim wasn't that nervous about giving the speech so much as he knew he needed to impress the Saudi Princes who would be in attendance. The G8 summit group had a management team hired to organize and prepare each meeting. Cynthia, the elected manager for this particular meeting, went on stage first and went through the typical housekeeping requirements. She introduced herself and her team, thanked everyone for attending, and let them know that if they needed anything at all she'd personally be available for the duration of the meetings. Cynthia then went on to point out everything from where the washrooms were located to the amenities of the beautiful Four Seasons hotel. Finally, she started her introduction of Jim. She provided a background on his career and embellished as much as she could in regard to his efforts in creating and maintaining renewable resources.

Cynthia then cut right to the chase by stating, "so with that introduction and without further ado, our keynote speaker for this event… please welcome Mr. Jim Dunsmuir."

Jim strode purposefully onto the stage, shook Cynthia's hand, made the appropriate acknowledgments for her very humbling introduction and started in on his speech. As always, the background effects that Alexandra was so good at creating for him stole the show. His words basically highlighted the multimedia presentation as opposed to the other way around. Jim could see his speech holding the attention and even provoking thought in his small but powerful audience. When he hit his key line, "The industrial world takes it for granted that our most powerful manmade resource can be created completely by renewable resources and *the titans* don't care…." He truly felt he made an impact, he could feel his audience agree with him and that fueled him on to a very strong finish that the crowd took to heart. As he was saying his thank you and goodbyes, the digital presentation ramped up to a solid symphonic ending that visually depicted nature at its finest.

Jim was clapped off stage as Cynthia reappeared to keep the meeting moving forward. As Jim was leaving the stage, Cynthia shook his hand, congratulating him on a great speech. As he made his way backstage, Garcia threw her arms around him in a big hug. It was their first public display of affection. The hug must have felt right because Jim didn't think a thing about it until sometime later.

They'd decided that following the speech they'd hang out at the symposium for an hour or so to mingle with anyone who wanted some time with Jim. He wasn't scheduled for any further involvement in the conference so they planned to head out and, in true showman's terms, leave them wanting more. The plan then was to fly back to Greenland and get back to work finishing up the proposal and making last-minute revisions based on any new information that came from this speaking engagement. They were then scheduled to fly back to Saudi Arabia for the official presentation in a week's time. Once they'd mingled and sampled the buffet table, Jeff, Jim and Garcia were ready to head out. The hotel supplied them with a small security detail that was more show for VIP clients than was actually of use or needed in the area, however with the dignitaries involved in the G8 meeting, the Crown Prince had authorized a highly trained security force to escort the meeting's high profile participants, of which Jim was one. The detail consisted of three men who led them out of the hotel and into the parking area.

CHAPTER 63

Jeff knew where Jim's car was parked and had been working out his timing on the street. He'd need to fall in line with the sidewalk traffic as it passed along the hotel parkade. Jeff knew he'd need to get a few steps behind Jim's entourage to stay out of their peripheral vision. He'd then have to shield the Cocktail with his body from people behind him and to the side. He had a lot of practice doing this with his gun during his detective days. Next he'd need to light the fuse under his robe and perform an invisible underhand toss that no one could see him do, which would not be an easy task. Jeff had now walked the set course seven times and gone through the motions of lighting and throwing the bomb each time. He was now waiting as inconspicuously as he could off to the side of the street. He wanted to move and to practice one last time but he couldn't risk missing the one and only opportunity he'd get. Jeff knew he may have a long time to wait but missing his chance wasn't an option so he had to be patient.

He'd been waiting for just over two hours when the back doors to the hotel opened. A well-dressed security guard led the way with Jim, Garcia and Jason in tow, followed by two more guards cut from the same cloth as the first. It was a now-or-never potentially life-changing event for him, either way. The pay day potential was huge however the risk of punishment for attempted murder, even if it wasn't an actual attempt, in Saudi Arabia no less, was terrifyingly unimaginable. Jeff had been part of many ops in the police force, had been in life threatening situations, had also preplanned and practiced this scenario many times, so he just let his training and instinct take over.

Jeff calmed his mind, tried not to over think and started walking. He was dressed like a local, so he made sure to walk with confidence and purpose like he knew where he was headed. There was a steady flow of pedestrians as was expected in a city of eight million. Jeff fell in step with them, shifted himself into a position he felt would be best to deploy his weapon without being seen and started to work on timing. He knew he had to light the bomb in fifteen steps then throw in twenty-three. Time had never gone so slow for him in his life. At eight steps he opened the velcro in his robe, at ten he reached inside with his hand lighter at the ready. He lit the lighter at eleven steps and put the flame to the wick at twelve. The rag started burning fast he turned his body away from the crowd and tossed the bomb up in a high arch right on his twenty third step. All in one motion he threw the bottle and then fell back in line with the pedestrian traffic. The flame from the wick was not as noticeable in the bright desert sun as it would have been at night. Out the corner of his eye he watched the bomb fly up in a high rainbow arc; to Jeff the flying bottle was as obvious as a sore thumb, however no one else seemed to notice. The bomb flew up over the heads of the small group and smashed into the ground right in front of the lead officer. The Molotov Cocktail worked perfectly. It exploded in a huge flame and burst fire in all directions, hitting no one. Jeff reacted with the crowd on the street as the security officers screamed, he watched as the officers grabbed Jim and his crew and forcibly ran them back inside the building to find safety.

When the bottle smashed against the ground and flames burst from the point of impact, Jim and the whole group slammed to a stop. Once the realization came over them that they were under attack they back pedaled away from the explosion. Garcia was transfixed on the fire, Jim grabbed her arm and pulled her towards him. Jason was in the process of turning back towards the hotel when the security guards took action, the three men encircled their clients, grabbed them by the arms and guided them back into the hotel at a run. Once back in the confines of the hotel they were immediately checked over by the health care professionals that were on standby for the summit. It was quickly determined that none of them were hurt or burned.

SUSTAINABILITY

Following medical clearance, the security detail was ordered to escort Jim, Garcia and Jason directly to the roof of the Four Seasons Hotel where the Prince's helicopter awaited to fly them to the airport. As it turned out, the Crown Prince decided not take any chances with one of his VIP guests, so he had the pilot fly them all the way to Switzerland in his helicopter and then from Switzerland back to Iceland on his private jet. He made his security detail travel with them and then had his personal assistant pack up all their belongings from the hotel and courier them directly back to Iceland.

CHAPTER 64

As Richard and his men made their way from Seattle to the Hamptons they were on a nervous high. The Fairchild operation was now behind them and so far they had gotten away with it. No one had been seriously hurt, no money was lost and both victims were released voluntarily. As former policemen, the guys knew there would be new priorities and emergencies taking over an already busy police department, but the file would remain open for as long Peter forced the issue and until some type of resolution could be found. They all knew that no crime is perfect and even though it went off as well as it could for them, it would be a couple years until they could feel safe again. Richard and Kelly had discussed the risks between themselves, eventually determining that they likely had more to worry about if Peter decided to hire his own investigators to try and figure out what happened than from the overtaxed police force. They knew Peter's vengeance would be a lot more severe than jail time would ever be, but it was too late to worry about that now. They needed to focus themselves and their team completely on threatening and scaring Chris Buchanan off the Neom project. To accomplish that meant they needed to check their emotions and be all business or they'd risk messing up the whole operation. Although not as potentially dangerous, this plan would take place in public surrounded by many witnesses. Richard wanted to push his men through and finish the op while they were still on an adrenaline rush; it was either that or give them time to crash, recuperate, and rebuild, and he knew they'd all just rather get this done.

Richard's thoughts shifted to Jeff, grateful that he was now safely airborne returning to the States following the successful completion of his mission in Saudi Arabia. Jim Dunsmuir, along with some of his key personnel, had been threatened to stand down from the Neom project.

CHAPTER 65

Mike and his family had successfully moved into the Hampton community and were well situated. Without officially getting into Chris's social circle, it had been easy enough to find out all there was to know about Chris's activities, or anyone else's for that matter. The community was small enough that everyone knew what everyone else did and it was always a topic of conversation at the right coffee shops.

There was an annual summer carnival, one of the biggest beach fairs of the year, happening this upcoming weekend near the Buchanan acreage. Chris had made it tradition to attend with his family every year for the past decade. From the information he could gather, Mike had determined that Chris would once again attend the event with his family. One of the most popular attractions was the Ferris wheel and social media had shown that Chris and his family rode it together every year without fail. Without being able to predict the future, Mike made an educated guess that this ride, at this event, needed to be the plan "A" attack on Chris Buchanan. Mike and his team would follow the family through the park and look for opportunities to attack the Buchanans, however the main objective would still be to take them at the Ferris wheel line up.

As per the plan, Mike had flown in on a private jet, returned to his rental home, and began finalizing plans and preparing for the next day's mission. Richard, Kelly and Joe rented rooms for cash in the most off grid hotel they could find in the Hamptons. This was no easy feat on a weekend during midsummer in arguably the best resort town in the world. They were each forced to stay in a different hotel just to find vacant rooms.

In an effort to create an airtight cover should an investigation ever be convened following this operation, they wanted to leave as minimal a trail as possible of their existence in the Hamptons. Their alibi would include wanting a low profile while they investigated concerns for numerous clients in the area. The alibi would be partially truthful in that immediately following their attack on Chris they would begin investigating real cases for other people in the area who had hired them. In order to further cover their tracks, they rented the hotel rooms for a full month.

Mike had scaled maps drawn of the carnival floor plan. He sent a detailed text of the plan along with the floor plan drawing to each of the men's burner cell phones. There was one entry and exit point to the event and he scheduled each person's arrival about twenty minutes apart. Each guy would take a separate route through the park to better understand the layout of the carnival's midway and to learn his specific exit route following the operation. The carnival was a large family event that single men didn't often go to by themselves. Mike would go with his wife and then they'd split up once inside the park. She only knew that Mike needed her to help his cover and then he'd need to go off on his own to work. Kelly, Richard and Joe would all enter the park separately and would do their best to dress to look as though they fit in. Summer clothes for men in the Hamptons involved dressed down versions of business attire. Open collar shirts, rolled up sleeves, linen jackets, soft pastel colors and loafers... a quick change of clothes and just like that each former cop looked like a relaxed Hampton dad who was taking his kids out for a day in the park. To further hide their identities, each man donned a stylish hat that matched the outfits and added just a little extra cover. At an event like this security would be tight, forcing the team to do all they could do to avoid cameras and video. Besides security surveillance, every family would be photographing each and every detail of the time they spent together on a day like this and of course every single person from age five and up would have a camera phone. Being the Hamptons, no one really expected any trouble so there wouldn't be any specific focus on trying to catch any shady characters, but investigations later would easily be able to find people and suspects in the back grounds of security footage and people's personal photos. In order to avoid unwanted suspicion, Mike had to build some fluidity into his plan. The men had the outline of a general plan in place and would keep a perimeter around Chris and his family as they moved through the park waiting for Mike to send out the text for them to deploy.

CHAPTER 66

"These threats are real and way more serious than we first thought in Vegas," Ramsey sounded surprised in his conference call with Jim who had phoned him from the Prince's private plane as it flew Jim, Garcia and Jason back to Iceland. "Whoever is trying to back us off this project has been able to get to you with little trouble and seems to have very thorough and well-executed plans of attack. I've been keeping in contact with the police and there's been no leads whatsoever in Vegas and even though the princes from Saudi Arabia looked after you very well following the bombing, it's very doubtful we'll ever hear word on any kind of investigation, if one even takes place," Ramsey said cynically, making clear his doubts about the justice system in Saudi Arabia. "I think we need to talk this over as a team and decide if we still want to proceed with making a bid on this project. We know what a potentially world changing project we could create if we're successful in winning the contract, but I'm not sure it's worth risking our lives over."

"Jim, Garcia, Jason are you okay?" Lois asked when Ramsey had finished, sounding deeply concerned. "Something like this goes beyond an initial scare. We're not programmed to deal with death threats, we don't know the effect this incident will have on any of us, but especially on you guys being directly involved. Your body and minds are going to crash in the next few hours, the adrenaline leaving your systems will finish you off, and you'll need two days of recuperating just to get back in shape. Until then most likely you'll feel exhausted and will be susceptible to negative thoughts and even viruses like colds and flus. You'll need to be as healthy as possible to build yourselves back up. I've already been in contact with some army psychiatrists to find out what they do to treat and diagnose PTSD in soldiers and civilians exposed to lethal danger for the first time. With any luck I can get you well on your way to a full recovery before anything negative takes hold."

As usual, Jason was quiet, Garcia was visibly shaken and sat clinging to Jim's arm, listening but not really in the moment. Recognizing their inability to converse, Jim responded for them all. "Ramsey, you're right. We'll need to take this threat way more seriously than we did in Vegas. Obviously we've left ourselves open for physical attack. We took all those precautions to shield ourselves from industrial espionage but never considered protecting our people physically and that can't happen again. We've dealt with harsh business and government practices before, but this is a whole new level. Lois, thanks for making those contacts with other psychiatrists. I need you to set up meetings for all of us as soon as we get back as we will need you to help us deal with this. Of course, I'm open to a team vote of some kind but at this point my plan is to very much walk into the Prince's Castle next week and present our plan for their consideration. We've worked too hard and the world has too much to gain if we're the successful bidders not to go ahead as planned." Still fueled by adrenaline and anger that his team had come under attack, Jim continued. "I find it interesting, as Ramsey pointed out, that three of the four bidders have now been attacked and, despite it being his own doing, Peter Fairchild has now been taken out of the running all together. There has to be a conspiracy at foot and we need to figure out how to deal with it which means we will have a lot of work to do when we get back. We'll be landing in a few hours so can you guys arrange to pick us up at the airport and get us home? Alex, can you and Lois work together to get us all the nutrition and supplements we need to bounce us back into shape? Start with snacks as soon as we get back and include breakfast in bed tomorrow morning, then plan for a working dinner meeting, we need to figure this out." Jim's natural leadership instincts took over.

"We'll get it done," Ramsey stated. "You guys try and relax the rest of the way home and we'll talk in a few hours."

"Agreed. Not sure how easy it will be to relax, but

we'll try, so unless anyone has anything else to add, we'll say good bye," Jim said. Everyone shook their heads and they signed off the line.

Back in the office, Ramsey, Lois and Alexandra looked at each other after they hung up. "Jim is going to push us forward on this," Lois predicted. "I can hear it in his voice that his mind is set. We're either going to have to vote him down or back him one hundred percent because if he didn't need our support completely before, he needs it now."

At thirty-six thousand feet, Jim started to feel the effects of jet lag and diminishing adrenaline. Garcia and Jason were already sleeping so he tried to calm himself down enough to relax but wasn't quite there yet. His body was dead tired and he knew it would take all his will power just to stand up right now if he had to. He was incredibly thankful for the private plane because he was able to stretch out and work on settling down. Jim knew enough not to make any decisions in the state he was in, but he did try to rein in the chaos of his jumbled thoughts. First and foremost, he needed to figure out a way to measure the true risk to himself and his team if he kept them in the running for the Neom bid. As he was thinking this, his mind drifted to Garcia. He was worried for her and felt bad for bringing her into this. He couldn't wait to get her safely home once they landed in Iceland. Focusing on spending time with her there, the thought brought peace to his mind and he drifted off to sleep, unaware that the mere thought of Garcia was enough to help him relax.

CHAPTER 67

The day had finally come for Mike to put his plan in place. His team's first three missions had gone off without a hitch and now it was his turn. They were down to the wire, it was a week before the Neom presentation in Saudi Arabia and they had one more competitor to scare away from pitching his bid. After weeks of planning and attending to details, Mike was ready.

Richard, on the other hand, was stressed. George had been on him constantly the last couple days. George's demands were nothing less than threats. Not once had he expressed gratitude that three of the four missions had been successful or that no one was hurt and Richard's guys hadn't been caught, he just demanded that Chris be forced out and that they got it done soon. Rich decided to keep George's threats to himself, he knew his guys were up for the task, but also knew it'd been a long few weeks and they were on the edge of breaking. If he added George's threats onto their already frazzled nerves, it would only add pressure to an already risky plan, so as the leader and the boss he decided to keep the information to himself and encourage the men instead. Richard pulled his burner out of his shorts pocket and sent a message to all.

"Okay guys, bottom of the ninth, we're way ahead in the game. We don't need anything out of the park, just a bunch of base runs and we win. Take it slow, Mike is point, he knows the target and the grounds. Lots of distractions around today so use something that will keep your minds focused. We all know our positions. Let's go guys, batter up."

Mike and Marcy were already in the park; they'd entered early so Mike could get a good feel for the grounds. Using the natural cover of a happy couple enjoying the park's atmosphere, Mike identified and reconfirmed the details and locations outlined in his plan. He was feeling confident. As they made their way to the live arts section of the midway, Marcy split off from Mike, knowing he had a job to do. In truth she had a strong interest in culture and was excited to take in as many of the shows as possible before needing to meet Mike in the car at the pre-arranged time.

Mike continued on his own down the midway to the casino area which was just starting to wind up. The casino offered the usual games of chance, everything from cards to roulette tables, but this one also had mini scale horse, dog and, in true Hampton style, sailboat races for people to bet on. This was the perfect spot for Mike to work from; there was a shaded restaurant area that had views of the main entrance and the gaming floor. Mike was able to blend into the scenery by joining the men already sitting on coffee row. From his vantage point Mike had a clear view of the park entrance and would know the moment Chris and his family entered the park.

Once he was in place, he replied "to all" in Richard's text saying he was set and ready. Mike's text was the cue for the others to join him in the park. Kelly came first and immersed himself in a group of people who got off a bright red tour bus. He snuck into the middle of the pack, trundling along with the herd, keeping his head down under the brim of his Lacoste ball hat. As far as Mike could tell there was only one set of cameras located strategically above the turnstiles to view the patrons as they entered and exited the park. If the guys continued on and followed Kelly's lead it was doubtful anyone would ever be able to pick them out on a camera replay.

Richard joined a group of people he assumed were attending a family reunion, it was a boisterous group of people busy talking forward and back to the people ahead and behind them in the line. Richard acted a little more animated than Kelly had so he would appear to fit in better with the group in the event there was ever a camera search. Richard also remembered to keep his head down and had covered his hair colour with a preppy plaid ball hat to further help hide his identity. Joe followed in a group much the same as Richard did about fifteen minutes after that.

When all the guys were in, they each strolled the park, reviewing the locations of the attractions and thinking through the possible contingency plans in the event things went sideways. They eventually converged on the area surrounding the Ferris wheel where they ultimately planned for the operation to go down. Once a recognizance of the grounds was complete, they each found a place to sit and portray the illusion of relaxed yuppies sipping their coffee until Mike sent them into action. With his team in place, Mike settled himself into the old stake out mode he'd mastered on the police force. He knew he could be waiting anywhere from twenty minutes to three hours for Chris and his family to arrive. He'd have to stay vigil and not let himself get over-excited at the risk of crashing mentally and physically before the operation went down. To help everyone stay sharp while they settled in to wait, Kelly shot out a text taking bets from the guys on estimated arrival times for the Buchanans. In the end it was Richard's guess that was closest and he won the fifteen-dollar pot. At the two-and-a-half-hour mark, Chris and his family arrived with a few friends and relatives. Mike observed the jovial group as they stumbled through the gates and headed towards the main street midway.

CHAPTER 68

Upon seeing Chris and his companions enter the park, Mike quickly sent out a text informing his crew of the situation. As their group took in the event, Chris and his wife followed behind, holding hands and smiling. They all headed for the snack bar and bought ice cream sandwiches, churros and every kind of soda imaginable. The group huddled up to eat and plan the day, then took off in different directions. Chris and his wife strolled off towards the boardwalk that led to the pier. Ten minutes later, they were at the end looking out over the ocean. Their kids Everette and Lacie were tagging along behind, but being kids they were running all over the dock, looking out over the edge, talking to the fishermen, and looking at all the hooks each one had.

Kelly followed along well behind the family. The park was not overly crowded, so he was easily able to keep them in sight. He slowly ate an ice cream cone as he walked along behind them, pretending to window shop in the different stores along the promenade. From different vantage points around the park the men all watched the family move down the pier enjoying each other's company. What they were about to do made Richard's stomach turn. He felt way worse for taking part in this mission than he did for his involvement in the kidnapping of Peter Fairchild. His team's violent actions were about to greatly upset many extremely nice people who didn't deserve it, not to mention ruin the family's yearly tradition and make them suffer PTSD for years to come. The only solace Richard could take in what they were doing was that he had no doubt in his mind that if he'd said no to George then George would've found and hired a group of men to execute these missions who would've had little to no regard for their victims' personal safety and wouldn't have sworn to abort any mission where one of the victims could be seriously hurt or killed. Beyond that thought, he needed to keep himself machine-like and focused on his mission or he wouldn't have the nerve to go through with it, especially when he saw how happy the family was together.

As the Buchanans came back down the pier, Richard moved in as the main shadow. Together the group had slowly meandered through the attractions, taking time to enjoy the atmosphere and now seemed to be heading in the direction of the Ferris wheel, which Mike had deduced was a yearly tradition for the family. As the Ferris wheel came into view they discovered the line up to be at least a half hour long. Richard began to worry that Chris and his family would decide not to bother with a wait that long, but like everyone else they happily lined up to wait their turn.

Once the family was in line it was time to put the plan into action. Mike swung into position at the end of the line. The waiting area was designed to have the patrons looking towards the park and the base of the ride, which was perfect for Mike and this part of his plan. Mike texted the others to say he was in position, gave them five minutes to take their positions, and then he was starting. The five minutes felt like an eternity, but Mike knew accuracy was critical so he set the timer on his phone and when the countdown hit zero, he put in motion the first step of his plan. As inconspicuously as he could, he threw a paper weight with a note wrapped to it that hit Chris right in the neck and fell at his feet. Mike had a few extra notes ready to go in case Chris didn't take the bait on the first one but like most people would have been in that situation, Chris was curious.

When he felt something hit him in the neck, Chris looked around to see what it was and that's when he noticed the strange object lying on the ground. Chris bent down and picked it up. His wife was mid-conversation with someone in line beside him, which worked in the team's favor, so when Chris opened up the note and read it he was easily able to slip it into his pocket without her reading it. Upon reading the note, Chris's face went white and he was visible shaken.

The note was simple, to the point, and effectively

terrifying for a father. "This is no joke, Chris Buchanan. Marcie, Everett and Lacie are in our sight. Pretend to be sick, sit out the ride on the bench right across from you. Make sure your family goes on the Ferris wheel and no harm will come to them. You'll receive further instructions at the bench."

Chris's ashen face and flustered manner easily allowed him to play the sick card. He whispered the news to his wife, she looked at him quickly with concern, but then nodded. She put a motherly hand on Lacie's shoulder and turned to continue her conversation. Kelly timed a walk behind the bench and placed a burner cell phone on it just as Chris turned away from the bench to sit down. Once sitting, Chris looked around and immediately noticed the phone beside him. He picked it up immediately when the quiet buzz went off indicating there was a text message.

With mounting dread, Chris read the threat that Mike had sent. "Chris you have two options. Option one, respond that you will drop your bid for the Neom project and inform the Princes that the plan does not fit your business profile at this time. Option two, we kill your family. We got to you this easy we can do it again. If you so much as leave the Hamptons prior to the bid next week or if we don't hear you've formally withdrawn your proposal, serious harm will come to those you love. Respond now."

Chris was shocked and visibly upset but he was not about to let bullies push him and his family around. He grabbed the phone and punched in an angry message back. "I don't back out of anything. First why should I believe you? Second, I can pay you more than you were given to attack my family."

Expecting this to be Chris's initial response, Mike was prepared with a response. "Chris this is not about money or business. This is about power. We have all the power right now and here is the proof of how close we are to you and how serious this is. Look up and find the man in line with the Red ball cap who is just behind your wife and kids. If you move from this spot they'll pay for your actions. The man in the hat has a gun and is a professional. I've just ordered him to shoot the man three people back in line from him. He's facing away from you right now and is wearing a black hat and a grey dress shirt. In twenty seconds, you'll hear the sound of a hoarse clap, which is actually the sound of a silenced Berretta M9A3. The man in the black hat will grab his arm about two seconds after you see a pink mist fly from his arm. My men will grab him and haul him off the grounds without anyone being the wiser. You'll have one minute following that time to respond to this text indicating that you're withdrawing from the Neom race or the next bullet goes in Lacie. This isn't a negotiation. It will happen, so choose wisely."

Chris couldn't believe his eyes. He had only asked one question and now someone might be shot. He looked up, saw the red hat indicated in the text, then looked back and saw the man in the black hat. His mind racing, he started searching the crowd for the security he knew had to be in place and was about to stand up and go for help when he remembered the part of the text the consequences of leaving the bench. Chris froze in place. Twenty seconds to the mark he heard a muffled clap mixed in with the crowd noise and he saw pink fly from the man's arm, then two hands seemed to come out of nowhere, grab him around the shoulder and haul him off into the crowd.

Horrified at what he'd just witnessed, and sick to his stomach that his family was so close to a cold-blooded gunman, Chris took a deep breath to try and calm himself. He looked back down at the phone to read the new text. "One minute and counting, Chris. Decide now."

Frantic to save his family and get them out of harm's way, Chris didn't need a minute. He didn't even need a second to make a decision like that. "You win," he texted. "I am out I'm out. Call them off."

Mike responded instantly. "Good choice, Chris, we have a deal. Your family is safe for now, if you renege on your end and fail to drop the Neom bid, Marcie, Everette and Lacie will pay for your decision. Now put the phone and note down on the bench and gently drop them off the back of the seat, so no one notices them. Then go tell your wife you feel better and will join them on the ride after all. Breath a word of this to no one, ever. Or we'll be back." Satisfied that he'd effectively terrified Chris, Mike sent the last message with a grim smile. He knew he'd won, but at what cost to a man whose only thought was for his family?

Chris, still visibly upset, responded with a simple, "k" and then very shakily pulled the note from his pocket, placed it on the bench and put the phone on top of it. Then he looked around and nonchalantly pushed both items onto the ground behind him. Chris then stood up and walked back to the line without looking back once. His mannerisms alone displayed the magnitude of love and fear he held for his family.

Richard's observations of these actions led him to fully believe Chris was out of the bidding race as he promised he would be. The men could tell Chris was deliberately standing with his back towards the bench. It was at this time that Kelly took the chance and walked through the area behind the bench, casually leaned down to 'tie his shoe', picked up the phone and note and kept on going. The other men watched Chris continuously through Kelly's recovery mission and all could testify that Chris never looked back or even attempted to see who was behind the threats made against him. Now that the mission was over, Richard oversaw each of his staff member's retreat from the park. When it appeared everyone was safely out and on their way, he relaxed a bit and watched Chris interact with his family. To Richard it appeared that Chris had completely forgotten about the threat and was now totally immersed in enjoying his family. While watching the scene he realized how fake their acting must have looked to anyone who'd been watching objectively, but for a man who loved his family completely, any threat looked real and nothing would be worse than losing those he loved. Seeing the joy Chris seemed to share with those he cared for made him think of Sara and wonder if he could ever get to that point in his life.

CHAPTER 69

Richard was the last to leave the park. As he settled in his car and started it, he pulled out his phone and sent one last text from this number. "Good work, men. Is everyone away safe? Remember, phones go in the ocean, clothes go in dumpsters. Any questions?"

Everyone responded with a yes, except Joe, who responded with a wise crack that helped relieve some of the tension they'd all been feeling. "Understood, Richard. Unless you want me to keep this black baseball cap of mine for a souvenir of the day you shot me?"

Then others jumped in with responses saying that next time it was their turn to shoot Joe because all of them had wanted to do it for a long time. Dark humor, but the edge was off at least, Richard thought.

Richard responded with a smile that felt natural and

light for the first time in weeks. "Sorry, boys. Being the boss has to have some perks."

Even though their acting had been bad, it was a quick attack that seemed to have worked. Richard would report to George that they were done and all the missions had been successful so it was up to him now. As he reflected on this last mission he thought the timing had gone pretty well. Joe had a very loud, very small Bluetooth speaker in his pocket, on which they played the pre-recorded sound of a silencer shooting a bullet. When the timing was right, Richard, wearing the red hat, hit send on his phone. The gun shot came out of Joe's jacket pocket aimed right at Chris sitting on the bench. Joe had been practicing spraying a blood type mist, jerking his body and then grabbing his arm following the sound of the gun shot. Kelly simply reached out facelessly from behind the crowd and pulled Joe away out of Chris's view. Mike should actually start writing action scenes for Hollywood, Rich thought dryly, and Joe could star in them. In order to complete the alibi, the men would now stay around and do some investigating in the Hampton area to complete their cover. They were simple jobs for the most part and would wrap up within a month or so. Following that, Richard would enlist Kelly and they'd lighten the load on the men a bit and give them some time off where they could spend some extended time regrouping. Richard let his head fall back against the back of the car seat before he began driving and allowed himself a minute of deep breathing. Finally, it was over.

CHAPTER 70

Jim, Garcia and Jason were greeted by the others at noon the following day when they got to the office with a catered meal and plan.

"Jim," Ramsey initiated the business conversation once the welcome-back pleasantries were out of the way. "Are we correct in assuming you still want to continue moving forward with bid for the Neom contract?"

"Absolutely I want this," Jim confirmed unequivocally. "The project is bigger than me and it's bigger than Neom. It'll change the world. Our design will globally enforce that renewable energy is efficient, reliable and, most importantly, profitable on a large scale. By showing profit at that level the governments will see that oil no longer has to be king and a healthy mix of both resources will take the planet safely into the future. The more I think about it, the attacks on us were scary, but superficial. Obviously whoever did it had us in their sights dead to rights twice and could have easily taken me or half our team out, but they didn't. I'm not sure why, but I think it was just scare tactics and now we say screw 'em and move forward. But I can't do it without all of you. We need to discuss this and decide as a team." Turning to Garcia and Jason, Jim looked to them first for their vote. "Garcia, Jason, you were with me through all of this, how do you feel? Do you think we should stay in the running or should we back out?"

Garcia didn't want to answer, as the newest member of the group and now Jim's girlfriend, she felt they all thought she would back him and probably didn't deserve an opinion at this point. Fortunately she was saved from having to speak first when Jason, who rarely offered his opinion about anything other than work, spoke up. "I'm with you, Jim and have been ever since you sold me on this idea in China. This project is world-changing; it's reenergized me. If you're still in, I'm still in. One hundred percent."

Jason's words were enough to reignite everyone's dreams and ambitions for the project. Without further discussion they immediately began moving forward, streamlining and putting the finishing touches on Jim's speech for the princes. The team double-checked the fine details, including everything from the financial estimates to the voltage drop and everything in between.

Jim, Lois, Jason and Ramsey would be flying back to Saudi Arabia in two days' time. Jim would practice the speech as many times as possible in the next couple of days, letting the rest of the team evaluate his delivery and ask him tough questions to prepare. The dress rehearsals were good practice but Jim knew no amount of practice could completely prepare him for the nerves he'd experience when presenting in real life. Jim hoped he was ready, he wanted this so badly. Jim was excited but exhausted as they packed up the office for the night. He was ready to go home, knowing he needed a good night sleep. When he and Garcia returned to her cabin for the night, they both realized they were ready for bed. Ramsey and Lois had stayed longer in the office discussing the events and trying to decide if they'd made the right decision. Eventually they came to the same answer. This project and its proposal could not be done halfway, they either needed to be all in or out. Since they had said they were in, they encouraged each other back into the right head space and went home excited for the upcoming days.

CHAPTER 71

Richard called George to report in on the success of their operations and to feel George out for an evaluation on how he thought the missions had gone. George was very complimentary toward Richard and his team, he said that if he won the bid, they'd have more than earned their money. Richard knew George was running on a high as well, half of his competition for probably the biggest job he'd ever do had now disappeared. George would be flying into Riyadh the next day and Robin Harms, his right-hand man, would be joining him personally to help with the presentation to the princes.

After talking to George, Richard called Sara. He didn't realize how much he missed her until the phone was ringing and he heard her voice on the other end of the line. She seemed excited to hear from him too and this further increased his good mood. Richard was beat from the stress of the last couple of weeks, but he'd do anything to see her now. Eventually they got to talking about Sara's upcoming holidays and they decided to meet up in a beautiful resort in middle America, basically take a holiday off the grid. Sara thought a holiday like that would be ideal, the slow pace would give them a chance to get to know each other better, and it would be nice to be able to travel in a country without having to worry about dangers around every corner. She was so ready to breathe the fresh country air.

CHAPTER 72

I t was taking longer for this day to arrive than any other great day the princes had ever anticipated in their lives; as they left the Crown Prince's downtown office in the back of the onyx black, twelve thousand pound Pullman Limousine heading for the Riyadh Four Seasons Hotel, Princes Sallmala and Shallen reflected back on what they had been anticipating for months.

Finally, their new city was about to become a tangible project and go beyond a conceptual idea. Yes, it was only awarding the electrical supply contract, but once this happened, they'd be on their way towards creating Neom and there'd be no turning back. They were disappointed they'd lost half their bidders on the project, but knew with a project this big it was going to take companies and men who could persevere. If two of the companies couldn't even make it to the bidding process, it was obvious they could never be trusted to construct the electrical infrastructure for a city that would have a larger population than many countries.

Their choice was now solar or geothermal power sources, both of which had been determined acceptable renewable energy sources by the Crown Prince, and he'd instructed the men to choose the one they felt would be most appropriate for their country. The King wanted his new city to be glorious and the Princes were going to make it just that. The scales were tipping in favor of Jim Dunsmuir at this point. The man was an international hero, he'd just given a tremendous speech on renewable energy at the World Summit in Saudi Arabia, following which there had been a terrorist attempt on the lives of him and his staff and yet he was still fully ready to return to the scene of the crime and compete for the contract.

"It's men like Jim that we want involved in our city," Sallmala was saying to Shallen. "Mr. Dunsmuir isn't doing this for money and he doesn't need the work. Obviously it'd be an ego trip for him, but it's more than that. You don't risk lives of your closest friends and family just for your ego. He's a true philanthropist, he wants to make the world a better place. Not many decadent Westerners would return to our country after the reception he got last time. In truth, we still owe him. He was a guest in our country and we allowed an attempt on his life. The embarrassment for us is great in this matter yet he has not tried to use it to his advantage at all."

"I agree," Shallen agreed without hesitation. "Jim is the one we want but we still need to do what's best for the country and the new city. Solar power is virtually maintenance free, we have acres of unusable sand ground coupled with the year round blazing desert sun. I'd be shocked if solar isn't at least fifty percent more efficient than geothermal power would be in be long run. Mr. Dunsmuir has to know that, though, and he'd be a fool to present us with a bid that couldn't compete. He must have something up his sleeve he thinks will match the efficiency of solar power."

"Both Dunsmuir Energy and Blade Solar arrive tonight, and although it's not fair to them, we need to make a bit of a spectacle of the bidding war. Both groups will be set up in the same hotel. We'll hold a media covered event tomorrow afternoon where everyone will be formally introduced after the Crown Prince announces the official beginning of Neom. We'll then follow up the conference with a private black tie reception at the Crown Prince's palace tomorrow night. Following an evening of socializing, we'll hold a semi-formal brunch the next morning back at the Four Seasons and then move right into project interviews." Sallmala reviewed the schedule they'd decided on when they'd realized they were down to two companies. "Let the games begin."

CHAPTER 73

Jim decided to ask Garcia to accompany him back to Saudi Arabia for the bidding process. Despite the fact that she'd been a target of a bomb because of him the last time she'd been there, she had still accepted the invitation and joined him along with Lois, Jason and Ramsey. The group flew into Heathrow from Iceland then chartered a private jet to Saudi Arabia. It was a six and half hour flight from Heathrow to their desert destination, and short of eating, the team used every second on board the luxurious plane to further prepare Jim for his presentation. Upon arriving in Riyadh, Jim's plane landed and taxied right into Sallmala's private hanger where they were met by a security team and escorted from the plane directly into Sallmala's Mercedes. Sallmala was waiting for them in the back of a magnificent limousine, while servants transferred the luggage from the plane to the car. Sallmala apologized formally once again on behalf of the Crown Prince and Saudi Arabia for the violent ordeal they'd endured on their last visit and assured them security would be tenfold what it was for the Summit meetings.

"It was a hell of an ordeal, for sure," Jim rationalized, "but things happen. People are unpredictable. My team and I accept your gracious apology and assure you that I don't hold you or the Crown responsible for the incident." Having the Princes beholden to him could be helpful to his cause, but Jim knew that if they felt he was trying to use the situation to his advantage they would hold it against him.

"We're headed back to the Four Seasons," Sallmala informed them. "We have floors blocked off for you and your competitor." Sallmala then went on to explain the agenda for the upcoming couple of days.

CHAPTER 74

George Anderson had also chartered a private flight for himself and Robin. Their flight time was about the same length as Jim's had been but they were flying in from the West. George's trip from Tangier to Riyadh was smooth, he and Robin didn't work as intently on preparing the Neom presentation as Jim and his team had. The duo had pressing work to complete on the Morocco solar project before they could concentrate completely on Neom. Upon landing in Riyadh, they too were escorted directly into a private hanger but this one belonged to Prince Shallen. In an almost identical manner, George and Robin were escorted directly from their plane into the back of Shallen's one point five million dollar armored limousine. The car was an identical twin, save the license plate numbers, to the Mercedes Sallmala had used to pick up the Dunsmuir Energy crew. All of the top ranking

Saudi Princes were afforded the beautiful Mercedes cars while the Crown Prince himself rode in a fleet of bright white custom designed Rolls-Royce Phantoms.

Shallen used the ride to the hotel to explain the agenda for the next couple of days to George and Robin. Although not happy with all the social events surrounding the bidding process, George was smart enough to feign excitement and accept the invitation to all the events. Once checked into their hotel, George immediately went to Robin's room and the two men began strategizing. They had to prepare for the meet and greet with the media the next day, then for the reception at the Crown Prince's Palace and finally for the bidding process itself. George knew that Jim Dunsmuir was heavily favored being that he had just spoken in Riyadh a few days ago and, as far as Jim and the Saudi's knew, Jim was almost murdered while he was supposed to be under the Saudi's personal protection. George knew the Saudi's would feel deeply embarrassed over the event and would now be doing all they could to make it up to Jim and his team. George would have to be charming, charismatic, and likeable in the social settings and then really impress during his interview because he knew Jim would out shine everyone during the social events. As he and Robin were putting the finishing touches on their presentation, inside his head George was weighing out the risks of running one more personal threat against Jim. He wanted Jim out of the running but he just needed to figure out the right threat and how to action it within the next day and a half.

CHAPTER 75

"I was worried I'd be shaking scared once I got back in this hotel," Garcia said to Jim as they settled into their room, "but I really don't feel nervous at all. Mind you, I'm not sure the president of the United States gets this much security! Sallmala has really gone all out to protect us. We're on the top floor of the Four Seasons in a hotel room that's bigger than most houses and furnished like a palace complete with bullet proof glass and guards outside our door. Sallmala said the floor below has been completely vacated and is under constant supervision by his security team."

"I feel the same way," Jim replied, "I'm not sure if it's the adrenaline from this deal, but I'm not in the least bit worried or thinking about what happened last time." He turned away from the suitcase he had been unpacking. "Come on, we need to meet the others in the restaurant.

It's going to be a long day tomorrow and I need all the energy I can get for the next couple days so I want to eat and get to sleep early."

"I hope you don't want to get to sleep too early when we get back," Garcia said with a tantalizing smile as she pressed herself up against him and kissed him longingly.

"Well maybe not right to sleep," he grinned and whispered into her ear as he returned the embrace.

Lois, Jason and Ramsey were already in the restaurant with a table next to a massive window overlooking a finely crafted swimming pool. The dining area was immaculate and obviously recently renovated in a luxurious contemporary style. The theme was dark wood bordered with soft decorative lighting and gold accents, as the couple sat down Ramsey was quick to point out that their competition was sitting at the other end of the restaurant. Jim took a quick look and noticed George and Robin were already eating their main course and seemed to be ignoring them so he turned back and said, "Let's eat."

Their food was exceptional and they kept the conversation light. Lois spoke about plans for her and Garcia to go shopping first thing in the morning to find clothes suitable for the Crown Prince's reception the following night. She had already spoken to the hotel staff and they would have the men sized up for tuxedo's right at the hotel but the women would have to go out shopping. Sallmala had already appointed a personal assistant to take her and Garcia to exactly the store they would need to go to for an appropriate wardrobe.

"Remember, folks," Ramsey reminded the team, "Neom is a major undertaking for the country so although we're all in a hurry to get to the bidding process, we need to play our part in the celebration. Our participation will go a long way towards earning respect and acceptance, which will bode well for us in our final goal."

As they stood to leave, Jim cleared his throat and said with grave sincerity, "Before we go, I just want to say that no matter the outcome in the next two days, I wouldn't change this experience or this team for anything. Thank you all for all your work and your commitment to this project." Not wanting to create an emotional scene, Jim reached for Garcia's hand and they headed off to their room before the conversation got any deeper.

CHAPTER 76

Ramsey had been right about this bidding war being a cause for celebration. The next day was a complete circus for the team. Lois and Garcia were awake at six so they could be shopping by eight when the stores opened. The women were so thankful for the personal shopper Sallmala provided them as the style requirements appropriate for an audience at the Crown Prince castle in Saudi Arabi were quite different than how they would dress for an important event in America. They picked up three outfits each. For the media meet and greet, Lois had a dark chocolate color abaya while Garcia's was a lighter colored khaki. In American terms, the best way to describe the clothing was to call it a long, loose fitting trench coat that when done up correctly covered the woman's body from neck to toe. Each woman accessorized with a white silk scarf that covered their hair, ears and necks as well. The women laughed when they were told this was the informal wear. For the formal reception at the palace, each had an almost identical abaya, both in black with dark green silk head scarves. The women would be allowed to show their faces as opposed to the traditional eyes-only head wear of the country. Finally, for the formal bidding process itself, each had a third abaya similar to that which they would wear to the media event as it was a more relaxed event. The men were, of course, acceptable in their traditional formal Western wear with tuxedos for the black tie reception.

The media reception took place in the Four Seasons ball room which was a complete opposite in comparison to a western style press release. Blade Solar was up first. They sat down formally with three reporters, one from the television network, one from the newspaper and one from the radio station. The reporters were allowed to ask a series of questions that were given to them by Sallmala and Shallen just before the interview started and the two Princes were on hand to make sure all went as prescribed. Once George and Robin were finished, it was Dunsmuir Energy's turn and they traded spots with George and Robin. Neither were allowed to hear the other party's responses. Following the interviews both groups were taken back to the restaurant where they were formally introduced to each other and while they ate a pre-ordered meal, Sallmala and Shallen explained the formalities and expectations that would be required of guests at the Crown Prince Palace for the evening.

Once their meal was complete, Jim and his team

returned to their rooms to prepare for the evening. Sallmala would once again chauffeur the Dunsmuir Energy team while Shallen would escort George and Robin. Both parties were required in the lobby for pick up at seven o'clock.

Jim asked Lois, Jason and Ramsey up to his and Garcia's room for a drink and quick meeting before they went to get ready for the evening. "Obviously these meetings are going to be quite different than we're used to in the States," Jim was saying as he poured drinks for everyone. "So we'll have to prepare ourselves. It seems all events will be extremely formal and prescribed. Let's make sure our comments and statements are respectful and conservative at all times. Garcia and Lois, I know you don't agree with this, nor do we, but despite the extreme steps forward the King has taken in female equality, the country is still far behind the rest of the West in its acceptance of women as equals. If we're going to win this contract, we'll need to fit in and make a good impression. I'm sorry but that means we'll have to follow the customs of the country as Sallmala laid out for us. This simply isn't the time or place to fight for women's rights," Jim said, chagrined that he had to take that stance.

"It's alright Jim," Lois reassured him. "Garcia and I discussed customs this morning as we were trying on the full length body covers we have to wear to these formal events. Thanks for acknowledging us in this, but our political feelings against oppression are nothing compared to the good this project can do for the world. We couldn't be more excited to participate and do our part as small as it may be here."

Garcia nodded in complete agreement. "And while this may not be the time to fight against women's oppression, that may be one more way this project will change the world in years to come," she said with conviction.

"Thanks," Jim said, appreciating their understanding. "Ok, team. Let's get ready. I've got a feeling tonight is going to be a spectacle like none of us have ever seen."

CHAPTER 77

When Sallmala picked Jim's team up at the hotel door he explained the trip would take about an hour and half to get to the Al-Yamama Palace just outside of Riyadh. By the time they arrived at the palace, night had fallen but the court yard was lit by high mast lighting the likes none of them had ever seen. The grounds were so perfectly manicured Garcia thought it would be doubtful if anyone could even draw such precise lines. Perfectly sculpted statues, a water fountain that rivaled the Bellagio in Las Vegas and the home itself perfectly centered amongst it all. Sallmala led them out of the car when the driver stopped in front of the massive palace doors.

Over the last twenty years, money, power and status had given Jim access to the finest and most luxurious private events and institutions the world over but never had he seen anything like this. One grand palace afforded as a private home for the king. The luxury of the grounds and palace was absolute. Neither Buckingham Palace nor the Palace of Versailles could match the meticulous effort put into every square inch of this grand residence.

Jim put his arm around Garcia's waist as the group began the ascent up the marble staircase to the entrance. Two uniformed servants opened the doors for them to enter where they were promptly met by a servant in a different dress uniform who greeted them and took their coats. Once their jackets were taken they were approached by two more servants bearing drinks.

Jim, Jason and Ramsey were offered champagne while water was provided to the women. Sallmala explained that the group would need to be divided from there on out, the women would be taken on a tour of the palace while the men went on a separate tour and eventually be introduced to the Crown Prince. Garcia could see objection forming on Jim's face and promptly took charge of the situation. "That sounds wonderful," Garcia said with convincing enthusiasm, "I can't wait to see this lovely home." Smiling reassuringly at Jim, Garcia turned and linked her arm to Lois's, ready to follow their tour guide. Her quick action prevented Jim from saying anything which may have offended any of the palace customs.

Recognizing Garcia's intent, Lois was quick to follow suit and started moving off with their guide. "You guys enjoy the tour. We'll meet up with you after."

Jim was stunned by how quickly he had almost forgot himself and where they were. Garcia had read the situation correctly and had adeptly stopped him from saying something about the women coming with them. Ramsey quickly picked up on the girls' plan and took charge, giving Jim a chance to regroup.

"This is an amazing place," Ramsey said, turning Sallmala's attention away from Jim's speechlessness. "It's beyond words, Sallmala. What type of tour are we going on exactly?" He was relieved when Sallmala replied without any indication of having recognized what had almost transpired with Jim's reaction to the women being separated from him.

"It's an executive tour. You'll see rooms filled with priceless treasures, some rooms themselves are works of art decorated in pure gold and jewels of such quality that most people in the world will never see. Plus, you'll tour the entertainment rooms. Everything from full working nightclubs to indoor car racing. The palace could be an indoor city," he said with pride.

As Sallmala took them through another set of doors into a grand receiving room, they were merged in with many other guests including George Anderson and Robin Harms who were in tow of Shallen on their own tour. The men were polite and professional as they shook hands all around. Then the two royals mixed their groups and took them on tour of the palace together.

An uncomfortable situation for Jim and his team was a strategic one for George, who knew this was his last chance to get at Jim before the bidding. George was going to have to bide his time on the tour and wait patiently for an opportunity to make his play. George started with a false offering of civility to break the ice, trying to get everyone to relax and hopefully lower their guards.

"Looks like we're friends today and enemies tomorrow," he joked with a smiled directed towards Jim in hopes of getting Jim on side for a truce, for the night anyway.

Not having much choice, Jim responded in kind. "Yes a cease fire for the evening," he said, seeming to follow George's lead. The men all laughed.

When the laughter subsided, Sallmala spoke. "Thank you, gentlemen. Your civility is appreciated. The construction of Neom is a huge leap forward for our nation and we'd like to celebrate its beginning tonight. It looks like you all have champagne so let's begin our tour. We'll start on the main floor it's where all the meetings and affairs of state happen, where mostly only top Royal family members and diplomats from important countries get an audience in the palace. It's even an honor for Shallen and I to be here tonight. We'll get through this floor quickly, as we move up floors the palace becomes more of a house and that's where all the really good stuff is."

CHAPTER 78

espite not being included in the men's tour, Lois and Garcia found their separate tour very fascinating. They were taken through what their guide called a private infirmary that was for the King's use only. The area the tour guide called an infirmary, seemed like a fully staffed, fully functional hospital complete with its own MRI and top of the line equipment. From the health care area, they were led into an indoor tropical garden paradise that rivaled the best views Hawaii had to offer. It was explained to them that the green house was a working tropical climate. There were special lights that acted as the sun that would gradually rise each morning in the East and fade out to a sunset each night in the West. The air and climate was programmed to rain and hold moisture at the levels of a tropical country so the green house could sustain the environment year round. The garden area itself was more like a town than a greenhouse. It was all so unbelievable and both women were once again astonished at the luxury afforded to the royals.

CHAPTER 79

A s they rode the elevator to the second floor, a plan was forming in George's head. He now knew how he was going to get Jim alone and what he was going to do. The elevator opened onto what could only be described as a large hotel lobby. In essence that's what it was, there was uniformed staff, a reception desk, and all kinds of computer banks and information areas. The Princes explained to the men that this floor was the hub of the estate. It was highly secured and everything from food orders to visiting presidents were processed in and out of the palace from the area. As with every other area they saw in the palace so far, no expense had been spared. Massive ballistic proof windows lined the walls, the ceiling was every inch of thirty feet high and adorned with breathtaking hand-painted murals that spanned hundreds of feet while still looking completely life-like right down to the smallest fingernail. Despite their differences and their reason for being there, the men were lost in the beauty the castle offered. Being engineers and builders themselves, they were a group who understood and respected the work that must have gone into the design and build process of the great estate and were rightfully in awe of it.

"Now if you'll follow me back to the elevator, we'll move on to the third floor," Shallen said after an extensive tour of the second floor. George and Robin were behind Shallen, followed by Sallmala, Jason and then Jim and Ramsey who were side by side talking as they closed up the rear of the group. As soon as they were in the elevator, George stood next to the buttons and discreetly pressed three. Just as Sallmala stepped through the elevator door, he pushed the door close button on the elevator and faked a fall backwards right into Jim, simultaneously pushing the two of them back out of the elevator as Ramsey stepped into the car and the doors closed.

CHAPTER 80

Jim was staggering to regain his balance when George grabbed him, slammed him against the wall, leaned in close so he could whisper in order to avoid unseen listening devices. "Listen, pretty boy. I don't give a shit who you are or what your reputation is. I want this contract. If my men can get to you that easy in Vegas and Saudi Arabia, there's nowhere you can hide and this time I won't tell them just to scare you. Lose the contract tomorrow, in a way that raises no suspicions, or Garcia dies a painful death followed by your pal Ramsey. I kidnapped Peter and his daughter and scared Chris off so don't think for a second I won't follow through with this. She's dead the day after I lose the contract and Ramsey the day after that. Plans are already in place. I just need to call them off, which I'll do if I win. Now let's get back on the elevator and join the group." Seeing Jim's ashen face, he quickly ordered him to smile. "We're friends tonight, remember?" He threatened menacingly.

George's fierce look immediately dissolved into a friendly, sheepish grin as the elevator doors opened. He apologized to the others who peered out in confusion from the elevator. "God, sorry about that folks. Damn clumsy of me! Let's move on with the tour," he said as he laughed and clapped Jim on the shoulder guiding him into the elevator car ahead of him.

Jim was shell-shocked and furious. George had basically just admitted to being behind all the violence that had been surrounding the Neom electrical bid over the last month. Could it be true? Would someone actually go that far just for a contract? He'd seen dirty business first hand over the years but nothing like this. For the rest of the tour he mulled over the threat. If it was true he had no time to protect Ramsey or Garcia, nor was it worth the risk. If George had been able to toss a Molotov cocktail at him the last time he was in Riyadh under the protection of the G8 summit, he could obviously attack him again this time with ease. George was playing poker on a multibillion dollar deal. The man was obviously insane and Jim had very little time to decide if George was bluffing or not. Just the fact that he was willing to attack him in the palace, surrounded by security, made Jim think he wasn't bluffing.

Ramsey could tell his friend was off from the second he got back in the elevator and asked Jim about it as soon as they had a chance to be alone. "What's going on? You ok?" he asked. "God you look like you walked over your grave! Come on, Jim," Ramsey admonished. "We need your charm here, we haven't won yet."

"I know Rams," Jim tried to shake off the shock and fear that were threatening to paralyze him. "I just started thinking about the process tomorrow and was running it over in my head. This tour is great but I just want to get to tomorrow already. Sorry I'll get back on board."

"It's all right," Ramsey said, "I get it. Let's roll through this night and move on."

Jim was glad Ramsey thought it was just his nerves getting to him. He needed space to think. Recognizing what his friend needed, even without understanding the actual reason, Ramsey stepped up and entertained the Princes for the rest of the tour and through the dinner. As it turned out the women were not even allowed to come back to join them for the main meal nor to meet the Crown Prince. The group was not brought back together until the end of the night when they were back in the entrance waiting for their coats to be brought to them. Garcia quickly rushed over and hugged Jim. As Jim looked over her shoulder in the embrace, George was staring right at him. When the men locked eyes, George winked at Jim to remind him of exactly what he was threatening. Jim's whole body went rigid. When she felt his body tense, Garcia jumped back and quickly asked, "What is it? Are you ok?"

He looked down at her and said loudly enough for George to hear. "Yeah, I'm just tired. Let's get out of here." He turned her around, encircled her waist with his arm, and headed for the door. With a puzzled look on her face, Garcia followed along.

CHAPTER 81

Jim never slept all night. He'd come to the conclusion that George would act on his threat, and despite the financial loss, and what was worse, the loss of his dreams, he knew he had to lose the contract. George had been pretty clear that he needed to lose without drawing attention to the fact that he did it on purpose, so he couldn't just withdraw or tell the Princes why he was stepping down. He was finalizing how he would lose in his head while he and Ramsey waited outside the board room door for their turn to present their electrical proposal. Blade Energy had been up first so George and Robin were in presenting the solar power option to the Princes and had been in the room for about an hour so far. Jim was expecting George to exit any minute. Neither he nor Ramsey were talking at this point. Both were sipping water and intently going over the presentation in their heads. Jim was starting to feel sick about sabotaging the work his team had done, but knew that he had no choice.

About twenty minutes later, the heavy dark wood board room door opened and one of the Prince's assistants lead Robin and George out of the room. The assistant was about five feet tall, a twenty something who spoke perfect English, was clean cut and conservatively dressed; a perfect representative for the Princes. He thanked George and Robin for their time and asked if they needed anything else before they left. When George said no, the young man turned to Jim and Ramsey and asked them if they were ready.

Before walking away, George walked over to Ramsey and offered his hand. "You know, Ramsey, I have heard so many good things about you. I've studied your career in depth and I feel like I'd know you anywhere. You ever get tired of working for this guy," George said pointing his thumb at Jim, "give me a call."

Floored by the unexpected unprofessionalism of a business magnate trying to poach him away from his business partner, he stuttered in response. "I'm good where I'm at George."

Jim knew that George's attention to Ramsey was a direct reminder to him about George's threat and as he was walking away, George locked eyes with Jim and added one more subversive warning. "Good luck in there Jim. And say hi to Garcia and the rest of your team for me. I may never see them again."

"I hope you don't either, especially if you're going to offer them all jobs," Jim said, his joke falling flat. Then when George left, he turned to Ramsey and began to put into motion the plan he'd come up with late last night. "I'm doing this alone today, Rams. I've been thinking about it and I need to win or lose on my own. I can't put your reputation at risk."

"What the hell are you talking about Jim?" Ramsey said with incredulous anger. "My reputation? Don't be crazy. You know you need me on this. Come on, let's go."

"Don't make a scene. I'm going in alone or I'm not going in at all," Jim said, sounding like an unreasonable child. "I've been thinking on this all night and it's what I have to do. Don't fight me on this. It's either me or you, Ramsey. Speak now."

"You know it can't be me," Ramsey exclaimed. "What's going on? Don't do this, Jim. We're a team."

Ignoring Ramsey's imploring request, Jim turned to the assistant and said, "I'm ready, young man. It's just me."

Even the assistant looked surprised but his professionalism quickly kicked in. "Of course sir, ready when you are."

Without looking at Ramsey, Jim followed the young assistant into the room and closed the door behind them, leaving Ramsey standing in the waiting room, shocked and furious.

CHAPTER 82

When the assistant let Jim out of the board room an hour later, Jim's face was sickly pale. He walked right by Ramsey's chair without acknowledging him and went straight to his room. Garcia was there waiting for him with champagne on ice, ready to celebrate the culmination of all their hard work to this point. Like Ramsey earlier, she was shocked when he asked her to leave so he could be alone. When she resisted, he snapped at her.

"Please, Garcia just leave me."

Realizing he was serious but not without feeling hurt, she slowly left the room and headed over to Lois's. By the time Garcia was knocking on Lois's door, Ramsey and Jason were already there. All of them looked sick and no one was saying anything.

Garcia looked at Lois, who confirmed her worst

suspicions. "The word is out. Blade Solar won the contract."

"He wouldn't let me go in with him to the presentation. How did he expect to win this thing alone?" Ramsey asked, shaking his head.

"What do you mean?" Garcia asked. She was desperately trying to get up to speed. "Jim basically just kicked me out of our room and now you're saying he wouldn't let you go to the presentation? What's going on? Something isn't right."

"I don't know, but it's over. We're done. It's been announced," Ramsey replied in defeat.

"I didn't know, I can't let Jim be alone now," she exclaimed and went running back to their room. By the time she got there, Jim was already gone. She went looking for him and eventually found he'd taken off straight to the airport and had Sallmala book him a private flight straight back to Iceland.

The team was shocked. They knew losing would be devastating but Jim's earlier actions and this unprecedented reaction to the news of their loss was so out of character for him that it was disturbing.

CHAPTER 83

"This just isn't like Jim," Ramsey mused aloud. "He's been off since about halfway through our tour last night, not to mention refusing to let me participate in the presentation, and then kicking Garcia out of their room. And he would never normally abandon his team, even in the face of a loss. Something isn't adding up. Lois, you guys book us flights back to Iceland. I'm going to see what I can do about saving face for us here with the Princes. Who knows what other project might come up and we don't want Dunsmuir Energy to fall out of favor."

To his relief, Ramsey discovered their company's reputation continued to be in good standing with the Princes. He was sure to make it known Dunsmuir Energy would be more than happy to work with them on any other project that may come up in the future and then thanked them for their time and hospitality. Sallmala then walked with Ramsey to the lobby where he was scheduled to meet the rest of his team for their trip to the airport.

"I'd love to hear any feedback on how we could improve our bid if there is a next time or to know how far off we were on this one," Ramsey said to Sallmala.

"We'll be sending out that exact information shortly," Sallmala replied. "Jim asked for it to get emailed directly to him. I'd say it should be out in a couple days or so."

Ramsey thought it was odd Jim would get it sent directly to himself, that was not the way they usually worked, however he didn't want the Prince to suspect any disconnect in the company so he thanked him and shook his hand as they parted ways in the lobby. Jason, Lois and Garcia were waiting for him expectantly but all he could tell them was that it seemed that Jim left everything in order with the Princes. He further explained that some information was to be coming to Jim in a couple days to explain the results.

"No sense standing around here," Jason reasoned when the group seemed to be stuck in surprise and indecision. "The quicker we get to the airport, the quicker we get home." Jason grabbed up his suitcases and headed out to the waiting car with the others in tow. It was a quiet car ride to the airport and almost as quiet a flight back to Iceland. Sallmala had them flown directly to Iceland on his private jet. The team was exhausted and slept on and off most of the way. They made a few attempts to contact Jim, who never answered his phone, and eventually they resigned themselves to waiting till they got back to talk with him.

Jim was waiting outside his car when they got off Sallmala's plane. They loaded their luggage in the back of the large SUV, climbed in with him and headed back into Reykjavik. "I know you must be wondering," he said as he pulled over into a large parking lot. "Let me explain."

Turning around to face everyone in the car, Jim explained how George faked the fall out of the elevator and how he then proceeded to threaten to kill Ramsey and Garcia if he didn't back out of the bid. He told them how George knew enough about the Vegas and Saudi assault to convince him that it was George who was behind it, not to mention that George admitted to the kidnapping of Peter and his daughter along with threatening Chris Buchanan and his family, which explains why they dropped out of the race. Jim said he weighed out the options and looked into George's past as much as he could in the time he had and determined he couldn't risk their lives. He further stated he was so angry that he had to get out of Saudi Arabia to prevent himself from retaliating in a way that could put someone in jeopardy.

Jim's team was understandably furious at the news and wanted war. It was Jim who lent a sense of calm to the group. "Guys, it's ok. I've had more time to think this through than you've had so hear me out. This might actually work out for the best. Trust me, I was as angry as you are now, but think of it this way. Now we can concentrate on the project solely in Greenland. I'd been thinking about this anyway as a backup plan for if we happened to lose in Saudi Arabia. If you guys are on board, it still has the potential to be world-changing just not on the scale we originally planned. Second, Lois I want Ramsey to take over my role in the company, so I'll need you to help us find a replacement for him. Business is obviously changing and we just found our vulnerability. My new role is going to be setting up better security for the business and for our team and planning an offensive to head these type of attacks off. Obviously these large projects don't get chosen for best product alone. Luckily we have the resources and the talent to shift and get ahead in this. Further, Lois and I'll build and improve our reputation in world. Lastly, off the side of my desk I will be working the long game towards bankrupting George Anderson. I won't stop till he's finished. No one will threaten us like that again," Jim stated adamantly.

Without officially knowing it, Jim's plan resurrected and saved his team. He gave Ramsey a new position of power and distributed positive challenges amongst the rest of the team, including himself. With the exception of the attack he was planning on George, all was for the direct good of the company and its staff. Even the idea of the attack on George itself quelled the anger of the team and gave them hope of retribution for their loss.

The End

RICHARD EMERSON RETURNS IN "MOONSHINE"

Richard Emerson was enjoying a well deserved break with his new girlfriend Sarah the couple was spending two weeks touring the American mid-west. Sarah had been living in Africa, working for George Anderson a highly successful entrepreneur who ran a solar power business that recently won a contract to provide solar power to a new city that was about to be built from scratch in Saudi Arabia.

Sarah's boss had hired Richard and his company, Trade Link Security to follow his competitors and do some industrial espionage for him. As the competition heated up he'd upped the ante and coerced Richard's firm into performing some less than legal operations for him in order to dissuade his competitors from bidding for the massive electrical contract.

Being used to the bustle of New York City as a police officer and now running a successful security firm a trip to America's Heart land had been just what Richard needed. While on vacation Richard was contacted by a man named Scott Simmons. Scott turned out to be a successful club and sports lounge entrepreneur who owned numerous establishments up and down the American East Coast. Scott had a gut instinct that his bottom line was starting to slip and wanted Richard to try and figure out why. When Richard questioned Scott on this Scott stated that he'd been recently out bid on a property by a competitor who didn't have the holdings nor the buying edge to afford to make money on the property for the price he paid. Scott was adamant that something was up because he knew the price points for his business, and this wasn't adding up. He of course wanted Richard to start immediately, Richard and his team were just breaking out of small-time investigations and moving into the corporate sector which he and his crew found way more interesting. When Scott indicated that Richard would likely find his competitor had organized crime connections Richard became even more intrigued. Richard was not about to give up on his time with Sarah so he told Scott he would contact him in a weeks' time and then he and his men would be out to meet with Scott and dive into a full investigation for him.

Printed in the United States
By Bookmasters